Danica Win[...]estselling author who [...] with their ability to drive emotion through suspense and occasionally a touch of magic. When she's not working, she can be found in the wilds of Montana, testing her patience while she tries to hone her skills at various crafts—quilting, pottery and painting are not her areas of expertise. She believes the cup is neither half-full nor half-empty, but it better be filled with wine. Visit her website at danicawinters.net

Jane Godman writes in a variety of romance genres, including paranormal, gothic and romantic suspense. Jane lives in England and loves to travel to European cities that are steeped in history and romance—Venice, Dubrovnik and Vienna are among her favorites. Jane is married to a lovely man and is mum to two grown-up children.

HIDDEN TRUTH

DANICA WINTERS

COLTON 911:
FAMILY UNDER FIRE

JANE GODMAN

MILLS & BOON

First Published in Great Britain 2019
by Mills & Boon, an imprint of HarperCollins*Publishers*
1 London Bridge Street, London, SE1 9GF

Hidden Truth © 2019 Danica Winters
Colton 911: Family Under Fire © 2019 Harlequin Books S.A.

Special thanks and acknowledgement are given to Jane Godman for her contribution to the *Colton 911* series.

ISBN: 978-0-263-27453-0

1219

MIX
Paper from
responsible sources
FSC® C007454

This book is produced from independently certified FSC™ paper to ensure responsible forest management.

For more information visit: www.harpercollins.co.uk/green

Printed and bound in Spain
by CPI, Barcelona

HIDDEN TRUTH

DANICA WINTERS

To Mac, thank you for teaching me the meaning
of true love.

Acknowledgements

This series wouldn't have been possible without a great
team of people, including my #1k1hr friends, Jill
Marsal and the editors at Mills & Boon—thank you for
all your hard work.

Also, thank you to my readers. You keep me writing.

Prologue

She clicked open the tabs of the gun case, exposing the M24 sniper rifle. It was a thing of beauty. Even without firing a single round from this particular gun, Trish Martin could recall the precise feel of pulling the trigger, smelling the spent powder and watching as her enemies fell to their knees.

There was no greater feeling in the world than a justified kill. The men standing around her, those dealing in death, would be easy to strip from this earth.

She ran her fingers down the synthetic stock, taking in the slight imperfections on the newly manufactured gun. This one would be for a different kind of kill, a long-term tactical assault, rather than a one-and-done straight to the head.

Some people were only too happy to judge her and her family for the work they did, but she didn't care. She didn't care that she was out there protecting the ones who didn't appreciate it right alongside the ones who did. She was a hunter, a predator, who fought for her territory and for life as she knew it.

The shroud of darkness wormed its way around her as she waited for the Bozkurtlar, or what some people called the Gray Wolves. To call them a Turkish crime syndicate was an understatement. No, they were so much more.

They were the reason she and her family were here in Adana, the reason she couldn't sleep at night, and the reason there were so many unmarked graves scattered around the Turkish hillsides. Their name suited them. No matter where in the world they were, death and mayhem followed.

That would all end soon.

She heard the sound of footsteps on the concrete floor and the clink of the metal door closing behind the group. From the sound, there had to be at least ten men. If anything went wrong…

She looked around her. They had made a mistake in agreeing to meet them in this shell of a warehouse. There weren't nearly enough hiding places or corners where she could find cover if she needed to. And there wasn't anywhere for her brothers to hide within the building. Without a doubt, the group's intention had been to isolate her and to strip her of any way to double-cross them.

"Ms. Stone," a man with a thick Turkish accent said from behind her. "I hope you aren't planning on brandishing that weapon. We're here to buy new, not used."

She stood up to face Fenrisulfr Bayural. He was nearly a foot shorter than her, but what he lacked in height, he made up for in his stance. When he stared at her, his golden-hued eyes took on the darkness that surrounded them, making her instinctively twitch for the gun at her side.

She stared down at him, forcing herself to act far

more confident and self-assured than she felt in his presence. He couldn't sense weakness in her. If he did, he and the bodyguards around him would certainly pounce. When it came to running guns, buyers tended to get skittish.

Two years ago, in Egypt, one of her team's sting operations had ended with a shipment of American weapons falling into the wrong hands—and the men on her team being murdered. They were part of the reason she had ended up here—men, especially those with a Napoleon complex, tended to be more than happy to play nice with a hot brunette. But she'd be crazy to think her looks would keep this from becoming a firefight.

"We sell nothing but the best. You'd be a fool to think anything less," she said.

"Good. But will you also be providing more advanced weaponry or just the ARs?"

He wanted the launchers. Of course he did. But rocket launchers weren't something that they readily had on hand. Yet what he didn't know wouldn't hurt him. For now, she just had to play along and make it out of this room alive.

"How many did you want?"

"Four thousand RPGs and ten thousand ARs. I need my men to have adequate coverage when they attack Ankara."

As he spoke the name of the city, she felt the warmth of the mic strategically stitched into her jacket. They had their location and an estimated number of enemy combatants—admittedly, a number far greater than they had anticipated. But perhaps it was Bayural's plan to inflate the numbers. In the event any of their dealings leaked, he would appear far more powerful than he and his group really were.

"What do you have available for us?" Bayural crossed his arms over his chest, covering his vital bits as he prepared to negotiate his price.

No matter how he tried to protect himself, once her brothers bore down there would be no protection great enough. His life would be theirs for the taking.

"The Type 91 Kai MANPAD rocket launcher will do everything from annihilating a door to wiping almost an entire city block clean with its shoulder-launched surface-to-air missiles. They're easy to carry, cheap and fast to reload. Everything you want." She chuckled slightly as she realized how much she sounded like a used car salesman instead of a trained killer. Her mother would have been so proud.

Bayural squatted down and picked up the sniper rifle. He lifted it up as he stood and shifted the gun in his hands as though he was weighing it. "Hand me a round," he said, turning toward the guard to his right.

The man pulled a round from his pocket. Bayural jacked the round into the chamber, smiling at the metallic click and slide sound the gun made.

No. He couldn't be allowed to actually shoot the rifle. It would be too dangerous. They were here to keep the general public from falling into harm's way, not to place them into greater danger. "The gun is solid. The shipment will be solid. Our team, Black Dragon, will get them to you by tomorrow." She tried to sound nonchalant as she slipped in their fake name, the code word. Her team would be here any second to strike these bastards down.

Finally, they could cut off the wolf's head.

"Tomorrow? I want them within the hour." He lifted the rifle, pointing it directly at her center mass as he peered down the scope. "You can do that, can't you?"

She glanced toward the far wall, hoping like hell that she would see the laser signal letting her know her brothers were in place, but there was nothing.

"When can we expect your shipment?" Bayural pressed.

"First, I want my ten million."

Bayural smiled. "Ten is too much."

"With everything happening in Syria, prices have gone up for your standard RPGs. You know as well as I do that the market is at least two Gs per RPG. As for the ARs, you are getting a screaming deal. That's less than two hundred a gun. We could get five if we went somewhere else."

He nodded slightly. "I'll give you a G per RPG."

She laughed. Even if she had really had the weapons, there would be no way she would go for such a ridiculous deal, but she had to keep up the negotiation until her brothers arrived.

"Or we will give you two if you can have our shipment to us within the hour." Bayural's pitch rose, like he was growing more nervous with each passing second.

His bodyguard leaned in and said something in his ear, something far too quiet for her to hear. Bayural's eyes widened and his brow furrowed. Whatever he said, it wasn't good news.

Her chest tightened, and her Kevlar vest suddenly seemed all too heavy.

Her brothers should have been here by now, at her side. "We can do the hour, but I'll have to talk to my team. Your order is larger than we were anticipating."

This was falling apart. Fast. She had to get out of there. She scanned the room for her planned exit point. The door to the alley was closed, barred from the inside. There was nothing to use as cover. It would take at least three seconds for her to get to the location, two to get the door open. Five seconds. Basically, a lifetime if they opened fire.

He clicked off the safety, the gun's barrel steady as it pointed at her. "Is something wrong, maybe you have something you want to tell us?" His voice threatening.

"No," she said, trying to appear relaxed as she took a step back. "But if you wish to have the deal go through, you need to lower that gun."

Bayural lowered the weapon slightly and motioned toward her with his chin. His guard took a step closer.

"What are you doing?" she asked as the guard grabbed her wrist and pulled her arm behind her. Her shoulder pinched as he lifted her hand higher, forcing her to submit.

Her instinct was to struggle and pull free, to launch into an attack. To get the hell out of there. But no, she had to trust her team. If they were waiting, there had to be a reason. They were trying to get more information. They must have needed more. She had to believe in her family.

"Back off," she growled at the guard. "Let go of my arm or the last thing you will see is me ripping it off and shoving it down your goddamned throat."

He lifted her wrist higher, forcing her to lean forward from the pressure.

"Bayural, get your man—"

"To stand down?" Bayural said, finishing her sentence. "Hardly. Who the hell do you think you are to command me?" He dropped the rifle to the ground and looked to his guard. "Break the stock."

She looked at the base where she had just run her fingers. The imperfection suddenly seemed so much larger.

The guard picked up the gun and smashed it against the floor again and again until cracks formed in the plastic. He batted it against the concrete one more time, sending the small GPS tracker her team had planted in the plastic skittering across the floor.

"You, your brothers, your sister, your team… You're dead."

"You may get me, but you'll never get the rest of them. We're survivors."

"Even if I have to spend the rest of my days on this earth hunting every one of your family members down, I'll do it. When I'm done, you and your kind won't even be a memory. You will be nothing."

There was a smatter of gunfire outside the corrugated steel building. A round pinged against the metal siding, the sound echoing through her.

With her free hand she reached down and pulled the knife from her boot. She jammed it deep into the guard's foot. The man screamed, letting go of her arm in a panic to remove the blade.

She grabbed her sidearm, taking aim at Bayural and pulling the trigger. The round ripped from the barrel, striking the man in the chest. Buyural didn't seem to notice the hit. He must have been wearing a vest.

The guards around him pulled their guns as she turned to find cover. Anything. Anywhere. She had to get the hell out of there. Now. She rushed toward the door as the sound of gunfire rained down upon her. The first round struck her in the thigh, ripping through her muscle with a searing heat, but there was no pain. Her ravaged thigh tripped her, the muscles failing to follow her brain's command. Her body fell to the floor, but she pressed on, dragging her injured leg behind her as she crawled toward the back door.

The door flew open, and standing in the nearly blinding light was her brother. "Trevor!" she screamed. "Get the hell out."

He ran toward her in what seemed like slow motion, but as he took two steps, the next round struck. Wetness. Warmth. Something had splattered her cheek.

She stopped struggling as she pressed her fingers to her face and traced the spatter to the gaping hole in her neck. No. This couldn't be real. This couldn't be happening. Not like this. Not now.

She sank to the floor as the blood poured from her.

The concrete was cold against her face as she watched the pool of red grow. The world narrowed to a pinpoint until all she saw was Trevor. His face. He'd always been so handsome. So dangerously handsome. She'd miss her brother.

She'd miss them all.

Breathe. All she had to do was breathe. But as she struggled to fill her lungs, there was only a strange gurgling sound.

She had been wrong to think this operation would be easy. Nothing in their lives had ever been simple. And now that misjudgment—and her desire to trust— would prove fatal.

... ... him
... ...

Chapter One

There was a single question that Trevor Martin hated above all others: "Who do you think you are?" It only ever meant one of two things—he was about to get slapped by a woman or he was going to have to knock some sucker out.

It wasn't the question that bothered him so much. On the surface it was just some retort people came up with when they didn't know what else to say, but when he heard it, he heard it for what it really was—a question of who he was at his core. And when he thought about that, about what made him the man he was, he wasn't sure that he liked the answer.

That self-hatred was one of the reasons he had taken a leave of absence from his contract work with the CIA. His entire family needed a break from the family business, so they bought the Widow Maker Ranch in Mystery, Montana. It was supposed to be an escape he so desperately needed from the thoughts of all he had done wrong in his life. Instead, it was as if the rural lifestyle and the quiet mountain mornings only made the self-denigration of his character that much louder.

He'd only been there a few days, but he couldn't help

but wonder if maybe he'd made a mistake in coming to this forsaken place where he was constantly shrouded in clouds and imprisoned by the brooding mountains. Everything about the ranch made him long to stretch and push the world and his thoughts away—if only it were that goddamned easy. No matter where he went or what he did, his memories of the days he'd spent in his family's private security business, one they called STEALTH, constantly haunted him.

And here he was the bearer of bad news once again.

If he were being honest, pulling the trigger and tearing down an enemy combatant was a hell of a lot easier than what he was going to have to do. He spun the motorcycle around in the dirt, kicking up dust as he screwed around and tried to focus on something he loved instead of something he was going to hate.

After a few more doughnuts, he got off his Harley and pushed the kickstand into place with his foot. Taking off his helmet, he set it on the seat, though a part of him wondered if it wouldn't have been better for him to wear it as some kind of shield from the battle that was likely to ensue.

Running his hand over his too-long locks, he pushed them out of his eyes and tucked them behind his ears.

There were times, just like this one, that he wished he were back in a war zone and had a staff of people under him who could handle this kind of thing.

All he had to do was say his piece, give them the letter, and he could get the hell out of there. He just had to go in and do his duty. The moment he and his brothers and his sister had purchased the land, they agreed that this would be a part of the work that would need to be done. Unfortunately, he had drawn the short straw.

He had never seen a picture of the house in question, but the shack in front of him was a squatter's paradise and far from what he and his family had imagined. The roof was a collection of corrugated steel in a jumble of different colors, and the siding, what was left of it, had started to rot and several pieces were only half-attached. Even the front door was cockeyed, listing to the left so far that there was at least a two-inch gap at the top.

Whoever resided there must be hard up. Maybe they had been hoping they were far enough out of the way at the farthest reaches of the ranch that they would go completely unnoticed. Thanks to the neglect of his cousins, the Johansens, whoever was living in this place had pretty much free rein—and their plan for disappearing in plain sight had worked. And from the state of the house, it was clear it had been working for a long time.

The forest around the house was filled with junk, everything from antique wringer-style washing machines to the rusted-out shells of farming equipment. From the state of disrepair, it seemed likely that this had once been the dumping ground for the ranchers of years past.

He walked toward the door. Behind him a twig snapped and the sound was answered by the chatter of a pine squirrel high up in one of the trees.

He wasn't alone.

If he turned around now, it would give away that he was aware he was being watched. For all he knew, the inhabitants of the shanty had taken to the woods at the sound of his bike as he'd made his way down the makeshift road that led up to this place. If he just kept walking, it would give him time.

He started again, looking for a window or something he could use to catch a glimpse of whoever was lurking in the shadows around him.

They couldn't get the drop on him; he wouldn't allow it. He'd made it through years of toeing the line between danger and death, and he wasn't about to get tripped up and find himself on the losing side now. Not when he'd come here to make a real home and a real life for himself.

He stopped at the front door of the squatters' shack and started to knock.

"They're not home," a woman said from somewhere in the distance, her voice echoing off the timber stands around them and making the source of the sound impossible to pinpoint. "And they would have been long gone regardless, thanks to your crappy driving."

He turned in the direction the voice had come from and relaxed a bit. She probably wasn't going to try to shoot him—if she had wanted, she already could have drawn on him—but some habits died hard, and he lowered his hand to the gun that was always strapped on his thigh.

Standing in the shadows at twelve o'clock, her back against the buckskin-colored pine, was a blonde. She was leaning back, her arms over her chest like she had been there for hours getting bored. Even feigning boredom, she was sexy as hell. She had the kind of curves he had spent more than one lonely night dreaming about. And the way her white T-shirt pulled tight over her leopard-print bra… His body quivered to life as he tried to repress the desire that welled within him.

"You know where they went?" he asked, trying to be a gentleman and look at anything besides the little polka dots that were almost pulsing beneath her shirt.

She smiled as though she could see the battle that was raging inside him between lust and professional distance. "Have you met the Cussler boys before?"

"How many are there?"

She pushed herself off the tree. "If you stop thumbing that SIG Sauer at your side, maybe we can talk about it. Men playing with their guns make me nervous."

"You around men and guns a lot?" he asked, but the question was laced with a provocative tone he hadn't intended.

She walked toward him, and from the way she moved her hips even he, a man who had slept with only a handful of women, could tell that she had heard the inflection in his words as well…and she intended to do something about it.

He raised his hands in surrender. That's not what he'd come here for, not that he would have minded kissing those pink lips, not with the way they gently curved in a smile but hinted at something dangerous if they were allowed free rein. With the raising of his hands, she stopped and her smile faded. There was a small cleft in her chin, and damn if it didn't make her look even cuter than she had before.

Once, when he'd been young, his mother had told him, "Dimple in the chin, devil within." From the look in her eyes when she was staring at him and that damn bra she was wearing, there was plenty of devil within her.

"Are you Trevor?" she asked, not moving any closer.

He took a step back, surprised that the woman had any idea who he was. "Who are you?"

This time, she was the one to wave him off. "Your brother hired me to keep house—starting here. He didn't tell me that I was going to need a backhoe and a dump truck."

Either she had accidently forgotten to supply him with her name, or there was a reason she was keeping it from him.

It hardly seemed fair she should know anything about him when this was the first he was hearing about her.

"You from around here?" he asked, motioning vaguely in the direction of Mystery in hopes she would loosen up with a little bit of small talk.

"Actually, I'm kinda new. Was looking for a slower pace of life."

"Well, it doesn't get a whole lot slower than here," he said, a darkness flecking his words. He hoped she didn't read anything into his tone. He didn't need to get into some deep discussion with a stranger about the merits or pitfalls of a place where he doubted he was going to stay.

"If you think it's slow in town then you haven't spent enough time in the mountains. These mountain men are about as fast as cold molasses and a little less intelligent. If you ask me, their family tree is more of a twig."

He laughed. "So where are you from...and hey, what's your name again?" he asked, trying to play it off like she had told him and he had simply failed to remember it.

She gave him an impish smile, and he could have almost sworn that she fluttered her eyelashes at him. "Sabrina. And I'm from all over. Kind of an army brat, but my last stop was Schofield."

Instinctively, he glanced down at her arms. She was pale and far from the buttery color of someone who had spent their days in the Hawaiian sun. She had to be lying.

On the other hand, maybe he was reading far too much into her and her answer. Maybe she just valued her privacy like he valued his. Besides, if he was going to transfer into the civilian world, he would need to stop thinking everyone was out to conceal the truth from him—not everyone was his enemy, especially a housekeeper in the little town of Mystery, Montana.

But he'd been wrong before, and that failure to see danger had gotten his sister killed. He couldn't let his guard down. Not now. Not ever.

"Your father in the marines?" he asked.

"Schofield is an army base. I wouldn't make that mistake around a vet, if I were you." She sent him a dazzling smile.

She had passed the first test, yet something about her just didn't feel right—just like everything in his life since his sister Trish had died.

"How long have you been waiting on the Cussler boys?"

She shrugged. "I only got here a few minutes before you. To be honest, I was trying to figure out where to start the cleaning."

"So, they're gone?" His job of kicking the family out of their shanty was proving to be a whole lot easier than he had expected.

"They're not here, but I thought you had already come to kick them out. At least, that's what your brother led me to believe."

He was supposed to be here an hour ago, but he hadn't known his brother was sending a crew behind him or he would have been on it. "And you haven't seen any sign of activity?"

She shook her head. "But like I said, I only got here right before you."

He walked up to the door and knocked. There was the rattle of dishes as the mice, or whatever vermin it was that lived in the place, scurried over them. He went to knock again, though he was almost certain they were alone, but as he moved the door creaked open.

"Hello? Someone home?" he asked, walking in.

The place was dark and as he entered, a putrid smell wafted out—the brothers mustn't have been there in some time, or they were even worse at keeping house than they were at building one. He stepped in and the cobwebs in the corners of the front door clung to his face. He tried not to be squeamish as he wiped them away. No matter where he went in the world or what he was doing, he'd always hated that feeling. No amount of training or conditioning could get rid of the instinctual revulsion—and that was to say nothing of the inhabitants of the webs.

"Trevor," Sabrina said breathlessly from behind him. "Look."

He dropped his hands from his face and gazed into

the dark shadows where she pointed. There, sitting against the corner, was a man. His face was bloated and his lips were the deep purple color of the long dead.

Trevor clicked on the flashlight on his cell phone and pointed it toward the man as he moved closer. Above his right ear, at the temple and just below the dead man's ruddy hair, was a small bullet hole. There was no exit wound on the other side. The man's eyes were open, but they had started to dry and shrink in the socket, in sharp contrast to the rest of the man's features.

"Do you see a gun anywhere?" Trevor asked, flashing the light around as he looked for the weapon that could have killed the man.

"No," she said, but she stood in the doorway staring at the man. She covered her mouth with the back of her hand as though she were going to be sick.

Trevor rushed over to her and wrapped his arm around her. "Come with me. Let's go back outside. It's going to be okay. You're all right. Everything is going to be fine."

She turned her body into him, letting him pull her into his arms as he moved her out the door and to the fresh air of the forest. He had been right—she would be just fine; from the way she felt in his arms, he was the one who was truly in danger.

Chapter Two

Sabrina had no idea why she had reacted that way. The man was hardly the first dead body that she had come across, and yet it felt like the first time. Maybe it was the way he seemed to be looking at her through those cloudy eyes or the smell of the body that had been left sitting in the heat of the fall, but she just couldn't control her body's reaction.

Damn it. Every time she started to think that she was strong, she did something like this.

Although maybe it wasn't a bad thing that she had reacted as she had. She had gotten to play up the lady-in-distress angle. If she had to be undercover for any amount of time, it was going to be immensely easier if she had one of the brothers under her spell.

She just had to remember to keep him at arm's length; the last thing she needed to do was let her emotions come into play. Emotions only had a way of getting her into trouble, and she was in enough as it was. They were the reason she was stuck in this place…and out of the direct line of sight of her superiors. Though she was certainly under their thumb.

Trevor was just another case, another investigation

she had yet to complete. In a month, if everything went according to plan, she would be out of here and set down in a new little nowhere town in the middle of America investigating another possible threat to homeland security.

Trevor rubbed her back and as he held her, his chest rose and fell so rhythmically that she found herself mimicking his movements. He was like a man version of a white noise machine, and just as soothing.

If she had to guess, between his dark brown hair, his crystalline blue eyes and a jawline that was so strong that it could probably cut glass, he was all women's kryptonite. He probably was the kind of man who had a woman every time he went downrange.

She pushed herself out of his arms and sucked in a long breath as she tried to completely dissociate herself from him. The last thing she needed was to share anything with him—even his breath.

"Are you feeling better?" he asked, looking at her like she was a bird with a broken wing.

She nodded. "I don't know what that was about. I'm sorry."

"That was about a dead man," he said, shock flecking his voice. "It's not something one sees every day. I would have been more worried if you hadn't reacted that way. Shock can be more dangerous than most flesh wounds."

Crap... She couldn't give herself away. Of course he would think she was a newbie to this kind of thing. She had to remember the role she had been sent here to play. A role that required that she be seen little and heard even less. What a joke for her superiors to play...

they knew just as well as she did that silence wasn't her strong suit. She wasn't the kind of woman who was going to let anyone push her around, tell her what to do or require that she "let the men do the real work."

Her skin prickled at just the thought of the last time she had heard someone mansplain to her.

Trevor touched her arm. "Sabrina, you with me?"

"Huh? Yeah." She looked at him and forced a smile.

"Why don't you go and sit down," he said, pointing toward his motorcycle. "Or I guess you can lean." He gave her a guilty smile, realizing what an absurd idea that was.

"I'm fine. Do you think you should call the police?" She motioned toward the shack with her chin.

She would rather not have any local officers running around the place and mucking up her investigation or compromising her position.

Yet they couldn't hide a dead body…

Or could they?

If they swept this under the rug, it would give her more access to Trevor and his family without the threat of outside interference. It would definitely speed things up for her. If the police started poking around, the Martins would clam up and go even deeper into hiding.

And really, who would care about one mountain man who had turned up dead? He was totally off the grid, and as far as the government was concerned he was a nonentity. In fact, the only thing that his brothers, and folks like him, were known for were extremist ideals and a penchant for causing trouble.

Yet she couldn't be the one to bring up the idea of hiding the very dead Cussler brother.

Trevor stared in the direction of the shack. "We should call somebody…"

The way he spoke made her wonder if he was thinking along the same lines as her. No doubt, he didn't want anyone poking around, either.

"But?" she asked, prodding him on.

"I bet his family would go bonkers if we brought law enforcement out here. And the last thing this ranch needs is more craziness from the locals." He frowned. "We are just trying to fit in here. We don't want to draw unnecessary scrutiny from our new neighbors."

"Well, if you think that the Cusslers would appreciate us not—"

"Yes, I'm sure they would want to keep this a family issue." Trevor sounded sold on the idea.

She wanted to point out the possibility that the other members of the Cussler clan may be lying dead somewhere out in the timber as well. Otherwise wouldn't they have already buried their brother's body?

Yet she didn't want to press the issue. Not if it meant there was a possibility he would change his mind and call the police. Not that he would. She had the definite feeling he wanted to sweep this man's death under the rug just as much as she did.

"I'm going to go back in and take a look around," he said.

"Why?" she asked, before thinking.

He looked at her as though he was trying to decide how much he should open up to her. "If we're not going to call someone out here, we need to make sure that this isn't the work of some serial killer or something. You know what I mean?"

"You think he was murdered?" she asked, trying to play up the innocent and naive angle.

"My hope is that this is nothing more than a suicide. I just need to make sure."

She doubted that was really why he was going back in. He was probably looking for something more, something that would guarantee they wouldn't find themselves in deeper trouble if any of this ever came to light.

"You wait here. I'll be right back."

She grimaced. He hadn't really just tried to tell her what to do, had he? If he thought she was some kind of chattel that he could just order around, he had another think coming.

"Okay." She sighed as she tried to calmly remind herself he wasn't bossing her around out of some need for control; rather, it was his need to protect. "But be careful in there. If I know one thing about these kind of recluses, it's that they have a reputation for hating outsiders. They may have set up some kind of booby trap."

He stared at her like he was trying to figure her out. The look made her uncomfortable. "Got it, but I promise you have nothing to worry about when it comes to my safety. I have experience with this kind of thing."

His alleged role in peacekeeping and his family's Blackwater-type company was known, but she was surprised he was admitting any of it to her. Maybe her investigation wouldn't be as difficult as she had thought. Hell, if things went her way she could have all the answers she needed in a matter of days.

Then again, things would have to go her way, and life hadn't been playing nicely with her lately.

Trevor slipped back to the shack, holding up his phone as a flashlight as he made his way back inside.

She moved quietly after him. Maybe she could see something that he would miss, something that would prove the brother's death was nothing more than a suicide so they could put this all to rest.

As she walked toward the shack, she stopped. No. She couldn't pry. She couldn't get any more involved with this. If she went in there and did find something, there was a high probability that she would slip up and say something that would give away her background. He couldn't know anything about her position in the FBI.

She walked around to the back of the shack to where an old push lawn mower sat. There, on the ground beside it, was a puddle of dried blood. Pine needles had collected at the edges, making the pool look like some kind of macabre artwork.

She opened her mouth to call out to Trevor, but stopped. No. She couldn't tell him.

From the state of the body in the house, there was little possibility this blood belonged to the dead man. If someone had shot him out here and moved him, there would have been drag marks or some indication that the body had been staged. Though she hadn't spent long in the room with the dead man, she had noticed the blood leaking out of the wound at his temple. If she closed her eyes, she could still see the trail as it twisted down his ravaged features and leaked onto his dirty collar, staining it a ruddy brown. He couldn't have been moved postmortem. No, the blood pattern didn't match.

Which meant this blood had to belong to another person. And based on the volume of it on the ground, they were possibly dealing with more than a single death.

Crap.

She stared at the dried blood. Kneeling down, she scooped up a handful of the sharp, dried pine needles that were scattered around. What she was about to do could end up going all kinds of ass-backwards, but it had to be done for her, for her investigation and for her chance at getting her future back. There was nothing she wanted more than to rise in the ranks, and sometimes that meant that sacrifices had to be made.

She threw the needles atop the blood and stepped onto them. She kicked away at the dried blood, earth and needles until there was nothing.

It felt wrong to destroy evidence, but at the same time a sensation of freedom filled her. It was refreshing to break the rules and to make her own in name of the greater good.

Walking around to the door of the shack, she poked her head inside. Trevor took a step deeper into the shadows around the dead body. He knelt down and moved aside a piece of discarded cloth on the floor. He chuckled.

As he stood up, she saw a gun in his hand. He wiped the grip and the barrel down with his shirt, as though he was stripping it of any possible fingerprints.

There was only one reason he'd wipe the gun down— he was trying to protect the person who had pulled the trigger. Maybe that person was him.

Hell, he had probably come in here and killed the brothers in an attempt to get rid of them once and for all. Then he had waited for her to arrive before he rode up on his Harley like some kind of badass playboy.

He'd probably wanted her to see the man's body first. He'd wanted to come off as innocent. He'd wanted to take her in his arms and act the hero.

And she had allowed the bastard to set her up.

Chapter Three

Trevor walked up the front steps of the ranch house and waited as Sabrina parked her car and made her way over to him. He had told her that she could have the rest of the day off. She didn't need to come back to the main house with him—she could return to the old foreman's place, which was hers now—but she hadn't accepted his offer. Instead, she had only said that she had work to do.

Actually, it was the only thing she had said. The words had rung in his ears the entire ride back to the main house. There had been something in her sharp inflection that told him she was angry about something, something he was missing—and that there was danger afoot—but for the life of him, he didn't understand.

It was like he was married all over again, his life awash with unspoken anger and resentment. The memory of standing at the front door of his apartment, watching as his wife bedded another man on their once-pristine leather sofa, made a sickening knot rise in his belly.

Once again, just like before, he was forced to be an unwilling participant in things unspoken.

Hopefully this time he would be able to stop his life from falling to pieces in front of him.

She came to a stop beside him, but she was putting off a distinct "don't touch me" vibe.

He must have crossed some invisible barrier when he'd pulled her into his arms back at the shack, but it hadn't been his intention to make her feel uncomfortable. He had just been trying to help, to lend a shoulder to a woman in need, not to tick her off.

"Did you talk to Chad yet?" she said, glancing down at her watch like she was checking just how much time he'd had before she arrived.

He shook his head. Truth be told, he had been hoping she would keep driving instead of turning off on the little dirt road that led back to the ranch. It would have made sense, her running away after seeing the Cussler brother rotting in his chair.

And if she had kept driving, he could have had the real conversation he needed to have with Chad without worrying about what she would hear. Now he'd have to play it cool until he could get his brother alone and he had the chance to find out exactly what he knew. No doubt, Chad would have dealt with that man's remains as he had and left them out there for the Cussler family to handle.

They didn't need to draw undue attention. They needed to fly under the radar and off the grid for as long as possible.

He cringed at the thought of having to move again.

Getting out of Adana had been a nightmare after Trish's death. When they made their move to Montana, they sent misinformation on the dark net to make it seem like they were moving east to Thailand. They had no doubt that Turkish mobsters were just waiting for their chance to kill the rest of the family.

As long as nothing came out, they'd be safe for a while. It was the reason they had chosen this speck on the map. Plus, they'd have the cover of the United States and the amnesty that it offered if anything blew back on them. He and his family had done so many covert ops for the former president that they would always have government backup.

Or so he hoped.

Chad came sauntering out of the kitchen, a hot dog in his hand. He glanced from Sabrina to Trevor and gave him a raise of the brow as he stuffed the rest of the hot dog into his mouth, leaving a blob of mustard on his lip.

"I see you're already living the high life, brother," Trevor said with a laugh. "You want me to go in and get you a Budweiser, too? Nothing says American like a hot dog and a beer."

Chad swallowed the bite. "Not all of us developed a taste for world cuisine. You can't tell me that dolma is better than a good hot dog." He wiped off the speckle of mustard at the corner of his mouth with the back of his hand. "What do you think, Sabrina? You vote American food?"

She shrugged like she couldn't give a damn less. "Either, so long as I'm not cooking it."

"And that right there is the reason I hired you. I've always liked a woman who was as smart-mouthed as me. You are going to fit right in." Chad laughed. "Did you guys get the squatters handled?"

"Not exactly," Trevor said. He cocked his head toward Sabrina in a silent message to Chad.

Chad's smile disappeared. "Sabrina, do you mind getting started with your cleaning up here in the kitchen? 'Fraid I may have made a bit of a mess in there."

She opened her mouth to speak, but stopped and instead gave Trevor a look as though she hoped he would step in and allow her to take part in their conversation.

"Uh, actually…" Trevor stammered. "Sabrina, you must be pretty tired. Like I said, if you wanted to head back to your place—"

"No," she said, taking off her jacket and hanging it in the coat closet just inside the door. "I'll get started in the kitchen. I have a job to do, and this place isn't going to get any cleaner if I just go back to my place."

Sabrina strode into the kitchen and the door swung shut behind her.

"Let's step outside," Trevor said.

Chad followed him out and Trevor made sure to close the door behind his brother. He glanced in the front window of the house to make sure that Sabrina wasn't anywhere in sight. Thankfully, it looked as though she was in the kitchen.

"What in the hell were you thinking sending that woman out there?" Trevor asked, turning back to his brother. "Do you know what the hell I found in that shack? And because you were in some freaking hurry, Sabrina saw. Now she's a possible loose end."

"First, you were supposed to get out there long before her. You don't get to make this my fault. You should have stuck to the schedule."

"Had I known you were sending someone out behind me, I would have. How about you learn to freaking communicate?" Even as he said it, he couldn't help but feel that he was the pot calling the kettle black.

"What exactly did she see?" Chad asked, taking a step back from him like he was afraid that Trevor was going to take a swing.

"That damned Cussler guy was splattered all over the walls. Been dead at least two or three days." He pointed in the direction of the shanty. "I had to convince Sabrina that the dude was better off if we just left him and waited for the family to come back and collect his remains."

Chad turned around as he ran his hands down his face. He stomped as he turned back. "Are you kidding me? We haven't been here a week and there's already a dead bastard in our back forty?"

"You should have just left me to handle my end of things, man. I had this taken care of. All I needed was a little time. But no, you wanted to rush things. To make sure everything was cleaned out and taken care of before Zoey and Jarrod arrive."

"You know how they can be—they were even more adamant than I was about the absolute need for privacy here. This family is all we have, Trevor."

"You don't need to tell *me* that."

Chad took in a long breath as though he were trying to collect himself. "So, was the guy's death a suicide or what?"

"There's no goddamned way. Someone shot him." He thought of the handgun he'd left sitting on the ground beside the dead man. "The gun was too far away from the body. No major stippling around the entrance wound, and the bullet had lost enough velocity that it didn't even travel through the entire skull—there was no exit wound. I'm guessing whoever pulled the trigger had to be at least ten to fifteen feet away."

"And where did you say you found the man?"

"He was sitting up in a chair, like someone got the drop on him. He didn't even have time to stand. He didn't see it coming."

"What about the rest of the hillbilly clan…did you find them? They alive or dead?"

"Hell if I know." Trevor threw his hands into the air. "I'm hoping that they just ran off. We don't need a dead family on our hands."

"Did you get a chance to look around?" Chad asked. "Wait, did you and Sabrina call in the locals?"

Finally, Chad was beginning to understand the implications of his screwup. If only he hadn't been in a hurry, they wouldn't already be compromised.

"Sabrina went along with keeping it quiet, but I don't know how long she'll be up for maintaining that." He glanced back inside, but the beautiful and stubborn woman was nowhere in sight. "She hasn't been acting right, ever since…" *I held her in my arms.* He didn't finish his thought.

"Huh? Ever since what?" Chad pressed.

"Since she saw the body. I'm afraid she may be a liability."

"What are you saying?" Chad asked. "You think she needs to disappear?"

"No," Trevor said, almost the same moment his brother had uttered the question. "No. We can't harm her. She hasn't done anything wrong. And who knows, maybe I made a mistake in thinking she can't be trusted. Maybe she won't be a problem."

Chad shook his head. "What if she does tell someone? What if it comes out that we tried to cover up a man's death at our new ranch?"

Trevor stared at his boots. "She wouldn't…"

"Dude, if she tells anyone… First, we are going to look as guilty as hell. Second, our faces are going to be spread across the world in a matter of hours."

"She won't say anything."

"And how are you going to know if she does or doesn't? For all we know, she's in there texting her mother's brother's cousin about what you guys found. Hell, she could be sending pictures of the dead guy." Chad paused. "You know that I don't want to hurt an innocent woman. Not after what happened in Turkey… And Trish…" Their sister's name fell off his brother's tongue like it was some secret code, some unspoken link between past and present.

"Then let's leave her be."

Chad shook his head. "No. If you don't want to neutralize the threat, you're going to have to watch her like a hawk. Every move she makes, you need to be there… hovering."

"And what about the squatters? The body?"

Chad sighed. "What about it? Like you said, let that guy's family handle it."

"And what if they do, and they call the police?"

"If they haven't already, they aren't about to now." Chad stared at him. "For all we know, one of them is the one who pulled the trigger—or else they're lying out there in the woods somewhere, too. Either those bastards are on the run or they aren't going to be spilling any secrets any time soon."

"Do you think I should go back out there? See if I can find them? Make sure that they're going to stay quiet?"

Chad stared out in the direction of the main pasture, but Trevor could tell that he wasn't really looking at anything. "I'll talk to Zoey and see if we can find out a little more on these Cussler guys. I want to know how many hillbillies were living out there, and who would have wanted them dead. I want to make sure that whoever is responsible for pulling that trigger isn't about to bear down on us."

His brother was right. They needed to make sure they weren't about to be ambushed.

"Most importantly," Chad continued, "I want you to keep Sabrina quiet. If you don't…you know what's at stake."

"She won't be a problem." Trevor paused, thumbing the gun at his side and letting it comfort him from his barrage of thoughts. "Hey…you don't think these Cussler guys have anything to do with STEALTH, do you?"

Chad shook his head, but from the way his face pinched, Trevor could tell that he was wondering the same thing. "Bayural and the Gray Wolves couldn't know that we are here. Zoey has made it her business to make sure of it. Everything we did has been in cash, or through Bitcoin. We're covered."

"Just because our sister is a computer whiz, it doesn't mean that we are safe. You know how easy it is to find someone, especially a group like our family. One stupid random selfie with us in the background and we're in danger. They are using the same facial recognition software that we are."

"Zoey has this under control," Trevor said, trying to give them both a little comfort—it had always been his job to keep the peace within the family, a job that had proven harder than ever thanks to his failure with Trish. His mistake was something that neither he nor the rest of his siblings would ever forget. "Besides, Zoey has made it her personal mission to keep them chasing fake hits around the globe. From what she said this morning, she currently has us pinging at a marketplace in Cairo."

Chad chuckled. "God, can you imagine those bastards' faces when they realize that they've been set up? I would almost pay to see it."

There was the clatter of pans hitting the floor from inside the kitchen.

Chad bounded up the porch steps and cracked the door. "Sabrina, you okay in there?"

"Fine, just fine!" she called back, sounding harried.

"Where did you find this woman?" Trevor asked, motioning toward the house.

"She came recommended from Gwen when we bought the ranch. They hired her when they were getting the ranch ready for us to take it over."

"So, just because our cousin—whom we barely know—thinks this woman is trustworthy, you took her word for it?" Trevor was surprised. Chad wasn't one for details but he was normally careful about who they brought into their lives.

"Brotato chip, you seriously have to pull the stick out of your ass. You're starting to act like Jarrod."

He was nothing like their oldest brother. Jarrod had been a lone wolf since the moment he called upon them to take their positions within the business. After he had set up STEALTH he hit the road, looking for assignments from various governments.

"I hope Zoey looked into her background," Trevor pressed.

"Of course. Zoey said she was clean, nothing too much to tell. Looks like Sabrina had been travelling around the world with her military family until she turned eighteen, just working odds-and-ends jobs since then."

It was in line with the little Sabrina had told him, but something still felt wrong. Trevor glanced toward the kitchen where Sabrina was working. Maybe someday, if he could just ease himself back into being a civilian, something might start feeling right.

A man could only hope.

Chapter Four

She sat in the corner of the barn, letting the streak of morning sun that was leaking through the siding spread over the tips of her boots. Though the beam had to be warm, she couldn't feel it through the leather. Maybe the sun was just like the rest of her life…pretty to look at, but completely devoid of feeling.

Then again, yesterday had been full of them—at least when it came to Trevor. She glanced down at her phone and his picture. The photo was sharp, black-and-white, typical of the FBI. And yet it didn't really capture the man she had met. No, in real life he was far less imposing than he seemed in the picture. The photo failed to show the way it felt to stand there encircled in his arms, and then to realize that he had been playing her from the moment they met.

She flipped to the email from her handler, Agent Mike Couer, and stared at the man's instructions. She'd have to play nice, get along and then get out of there. If she didn't screw this up, she could be in and out without the Martins even knowing who she was or what she did. She'd made it this far; as long as she didn't get wrapped up in another set of arms, she'd be just fine.

For a moment she considered calling Mike and telling him about the body they had found, but she stopped. There wasn't enough evidence to track this back to the family. Sure, she could probably take Trevor down for the murder, but that wasn't what she was here for; no, she was here for them all. They had to be stopped before they put any more weapons into the hands of terrorist organizations…and that was to say nothing of the lives that they themselves had snuffed out. This family was likely responsible for the deaths of thousands of people, if not tens of thousands.

The thought made the anger bubble up inside her. These days that feeling, that fire, was her only constant companion. Without it, she wouldn't know who she was. It was that feeling that propelled her forward, past the crap in her personal life, and helped her to focus on her prime objectives. Her life wasn't hers to live. Her life belonged to the people of the world, people who deserved to be kept safe and out of the line of fire of the Martins.

Stuffing the phone back into her pocket, she made her way into the house.

She just needed to get her hands on as much information about the incident in Turkey as possible. There were reports of photos, pictures proving that the STEALTH team had been involved in the illegal gun trade, and during the event civilians had been shot and killed. If she could just prove it, or find evidence that the family was part of organized crime, not only would her past indiscretions at the agency be forgiven, but she might also find her way out of the remote offices and back to DC.

The house was silent as she weaved between the

moving boxes. Trevor and Chad had been vague in their plans for the day, but she expected nothing less. No doubt, they were at the shanty taking care of their mess. She should have been out there with them, getting information about their possible involvement with the dead man and his family, but she hadn't found a way to get herself invited along. And really, even if she caught Trevor red-handed with this murder, where would it get her?

He was good at keeping people in the dark, but his family wasn't as good as they thought they were. She'd get what she needed. She always did.

Trevor's bedroom door was closed, but his room seemed like as good a spot as any to start. She opened the door. The room had nothing but four boxes, a desk, and a mattress and box spring on the floor. At the head of the bed, there was a rolled-up mummy bag sitting on a large body pillow.

Apparently, even though he had nothing, he was a man who still liked to make his bed in the morning.

Grabbing a box, she set it on the bed and pulled off the tape. As it opened, the scent of sand and sweat rose up and met her—the smell of war.

Well, she could fight, too.

She pulled out a set of fatigues. They were green and brown, a throwback to what Americans once wore in the jungles of Vietnam—not what she would have expected from desert warfare. The last time she'd seen an operative wearing this was in northern Africa. Some of the insurgents there loved to use the fatigues almost as their own personal calling card. They had even taken to calling themselves al-Akhdar, or "the Greens."

It didn't surprise her that this man would have found himself alongside such an infamous group. From what little she knew about them, the Martins had a way of being in prospective war zones even before the leaders of the country knew they were under fire.

She lifted the uniform out of the box and hung it up in Trevor's closet. Though she never had time to clean her own apartment back in Washington, coming in undercover as a cleaning lady had its benefits. She could almost openly go through whatever she wanted under the guise of her newfound job.

It didn't take long to empty the box and move to the next, putting away things as she came across them. Though she hadn't expected to find much in the boxes, she had hoped that maybe he'd tucked something away—a picture, some sentimental token—but there was nothing. In fact, aside from his picture and the few boxes that were in the room, there was little to prove that this man truly even existed.

The only things she'd been able to glean so far, thanks to what she'd managed to overhear from the brothers this morning, was that the rest of the family—Zoey and Jarrod—would be arriving sometime soon. When they got there, she would have little time alone in the house. She'd have to work fast.

After going through what amounted to four boxes of random clothing and a set of encyclopedias that she was sure dated from the 1980s, she folded up the boxes. Carrying them under her arm, she stepped toward the door. As she moved, she noticed a gap between the head of the bed and the wall. It wasn't much, just a couple of inches.

Making her way over to the gap, she pulled back his pillow, exposing a long black gun case.

Now we're talking.

She pulled out the case, gingerly setting it on the bed and clicking open the tabs. In the belly of the case sat an M107 .50 caliber. She'd only seen a few of these in her days, and they were always in the hands of snipers—army snipers, to be exact. She snapped a quick picture of the gun and its serial number, but made sure not to touch the weapon. She sent a quick message to her people at the Bureau, hoping that one of them could pull up something.

He had played her when he'd brought up Schofield. He must have been testing her. Which meant there had been something about her that made him think that she couldn't be trusted. Or maybe he mistrusted everyone. She racked her brain trying to think of something she had said or done that could have blown her cover, but nothing came to mind. She'd played it pretty cool...except for the girlie bit.

Or perhaps he wasn't Army after all. If his family had in fact been running weapons, as they assumed, then maybe this was just one from their catalog. There was little reason for Trevor to have such a specialized weapon out here in the Middle of Nowhere, Montana. Unless he feared for their safety, or he thought he was one phone call away from having to kill someone.

She was probably right in assuming he was the type who was always looking over his shoulder. It probably came with his kind of game.

Maybe it was that she simply saw some of her own life mirrored in his. Over the last year, thanks to her little slipup—okay, major setback—she had been away from home and the Bureau nearly the entire time. In fact, there had been only three days that she was in the office. One when she went in to see *him*, one when she was called into her superior's office and told she would henceforth be working remotely, and then when she was packing up her desk. Ever since then, she'd been living out of hotel rooms around the world. Everything in her life had been temporary and single-use.

She ran her fingers through her smooth hair. Since she'd taken residence at the Widow Maker Ranch she'd finally gotten the chance to buy and use real shampoo again, and not be stuck with the cheap stuff that was always in the guest basket at the hotels where she stayed.

Compared to Trevor's constantly on-guard life—a life that required high-caliber rifles and owning nothing but a smattering of dusty old clothes—a few split ends seemed to pale in comparison. At least she had a certain amount of freedom. For the most part, she could check out when she was off duty.

For a split second, she felt a niggle of pity for the handsome Trevor Martin. He was never going to be able to live a normal life, not doing what his family did. They would always be hunted. And forget about having a love life.

The pity turned to something else, something entirely too much like disappointment.

She was just being silly. What was going on with her since she met this man? It was like she had never been around a good-looking, dangerous, Harley-riding, perfectly built badass before.

She closed the gun case, slipping it back in exactly the same position she had found it.

No doubt with her unpacking his room and all, he would probably assume she had seen it, but she didn't want to make it blatant. And hopefully he would brush it aside, thinking she was the kind of woman who knew nothing about guns.

Her secret made a smile flutter over her lips. There was just something thrilling about being something and someone that no one expected at first glance. It was almost like a superpower...if she were a superhero, she'd have a cool name. No, better than cool—she'd want something enigmatic, mysterious. Something like the Shadow Defender, keeper of secrets and protector of the innocent.

She giggled as she walked out of the room, running smack-dab into Chad. Looking up, she tried to cover the guilt that was no doubt marking her features. Damn it, how had he gotten in without her hearing anything?

"Hey," she said, stepping around him. "I thought you guys were out for the day."

Chad glanced toward his brother's room. "Uh, yeah. What were you doing in there? Does Trevor know you were planning on going in there?"

She gave him her most alluring smile, hoping that she could bring down his suspicions in true female superhero style. "I just thought I'd get a move on unpacking all the boxes. I was going to go ahead and hit your room next. That way you guys have a comfortable safe haven to come home to at the end of the day." She shifted her weight, subtly exaggerating the curve of her hips. "There's nothing worse than a barren room."

Chad's eyebrow rose.

Crap, hopefully he didn't think she was making a move on him; she hadn't meant anything. No, not when it came to him. Chad was good-looking enough, but he wasn't nearly as handsome as Trevor. She thought back to the way Trevor had taken off his helmet and swept the long hair from his eyes. If he had a fan blowing on him, she might as well have been watching a freaking modeling shoot.

She turned before Chad could get any clue as to what she was thinking. The last thing she really needed was either brother assuming there was any possibility of something more than an employee-employer situation.

"Sabrina?" Chad called after her. "If you don't mind, I'll go ahead and unpack my things. No need for you to worry about it."

She waved behind her, not bothering to look back. There went her chance, at least for now, to get into his room. At least she had a starting point to her investigation. If she ran the serial number on the .50cal, maybe she could pull up something. If she was lucky, there would be some agency out there tracking the gun, but based on what had just happened, luck wasn't on her side.

She made her way to the newly remodeled kitchen, which still smelled of paint. As she pulled a box of Cap'n Crunch out of the pantry, the back door opened and Trevor strode in. He was sweaty and shirtless, wearing only a pair of running shorts and tennis shoes. He stopped and stared at her for a moment too long before he shut the door. Apparently he hadn't been planning on bumping into her, either.

He wiped his forehead with the back of his hand as he walked over to the cupboard by the sink and grabbed a glass of water. Since his back was to her, she could make out a droplet of sweat slowly twisting down the thick muscles along the tanned skin of his spine. The bead moved slowly, making her wonder if it tickled.

"I see you're one for a healthy start to the day. I like it," he said, filling up his glass and turning around with a cheesy, oh-so-cute smile on his face.

"The Cap'n and I have a long-term relationship," she said, hugging the box to her chest like it was a bulletproof vest. "He knows just how to make me smile."

"I hear you. I'm a sucker when it comes to food."

"You know what they say about the way to a man's heart," Sabrina said, but as the words escaped her, she just as quickly wished she could rein them back in.

Why couldn't she just be normal around this guy— flirty, yet out-of-bounds? Instead, here she was saying things that she couldn't have imagined herself saying when she was forced to take this assignment.

"In that case," Trevor said, grabbing a towel and dabbing at his forehead, "would you mind pouring me a bowl? I'll be right back, just going to go put on a shirt." He flipped the kitchen towel over his shoulder.

Hold up, had he really just implied she could make her way into his heart? No. He couldn't have meant anything like that.

As he walked away she once again found herself staring at the little bead of sweat, which now sat at the subtle indent that marked the place where his hips met his back. Her gaze moved lower as he walked away.

His shorts moved in perfect harmony with his round, toned behind.

Yeah, she could touch that. Chances were, he would fit perfectly in the cup of her hand.

Wait, he was playing her. She couldn't fall for his abundant charms or his easy grace. No.

She turned around and grabbed a bowl from the cupboard and poured him some cereal, carefully setting the milk on the table beside it so he could add it in when he came back.

Her phone pinged with an email. Checking around her to make sure no one was near before opening it, she unlocked her phone. There was a message from Mike. Just seeing his name pop up on her screen made her stomach clench. Just once, she would have liked to not have that feeling. It was stupid, really. His name would always pop up. He was too involved in her life for him to just disappear. If anything, she was foolish to think she would just get over him and be able to go back to work and pretend that nothing had happened between them.

Maybe she would have been better off quitting her job and moving on to something else, but she had told herself she was a big girl—able to handle anything that life threw at her, that she would just have to accept the consequences that came with her choices...and yet she seemed to always die just a little every time she saw anything to do with her former flame.

She hated him. Everything emotional he represented. He was the embodiment of all of her worst flaws—her inability to say no, to make people unhappy, and the weakness she felt when it came to the needs of her heart.

If only she could turn the damned thing off, be cold, distant, professional.

Opening the email, she read the encrypted note:

Dear Ms. Parker,

In regard to your findings at your current posting, we are and have been aware of your assignments' past—including jobs dealing with long-gun usage. I'm glad to see you are finally making headway. Too bad it has taken you this long.

If you fail to meet the goals and standards set forth in your proposal in a timely manner, the SAC has let me know that they will be forced to look elsewhere for a UC who is better qualified. You have a week.

—M.C.

What a bastard. Mike had known what Trevor was and he'd left it out of the case files he'd handed her. He was trying to get her fired.

Of course.

What had she been thinking, assuming her sentence would be simple banishment to a remote office as an undercover agent along with her former flame? The special agent in charge, or SAC, whom they'd been forced to report to regarding their relationship had put them together out here in the middle of nowhere, hoping that they would learn to get along and develop a new sense of trust with each other. But the move had been ill-advised. As it was, she had a feeling she was in a dog-eat-dog battle with her ex, and only one would leave this kennel alive.

No big deal. She could do this. In fact, there was no

better impetus for her to kick butt and take names than someone thinking she was incapable—or, in this case, Mike thinking he had the upper hand and assuming he could get rid of her that easily. She would show him, and the rest of the Bureau, exactly what she was made of.

The door to the kitchen opened and Trevor walked in. His smile had disappeared.

"Were you looking for something in particular?" he asked, the playful edge in his voice completely gone.

"Excuse me?" she asked, feeling the blood rush from her face as she stuffed her phone in her pocket.

"You went through my things. Why?" he said, staring at her.

She paused, thinking about every syllable before she spoke. "Your family hired me to do a job. I am here to help you get this house in order." She walked to the drawer and pulled out a spoon for him and set it down on the table beside his bowl like it was some kind of olive branch. "I have no interest in disrupting your life or invading your privacy," she lied, forcing her face to remain unpassable.

"Then why?"

"I told you why. I want to help." She sat down at the table, hoping he would recognize her contrition. "Look, I understand you're nervous. But about the man we found yesterday…"

Some of the anger disappeared from his face. "Did you tell anyone about the body?"

She shook her head. "Like I said, I am here to make your life easier, not cause more problems. If you don't want me to go in your room anymore, I won't." There wasn't anything in there she was looking for anyway.

He sighed. "No, don't worry about it. I guess I'm just a little jumpy. I'm not used to civilian life."

"That's okay. We're just going to need to start learning to communicate a little better with each other—especially when it comes to our boundaries." She motioned for him to sit.

He picked up the spoon as he sat down, finally a bit more relaxed in her presence.

Maybe she wasn't so bad as a UC after all—given time, she would get exactly what she needed.

Chapter Five

Trevor didn't quite know what to make of her. On one hand, Sabrina seemed to be everything a cleaning woman would be—focused, driven and into all of his things. On the other hand, the mere thought of someone poking around his house made him clench. He hadn't had a woman taking care of his life for him since... well, he was a child.

Done with breakfast, he walked back to his room. He hadn't had a closet, at least one that wasn't in a hotel or rented room, in forever. It was strange to think he actually owned something. In a way, it felt like a leash tying him to this place.

He had spent entirely too much time being out in the world and on his own to adjust to this kind of lifestyle overnight, but he had to admit that it would be nice to just hand things over to someone else for a while. For once, he could just focus on living.

A pit formed in his stomach. He'd been working in the shadows for so long he wasn't quite sure what living actually meant. The only thing he knew for sure was that he didn't want to be alone.

He thought of the way Sabrina had looked over

breakfast, her long hair falling down in her face like gentle fingers that longed to caress her cheeks. He'd wanted to reach over and brush the tendrils out of her face, but as much as he had desired it, to touch her seemed wrong...especially after what had happened at the Cusslers'.

No matter how beautiful she was, she was clearly not interested in him. And yet if there was one reason he was glad to be leashed to this place, it was because of her.

But could he trust her?

He closed his bedroom door and walked to the head of the bed. Lifting out the gun case, he looked at the latch. The hair he'd left tucked in the lock was gone. She'd seen his gun.

No wonder she had been so strange with him, nervous even. He could only guess what she thought of him. Hopefully she thought he was just some redneck with a penchant for high-end weaponry. Or better yet, she hadn't a clue what she was looking at.

He pulled a hair from his head and put it back in the latch, setting the booby trap again. If she came back... well, they were going to have to have a longer talk. He'd show her exactly how well he could communicate.

Slipping the gun case back, he sat down on his bed and pulled out his phone. Zoey had sworn that she'd looked into the woman's background, and he trusted his sister's judgment and aptitude when it came to technology...and yet, every cell in his body was telling him that Sabrina wasn't all she seemed to be. Zoey had to be missing something. He didn't know much about housekeepers, but it couldn't have been normal for them to open a gun case…that was, unless they were going to strip it down and clean the gun, or if they were looking for something.

Whatever she was looking for, she wasn't going to find it in his gun case. The only thing she'd find there was a recipe for disaster.

He unlocked his phone and went to his secondary email. Ever so carefully, he wrote:

Dear Ahmal,
My team will be in place Wednesday night for the hand-off. Johnson and Beckwith. City Centre. Seven o'clock.
T

If Sabrina was a spy, she'd have it read within the hour. If she was a decent spy, she'd have men in downtown Seattle Wednesday at seven.

He emailed Zoey using his private server, letting her know to keep eyes on the fake drop.

The pit that had formed in his stomach started to dissipate. For now, he'd done all he could to put his mind at ease…at least when it came to Sabrina.

He still needed to get to the bottom of the Cussler murder.

Crap. What if she is tied to the murder?

No. He shook his head at the very thought. She was suspicious, but she didn't seem like the type who would kill people. He'd seen those types more than he could count, and she didn't carry the same darkness in her eyes.

If anything, her blue eyes were like the sky…open, bright, and full of promise. And the way she sometimes looked at him, when she was unguarded it was like she wanted…well, she wanted *him*.

Yep, he was definitely losing his edge.

He needed to get to work.

As he made his way from his room and the traps he secretly hoped she wouldn't step into, Sabrina was whisking her way around the living room, dusting.

"I need to head up to check out the Cusslers. You wanna go with me?" he asked, trying not to notice the way her jeans hugged her curves as she bent over to dust the bottom of the built-in bookcase next to the television.

"Sure." She turned and smiled. "I don't know if you know this, but there is only so much of a mess that a man and his brother can make in a house. I swear, I've dusted this room at least three times in the last day. I could use a break."

He chuckled. "I can't say that I've dusted three times in my entire life. What's the point? It's just going to get dusty again."

She laughed, the sound high and full of life, and it made his longing for her intensify. It would have been so easy to take her back into his arms. She was…incredible.

Maybe being around her today was a mistake, not only professionally but personally as well.

"I…" he started, but the sound came out hoarse and he was forced to clear his throat. "Sorry. I was just going to say, I was thinking about running over to see our cousin at her family's ranch, Dunrovin. Maybe we could borrow a couple of horses and ride around the property and maybe a bit up the mountains behind the squatters' place…see if we find evidence that could help us get to the bottom of this guy's death."

Her face pinched for a moment, but then her smile returned…this time not quite reaching her eyes. "I haven't been on a horse in years, but I'd be happy to help you out. Investigating a murder is far more fun than cleaning a house." She walked to the coat closet and grabbed a jacket before turning back to him. "Wait, should I not say that? You being my employer and all?" She gave him a melting smile.

It worked.

"I'm not your employer…that would be my brother." He took her jacket from her and lifted it so she could simply slip her arms into it. As she moved under his hands, his fingers grazed her skin, sending sparks shooting through him.

He tried to ignore the way she made him feel, but the more he ignored it the hotter the sparks seemed to burn.

He walked a few steps behind her on the way out to his motorcycle. For a moment, she stood staring at it. "Um, do you just want to take my car?"

He checked his laugh. "What? Are you afraid of a little danger?"

Sabrina gave him a cute little half smirk. "There is a difference between danger and a death wish. Do you know how many people die each year on these things?"

Though he couldn't deny her logic, she wasn't seeing the bigger picture. "I've always thought life should be lived to its fullest. Sure, you can stay in a safe little bubble and live an extra day, or you can grab life by the horns and ride it for all it's got."

She laughed. "Of course, you would say that…if

you want to ride, feel free, but I'll be following you in my car."

In a strange way, he found comfort in her refusal. Clearly, she wasn't the kind of woman who sought an adrenaline rush...or who wanted to court danger. Rather, she seemed to want to play by the rules. No one who lied for a living played by the rules all the time. There was a certain level of gray that just came with the life. He couldn't count the number of times he had been forced to break the law in order to serve the greater good. It was one of the things he had missed most about standing in the countryside of Turkey, running guns over militarized borders and taking down men who deserved to die a thousand painful deaths in recompense for the horrendous crimes they had committed.

Trevor had always considered himself to be on the side of righteousness when he'd been in the thick of things, but now...looking back, he couldn't help but wonder if he had made mistakes. There had been plenty of times when he didn't have to pull the trigger, when he could have let his target go...and yet, he'd never flinched. For him, there was never any hesitation. He was just there to do his job, do right by his family and get home safely. He'd never questioned his orders or his assignments. But what if he should have? What if he had killed innocents?

"Let's go ahead and take your car. I don't have a helmet for you anyway. And the last thing I'd want is for you to get hurt." He motioned toward her beat-up Pontiac. The paint was chipping around the wheel wells, and what paint remained was bubbling with rust. Clearly not a Bucar—a Bureau car—so she couldn't have been sent here by the Feds. That was, unless they had put her in this junker so she wouldn't fall under any unwanted scrutiny.

They did undercover well, but they weren't this good.

Besides, what could he possibly be under investigation for—they worked for the CIA. However, in the US government, they were notorious for the right hand not knowing what the left hand was doing...and it had only gotten worse with the new leadership in the Oval Office on down.

Then again, she could have been working for a foreign government. The Gray Wolves were known to have people planted throughout the Turkish government, and he wouldn't have doubted that they also had government allies in and around Europe.

He sighed as he opened her door and helped her into the car. He was making something out of nothing. Though he wasn't completely innocent, he wasn't guilty, either. He just needed to relax.

He walked around to the passenger side and stopped for a moment, trying to contain the writhing ball of snakes that were his feelings. Even if an innocent person had been killed, it hadn't likely been by him. He'd only fired on his enemies, but...they had been in an enclosed space. What if a round had ripped through the building and somehow struck someone outside? It had been known to happen.

In his time in the military, they'd touched on the topic of collateral damage time and time again. He'd always told himself that he was above making mistakes, especially ones that involved lives... but now he couldn't help questioning himself.

He'd let his sister down. He'd let her die. What if he'd killed someone else's family member in the process?

He closed his eyes, but the second he closed them he saw Trish's face, looking up at him as the pool of blood around her grew. He'd tried to save her. He'd killed at least five men getting to her, but by the time he'd gotten her to safety, it was already too late.

Every night since he'd gotten back to the States, he'd had the same nightmare—him doing those damned chest compressions on Trish. Waiting for her to take a breath. Checking her pulse. And watching in terror as he realized she was gone.

He was living in his own personal version of hell.

He'd never forgive himself.

All he could do now was protect the family he had left. And that started with making sure this Cussler guy's family wasn't going to come after them or bring the law down on them. They didn't need any more trouble.

As they drove to Dunrovin, he caught himself glancing over at Sabrina again and again. She seemed to be concentrating entirely too hard on her driving. Her eyes were picking up the light as it streamed in through the windshield, making them look even brighter. And now, in the sun, he could see the fine lines around her eyes and at the upturned corners of her mouth—the lines of someone who loved to laugh. In a way, it made her seem even more beautiful. Whoever had her on his arm was a lucky man.

"Have you been to this place before?" he asked, forcing himself to look away.

She nodded. "Yeah, I helped Gwen move their stuff

to the new place when she and her mother decided to sell you all the ranch. Dunrovin is really nice. They've had some trouble in their past, but now they are up and running and doing well as a guest ranch."

They must not have the same problem with squatters that they were having at the Widow Maker. "Hey, you never did tell me what you knew about the Cusslers. I tried to look them up this morning, but it doesn't appear that they have left much of a paper trail."

"I don't know much, just what Gwen told me in passing."

"So she knew there were people living out there in the boondocks?"

Sabrina passed him a guilty look.

He wasn't sure if he should be annoyed that his cousin hadn't taken care of the problem before they arrived, or if he should be concerned. Gwen must have known the danger. Maybe she had avoided them out of fear.

He just loved walking into a hornet's nest.

"Do you know how many folks we should be worried about out there?"

"From what I know, which isn't too much, it sounds like there were just some brothers. I'm assuming that the man we found is one of them."

"Were any of the brothers married?" he asked.

"I don't know. They were all pretty reclusive, but with that came an ability to live off the land. Whoever is left out there, they are certainly more than capable of surviving."

He nodded. He wasn't worried about their ability to survive—in fact, he was about as far away from that concern as humanly possible. They were just looking for more potential threats. Hopefully he wouldn't tangle with the remaining brothers, their wives, kids, grand-kids, dogs and who knew who or what else. He had been in that situation before. Family dynamics always had a way of complicating any situation.

When they found the rest of the clan—rather, if they found them—he could speak to them and discover what happened. Maybe he was making something out of nothing. Maybe the Cusslers had gotten in a fight, and the man he'd found had been on the losing end. Hope-fully, this had nothing to do with the Gray Wolves, or Trevor's family's long-term safety.

"I'm not sure if you're aware," Sabrina started, sounding nervous, "but Gwen's husband, Wyatt, is the local sheriff's deputy here."

"Sabrina, can I ask you something?" As he asked, he second-guessed himself.

"Hmm?" she said, looking over at him and away from the road.

"I appreciate you not wanting to make waves with this guy's death…but why—"

Her face pinched as she interrupted him. "Let's just say that I don't want to draw any unnecessary atten-tion."

"Why? Are you on the run from the law or some-thing?"

She laughed, but the sound was tight. "Hardly. I just don't like drama. I've had enough of that over the last couple of years." She tapped her fingers on the steering wheel nervously. "And as much as I think murderers should be held accountable, this guy didn't seem like the type that would want someone digging too deeply into his life."

To a certain degree, he agreed with her. However, everything just felt off about her answer. She was hiding something.

"If you don't mind me asking, what kind of drama have you been going through?"

She nibbled at her lip, like she was deciding whether to tell him the truth. It all came down to this—if she opened up to him he would finally be able to trust her. If she didn't, well…

"Let's just say I found myself in a relationship with the worst possible man."

Oh.

She was wounded. Now she was beginning to make a little more sense to him. He could understand some of the fear and pain she was feeling.

"I get it." It was the only thing he could think to say. What he really wanted to do was to pull her into his arms and make her feel better. Together, they could heal from the traumas of their past.

Sabrina chuckled. "What about you—any skeletons in your closet?"

He visibly twitched but tried to cover it up by casually scratching at his neck. He wasn't sure he was ready to tell her about his own failed relationships. "I… I used to be married."

Instead of coming at him with questions, as he assumed she would, she sat in silence for a long time letting the road roll by.

"I hope you know you can trust me," she said, finally breaking the silence between them.

This time he didn't even try to cover up his twitch. There was no way she could possibly read his mind, and yet here they were. "The rifle at the head of my bed..."

She tensed, her hands wrapping tight around the steering wheel until her knuckles were white. "Yeah, I was going to ask you about that."

At least she wasn't denying or trying to hide the fact that she had gotten into his gun case. He could respect her honesty.

"I spent quite a few years in the army before we started in the investments game. I guess some old habits die hard."

He was grateful as a ranch came into view in the distance. There was a long row of stables, a main house and a bright red barn. The place looked like something out of *Town & Country* magazine. "Is that Dunrovin?"

Sabrina nodded. "You should see this place at Christmas. Gwen showed me some pictures of last year's Yule Night Festival. There were Christmas lights everywhere, the whole shebang."

He had no idea what the Yule Night thing was, but he was glad they were no longer talking about their pasts.

As they drove up and parked in the gravel lot of the ranch, a group of mutts ran out to greet them. Well, mostly mutts. Among them was a small Chihuahua barking maniacally at their approach. In fact, the little dog seemed to be the leader of the pack, egging on the rest of them in their cacophony.

"Looks like we got the royal greeting," he said with a chuckle.

An older woman walked out from the ranch's office, waving at them as they approached. Behind her was a woman with long, wild blond hair whom he recognized as his cousin Gwen. He hadn't seen her since they were children, but even the way she moved, with an air of confidence and grace, hadn't really changed.

The older woman called the dogs off and herded them into the office, closing the door behind the pack and then turning back to Trevor and Sabrina. "Welcome to Dunrovin. It's a pleasure to finally get the chance to meet you, Trevor. I've heard so much about you from Gwen," she said, extending her hand as he made his way up the steps.

"The pleasure is all mine..." He shook her hand as he waited for her to supply him with her name. Hopefully all she had heard about him had been positive.

When he and Gwen had last met, when they were both about eight years old. He had pulled her pigtails, which had quickly devolved into a wrestling match that ended with them both muddy messes. He could still distinctly remember the hay sticking out of Gwen's French braids and the stupid, victorious smile on her face.

"Eloise. Eloise Fitzgerald," the silver-haired woman said, giving his hand a strong shake.

"Hey guys," Gwen said with a nod. "I already have the horses waiting for you in the trailer. Are you sure you don't want me to go along with you on your ride? I know some great Forest Service trails. There's one up Elk Meadows you would love."

Eloise jabbed a sharp-looking elbow into Gwen's ribs and looked back and forth between him and Sabrina, like she was seeing something between them that wasn't there.

"Oh," he said with a chuckle. "We...no..."

"It's not that kind of ride," Sabrina said, finishing his sentence for him. "We are just going to go out and check some fences, then maybe head up the mountain for a couple of hours."

Gwen frowned. "The fences were in good order when I left."

Eloise looked over at her like she was clearly not getting the hint. "Don't worry about it, Gwen. You and I have plenty of things to do in the office today. In fact, I was hoping you could call next week's guests and confirm their reservations. Then we need to finalize the menus and talk to the kitchen staff."

Thank goodness for busy work.

"I'll be waiting for you in the office," Eloise said, motioning inside. "Shortly."

Gwen nodded as Eloise gave them a quick, knowing wave and made her way into the office. She was met with a barrage of barking.

"I hope you don't mind taking the old ranch pickup," Gwen said, walking them out toward the barn where a white pickup and horse trailer were waiting. As they grew nearer, there was the thump of hooves coming from the trailer. "I already put their saddles on, but you're going to need to cinch them tighter when you get there." She looked him up and down as though she doubted his abilities. "Are you sure you can handle this? If you need, you can give me a call and I can help you out."

He waved her off. He hadn't been riding in a long time, but he was sure that after a couple of minutes he'd be more than comfortable back in the saddle. "Nah, but thanks. If I need something, I'll just give you a ring."

"Just so you know, about half the back side of the Widow Maker is without cell reception—or it's sporadic at best. Make sure you're careful out there," Gwen said, giving Sabrina a look of concern. "If Trevor is anything like he was when we were kids, he's going to go all out and get himself into trouble. He tends to act first and ask questions later."

He laughed, the sound coming from deep in his core. "I'm not a kid anymore. You don't need to worry about me."

"I'm not worried about you," Gwen said, stepping closer to Sabrina. "I have this girl's life and the welfare of our horses to be concerned about."

Though she was just teasing, he couldn't help being rankled by her ribbing. "Look, if you don't want us to take the horses, it's okay. We can find some other way to do the work. Chad and I have been talking about getting four-wheelers. I was just putting it off until we knew exactly what—"

"Stop. It's okay," Gwen said, interrupting him. "I just want you to remember that we are in Montana, not New York. Everything isn't just a phone call away. I don't want you to go messing around up there and find yourselves in trouble. Believe it or not I love you, cousin."

"I love you, too, even if you are still a pain in my ass." He laughed as he wrapped his arm around her and gave her a quick side hug. "Hey, about the Cusslers... Sabrina said you knew a bit about them."

Gwen nodded, smoothing her shirt where it had wrinkled under his touch. As she moved, he spotted the band on her finger. "They would come to mind with the mention of a pain in the ass, wouldn't they?" Gwen sighed. "What did they do now? I want you to know, I tried to talk to them when I found out you were going to take over the ranch. They were less than welcoming."

Apparently, they had all been alive, which was more than he was currently working with. Yet he couldn't let Gwen know anything that would implicate her should something leak to the authorities.

"I believe it," he said, stabbing the toe of his boot into the gravel of the parking lot. "How many are living out there?"

She shrugged. "All I know for sure is that there were four brothers and a couple of women. But there could be more or less. They were a bit like rats, scurrying around and hiding whenever we went out there to try to talk to them."

Which meant that they may well have been around when he and Sabrina had gone out to evict them. He could understand exactly why they had been living out there for so long. It was hard to catch their kind.

He glanced over toward Sabrina, who gave him an acknowledging nod. Her face was pinched, like she was working hard to keep a secret, and somehow that simple look made something shift inside him…something like trust clicking into place. No, it was something else, something deeper, a feeling much too close to desire.

Like before, he wanted to tell her to relax and that everything would be all right, but if he'd learned anything in the last few months, it was that no one close to him ever walked away unharmed.

He couldn't allow himself to fall for her. And if he couldn't stop himself, he most certainly couldn't allow her to get any closer to him than she already was. If he could, he would fire her and send her far from this place…but Chad would have his hide.

"Do you know about how old they all were?" Sabrina asked.

Gwen shook her head. "The oldest brother was probably around forty. And the women… I don't know if they were wives or sisters, but they could have been anywhere between their twenties and forties. From the state of them, it was hard to tell."

"What do you mean?" Trevor asked.

Gwen twitched. "They hadn't bathed in a long time. Their hair was in mats. They looked absolutely wild. We wanted to help them, but what could we do? We were barely making it as it was. And like I said, the Cusslers were well beyond wanting or taking help."

"I get it, Gwen. After seeing their place…" Trevor stopped as he tried to prevent the memory of the dead man's sallow face from creeping into his mind. "Do you know if they get along?"

Gwen nibbled at her bottom lip. "From what I know and what my husband has said, it seemed as though they do. But there are whispers that there are other groups out there—families like the Cusslers who take to the hills."

"Do you know where they're living?"

She shrugged. "Nomads for the most part. The Cusslers just managed to find a spot to squat where they didn't face too much trouble."

"So they don't move around at all?" Sabrina asked.

"I think they may have a hunting cabin farther up the ridge. I assume they went up there whenever they were needing a fresh supply of game."

Trevor checked his excitement. Just because they found a possible location for the rest of the Cusslers didn't mean they were any closer to finding out who had killed the man.

"Now, I don't know if there is any validity to it, but I heard rumblings from Wyatt that the Cusslers were fighting another family out there. From the sounds of it, it was a real Hatfields-and-McCoys kind of thing— doesn't sound like there were ever any kind of winners." Gwen glanced toward the mountains that loomed over them. "It was just another reason for us to keep our distance, the last thing we wanted to do was get wrapped up in a never-ending war."

He held back a chuckle. His entire life was just one unending war. Whether it was here or on the banks of the Yangtze River, he'd always be fighting some kind of battle, but at least these kinds weren't the ones inside him.

He relaxed slightly.

If Gwen was right, they had nothing to worry about. The man was a victim of nothing more than a hillbilly civil war. But if she was wrong…if the Gray Wolves had planted a false rumor…

No, they wouldn't. It was too far-fetched. The Gray Wolves were smart, but like him, they wouldn't just walk into this community and start stirring up trouble. They would want to fly under the radar.

But he couldn't make another catastrophic mistake when it came to his family's safety—he couldn't live with himself if he lost someone else because of his failure to understand his enemy.

Eloise poked her head out of the office door. "Gwen, you coming?"

She tossed him the keys and he scooped them out of the air. "Thanks, Gwen."

She dipped her head. "Not a problem. Just be careful out there. I don't have a good feeling about this." She turned to walk away, but looked back at them. "You aren't planning to go out there to see the Cusslers today, are you?"

Sabrina slipped her hand into his, their skin brushing as she took the keys from him.

"Nah," he said, but even to his ears it came out sounding tinny and fake as he looked down to the place where Sabrina had touched him. "Fences today. Just wanted to know what to expect."

Gwen gave him a wide smile, like she actually believed his lie.

Denial just might have been his most powerful ally—especially when it came to his own feelings.

Chapter Six

Sabrina gripped the steering wheel hard, carefully maneuvering the truck and horse trailer down the bumpy road leading straight to the Cusslers' shanty. Every time the truck hit a bump and the mud splattered against the windshield, she cursed last night's rain, and she couldn't help but to look over at Trevor to see if he was silently judging her.

Truth be told, she hadn't driven a truck carrying such a heavy load before, but she would never be second to a man. She could do anything he could. She was tough. And what she didn't know, she would learn.

"Are you sure you don't want me to drive?" Trevor asked, holding on to the dashboard like it was his lifeline.

She gritted her teeth. "I've got this." As she spoke, the front right tire connected with a giant rock in the road, jarring them so hard it made her jump in the seat.

"Dude," Trevor said, looking back at the horse trailer they were pulling. "If you're not careful, you're going to end up rolling us."

Though she was only going ten miles an hour, she slowed the truck down even more. "Look, Trevor, if you think you can drive better than I can on this crap, be my guest. But it's not as easy as it looks." She motioned toward the muddy, pitted road in front of them. "Have you ever even driven a truck and trailer before?"

He opened his mouth to speak, but paused for a long moment as he stared at her. "I've done more of this kind of driving than I care to admit."

This was her chance—finally she could learn more about this man in a way that wouldn't seem suspicious.

"All that driving have anything to do with that gun I found in your bedroom?" she asked, raising an eyebrow.

He snickered. "You're awful curious, aren't you?"

Or maybe it wasn't her opening, after all.

"I just like to know who I'm working for…and whether I need to be concerned for my safety or not."

He slowly blinked, like he was trying his hardest to control every single muscle in his body. "The only people who should be scared of me are my enemies. You've already shown me that we are fighting on the same side. In all honesty, it's been a long time since I've been around somebody—other than my family—who hasn't wanted to use me to achieve their own gains. It's a bit of a relief."

A wave of guilt washed over her. Sometimes she hated the duality of her job. Here she was making strides professionally, and yet she found herself personally compromised. It would've been so much easier if she didn't like the man she been sent here to investigate.

Then again, perhaps his little speech was nothing more than a subtle manipulation, a tactic to lull her into becoming complacent. Well, if he thought she would be that easy to manipulate, he was wrong.

Or maybe she was just looking for a reason to stop herself from falling for Trevor. It was unprofessional in every way, to even think about having feelings for the handsome man sitting beside her in the truck. Yet a heart wanted what a heart wanted; if her heart was easily controlled by her mind, she would never have found herself in the backwoods of Montana.

This time had to be different. She couldn't let herself be sucked in by a man's charms; she had to remain distant. Untouchable.

"With time, Trevor, you'll find that I'm a woman who is different from the rest. I'm not the type to pander to a guy."

Trevor took his hands off the dashboard and leaned back in his seat, like he was trying to avoid the ricochet of her words within the truck's cabin. "You don't think I was already aware of that?" Trevor asked.

"Well, I just don't want you thinking that I was…" She paused as she searched for the right word. "I guess I don't want you to assume that I'm weak. You know, after what happened the first time we came down here to the Cusslers' place. I don't know what came over me. This time when we see this guy, I'll be ready."

Trevor looked at her for a long moment, almost as if he was trying to decide how to proceed. "Sabrina, it's okay to have a weakness."

There was a softness in his voice that made her wonder if there wasn't another layer of meaning to his words.

"Weakness is unacceptable. Weakness means we have to depend on those around us. Doing something like that means you open yourself up for disappointment, for hurt. Strength is the only way to survive."

"Do you mean in dating, or in life?" Trevor asked, as his hand slid slowly to the center of the bench seat.

"Both," she said, jerking the wheel as she dramatically tried to avoid another pothole, secretly wishing he'd be forced to hold on again so his hand wouldn't be so accessible. A girl only had so much restraint.

"Don't take offense, but…" Trevor sighed. "Well, you sound like a woman who's been hurt…a lot."

She answered with a dark chuckle. "If you had grown up in a family like mine, you'd see the world from my perspective, too."

"You mean because your family was military?" Trevor asked.

She was surprised he remembered anything about her. She'd have to be careful about what exactly she said to him. "The moving around and constant change was fine. Sure, it takes a special breed to be able to live that kind of lifestyle, but that wasn't what our problems really stemmed from. My dad was the kind who always wanted to be in control, and sometimes that meant acting in a way that is completely unacceptable by today's standards."

"Is that why you took the truck keys from me—you wanted to remain in control?"

"I took the truck keys because I saw you driving the other day. I wanted no part of that." She laughed.

The smile returned to Trevor's face and his hand moved a bit closer. "One time is not indicative of anything." He reached over and took her hand, like he finally was giving up on her making the first move.

His hand felt cool against hers, and she wasn't sure if it was because he was cold or if she was just blazing hot because of her nerves. She thought about disentangling their fingers, but as he started to caress her skin she couldn't find the willpower.

It felt so good to be touched. It was strange, but besides their hug the other day, it had been a long time since anyone really touched her. More, she was being touched by Trevor…the only man she had ever been instantly attracted to.

With most men, her attraction to them only occurred after months of them being securely planted in the friend zone. She hadn't really taken Mike's advances seriously for at least six months; that was until Mike had finally kissed her after a lunch meeting, and something inside her changed.

This thing with Trevor, it was…disconcerting, uncomfortable and strange. And yet so right. When she looked at him, she wanted to move closer. To touch more of him. To feel his arms around her. It was like he was the sun on her face after months of winter gray. As much as she loved the sensation, that spark, she hated it.

Many of her friends had told her stories about the elusive spark, and how they knew the instant they met someone that they loved them. All their talk had made her wonder if there wasn't something wrong with her— aside from her atrocious taste in her past boyfriends. She had tried to make herself feel better by telling herself that her friends were crazy, that nothing like that ever existed except in movies. Those sparks were just weakness…their body's way of opening itself up and revealing its most vulnerable part—the heart.

Right now, she wasn't sure if she was right or wrong, but she wasn't ready to give her heart to anyone…not after all she had put it through in the last few years.

"I'm a good driver, regardless of what you think." She forced herself to let go of his hand.

A silence widened the gap between them.

"Uh-huh," he said, sounding dejected as he put his hand in his lap.

Maybe it had been wrong to pull back from him. If she had stayed put it might have made it easier to learn everything she needed to know about his family, their work, their role in the murders and their gun trade. And for a while, she could have just lied to herself and told herself that this really was her life. She could play the housekeeper who was falling head over heels for the man beside her.

She groaned. Why did he have to make her feel this way? It was so much easier to live within the framework built by the FBI—where he was nothing but her assignment and she was safely detached.

If feelings didn't have a way of muddling everything in her life maybe they wouldn't be so bad, but as it was, feelings sucked.

As the little shanty came into view, with its rusty, corrugated steel roof filled with holes, she relaxed. She'd never been so happy to get to a dead body in her life. At least she'd have something to think about besides her feelings.

That was, if she could just control her reaction when she saw the man again. She couldn't be weak in front of Trevor. She had to prove to him that, like he said, a single event wasn't truly indicative of anything—it was an anomaly.

She pulled the truck and trailer down the drive leading to the pathetic shack and turned to Trevor. "I'll get the horses together and buttoned up if you want to go take a look around."

He gave her a look of disbelief, like he questioned who she thought she was giving orders to him. She'd have to reel that in a bit. No matter what she personally felt, she had to remember that she was supposed to be doing a job...a job that didn't include leading the charge in getting to the bottom of a hillbilly's murder mystery. She had bigger fish to fry.

"If you don't mind, I'll give you a hand," Trevor said. "With things out here so up in the air, I don't want to leave you alone. We don't know where those other Cussler boys are, or the women. For all we know, we're walking out into some kind of mountain men's civil war."

He wasn't wrong, but she couldn't seem to think straight thanks to his presence.

"You think his body's still inside?" she asked.

Trevor shrugged. "I'd be lying if I said I hoped his body was still in there. It would make things a lot easier if his remains are buried somewhere out in the woods."

Once again, they were skating down the slippery slope between right and wrong, but she couldn't disagree with him.

The horses nickered as she and Trevor stepped out of the truck and into the mud. Theirs were the only fresh tracks.

"It's okay, guys, we're gonna get you out," Trevor cooed to the horses as they stomped inside the trailer.

He walked around behind the trailer and opened the door. Carefully, they backed the horses out and walked them around and tied them up. He helped her put on the horse's bridle and cinch her saddle tight. He may not have gone on a horseback ride in a long time, but he seemed right at home taking care of the animals.

"Here, let me give you a leg up," he said, holding out his hands.

She didn't want to take his help. Not after she'd made such a show of taking over the driving. But the last time she'd ridden on a horse the owner had kindly given her a set of steps in order to get up.

She put her left foot in the stirrup and he helped her with her right. For a moment, his hand rested on her thigh as he untied the horse and handed her the reins, unclipping the lead rope.

"You got him. You gonna be okay?" he asked.

She nodded. She'd forgotten the thrill that came with sitting astride a horse. It didn't escape her that she was sitting on an animal who weighed a ton more than she did, but was just as stubborn. Hopefully today would go well and she wouldn't make an idiot of herself. All she had to do was pretend she knew what she was doing and soon enough she would.

At least she hoped.

"What's her name?" she asked as the horse took an unwelcome step away from the trailer. She checked the reins, trying to pull her to a stop.

"First off, he's a gelding, and I think he goes by Zane."

She wasn't off to a great start.

She ran her hands down his whiskey-colored coat. "You and I are going to get along great, aren't we, Zane?" She tried to sound more confident than she felt.

The horse took another step, and she tried to relax into the saddle. It was going to be okay; she just had to play it cool.

Trevor rode up alongside her. "And this is Donnie. They're both supposed to be great horses, so I think you're gonna do fine." He reached back and slipped something into the saddlebag.

Apparently, he could see exactly how uncomfortable she was. She readjusted herself in the saddle and tried to recall what she had been told about sitting up straight. She couldn't remember exactly how she was supposed to move with the horse. No doubt she looked like a sixth-grade girl at her first dance—gangly and out of rhythm.

And just like a sixth-grade girl, she wondered when she would finally get over her awkwardness. She was tired of always feeling like she didn't quite fit into any situation. Just once, she would've liked to let herself go and fully give herself to the world around her.

Thankfully, Trevor and Donnie took the lead and Zane moved in step behind them. They rode over to the shanty, where Trevor stepped down from his horse and handed her his reins. "You guys stay here and I'll go check on our friend. I'll be right back."

She looped the reins in her hand and stared at the cabin's blacked-out window. For a second, she considered getting down and going in with Trevor, but she stayed seated. Maybe it was weak of her to not want to see the dead man, but it saved her from making a fool of herself. It was probably the same reason Trevor had left her behind.

She couldn't deny the fact that he was thoughtful and kind, but she forced the thoughts away. No, he was a fugitive from the law. Her enemy.

She pulled out her phone—no signal. She hated the feeling of being cut off from the world around her. There probably wouldn't be a cell signal again until they were back at the ranch. She reminded herself that they'd be back tonight. Besides, Mike had made it clear that he wasn't keen on the idea of her checking in too often. If she was out of contact, at least she would be off Mike's radar.

And yet the whole situation made the hair on the back of her neck stand on end. She was completely on her own. If Trevor caught even a whiff of what she was up to, he could kill her and dump her body without anyone ever being the wiser.

She took a calming breath. No, she hadn't made him suspect anything. This would go fine. It would be suspicious if she tried to leave now. She just had to blend in and play along, gleaning information as they went.

There was the rattle of dishes from inside the cabin. "Everything okay in there?" she called.

"Yeah, everything's fine," Trevor answered. "The body's gone. Aside from him being missing, everything else seems untouched." Trevor walked out of the cabin and got back up into the saddle. He was frowning, and there was a distinct look of concern on his face.

"I bet it was one of the brothers. They probably saw us here the other day and as soon as we left they came in and got the body."

She thought back to the puddle of blood she'd destroyed behind the shanty. More than likely, the blood had belonged to one of the other Cusslers, and it wasn't until he'd been treated for his wound that the family could come and recover the body. And yet she couldn't tell Trevor what she really thought.

Trevor rode toward the trail that led up the mountain. "The only way we can be sure to know what is going on here is to find them. We need to talk to them and make sure they know they aren't welcome back. I can't have my family involved with whatever's going on out here. We don't do chaos."

She nearly chuckled. Her life was often nothing but chaos and one crazy event after another—just another reason they didn't fit. Not to mention she would be constantly keeping secrets from him. A relationship and life built on bedlam and secrets wasn't viable—she had learned that lesson all too well. And in her line of work, all she had was secrets. She could only imagine what would happen if she truly had to keep everything about her work away from the man she loved.

Wait, did she love him? No. It was impossible.

She had to pay attention to the work at hand and remember that she was going to bring chaos to his life no matter what he wanted.

"What else have you found out about their family?" she asked as they started ascending the trail.

"My sister, Zoey, she's a super nerd. Anything on the computer, she can do it," he said, his tone filled with unmistakable love and pride for her. "She's been looking into a few things for me, and so far, we haven't found anything of use. Though I can't say I was surprised."

"She found nothing. That's odd."

"There was just one headline, must have been from forty years ago—a man who might have been the dead guy's father was convicted on a murder charge. Apparently, he suffered from what the paper called insanity, but from what I can make of it, it sounded like he had undiagnosed schizophrenia. He spent ten years in an institution, then disappeared from the records."

She cringed as she thought of the antiquated institutions where those with mental health issues had been stuffed away. They were the thing of nightmares—corporal punishment, physical labor, isolation, lobotomies and even sometimes practicing eugenics. She could barely imagine the horror and the terror those who were forced to live in such a place must have experienced.

"As in he died? Or do you think he escaped?"

Trevor shrugged. "I would guess he died, but who knows."

Even if the man was alive, by now he'd have to be in at least his late sixties, and the last thing he would do is kill his own son. But then again, humans—and the atrocities they committed—constantly surprised her. Filicide wasn't that uncommon, even if she wasn't accustomed to seeing it. She'd heard about it in many other investigations—and it was increasingly common in cases where large amounts of money or corporations were involved…or in cases of mental illness.

On the other hand, she'd read study after study that had found that only a small proportion of schizophrenics were dangerous to others…and yet this man had already proven that he was in the small percentage that was willing to kill.

She nibbled at her lip. If she remembered correctly, children of a person with schizophrenia were 13 percent more likely to develop symptoms of the disease.

"Do you think he was killed by family, or do you really think it was someone else? One of the other squatter families?"

The leather of his saddle creaked as he looked back at her. "I hope it's one of those things. If not, we're going to have a significantly bigger problem on our hands."

"What are you going to do if these guys come back to the shack?" she asked.

"We will make sure they know they aren't welcome…we can't have people being murdered left and right on our land and we can't be compromised—" He stopped and glanced back at her to see if she was listening. "We can't have anyone or anything living at the ranch that is going to be a liability."

She tried to keep from cringing. "Gwen and her mother lived here for a long time. They managed to coexist peacefully with the Cusslers. Don't you think it's strange that all of a sudden people are turning up dead out here?"

"Gwen didn't tell you everything, did she?" He laughed. "Gwen's crew called the cops out here more times than I can count to evict the family. When that didn't work, they came out and bulldozed their little shanty—more than once. These suckers are like gophers. They just keep popping their heads up."

In a way, she couldn't help but feel sorry for the people who had been living out here on the land illegally; no doubt, if they had other options, they wouldn't have found themselves in the situation they were in. But perhaps she was giving the Cusslers too much credit. They were knowingly breaking the law, indifferent about the rights of others, disrespectful and possible killers.

She shook her head as she thought of the moral pluralism they were facing. Why could nothing be cut-and-dried? What she would give to go back in time, to live in her early twenties when she was smart and resourceful enough to be independent, but still naive enough to believe that everything in the world was simply black or white, good or evil. She longed for the days when she just made a decision and didn't second-guess herself or think of at least nineteen other ways to answer the questions posed to her.

"I'm sure Gwen doesn't feel good about what she was forced to do," she said, thinking of the moment she covered up the blood, and when she had come inside the shanty to see Trevor wiping off the gun.

"Like Gwen said, they were well beyond help." Trevor slowed down so they could ride side by side.

The terrain had flattened out and they were surrounded by a thick pine forest, a forest where anything or anyone could have been hiding completely undetected. Chills rippled down her spine as she thought of the danger that may well have been surrounding them. Trevor reached down and ran his fingers over his gun's grip as he also must have realized the farther they rode, the farther they were from help.

"Had you ever been to the house before, you know, before we saw *him*?" she asked.

Trevor shook his head. "No, but I'd heard about the place and I had been tasked with cleaning it up—just like you."

Was that what he had been doing with the murder weapon—cleaning up the place?

She wanted to ask him why he had wiped off the gun, but if she revealed what she had seen, it may well place her in danger. Trevor would never hurt her, but she didn't know if she could say the same thing about the rest of his family. If it was known she could act as a witness and testify against him—if push came to shove—they may decide to take her out. As it was, he had already hinted that they saw her as some kind of liability.

She was the only one outside the family, and outside the Cusslers, who knew about the murder.

She had known she was in danger before, but as she worked through her thoughts, the fear within her swelled.

"Is that why you picked up the gun and wiped it off?" If she was going to be in danger, she might as well at least find out the truth.

Trevor pulled his horse to a stop and she followed suit. He stared at her for a long moment, like he was thinking about exactly what he wanted to say. He had to realize there was no use in lying; obviously she had seen what he had done, and he was likely weighing the consequences and ramifications of her revelation.

"I don't know why I did that. I just—"

"Wanted to cover your brother's tracks?" she said, finishing his sentence.

"Look, I don't know where you got that idea, but Chad isn't the kind of guy who would just come out and murder somebody. We aren't that kind of people… we're just looking for a quiet place to retire and get out of the public eye." Trevor raised his hands, like he was submitting to her.

She wanted to believe him, but he and his family were likely nothing but a deadly force.

"But you weren't sure, or else you wouldn't wipe down the gun. There was no harm in just leaving it there if you knew he wasn't responsible."

He looked down at his hands as he rested them on the saddle horn.

"From the little time I've been here, it's obvious to me you guys aren't all you say you are—you're not just some investment bankers or hedge fund family or whatever." Her entire body tensed as she thought about how much danger she was putting herself in.

"Who is it that you think we are?" Trevor asked, catching her gaze. He looked torn.

"I don't know, but I want you to tell me." She was forcing him to completely trust her or else get rid of her.

She was playing the odds that he had strong feelings for her, feelings that he would give in to. It was just too bad that if he did open up to her, he'd end up getting screwed.

Chapter Seven

The last person who started asking questions about his family had ended up dead. It had been three weeks before the body washed ashore on the coast of North Carolina. They handled security breaches in such a way that he was surprised anyone had ever found the body at all.

He couldn't let anything happen to Sabrina. She wasn't like the man before, who had been investigating the family for the French government. She was innocent and unfortunately too observant and smart for her own good—and for his as well.

"My family and I are from New York. Last year, our tech company VidCon went public and we sold our shares to an investor. We all had been working together for so long it just didn't make sense for us to go our separate ways, and we all loved the Widow Maker. We came here a lot as children and had so many good memories. Here, we could be together as a family, each building our own houses on the property."

He looked over at her to see if she was buying his story. From the sour look on her face, she wasn't.

"I know that's who you say you are, but most tech junkies I've met don't have sniper rifles in their bed-

room. Not to mention a closet full of military gear." She
looked at him like he was growing two heads. "I'm not
an idiot, Trevor."

"Yes, I was in the military. Where do you think I
learned how to run logistics for a company?" He had
to make her believe the story he was selling, otherwise
she'd be toast.

She nudged her horse forward, making him wonder if
she just couldn't stand being so close to him any longer.
He wanted to reach out and pull her back to him, to tell
her to stop thinking what she was thinking, that she was
wandering down a dangerous path—but he couldn't.

"I know you're not telling me something, Trevor.
You don't have to keep lying to me. I want to help." As
she spoke, he couldn't help but notice that she wasn't
looking at him.

They rode in silence as they moved off the property
and onto public lands, Sabrina leading the way, for at
least three miles. He didn't know exactly where they
were going, but it didn't matter; he needed all the time
he could get in order to make a decision about what to
do with her.

If he were smart, he would take care of the problem
that she was becoming with a single shot. He'd hate
himself for it, but he needed to protect his family. They
had to come first—they always came first. The dedication and loyalty they had for one another was the reason
they had survived in the business as long as they had.
He couldn't let a woman come between them.

And yet there was something about her that he was
inexplicably drawn to. Sabrina was the last thing he had
expected when he'd learned that she was the family's

housekeeper. She didn't seem to fit the bill of someone who would want to make her living by cleaning up after people. She seemed like the kind of woman who would find that monotonous. If anything, she seemed like a fit for a job like a district attorney or something…a job that would require she be able to speak her piece and then back it up with statistics and charts.

He could imagine her up in front of a judge and jury, arguing for the greater good. She'd definitely put him on the spot about that gun…and in doing so, she seemed to understand that she was going to draw scrutiny. And yet she still had the strength to face him head-on. That ability both captivated and terrified him.

"Sabrina," he said, finally breaking the silence between them as he rode up alongside her, "don't be upset with me. I'm sorry about what happened with the gun. I made a mistake. Just know it was made with the best intentions."

She sighed, letting the clatter of their horses' footfalls against the rocky scree path fill the air. "I appreciate your apology, but I don't like feeling like I'm being lied to. And if you're like me…or if you're feeling what I'm feeling…" She reached over and took his hand, the simple action surprising him. "You have to understand that all I really want is for you to open up to me."

He wanted to do that, to tell her everything about who he was, what he'd seen and where he'd been. He wanted someone to tell his fears to and his dreams, but that wasn't his life. It wasn't something he could offer another person. His life was complicated, so much so that regardless of what his heart wanted, he couldn't risk bringing another person in.

And yet he couldn't deny that he was feeling something for her—something he hadn't felt for a woman in a long time.

Not for the first time since her death, Trevor wished he could go to Trish to ask her advice. She would've known exactly what to do and the kinds of questions to ask. He missed her so much. His brothers and Zoey were great, but none of them had a relationship like he'd had with Trish. With her, he'd always been able to talk about anything—even feelings. He didn't delve into them often, and now that Trish was gone, he wasn't sure he was really up to talking about feelings ever again. They were just so damned complicated, especially when it came to the other sex.

"Sabrina, have you had a lot of serious relationships? I know you said you'd had a rough time with the last guy you dated, but have you dated anyone else for a long time?" *Ugh*. That had not come out at all like he'd wanted it to. It sounded so stupid.

She glanced over at him with a cheeky grin on her face. "I do know what a serious relationship is, Trevor." She laughed. "And yes, I've had a couple serious relationships. Why?"

"When you were in these relationships, did you always tell them everything?"

The grin on her face twitched. "What are you getting at, Trevor?" Her voice lost its playful edge.

He'd struck a nerve. She must have been hiding something about her love life. Maybe that's why she had come to the middle of nowhere to disappear. He'd dated enough in his lifetime that he could certainly understand the desire. There was nothing worse than heartbreak.

At least he wasn't the only one with a secret.

"I'm not saying that I think you're a liar or anything," Trevor said. "I'm just asking if there are things you choose not to tell—" *the person you love.*

He didn't dare finish his sentence. He was already close to implying that their relationship was something more. She didn't love him; she barely knew him. And yet…ever since they'd met he hadn't wanted to be without her. It was like her presence both comforted him and made him question everything. It reminded him of the first time he'd fallen in love, but then he'd been merely a teenager—he couldn't go back to being the boy he once was. He'd had too much happen in his life, too many heartbreaks and failed relationships. He couldn't allow himself to repeat his mistakes.

Her grin reappeared. "I admit nothing."

"Admit it or not, we both know that no relationship is completely without secrets. Sometimes in order to keep a friendship or relationship, or to make another person feel better, we omit things. It's human nature."

"Human nature or not, what you did at the shanty was more than just omitting a detail." She paused. "But here's the deal, I don't want you to lie—ever. I don't want you to omit anything. I want to be able to trust you."

Here he'd been worrying about trusting her, and apparently she'd been worried about trusting him as well. That made him chuckle. Maybe they were more alike than he thought.

As they moved higher up the mountain, snow dusted the scree. Even in August and September, snow was common in the high country, and it wasn't unheard of to get fresh snow in the higher elevations every month of the year.

Though he had brought a few essentials, in case of emergency, he didn't have enough supplies to last more than a day or two at most. When it got dark, and colder, the snow was likely to become a problem.

He didn't want to put Sabrina at risk. If something went awry, or if he got hurt, he didn't want to burden her with all that it would take for them to survive.

He thought back to his days in Afghanistan. At that time, he'd just gotten into the private security game with his family. They'd been at it for some time, but he'd finally reached an age at which his father agreed to bring him along. Being out there, in the countryside of a foreign nation where he didn't speak the language or know the customs, had been intimidating. It hadn't taken him long to learn that what they did tended to get people killed.

He winced, remembering the al-Qaeda hit man who got gunned down right in front of him for failing to light his commander's cigarette. Later his brothers had explained to him the commander had done it as a show of force, as a reminder that they were to do as he wished and play by his rules. The man had died because they were there.

He'd had to stay at that camp, pretending to be a bodyguard for the al-Qaeda commander, for two months. Luckily, he had gotten out of there alive. It had been one hell of a welcome into STEALTH.

After he left, they had traced the terrorist group coordinates thanks to the implanted GPS trackers in the weapons they had supplied. Some of the guns had spread as far north as Mirzaki and as far south as Bahram Chah. With the information they had accumulated, they gave the coordinates of the largest and most active terrorist cells to the DO, or directorate of operations. The next day, eight of the ten cells had been wiped off the map.

It wasn't the easiest or the cleanest way to track the movements of their enemies, but it had been highly effective. They were proof that boots on the ground were truly their government's most effective weapon. He was sure that they had saved thousands of lives.

What he'd done then was a thousand times more challenging than what he had to do now. And yet finding himself alone with Sabrina seemed to create an entirely new level of difficulty. Maybe it would be easier if they just dispelled the sexual tension that reverberated between them. If they just kissed, things would get easier, and hell…maybe he could go back to focusing on the task at hand. He kept finding himself thinking about them, about her, trust and feelings and not thinking about where they were or what they needed to be looking for. At this rate, unless the hunting camp had been built right in the middle of the game trail, he doubted he would notice it.

"Do you want to turn back?" he said, his breath making a cloud in the cold.

Her cheeks were red, like they had been nibbled at by the chill of the later afternoon. "No, I'm fine." Her words were slow.

"Let's take a little break." When they came up to a flat clearing, he got off his horse and held out his hand to Sabrina. Her fingers felt like ice.

He had to build a fire before hypothermia got the better of her. It had to be in the twenties, with snow starting to accumulate around them. While the snow would prove helpful in tracking, he had to get his head on straight before he was ready to continue.

Heck, maybe he was right in thinking about turning back. She was cold; he wasn't at the top of his game.

She hugged her arms around herself and did a little two-step move as she tried to get warm.

Yes, fire first.

He tied the horses up to a couple of pines and set about collecting anything dry that would burn. He made his way back to her with a collection of pine needles, pitch wood and branches. She had built a little teepee-shaped stack on the ground with her own collection of fire starters. A tendril of smoke was already puffing from the top of the stack, and there was a split log sitting beside it.

She looked up at him as the fire got going. "Oh, hey, thanks," she said, motioning to his redundant work. "You can set those right there," she said, pointing to the log.

Sometimes she had a way of making him feel so inept.

He dropped the kindling within her reach. She had her hands up, warming them.

"Where did you learn to do that?" he asked.

"Anyone worth their salt knows how to start a fire."

He raised a brow. He wasn't sure she was entirely right, but the comment intrigued him. She was definitely from a military family. Most people were vaguely curious about that kind of skill, but when it came to practical use, few had actually gone so far as to learn how to do it—especially in a wet environment.

"Did your dad teach you?"

"Are you asking me that because I'm a woman?"

"No." He sighed. "I'm asking because my dad taught me. When we came here for vacation, my dad loved to take us all out and spend time in the woods like this. When we got older, we were allowed to set our own camps, just so long as we were within yelling distance."

"Sorry, I didn't mean to be all defensive. It's just…"

"You're a feminist. There's nothing wrong with it. I can understand why you don't want to be underestimated."

"I don't know if I'd call myself a feminist or not. There are so many stigmas with that…but I do know that I'm tired of being put on a lower tier because I have ovaries."

He laughed, the sound echoing through the surrounding woods. "You are hilarious."

"There's nothing funny about being treated like you're not capable or that you should be subservient to a man. I think I should stand beside whomever is in my life, not behind him."

"That's not why I think you're hilarious," he said, picking up a log and moving it over by the fire so they could sit down together. "I guess *hilarious* is the wrong word. I just think you are amazing." He patted the spot next to him on the damp log. "I'd love to have you at my side."

She smiled, but it looked like she was trying not to. She sat down beside him. "You're not so bad yourself." She leaned against him, putting her head against his shoulder.

The action surprised him. He could make out the smell of the horse on her skin and the floral aroma that perfumed her hair, and the effect was perfect—a woman and a warrior.

"What about you?" she asked.

"Huh?" He tried to sit still, not quite sure if he should let her simply lean against him or if he should make a move and put his arm around her. The last time it hadn't ended so well.

It wouldn't be to his advantage if he made a move and it resulted in them riding back in silence. It would be one heck of a long ride.

"Were you really in the military?"

"Uh." His body went rigid. She had just given him a speech about opening up and being honest, but he wasn't ready for her to start asking questions. "I was in the army."

"So you were toying with me about Schofield being a marine base?"

He gave her a guilty smile. "Maybe a little?" He tried to sound cute and semi-repentant.

"I see. Okay." She nodded. "When did you get out?"

He shook his head. "I've been out for about eight years. I only did a four-year tour—that was more than enough time."

"What didn't you like?"

He didn't want to answer that question. Something about it was so private. It was like in telling her, it would bare some of his soul. And yet… "I loved the travel, but I found that it was too *political* for my liking." He thought of all the times he had traveled in order to fulfill contracts and take out foreign leaders.

She was quiet for a long time. He leaned over and put the log on the fire.

"Chad didn't send hot dogs with you, did he?" she asked with a chuckle.

The reminder of food made his stomach rumble. Though he wanted to sit there forever with her, he got up and grabbed his go bag. Coming back, he dug through it. "Here, I've got a granola bar. And there's vodka." He pulled out a silver flask.

"Vodka?" She laughed. "That sounds like the meal of champions."

"The granola bar is complex carbs. The vodka—aside from being the beverage of the gods—is great for medical purposes as well as for relaxing." He tried to sound serious, but his voice was flecked with playfulness.

"I see. In case we needed to get drunk and eat carbs, we're totally covered. You don't have a steak in there, do you?"

"I wish." He laughed as he sat down beside her and she put her head back on his shoulder.

Handing her the flask and a bar, she took them and then opened the canteen's cap and took a long swig. As she handed it back, he followed suit. The vodka burned on the way down. He wasn't much of a drinker, but being this close to her it felt like it was called for. Maybe, for once, he could just relax around her.

They munched on their bars and he threw the wrappers into the fire, watching as they melted into nothing. It could have been the alcohol, but he was mesmerized by the flames as they danced. They were so beautiful, and he was reminded of the fleeting nature of it…and the life that succumbed to its force. In a way, Sabrina reminded him of the flames. She was so wild, free and alluring. He could have happily gotten lost in her for hours.

She reached over and into the breast pocket of his jacket, took out his flask and took another pull. Reaching back over, she slowly put it back, letting her fingers move over his chest. His body sprang to life, and as she touched him, he longed for more.

He took her cheek in his hand, caressing her fire-warmed skin. "I was serious when I said you are amazing. You…you are something special."

She looked at him and he watched the flames dance in her eyes. As their lips met, it was as if the entire world lit up around them.

IT WAS HAPPENING. Really happening. Sabrina couldn't remember exactly how they had gotten there. As his tongue caressed her bottom lip, she gave herself to the moment and decided not to dwell on it.

He held the back of her neck, his thumbs caressing her cheeks as they kissed. The world dissolved around her. The only thing existing was him, his lips, his warm touch on her cold face and the feel of his breath against her skin.

If she could, she would live in this moment forever.

Unfortunately, he pulled back, ending it far too soon. His cheeks were flushed, and there was a thin gleam of sweat on his skin even though it was bitterly cold.

"I…we…" she stammered, trying to be logical about

what had just transpired between them, but all she could think about was how she wanted more—so much more.

Instead of saying anything, he reached into his go bag and pulled out a hatchet.

"Uh," she said, looking at the gleaming blade. "I didn't think the kiss was that bad. In fact, I was hoping you'd want to do it again."

He laughed as he put the blade behind his back and out of sight. "Crap, sorry! That's not it… I was just going to build us a little shelter."

"We kiss and you think *shelter*?"

He was such a dude. There she was thinking about feelings, and he was thinking survival.

Apparently, her kiss didn't carry the same magic it once had. In the past her kiss would have left a man thinking about nothing more than wanting the rest of her.

"I promise you…that's not it." He pulled his coat down a bit, covering his crotch. *Oh.*

Maybe she had a gift after all.

"You don't need to be embarrassed. I take that as a compliment." She gave him a coy look.

He laugh nervously. "Oh, believe me, I'm not embarrassed about anything I've got going on down there."

"Oh my goodness…" She laughed so hard her stomach hurt.

"If I have my way, you will see exactly what I mean."

"You have no shame, do you?"

He reached out and took her hand, giving it a squeeze. "Actually, I was thinking I'd build us a shelter so we could…get a bit more comfortable." He looked up at the sky where there were stars peeking through the dusk. "It's getting dark. Even if we turn around and start making our way back to the truck, we're going to be packing out in the dark. Our horse skills being what they are, I think it's best if we just wait out the night."

"That's the only reason you want to stay out here?" she asked, raising her brow.

"I have to take care of my lady first, then we can have the rest of the night to see where things go." He kissed her hand. "If you want, there's a couple of Mylar survival blankets in the bag. We can start setting up the lean-to." He started to say something else, but stopped. From the guilty look on his face, she could tell he'd been about to start giving orders.

He was learning that she didn't appreciate being told what to do. And the realization made her like him that much more. It was a rare man who wasn't intimidated by an independent woman.

"Don't go too far. If the Cusslers are close they'll come to investigate the fire," she said, looking into the shadows that surrounded them.

"I guess we'll need a door for our lean-to if we want our privacy."

The way he spoke sounded like he was joking, but she liked the idea. The last thing she wanted was to be spied on by a group of hillbillies in the middle of the night. Especially if things went to the place she wanted them to go with Trevor. She'd like to see exactly what he had been trying to cover with his coat.

They collected a few poles and set up a frame for their shelter. Trevor chopped off fresh boughs from the surrounding pines and, using them for the insulating materials, set them around the frame and on top to stop the snow from getting through. It didn't take long, but by the time they were done, she was starving. The granola bar had done little to keep the pangs of hunger at bay, but she could make it a day or two without food.

She sat down on the log by the fire and opened his bag. At the top was a handgun. The black steel immediately reminded her of why she was there in the first place, and all that hinged on her investigation of Trevor and his family.

If they had sex, it would compromise her in an entirely new way. If she did it, would be she doing it because she wanted to, or would there be a part of her that had sunk so low that she was willing to use her body to get ahead?

She hated the thought.

She pushed the gun aside and pulled out the Mylar blankets. Opening the crinkling, tinfoil-like material, she set the first sheet on the pile of soft boughs that would act as their bed for the night. If this was what they were going to sleep on, it was going to make for a loud night.

Trevor came over and took the second blanket from her. Using a bit of duct tape, he lined the top of the shelter with the Mylar sheet so the fire's heat would be reflected down on them as they slept. As he worked, she could make out the scent of saddle leather and sweat and the sweet aroma of campfire on him. She'd never thought she was the kind of woman who would find that to be an aphrodisiac, but it was just that…especially when a bead of sweat worked its way down his temple, slipping into the corner of his lips.

She wanted to take those lips again. Thankfully, one

of the horses chuffed. Getting up, Trevor followed suit, and they made their way over and readied them for the night.

As they finished, Trevor put his hands on his hips and stood admiring their work. Darkness had settled in on them, and with it came a whisper of tiredness. It had been a long, exhausting day, but she wasn't going to let it stand in the way...*if* she decided to act on her baser instincts.

She slipped her hand between his; her fingers were icy in comparison. "What, no door?" she teased, looking at their shabby-chic survivalist paradise.

"Well, I was thinking something in a teak...maybe mahogany." He let go of her hand and gave her butt a playful pat. "You are freaking funny, aren't you?" There was a brilliance in his eyes as he looked at her that made him appear even more handsome.

She had found herself an Adonis. Yeah, Mike had definitely set her up to take this fall.

But she was no Aphrodite and she couldn't fall in love with this ill-fated man. However, maybe just for one night, she could give in to her desires.

Stepping into the lean-to, she pulled him after her. The sheet crinkled under them as he lay down beside her. He unclicked his SIG Sauer P226 from his thigh and set it above their heads like an ominous reminder of the reality that awaited them when they stepped out of their silver wonderland. Wrapping her leg around his, she scooted into his nook and put her head on his chest. Maybe she could be satisfied with just this...the simple pleasure of lying in his arms.

Then again, there was something that seemed more

dangerous about sinking into the comfort and safety of his arms...sex was intimate, but listening to the beat of his heart would be far more bonding. And that bond, the sacredness that came with letting someone into her heart, terrified her.

He ran his fingers through her hair. If she hadn't been so nervous, the sweet comfort of his touch would have put her to sleep. And yet all she could think of was where her hand rested on his abs. As he breathed, she could feel the muscles expand and contract. A warmth rose up from his core, growing steadily warmer as her hand eased down his stomach. She was so close to him. All it would take would be one little flip of the button and everything between them would change. For one night, he could be hers and she could be his...in every way.

One little button. How could she have let her future come to rest on one little brass button? She'd been playing this game long enough that she knew what she was setting herself up for; she couldn't claim ignorance now. And yet she was still surprised how *authentic* it felt being with Trevor. If she was just *her* and he was just, well, *him*, they could have made the world theirs.

He cleared his throat and stopped playing with her hair as her hand moved down until her fingers grazed the rough fabric of his blue jeans. "Sabrina?"

She stopped moving and looked up at him, gently resting her chin on his chest. "What?" she asked coyly.

He gave a light nervous cough and didn't seem capable of continuing.

"Shhh," she said, pressing her finger to his lips.

He drew her finger into his mouth and gave it a playful nibble. Her thighs clenched at the pleasure of the slight pain. She withdrew her hand and rested her fingers on the fateful button. Reaching down, he stopped her for a moment.

"Are you sure you want to do this?" he asked, giving her a look that was a mixture of desire and concern.

She understood exactly how he must have been feeling, but at this moment logical thought was failing.

"I want you, Trevor. I've wanted you since the first moment I laid eyes on you." She moved atop him, straddling him as she flipped open the button and unzipped his jeans. She looked into his eyes. "What about you? Do you want me?"

"More than you can possibly know." He emitted a slight growl, running his hand over his face. "But you are going to be the death of me." He took hold of her hips and she ground against him.

She giggled, but at the back of her mind she questioned if he was right in his assumption—literally. She forced down the thoughts. Now wasn't the time to worry what would come of their forbidden relationship. Now was the time for pleasure.

Sitting up slightly, she wiggled down his pants. Standing over him, as much as she could in the enclosed space, she slipped off her pants and black panties and let them drop on the Mylar beside him. The fire reflected off the silver sheets around them, but the chill of the night pressed in against her nakedness.

He sat up, taking hold of her. His hands were warm against her ass. He gave her a wicked smile as he kissed the soft skin of her inner thigh. His lips were hot against her cold skin, and as he inched his kiss higher up her leg, she was sure he was hotter than the flames that danced on the Mylar.

She reached up as his tongue met her, and her hands brushed against the world of fire around her.

"Trevor," she gasped, as his fingers found her. "I need you. Please," she begged, running her fingers through his long hair.

He kissed her again, then took her hand and leaned back, leading her atop of him. She pulled him inside her and in one slow movement, he filled her. There was nothing more glorious than this night…*their* night. It would be one memory she would cherish for the rest of her life.

Chapter Eight

The sun was breaking through the trees, but as they rode deeper into the backcountry, all Trevor could think about was the taste of Sabrina. He sucked at his bottom lip. He'd never known a woman could taste exactly like peaches.

And the face she had made when he'd pressed inside her. Just the thought made his body spring to life. Dang, he would give just about anything to be back in that lean-to, holding her against his chest and listening to the sounds she made when she was satisfied.

Ever since they'd loaded up and hit the trail this morning, she had been quiet. If she was like him, it was lack of sleep catching up with her, but it still surprised him. Not that he'd ever done this kind of thing before, but when he had slept with women in the past, normally the next day they opened up and wanted to talk. Sabrina was certainly a different kind of woman, and she definitely kept him on his toes. It was one of the things he loved about her—she challenged him.

As they rode up onto the top of the saddle that bridged two mountains together, in the distance he could make out a muddy game trail. Thanks to the pristine snow around it, the muddy mess looked like a snake slithering through an Arctic playground. The trail had probably been made by deer and elk, but it seemed out of place in the high country.

While animals were sometimes at the top of the mountains this time of year, it seemed like they would have moved lower to wait out the cold snap. Unlike humans, they heeded nature's warnings.

If he and Sabrina had been smart, they would've never spent the night up in the woods. It had been an ill-advised decision. Even without the possible ramifications of sleeping together, the weather alone could have been extremely dangerous. Luckily the storm hadn't been that bad, but if it had, they could have been stuck out in the wilderness for days. Even now there was no guarantee they would make it back unscathed.

The cold air nibbled at his nose as they rode toward the serpentine game trail. The distinct odor of campfire drifted toward him on the gentle breeze. "Do you smell that?" he asked, unsure if it was his clothing that he was smelling or if it came from some unknown source.

"Smoke." She looked around, pointing toward the east. "Look over there."

There was a fine tendril of wispy smoke drifting up and over the edge of the mountain. They were close to someone. But in the millions of acres that spread around them, it was impossible to know exactly who awaited them. Hopefully it was the Cusslers, and they could finally start making heads or tails of the situation they found themselves in. Then again, it might also be the second hillbilly family. Either way, they could be walking straight into a trap.

The people who lived in this kind of environment weren't stupid about survival. If they had any indication that he and Sabrina were coming up the mountain to find them, they wouldn't have built such a visible fire. In the event it was an ambush, they were ill-equipped to succeed.

Or at least one of them was.

He'd fought this kind of battle more times than he could count. It always seemed like the odds were stacked against him when it came to looking at something like this on paper, but his training and his level of expertise always gave him an advantage. They just had to play it smart.

He motioned for Sabrina to stop, riding up alongside her and climbing down off his horse. To their left was a small drop-off. He led his horse down the embankment and into the small stand of timber. Sabrina followed suit. They tied up their horses and he grabbed the go bag. Pulling out the gun, he handed it to her.

"You need me to explain how to use it?" he teased.

She smiled at him, but there was a sassy look on her face. "Isn't someone feeling feisty this morning?"

"That's not the only thing I'm feeling," he said, pulling her close and pressing his lips to hers. She wrapped her arms around his neck and dug her fingers into his hair, making him nearly groan.

"Hey now," she said, pulling back from him. "This isn't the time or the place for fooling around."

He didn't want to point out that last night was just as questionable, so he stayed quiet. She slipped the gun in the back of her pants and covered it with her jacket. There was something about the way she moved that made it look like she had done that a million times before. There was no hesitation, no shock at the feel of the cold steel against her skin and no second-guessing herself before she put the gun away. She was some kind of housekeeper.

"How accurate are you thinking you can be with that gun, if it comes down to it?" he asked.

"Let's just say starting a fire and working a truck and trailer weren't the only things my daddy taught me to do," she said. "If I were you, I would make sure I wasn't the one standing on the other end of my barrel."

He laughed quietly, looking over toward the smoke as he realized that up here, with as little cover as they had, it also meant that sound would most certainly carry.

His phone buzzed in his back pocket. They must have found a tiny service signal. Moving to take it out and check, he stopped himself. "I need to take a whiz before we get started. Do you mind waiting here?"

"No problem," she said, waving him off.

It wasn't a great excuse, or charming, but it was the only thing he could think of to be alone for a few minutes.

He walked away from her and sat down behind a small knob on the hill where he couldn't be seen from above or below. Taking his phone out, he looked down at the screen. Chad had texted at least twenty times. Zoey had set up the fake drop in Seattle. They'd have at least a dozen eyes watching the place; if there was even a chance Sabrina wasn't who she said she was, he'd know.

Saying a silent prayer that he was wrong, he stuffed the phone back into his pocket. Last night had been inimitable, but he would love to try again.

But if Sabrina were working for some foreign government or the Gray Wolves, what had occurred between them would never happen again. More likely than not, his family would require that he take care of the problem. He couldn't stand the thought of hurting her.

He sat with his knees up, and he pressed his forehead against them as he closed his eyes. The cold snow was starting to melt and leach into his pants, making his butt cold, but he ignored the feeling. The biting cold was nothing compared to the gnawing he felt in his chest.

Hopefully he hadn't misplaced his trust when he'd put it with her.

For now, he could rest in the naive hope that he had found the one woman in this world to whom he could truly give his heart.

MEN. SOMETIMES THEY were so uncouth…it was like she was back in the good old boys' club that was a FBI resident agency.

As he walked away, she made her way down the embankment from the horses and found a little bush. As she unbuttoned her pants, her phone buzzed from inside her breast pocket. The sensation caught her completely off guard. She hadn't had service in the last day and it was a surprise that she even had any battery left, considering her phone had likely been searching for a signal since then. She pulled out her mobile, and looking over her shoulder to make sure Trevor was nowhere in sight, she punched in the code to unlock it.

Front and center in her inbox was an email from Mike. She opened it, and as she read, excitement and then a sense of dread filled her. Her team had intercepted an email sent from the Widow Maker. Apparently, Trevor and his team were supposed to make a drop in Seattle at seven tomorrow night. Mike wanted to know whether or not they were to move on the information.

She stopped reading and pressed the phone to her chest.

If that were true, then it was likely the reason Trevor had been only too happy to spend the night out in the woods. He'd probably wanted them to spend the night out here again so she was completely out of the equation. Maybe he still saw her as a security risk and wanted her as far from his dealings as possible. Then again, she hadn't given him any concrete reason, that she knew of, for him not to trust her. Besides, he would have to be at a meeting like that, wouldn't he?

She glanced back in the direction he had gone, but he was nowhere in sight.

Maybe Chad and the rest of the family were taking the lead on this one.

If the intelligence was legit, she needed to have a team there. Between the email and what they could glean from the handoff, her team would likely have more than enough for whatever prosecutor was put on their case. They could take down the family and put an end to their illegal gun trafficking once and for all. Then she could move on to another UC position. Maybe she could even get transferred away from Mike. She'd heard of some of her people taking remote location gigs; maybe she could get a little sunshine in and see the beaches of Colombia.

Going back to her phone, she told them to move on the intel.

If she was wrong, and Trevor or someone from his family had planted this for them to go on some wild-goose chase, her job would be on the line. The Bureau hated spending money and resources on anything that proved to be a dead end, but her gut was telling her that this was something they had to do. If she didn't act, and the Martins were in motion for a trade, then she'd miss her opportunity. Maybe it was a bit aggressive to jump on their first big break in the case, but if they could one-and-done this, she could go back to the agency with her head held high. Mike would have his deadline met and she would be the resident hero.

Besides, Trevor had probably set all this up...he'd brought her all the way to the backside of the moon knowing they were unlikely to have any digital reach. If he thought she was a threat, it was one heck of a plan. She'd been completely at his mercy. Why had she been so stupid in letting him take her on this ridiculous trail ride? She should have trusted her gut and found a way to stay behind. If he had gone without her, she could have been right there and dug deeper into the lead the IT crew had picked up. As it was, she might as well have been sitting on her hands.

She stuffed the phone back in her jacket and after doing her business, careful to keep the gun from falling in the snow, she made her way back to the horses. Trevor was already there, waiting for her. He had a worried expression on his face and after what she'd just learned, all she could do was stare at him. He was probably thinking about the deal he was going to miss.

The last thing she should have done was sleep with him. Heck, he'd probably even had that planned, too. Be cute, joke a bit, tell her she was beautiful, and she had turned to putty in his hands.

Why was she so stupid sometimes? She knew better than to let herself fall for a man like him.

She stretched, as if by doing so, she could wedge herself back into the box that was her role as a UC for the Bureau. There was a job to do. If she didn't think about the way his lips felt against her skin, or the way he sighed when he fell asleep, it wouldn't bother her too much.

He turned away from her and as he moved, there was a dark blue patch on his ass like he'd wet his pants. "You know," she teased, trying to relieve some of the stress that filled her, "most people take their pants down when they use the restroom."

"Oh…yeah…" He dropped his hands to the back of his jeans and gave a constricted laugh. "I slipped and fell down in the snow when I was trying to find a place. Nothing like a cold, chapped ass to remind you how good life is back at home." As he said the word *home*, his face pinched like there was something painful about the word itself.

She couldn't help but wonder if he really meant how good life was back where he could run guns once again.

She set her jaw. He was a killer. He put guns into the wrong hands, hands that were more than happy to pull the trigger even when the guns were pointed at the innocent.

He could act as endearing as he liked, but that didn't make him any less guilty.

She just had to remember not to be a fool—no matter how tempted she was to take on the enticing role as the woman on his arm.

No doubt he had one incredible, fast-paced and thrilling life. If only it was on the right side of the law.

Chapter Nine

She was acting weird. Or maybe he was, he couldn't decide. As they hiked toward the smoke, he couldn't make heads or tails of his thoughts. This was all driving him mad. At least he would soon find out one way or another if she could be trusted. He would have his answer and then they could move forward—or not.

The snow crunched under their feet, the sound reminding him of what needed to be done. All they had to do was get to the bottom of the Cussler brother's death for now. He could deal with the rest when he got home.

Yes, shoving the thoughts of her possible deception away...yes, that was the best answer. If he was acting weird, at least he could put an end to it this way and slide back into his role as one of the Martin brothers—tech billionaires extraordinaire, complete with a fictionalized military backstory...well, sort of fictionalized. Some of his experiences with the military had been all too real.

That's all this feeling was, his past coming back to haunt him. He was out of that game. Now he just had to look to the future.

If only it were that simple.

Becoming a civilian was proving to be far harder than he had expected it to be. He'd always thought that the people who had the biggest issues were also the ones whose egos wouldn't allow them to step away from the game. He'd never thought that *he* would be one of those people. Sure, his identity had been all spook all the time, but that wasn't who he *was*. He had always thought of himself as so much more…and yet he was constantly proving himself wrong. Even the way he made his bed every day spoke of his passion for a life that was no longer going to be his once he retired completely.

There was a click and slide in the distance, just like the sound of a round being jacked into a bolt-action rifle. He glanced in the direction of the smoke. They had to be at least a half mile away from the possible camp. They were surrounded by a blanket of white, interspersed with dots and jags of gray and black and trees that had fallen victim to a recent forest fire. In the world of white, nothing moved. Yet the sound had been nearly unmistakable.

He'd heard that grind of metal too many times in his life to get it wrong.

"Get down," he said, moving behind a piece of deadfall and motioning toward Sabrina to follow suit.

She looked at him like he had lost his mind, but she did as he told her and squatted down beside him. "What is it? Did you see something?" she whispered.

As the last syllable fell from her lips, a bullet whistled by them. Without thinking, he pushed Sabrina all the way to the ground so she was lying behind the log. Based on the sound and the percussive wave of the shot, whoever was shooting at them was uphill, not far. He knelt as low as he could, using the tree for as much cover as possible. He pulled his phone and using the selfie angle, he looked behind him.

At the top of the trail, he could make out the black tip of a rifle barrel.

They couldn't move. If they dared to go anywhere they would be an easy target for whoever was holding that gun. Their adversary literally had the upper hand.

"Can you see who it is?" Sabrina asked.

"Can't see their face, but whoever it is, they are using a high-caliber rifle. Any closer, and a tree just might not be wide enough to keep us safe." He moved to pull his SIG Sauer out of his thigh holster, but then he realized it was already in his hand. He had no idea when he had taken the gun out, and yet he was impressed by his body's autonomous reaction to gunfire.

Maybe being a trained mercenary really did have its advantages after all.

"Take out your—" Before he could say the word *gun* he noticed that, just like him, she had her weapon drawn and ready. The gun was pulled close to her chest and high, the position of a law enforcement officer or a well-trained marksman.

She had said she'd been trained to use weapons by her father, but she didn't appear to be a Sunday shooter.

She rolled and moved to look over the log. As she readjusted, another round pinged through the air. This time, it sounded like it struck something to their left.

"Do you think they're really that bad a shot?" he asked. "Or are they messing with us?" The question was as much a legitimate question as it was a test for her.

She looked up the hill, like she was gauging the distance. "The gun's caliber is too big to be using open sights—they have to have a scope on it. And if they have a scope on it, they could hit the hair on a gnat's ass at this range. They have to be messing with us. Either they're trying to flush us out, or they're sending us a message that we aren't welcome."

Test failed. She was definitely no Sunday shooter.

"You're right," he said, crestfallen. "Which leaves us with two options. We can fight—and turn this into a shooting gallery—or we can sit here and wait for them to get bored and leave. But if we wait, and they really are out to kill us, then they may well get the drop on us and move around until they have a better angle. We could be sitting ducks."

In a way, regardless of what the person shooting at them chose to do, he couldn't help feeling like he was a sitting duck with Sabrina. It seemed all too likely that she wasn't the woman she was pretending to be. Hell, she probably had gotten pinged on her phone the second he'd gotten pinged on his. Maybe she had heard something that had turned her off of him… Maybe she was already making plans for the fake drop in Seattle. That would explain why she was acting so weird.

He grumbled aloud. He couldn't fall back down that chasm, no. No more second-guessing himself. No more second-guessing her.

He had bigger things to worry about right now. He was being ridiculous by allowing his mind to wander. He had to focus.

The wind kicked up as quarter-size snowflakes cascaded down from the sky, making the entire world look like something inside a snow globe. It was his chance.

Though they only had small arms, he'd have to make a break for it.

"Cover my six," he said, moving his chin in the direction of the shooter.

"Are you crazy?" Sabrina asked. "If you go out there, you'll be an open target."

She wasn't wrong; there was little cover. "That's what you're here for," he said, smiling in an attempt to downplay the danger they were in and put her mind at ease. "You're going to have to put your money where your mouth is. You said you're good marksman."

"I didn't mean I was *this* good. They have to be at least fifty yards away—way outside my comfort zone." She grabbed his hand, stopping him from moving. "Don't go." There was a deep well of concern in her eyes.

He had to act for the same reason she didn't want him to go—he had to shield her, the woman he loved.

Not that she could ever know that.

Though if she thought about it, she'd probably quickly realize that he wasn't the kind of man who would risk his life for just anyone.

He moved his hand out of hers and snapped a round into the chamber of his weapon. "Start shooting in three...two..." He stood up and raced up the hill, firing as he zigzagged haphazardly over downed trees and rocks. The brush pulled at his feet, threatening to bring him to his knees and welcome him to his death.

Taking a hard right, he watched as the gunman's barrel came into view above him. He hit the ground as the muzzle flashed. The bullet thumped as it ripped into the tree base just inches from his head.

Gunfire rang out from Sabrina's direction. There were twenty-two rounds in each of his guns' magazines. They'd have to be smart about this.

As Sabrina fired, he jumped back to his feet. A couple dozen yards in front of him was a large boulder. It was a long way to go without cover, but he had to go for it. He sprinted as hard as he could up the hill. The shooter fired. The bullet pinged off a rock, ricocheting into the air.

He slumped down behind the boulder. His breath came in heavy gasps, but he barely noticed as adrenaline coursed through him. Sabrina was out of sight, tucked behind the deadfall. *Good.*

For a moment, the world was silent. Fat blobs of snow coursed down, one landing on his nose and quickly melting, like some warning to him about the impermanence and fickle nature of life. He needed no reminder.

Trish flashed into his mind. She would have loved this. There was nothing she jonesed for quite like a good firefight. She was probably looking down on him from heaven. The thought came with an ethereal bit of warmth.

He smiled up at the sky, knowing full well that it was probably nothing more than his mind playing tricks on him, but he didn't care. If there was even a tiny chance she was here with him now, he needed her to know he loved and missed her. Maybe he could even make things right by saving Sabrina now.

Raising his gun, he charged from behind the rock and ascended the hill. He expected gunfire to rain down on him, but as he ran there was nothing except the crunch of his boots in the snow. As he breached the crown of the mountain, he stopped. There was no one there. A little way down from where he stood was a stand of timber, thick and dense as it had somehow escaped the ravaging effects of the fire that had taken down its sister side.

Near him on the ground was the packed snow where someone had been lying down. A smattering of brass casings littered the ground. From the patch of packed snow, there was a set of tracks leading into the timber and then they disappeared between the trees. The shooter was probably watching him right now. The hairs on the back of his neck stood up as he realized how easily the shooter could set up again from behind a tree and take an open shot at him.

He moved to the patch of boulders they had been using as coverage. Whoever had been shooting must have planned out this location. In defense and offense it was literally perfect—high point, great coverage and the ability to blend in with the background. He couldn't have done a better job himself.

Whistling down, he motioned over the hillside for Sabrina. She stood up and he waved her forward, surveilling the area around her as she hiked up the steep hillside. His breath made a cloud in the air as he guarded her and the cold bore down upon them. It was colder up here, even more frigid than it had been the night before.

They'd gone a whole day without food and the water supply was running low; soon they'd have to start thinking about boiling snow. They couldn't afford to chase after whoever it was that had been trying to gun them down, but they were so close. They couldn't stop now.

Sabrina plopped down beside him, her breathing

heavy. "Holy crap, that hill didn't look that steep from the bottom. How did you run up it?"

He chuckled. "Someone taking aim at you tends to give you an extra incentive to move."

"You're hilarious," she said sarcastically, nudging his arm as she slipped her gun back into the waistband of her pants. "I don't see any blood."

"And I haven't seen anyone moving. Either they are hunkered down somewhere in that timber—" he motioned toward the stand down the hill "—or they high-tailed it out of here."

She motioned toward the curl of smoke rising up from the center of the timber. "Do you think we have enough rounds to go down there, poke around and see if we can flush anyone out?"

"I can't put you in danger. At least not more danger than we're already in—up here, in the middle of nowhere, if one of us gets hurt, we may never make it out."

"From the moment we left the ranch, we've both known that this was a high-risk situation." She moved closer to him and put her hand on his knee. "Even when things are hard, I'm not one who gives up."

"But this isn't a battle of wills, or resilience." He put his hand atop hers and traced the length of her finger with his. "This is possibly life or death, and I don't want anything to happen to you."

She gazed into his eyes, and as she looked at him he could see the start of tears. And yet the look on her face wasn't happiness; it was like she was torn. Maybe she was feeling just as confused as he was about this entire situation and how unlikely it seemed that they would end up together.

"Trevor, you…*we* are amazing. I know I shouldn't say this, but I've never met anyone like you. I don't know what it is about you, but even now just sitting here close to you, with bullets raining down on us at any minute… I dunno why, but I feel safe. More than that, I would be the happiest woman alive if I could stay out here and avoid going back to the real world if it meant I could spend another second with you." The expression on her face seemed to darken as she spoke, in contrast to what she was telling him.

"But?" He waited for the ax to fall.

She huffed. "But…" She paused, suddenly taken with her pants' stitches. "But I don't think we should be worried about it right now."

That wasn't what he was expecting her to say. He'd assumed she was going to tell him she wanted nothing to do with him once they got out of the woods, that she was quitting the ranch, or she had some deep dark secret that would keep them from coming together, but not this. As much as her avoidance was a relief, it was going to nag at him. There was something she wasn't saying, that she must not be ready to tell him. And yet he had to respect her needs and not push her to open up more than she was comfortable with.

She reached down in the snow beside them, digging in the white fluff like a nervous tic. Her fingers reddened as she moved them around in the snow, and it melted and stuck to her skin. Even though it was not his own hand, he could feel the sting of the cold, and he wanted to take her fingers and warm them for her so she wouldn't feel any pain. But he stopped himself. It seemed like perhaps he wasn't what she wanted.

She gasped, pulling her hand from its icy diversion. In her grasp was a spent casing. She flipped it over, reading the caliber stamped into its base.

"This came from an HK416," she said, staring at the brass in her hand.

There was no way she could possibly know about the Heckler & Koch assault rifle. It wasn't a particularly common gun, though they could be bought on the black market. "What do you mean? How do you know?" The knot in his stomach returned, larger than ever.

"This brass is nearly identical to a .223, but here." She handed the casing over. "If you feel the weight, it's significantly lighter."

He took the casing and rolled it around in his hand, but he wasn't thinking about the cold metal thing; rather, who the stranger was sitting next to him. He stuffed the round in his pocket and stood up.

"Why would it be lighter?" he asked, even though he already knew the answer.

"In 2012, the army commissioned manufactures to reduce the weight of the brass casings in this type of round by 10 percent. That means that this weapon most likely belongs to someone who is either active military or FBI." As she looked up at him and their gazes met, her expression changed from focused to guilty.

"Sabrina." He said her name like it was just as much of a secret as whatever she was hiding from him. "Tell me the truth. Who sent you?"

Chapter Ten

She had screwed up, royally. Her hubris had caught up with her and she had no one to blame but herself. Why did she have to open her stupid mouth?

Her investigation was over. She was done. Her cover was blown.

Sure, she could lie about why she was here, but even if he pretended to believe her he would never really trust her again. And if she came out with the truth, he'd inevitably run her out of his life like the infiltrator she was.

But she had to try to cover her ass and buy more time with him. Maybe she could salvage something from this investigation—maybe even clear his name and keep his family out of federal prison.

He opened his hand and helped her stand. "Just tell me." There was a deep sadness in his voice, and it broke her heart.

It hurt more than she ever would have expected. This wasn't her first investigation to go off the rails, but it had never happened like this before. In this moment, it was her life—her *real* life—that was most impacted.

If she told him the truth, maybe they could work together and come through this—but that seemed like one heck of a pipe dream. To hope for something like that was like having faith in humanity—a great philosophy, but rarely worked in practice.

She had been sent here to stop him from putting weapons into the enemy's hands, and yet as the minutes slipped by it was like her objectivity had collapsed. Her heart had come into play and she hated it.

"Trevor, I want everything to work out for everyone involved." She reached over and cupped his face in her hands. "None of this is what I expected when I came to the Widow Maker Ranch. I'm hopeful everything is going to play out all right, but I need you to tell me some things."

He nodded but remained stoic. "Is your name even Sabrina?"

She huffed. Of course he'd be questioning her from the ground up. If she was in his shoes she would be doing exactly the same thing. "Yes."

"And what happened last night… Were you just playing me?"

She stepped closer to him, their bodies brushing against each other. She ran her hand down his neck and rested it on his shoulder. "I'm not the kind of woman who jumps into bed with a man. Ever. There has to be something there, really there, before I'll even consider being intimate."

His lips pursed and he nodded, remaining silent. Stepping away from her touch, he turned around and slowly made his way toward the smoke rising up from the stand of timber. His hands were limp at his sides, and the gun nearly dangled from his fingers.

He was in shock, hurt and probably analyzing exactly how this was going to play out. She had admitted nothing, at least not directly, but he had to realize what a liability she was for him and his family. He made it clear from the very beginning that his family was the most important thing to him, and she had no doubt he was willing to do whatever it took to keep them safe. And that placed her in more danger than when an unknown gunman had taken aim at her. At any moment, Trevor could decide to take her out.

It was unlikely anyone would ever find her remains if he chose to kill her.

She started walking after him, following his footsteps in the snow. The trees moved in on her like brooding sentinels, as if they, too, were judging her for the role she had taken on with the Martin family. Trevor, more than anyone, should've understood what it meant to do a job like hers. He had a life filled with secrets as well. Secrets that she still wasn't privy to. And yet those same secrets could save them.

Trevor was growing ever more distant, and the shadows of the timber threatened to help him disappear. Right now, that was probably exactly what he wanted to do. In fact, it was almost exactly what she wanted to do as well. However, she didn't want to lose him. She wanted to keep on living this fictional life—a life in which she was free to love and she could put aside the possibility that he was her enemy.

"Trevor," she called after him.

He turned and waited for her to catch up. As she neared, she could have sworn there were faint marks on his cheeks where tears had fallen, but she hated to think she had elicited such a response from him—the warrior.

"Don't say anything." He raised his hand. "I need some time to work through all of this."

She nodded. "I'm serious, just know that I want to help you. We can be on the same side."

He turned away from her and kept walking; the subtle evasion amplified her pain. They walked in silence until they came upon a small clearing. At its center was a dying campfire. There was a collection of pots and pans, mugs, and blue plates. It looked as though at least five people had struck camp and had been eating breakfast when they suddenly fled.

The footsteps in the snow went off in all directions. If they followed each trail, they would be tracking for hours.

Trevor walked to the right, moving around the fire as he searched the ground. She made her way left, as she tried to focus on the work at hand instead of the conversation that Trevor didn't want to have.

Not far from the back side of the camp there was a smattering of blood upon the snow.

"Trevor, can you look at this?" She pointed at the ground.

He made his way over. A faint smile played across his lips. "Looks like we may have hit the shooter after all."

"Maybe we don't make such a bad team," she said, but the sentiment came out sounding more like a question.

He didn't respond, squatting down beside the bloodied snow. "This is definitely fresh. It's still melting. But based on the little amount of blood, I'm thinking we just winged him—or her."

"If we did hit one of them, they're going to be moving slow." She looked out into the timber. "We could probably catch up to them if we move fast."

Trevor sighed as he stood up. "Nah, I think we should head back." He brushed by her as he looked around the camp.

She should have been following suit, looking around to see if they could find anything to give them a clue about who had been shooting at them, but all she could focus on was Trevor.

The second they got out of the woods and headed back to the ranch everything would be completely over—her investigation, the case, her job and their relationship. But she couldn't blame him for wanting to get out of the woods and away from her.

They walked around the timber near the deserted camp for a bit longer, but time seemed to lose any reference. She kept looking to him, hoping the right words would find her, but none came. Between them there was only awkward silence smattered with unspoken feelings.

It felt like a breakup, even though there was nothing formal to end.

Maybe this kind of work, as a UC, wasn't something she was cut out for. Normally she was fine, but her emotions had never come into play. If she couldn't keep her heart out of her work, she had no business doing it.

She'd have to give Mike her notice as soon as she got back into service. Not to mention the fact that she'd have to tell them she had let them all down. Mike was going to have a field day with this. He'd always told her she was weak, and now it turned out that he was right.

Trevor finally stopped as they came back to the edge of the timber and to the camp. He looked in the direction of the shooter's perch. "How did you know about the HK416 being a FBI weapon? Is it because you're an agent?" He turned to face her, but from the emotionless look on his face she couldn't tell exactly what he wanted her to say.

A lump formed in her throat. She tried to swallow it back and to replace her nervousness with bravery, but it didn't work. She was scared for so many reasons, the biggest being that if she walked away from Trevor, she would be walking away from the love of her life. The thought tore her apart.

"I…" She struggled to find the right thing to say. There was no easy way out of this. "Yes, I was sent here because of what happened in Turkey. We have reason to believe that you were responsible for several civilians' deaths… That, and a few other things."

He reached over and braced himself against a tree. The bark crumbled under his fingers, littering the ground with the ashy remnants of what had been so beautiful only moments before. Everything was disintegrating.

"So you came here believing that I was some kind of monster?" There was a pained look in his eyes.

"No, I came here to find out the truth. And the moment I met you, I knew that things weren't going to be as black-and-white as I'd hoped. You are nothing like the man I expected to meet." She wanted to reach out and touch him, to reassure him that everything was going to be okay—but the truth was, she didn't know whether everything would be all right or not.

"And you know about Trish's death?"

She nodded. "What happened to her…from what I know, it wasn't your fault."

He leaned against the tree, crossing his arms over his chest. "You're only saying that to create a bond—empathize with your target, make them feel safe. I know your game."

His words tore at her, ripping away what little was left of her defenses. "I'm not playing a game. If I were, I'd never have told you the truth about me being an agent. Until very recently, I wasn't sure about you. But I've come to believe that you are incapable of hurting an innocent person." She couldn't stand it; she reached over and put her hand on his chest. His heart was thrashing beneath her touch. "Don't think I didn't notice that you weren't shooting earlier. You could've gone in there guns blazing, but you took the high road. That takes an entirely different level of bravery."

"That wasn't bravery, it was curiosity." He looked down at her hand but didn't move to take it. "I didn't want to kill the one person who could have possibly known about the Cussler brother's death. I have to know how close all my enemies really are." He moved away from her.

She'd broken the bond they'd had, irreparably.

"I know you probably don't believe me, but I'm not one of them. I have the power to condemn you—if I'd found evidence—and I also hold the power to clear your name. But I need to know some truths from you, something I can take back to my handler to prove that you're the man that I know you are—and not the gunrunning terrorist the FBI believes you to be."

His indifferent expression changed to one of complete shock as he opened and closed his mouth like he was struggling to find the right words. "How much do you know about me?"

The way he asked made her wonder if she had missed some glaring detail.

She'd already admitted her truth to him, so all she could think of was the old adage *in for a penny, in for a pound*.

"I know that you and your family are in fact a group called STEALTH. You've been running guns around the globe for a number of years now. I know, and the FBI has proof, that you are involved in the trade. I don't know to what degree, and I'm hoping our intelligence was wrong—that you are just the little fish and we are going after the whales. From what I've seen, you don't seem like the type of man who would put guns into the hands of those who wish to do the most harm."

"You're right, I don't want to hurt anyone who doesn't deserve to be taken to their knees. But being in the FBI, you have to know as well as I do that there are truly wicked people out there. And the only way to bring those kinds of monsters down is to send monsters after them…and just like you first assumed, I am that monster." He sat down on a log next to the dying campfire.

She didn't know what to make of what he was saying. Was he admitting his crimes? If so she had no choice but to turn him over when they got back to the ranch. Perhaps that was what he wanted, to fall on the sword and go to prison…otherwise, why would he have so easily admitted to his mistakes? And yet there was something about the way he spoke that made her wonder if there was more to the story.

"Why, Trevor?" She sat down beside him.

"Why what?"

"Why do you think you're a monster?" She tented her fingers between her knees as she leaned forward and looked back at him.

"I had nothing to do with civilian deaths in Turkey. Yes, I took down my enemy combatants—I've killed. And if you asked me if I'd do it again, I wouldn't hesitate to say yes. Especially when it came to trying to save Trish. I'll do anything to save the people I love," he said, a deep sadness in his voice. "But I'm also the man who is willing to run into a burning building and save the innocent. I'm the man people call in the dead of night when the demons seep out of the cracks and wish to do them harm. So you can judge me however you wish. I'm guilty of plenty of things that society deems wrong, but in my heart, I know that I'm the man who is doing what many others can't. I make the hard choices."

She sat in silence, trying to come to terms with the things he was saying. He wasn't like any gun dealer she'd ever met before—not that she'd met many. He didn't seem to be after money or driven by greed. Instead he seemed almost like her, focused on humanitarian need and the prospect of justice—but in the most unconventional way. And she still didn't understand how giving guns to warlords was saving the innocent. Was this an elaborate rationalization?

"Trevor, why were you running guns?"

He smirked and ran his hands over his face. "That's past tense. We don't do it now. We got out of the game after everything with Trish. So if you think you're going to help the FBI and federal prosecutors by coming after my family, it's nonsensical. We're out of the game."

She didn't know whether or not to bring up Seattle. He was lying to her—they were still very much active in the trade—but she couldn't reveal everything she knew. Not if there was a chance he was playing her for a fool. "But you admit you have been putting guns into the wrong hands?"

"Just like you said *trust me*, now I ask the same of you. What I did, I did because I had to. Yes, the ethics were somewhat ambiguous, but there were greater things at play than even you know."

"What do you mean?"

"I mean that you don't have all the answers, and neither do I. But I'm not the bad guy here. Just like you, I do what I have to do—sometimes at the cost of others."

"You don't care that civilians are dying because of you?" The question came out and slashed like a sword. She hadn't meant it to be as harsh as it sounded, but she needed to know exactly where he stood. Both of their futures depended on it.

He shook his head. "I know it doesn't look like it from the outside, but I wanted to keep people safe just as much as you do. When I realized I couldn't, that's when I came here. If I can't even keep my own sister safe, then I have no business out there. Thinking I could make a difference, it's almost the definition of stupidity."

"You're not responsible for your sister's death. I've seen the reports. Maybe they didn't have all the facts, or the answers, but I saw the forensic analysis. From where you were standing, you could have never gotten there in time to help. The shooter had the advantage."

"You may have seen the science behind everything, but what you didn't see was someone you love looking up at you and knowing that they needed your help, and yet all you could do was watch them die."

She wanted to hold him and tell him it would be okay, that time would heal. And yet he wasn't hers. They were enemies, at least in his mind. If she even tried to console him, it would come off as false—and only drive them further apart.

She couldn't make his heart feel something toward her that his mind wouldn't allow.

And as much as she knew she shouldn't reach for him, she did. She took his hand in hers and lifted it to her face. "Trevor, I'm so sorry. For everything. For Trish. For this. For the investigation. But you're not alone in your suffering. When I was young, I lived in Redmond—"

"On a military base, or was that a lie, too?" he asked, pulling his hand away.

He had every right to snap at her. "Some of what I told you was backstory, but there is some truth to it. I find it easier to have an identity that I can actually relate to. My dad was in the military. He was controlling and passionate about his Second Amendment rights— until he and my mother were found in a parked car at the bottom of Mount Rainier, murdered. I was sixteen."

They sat there in silence for a long moment. "I'm sorry, Sabrina. I know how hard it can be to lose people you love." He turned to her. "Is your parents' murder the reason you decided to become involved in the Bureau?"

She nodded. "After their death, I had nowhere to go. I was shipped around foster homes in the area for a while until I ended up in a nice couple's house in Redmond. The guy worked for a local law firm and the woman worked at the federal office. My guardian set me up with an interview at the FBI after I graduated from college. Go Huskies," she said, raising her hand in the air in feigned excitement.

"Did they ever solve your parents' murder?" he asked.

She shook her head. "And the files are buried. I've tried to look into them a few times, but I don't have the clearance."

"It sounds like there's more to your parents' murder than the Bureau wants you to know."

She chuckled. "We live in a world full of conspiracy theories, don't we?"

"They're not always theories. Sometimes the most outrageous things I see and hear are the truth." He picked up one of the blue camp plates like he was inspecting the edges. "As much as you want to get to the bottom of your parents' murder, you probably need to let it go. You're chasing ghosts, and when you do that you open yourself up for a lifetime of disappointment. One ghost leads to another, which leads to another, and then all you end up with is heartbreak and a life haunted by questions you'll never have the answers to."

"Sounds like that's something you have a little bit of experience in," she said, looking into his eyes.

"I don't want to talk about it, but people don't lead lives like ours if they have a healthy childhood." Trevor threw the plate he'd been holding and it hit the exposed ground opposite them with a clatter.

"Why did you do that? You know that had to echo throughout the entire forest." She motioned toward the plate.

"They wanted us to come here. They'll be glad to know we took the bait."

She looked around. From what she could see it looked like a regular old campsite. There were no booby traps or any other evidence that they'd been set up, so she wasn't sure where he was coming up with this idea.

Almost as if he could read her mind, he continued, "Did you notice everything around here is brand-new? If you look at our guy's tracks, his boot marks are still in perfect diamonds and squares. And that plate, and all the dishes, barely have any marks on them. And if you look at this makeshift camp, everything has been moved here within the last day or two." He pointed toward the ground. If they'd been here long, the ground would be trampled well beyond this.

"So what? Maybe they just got here. These people are travelers."

"If these are the Cusslers, or their enemies, they aren't the type to be running to Walmart to get cookware and boots very often. Either they aren't who we've been thinking they are, or we're chasing the wrong ghosts."

She couldn't think of anyone else who could have been behind this.

"While I have my fair share of enemies, they aren't people who would shoot at me and miss. The people who want to kill my family are the type who can kill from two miles away, like our friends in Turkey. Which means it's likely that whoever is behind this is after you. Who have you ticked off lately?"

No. He was grasping at straws. There was no way she was the target here. He couldn't turn this back on her. This was his mess. His family's drama. Not hers.

Unless everything wasn't on the up and up with Mike.

The brass they'd found, the new plates, the manic deadline and the threatening emails…the evidence wasn't in the Bureau's favor, but everything he was pointing out was circumstantial. Sure, she had enemies—who didn't? It didn't mean that anyone was after her.

And yet she had a sinking feeling Trevor was right.

Chapter Eleven

Trevor wasn't sure if he had assumed correctly or not but he could tell he had planted just enough doubt about her team to create a distraction. As soon as they got back, he would alert the family that they were under investigation. In just a couple of hours, they could bug out—and disappear once again. He'd always heard Crete was beautiful. He could use a little bit more of a tan, and he certainly wouldn't miss snow.

As they walked back to the horses, he tried not to feel guilty as he took in the view of her walking ahead of him. He would be lying if he didn't admit how much he enjoyed that picture. He loved the way her hips swung back and forth as she picked her way through the underbrush that led to the serpentine trail. He'd miss that almost as much as he'd miss feeling her breath on his skin when she fell asleep with her head on his chest. It had been a long time since he'd made love, but the things she had done with her hips were unlike anything he'd ever experienced before. He couldn't risk losing her.

If the situation had been different, she was definitely the kind of woman he could imagine settling down with. Then again, he was never planning to settle down again.

Maybe she was more the kind of woman he could imagine traveling the world with. A scene from the movie *Tombstone* came to mind—with Wyatt and Josie slipping away into the sunset aboard a cruise liner and setting out on a life of adventure together.

But she was his adversary. She was trying to take down his family. Or at least she *had* been. It had to count for something that she had outed herself to him. Working with the CIA, he knew exactly how much was at risk in doing so—and exposing the truth to him may have put her job on the line. She certainly couldn't continue their investigation—but just because she left didn't mean that his family wouldn't still draw scrutiny from the Bureau. Just for once he wished he could call his friends in the CIA and have them whisper the truth into someone's ear in order to get this all to stop.

He'd end up dead long before the truth reached the right people. The Gray Wolves had their men everywhere, and where they didn't have their own people, they had paid informants. There was a lot of money to be made if a person was the type who was willing to sell state secrets.

"Sabrina, can you think of someone who wants you gone at the FBI?"

She stopped walking and turned around to face him. "There's always someone who is breathing down your neck behind closed doors."

The pinched expression on her face told him he had struck a nerve. She definitely had enemies.

"Is there anyone you can trust inside the Bureau?"

She looked off into the distance, as if she were contemplating her answer. "I know you think you're onto something, but I just don't see anyone working this hard to get me fired. If my enemies wanted to see me go, all they had to do is fudge a little paperwork."

"It isn't that easy. I *know* it isn't."

She quirked her eyebrow. "And how would you know? Did your family do an in-depth study of the Bureau?"

He chuckled. "You and your BuCrew aren't nearly as secret as you all would like to think you are. Sure, you have great people in tech, but when it comes to the truth I'm learning that you guys are at least ten steps behind."

"And yet we knew all about you and your family's dealings." She gave him a smart-ass tilt of the head.

If only she knew the truth, she wouldn't be so glib. And yet he could never reveal his truth to her. It wasn't just his to reveal.

"At least you can find some comfort in the fact that your enemies don't want you dead, or else they are just crappy shots," he teased her. "If this is someone from the FBI taking potshots at us, with all your long gun training through Quantico, I'm sure your instructors would've been so proud." He laughed. It felt good to be able to joke with her once again.

"Hey now, we don't know for sure whether or not those were my people shooting at us. In fact, if those were *my* people then I guess they weren't really mine after all, were they?" she pondered aloud.

"You are ridiculously cute when you're being asinine. You know just as well as I do that it was your enemies up there—FBI or not."

"I just think it's too far-fetched. It seems more likely that it's someone who wanted to make it look like FBI or a government agency. Plenty of these off-the-grid types are anti-government. It's easy enough to get your hands on those types of weapons. You know all about it." She gave him a judgmental look.

He walked up beside her and slipped his hand into hers. "How about we put a bet on this? If we get to the bottom of this and it's someone close to you, you have to spend another night with me—we'll order room service."

She gave him a playful grin. "Since you seem so certain, if it ends up being someone involved with your family—which by the way, seems far more likely—then you owe me two things. One, you have to keep my secret, under threat of penalty of death, should you expose me."

He loved that she could threaten him with death and it turned him on. "And your second ask?"

"A favor yet to be named. Do we have a deal?"

"I don't make bets when I don't know what's at stake."

"It's a deal, or there's no deal at all." Her playful grin grew even more impish. "It all comes down to how much you believe in your theory."

She was calling him out—testing to see exactly what cards he had up his sleeve. "Okay, deal…but the second ask can't be for something I don't want to give."

"Again," she said, a look of pure innocence on her face as she cajoled him, "all or nothing."

"Then *all* it is." He didn't like the deal, but something deep in his gut told him that he was right and there was more to this than what they had first assumed.

The ride out of the woods took far less time than it

had taken them to ride in. As they passed by their make-shift lean-to, he found himself once again wishing they could go back in time.

He wasn't angry at her admission of working for the FBI, not as he watched her ride in front of him. She had a job to do, just like he did. And the fact that she had finally admitted the truth to him went a long way. She certainly didn't have to do that. And it proved to him, more than anything else she could have done, that he could trust her. In a way, it also made him wonder if she was just as emotionally invested in what happened in that lean-to as he was—which meant, she must have realized how impossible their relationship would be.

If nothing else, at least they could walk away from each other knowing that somewhere in the world there was a person who really cared for them.

The ranch was dead quiet as they rode up with the truck and trailer. Unsaddling the horses, they barely spoke. It was as if she knew just as well as he did that things between them were about to come to an end.

There was no way they could go back and pretend they weren't the people they truly were, the people they had revealed to each other up on the mountain. If only he could have told her his truth as well, that he was working for the CIA, and yet…he couldn't. If he did, it would serve nothing. She would still have to leave, but when she did she would be in even more danger than when she arrived. The people he worked for weren't the kind who liked leaving loose ends. They made Trevor and his family look like teddy bears in comparison.

Instead of taking the horses straight back to Dunr-ovin Ranch, they'd decided to head home. It could have been all the riding or all the emotions he experienced over the last few days, but when they hit the front door, he was exhausted.

When he walked in, Chad was sitting on the couch, watching ESPN. He looked up and his expression darkened as though he could see from their faces that something was up.

"How'd it go? Did you find them?" Chad asked, flicking off the television.

Sabrina glanced over at Trevor. "Hey, I'm going to run out and unload the horses and put them in the barn. You guys go ahead and talk." She gave him a pleading look, as though she didn't want him to tell his brother what she had told him, but also understood he couldn't let a secret that big just stay between them.

He hated being in this position.

"Okay, I'll be right out and I can help you grab the rest of the stuff out of the truck." Stepping closer, he was going to give her a quick peck to the forehead, and then stopped himself. Chad didn't need more fodder for the fight they were likely about to have.

As the door closed behind Sabrina, Trevor walked over and sat down on the couch beside his brother. His knees ached from all the riding, making him feel old and tired.

Chad leaned forward looking him in the eye. "Are you going to tell me what that was all about?"

And so it began.

He couldn't look his brother in the eye, and he wished Chad hadn't turned off ESPN—it would've made things easier.

"What do you mean?" he asked, trying to buy himself more time.

He had been trying to think of ways around this conversation for hours now, and yet at zero hour, he still couldn't decide exactly how he wanted to handle things with his family. They deserved to know the truth about Sabrina, and they absolutely had to learn that they were under investigation. In fact, if he were under investigation, it was likely that other UCs were trying to break into their lives—other UCs who probably weren't as softhearted and kind as Sabrina.

And yet it would be immediately clear who the UC was in their lives as soon as he started talking. He wouldn't be able to hide her identity. At least Chad wouldn't want to kill her since she was an agent for the FBI…hopefully. Even though she didn't have a clue, they were all playing for the same team.

He would just have to figure a way out of this that worked for everyone and kept his family and Sabrina safe.

"You know exactly what I'm talking about, Trevor." Chad motioned toward the barn. "What happened up there on the mountain? Did you kill the family—is that why she's acting all weird around you? Or did you guys bump uglies?"

"Dude, seriously?" Trevor said, trying to look as innocent as possible. "Would I be this quiet if I'd taken the family out?"

"Good point," Chad said with a nod. "So then, you banged her?"

Trevor shook his head but was careful not to look at his brother. His eyes would give it away. "Sabrina? She's a nice woman, but I have a feeling that she's not going to stick around here too much longer. Especially after what we found," he said, a bit proud of the way he'd maneuvered around lying to his brother. Some things were better left unsaid.

"Which was?"

"Somebody up there decided to spark a few rounds off at us. They were just warning shots, but somebody wanted us to get the message we weren't welcome."

He told him about the shooter and the campsite but left out his theory about who had been pulling the trigger and why. There was no use getting his brother up in arms about something he wasn't sure of just yet. All Chad needed to worry about was making sure that the affairs of the ranch were in order and that the Gray Wolves didn't find out where they were.

If nothing else, at least he could be fairly certain that it wasn't his family's enemies who were behind this and the Cussler guy's death.

"What, are you surprised that our squatters would have a problem with you chasing them down? Nobody likes being kicked out of their house," Chad said.

Now would've been the perfect time for Trevor to tell him the truth and explain all the problems they were facing, but he held back. "Chad, do you think we made a mistake coming back here?"

"What makes you ask that?" Chad asked with a worried expression on his face.

"Nothing," Trevor said with a shrug. "I've been thinking maybe the US isn't the best place for us. I know we thought we had amnesty here, but what if we don't? What if we peed in the wrong person's corn-flakes, you know what I mean?"

"Clearly you're not telling me something," Chad said. "When you left here yesterday, you are all gung ho and ready to start making a new life here—even though it was boring. And now it's like you had a complete change of heart. You have to tell me why."

Trevor got up from the couch and strode over to the bay window that looked out toward the barn. The lights were on and the sliding door was open. Sabrina was unloading Zane. He watched as she backed him out of the trailer. "Call it a gut feeling or whatever you want, but I just think that maybe it's best if we bug out for a while—go somewhere in the Cayman Islands or something. Think about it, we could be lying on the white sand beach and drinking a cold one."

Chad stared at him like he was trying hard to figure him out. "Dude, Trevor, if you did something to upset Sabrina, we can figure it out—we don't need to get out of here. There a lot of housekeepers we could hire."

"Have you talked to Zoey at all while we were gone?" Trevor asked, trying to change the subject.

"Zoey said she's been watching all the channels, but so far she hasn't seen anything that would indicate the Gray Wolves have any idea where to find us." Chad got up and walked over and stood beside him at the window. "I know you're nervous, maybe that's what's going on with you, but I'm telling you this ranch is about the safest place we can possibly be. At least out here we have less of a chance of the Gray Wolves buying out some government agency in order to find us. I mean who is out here who would give two craps about us?"

Trevor's stomach dropped. What if Bayural had bought out someone at the FBI? Maybe they had sent Sabrina here to make sure they stayed while they got everything in place to take them out. But then, if that were the case, wouldn't they have just taken out a contract with a merc?

"Let's get the hell out of here," Trevor said, turning his back to the window.

"What? And what about Sabrina?" Chad asked, not stopping to ask him what he was thinking. His brother knew him well enough that if he said it was time to go, it was time to go. He could explain it to him later.

"We'll take her with us—if she wants to go."

"I knew you banged her," Chad said with a satisfied laugh as they rushed down the hall to their bedrooms to grab their bug-out bags.

Trevor was pulling out the .50cal from behind his mattress when the front door of the house slammed open.

"Trevor!" Sabrina yelled, her voice frantic.

The Gray Wolves were coming for them; he could feel it even though everything hadn't yet quite clicked into place. "What?" He dropped his bag and his gun case and sprinted out of the room, pulling his SIG Sauer from his holster and readying himself for whatever—or whoever—he was about to meet at that door.

Sabrina was standing at the front door, her hands over her mouth.

He lowered his weapon when he saw no one was behind her. "Are you okay? What's going on?" he asked, the words rushing out like it was a single syllable.

"There…" She motioned behind her. "There's a man out there, inside the last barn stall. He…he's been shot."

"Is he still alive?" Trevor hurried to her as Chad came running down the hall and to the living room.

She shrugged. "There was blood everywhere. I didn't stay to check him out."

"How long have you been home, Chad?" Trevor asked.

"I got back last night at midnight. Haven't left since then."

"And you didn't hear anyone coming or going, any cars?" Trevor asked.

Chad shook his head. "It's been quiet. No one."

"Stay in the house," Trevor said. "Make sure you watch our six. Whoever shot the guy is probably still out there—and they are probably gunning for us as well."

As he ran toward the barn he couldn't help but wonder if he was wrong and their shooter was already long gone—he had to hope, but he wasn't going to risk it.

If Bayural or his men were here, they could have easily taken Chad out while he'd been sitting watching television in the living room. From the right vantage point, Chad would never have known that anyone was ever even out there.

Whoever was behind these killings was doing their best to frighten them into submission. He couldn't let the killer get away with their murderous rampage any longer.

"Did you recognize the guy?" he asked Sabrina as he followed her into the barn.

Sabrina shook her head as she pointed toward the last stall. "He's in there."

Zane was nickering, his sound high-pitched and scared as he trotted nervously around the stall. Just like Trevor, he must have been able to feel the danger in the air.

Trevor walked to the last stall, half-afraid of what he would find. The blood was splattered over the wood paneling and there was a bloody handprint smeared down the far wall. "Hello?" he called, hoping that the man would answer. But there was little chance that the man was alive on the other side of the gate.

There was no answer.

He unclicked the latch and opened the gate, stepping into the stall. There, against the wall closest to him and tucked back into the corner of the room, was the man. He had scraggly gray locks and hair was sprouting from his ears. On his neck was a long, puckered scar as though someone had once tried to cut his throat but failed.

His hands were covered in blood and palms up in his lap, and his head was leaning haphazardly to the side. There was something about the man's face that looked familiar. He'd seen those same eyes and that shape face before—in fact, he looked almost identical, albeit slightly older, to the man in the shack. Trevor had to be looking at another of the Cussler brothers.

He walked over to the man and placed his fingers against his neck, hoping against all hope that there would be some faint pulse, but he found nothing but a sickening chill. He pulled his hand back. Algor mortis had started to set in.

Trevor moved to the man's feet and pulled back the leg of his pants, careful not to touch too much and leave behind any trace evidence. The guy had been sitting with his knees up and, even though Trevor pulled at his jeans, his legs stayed bent due to the effects of rigor. He'd definitely been down at least a few hours. Around twelve and he would have been completely immobile, but there was still a bit of pliability in his limbs.

Who in the hell was killing this family? And had they planned to murder the man here or had the man come here to die after he had been shot—making it look like Trevor and his family were responsible for his death?

"Is he alive?" Sabrina asked, but there was a resignation in her voice that told him she already knew the answer.

He didn't respond. Sabrina stopped behind the opened gate and looked inside; her gaze moved to the dead man. Maybe the poor light in the barn was causing him to see things, but he could have sworn that her face had grown a shade paler.

"You don't have to be in here," he said, moving closer to her and taking her hand. "You don't have to pretend to be tougher than you are with me."

She opened her mouth to speak as she looked up at him. There was a renewed softness in her eyes, and the look reminded him of when they had been making love and her body had begged him for her release.

"It's okay," he said, giving her a soft kiss to her forehead. "I've got this."

She took a step back so the man's dead body was out of her view, but she didn't leave. "What are we going to do, Trevor?"

He hadn't gotten that far yet.

This really should have been a case for the local cops, but calling them in would lead to a whole slew of questions he wasn't ready or willing to answer. It would only land them in deeper trouble. Yet they couldn't just wait for this body to disappear like they had the last, not with so many possible variables.

His first thought was for her to call her people at the FBI, but if they were in any way connected to this case, they wouldn't be coming in as allies. They weren't an option.

He'd have to call in a few of his friends at the CIA. They didn't typically work within the borders of the States, but undoubtedly his people knew some folks who could help him sweep this man's death under the rug.

Though sweeping it under the rug last time had certainly done them no favors. They needed to find answers and fast.

"You don't think your brother has a hand in this, do you?" Sabrina asked, her voice soft and smooth as though she was trying to be careful and not sound too accusatory.

He appreciated her effort, but her question still ruffled his feathers. "Chad wouldn't be stupid enough to kill a guy and leave his body sitting out here."

"Unless he wanted to set us up. He doesn't have a reason to want to drive you off the ranch, does he?" Sabrina asked.

He tried to control the anger that rolled through him. "No. He didn't do this. He wouldn't do this. My family are the only people I can really trust."

She visibly cringed at his unintentional jab.

"I just mean that he wouldn't have let us walk out here and work in the barn if he'd left this guy to cool down before getting rid of his remains."

"But you admit your brother is fully capable of pulling the trigger?"

"Look, Sabrina," he said, running his hands over the stubble that had grown on his cheeks over the last few days. "Anyone is capable of killing under the right circumstances. My brother is perhaps more likely to find himself in those kinds of circumstances than most, but that doesn't mean he is an evil man. He doesn't just go around killing people."

"I'm sorry, I know you're right," Sabrina said, leaning against the doorjamb. "I'm just…tired."

"I know you want to find an answer to this that doesn't point back to your people at the FBI, but you need to stop looking in my direction in order to figure out who is behind these killings—at least in the direction of my family. I'm telling you, we aren't the ones keeping secrets from one another."

She nodded. "I'd be lying if I said I wasn't a little jealous. Your family…it's one of a kind. I would like to have a group of people who I could always depend on."

His anger dissipated. He knew what it felt like to be lost, so he could empathize with what she was going through right now. In fact, he had to wonder if he was the only one she could really trust.

It seemed crazy how far they had come since they first met each other. He would never have guessed that this was how they would've played out. Aside from the dead guys, he wasn't sure he would change anything. He liked the fact that she was nearly as dangerous as him.

"Did you figure out where he was shot?" she asked, clearly trying to change the subject.

That was something else he appreciated about her—she was just as avoidant of feelings as he was. Sure, it may not have been the healthiest response, but it certainly kept one from getting hurt.

He stepped closer to the man. There was a small hole in his jacket just over his heart. Flipping back the edge of the coat, there was a small wound in his chest. Blood had seeped out and run down from the wound and had pooled at the top of his large belly before slipping down onto his jeans. "Looks like it was a single shot. Likely at least ten feet away."

There was the crunch of tires on the gravel of the parking lot just outside the barn. Trevor flipped the man's jacket closed, and as he did so he noticed the smear of blood on his own hands.

As he turned away, he saw a small hole in the wall. Lodged in the soft wood was a bullet.

Sabrina looked at him. "You think we should go out there?"

There was the sound of footsteps in the gravel as somebody made their way toward them.

Trevor rushed out of the stall, wiping his hands on the backside of his jeans. As he turned to face the door, a man came into view. Not just a man, but a deputy sheriff. He was all brassed up, complete with a Kevlar vest underneath his uniform. He looked to be in his midthirties, maybe. His hair was shorn and starting to recede just above the temples, and his forehead was littered with the wrinkles of someone who worried often.

He forced a smile as he walked toward the man. Zane's whinnies intensified from inside the horse's stall.

"Hey, Deputy, how's it going?" Trevor said, trying to sound amicable.

The deputy gave him a two-fingered wave. "Good," he said, sounding as tight and rigid as the vest he was wearing. "Anything going on out here that I need to know about?"

Sabrina gave him a confused look. "Nothing I can think of, Deputy."

The man chuckled. "May I ask your name, please?" The question was more of an order than a nicety.

Trevor strode toward him, moving with as much confidence as he possibly could. He extended his hand. "The name's Trevor Martin, you?"

The man gave him a strong shake of the hand, so strong it came across as an act of dominance—as though he wanted Trevor to know that he was at the head of the hierarchy here. "The name's Wyatt." A smile broke across the man's face. "Did Gwen tell you I was coming?"

Sabrina stepped between them as she shook her head. "Trevor, this is Wyatt, Gwen's husband."

"Oh," Trevor said, a wave of relief crashing over him. "Nice to meet you, man. Gwen's a fantastic woman. I'm proud to have her as a cousin."

"She is that." Wyatt glanced around the barn. "It's been a long time since I've been in here. I helped Gwen and her mom get this place together so you guys could move in. Hope you found everything in order."

Trevor nodded, but his mind went straight to the dead man in the last stall. "Everything's been great, but we are still getting organized on our end. I'm thinking my sister and other brother should be descending upon the ranch in the next few weeks."

Wyatt nodded. "That'll be great. It'll be nice to have some more family close. I know Gwen's been awful lonely since her sister passed away. She's been looking forward to getting to know you guys a little better."

Trevor nodded. "I was so sorry to hear about Bianca's death. At least they caught the person responsible."

"Yeah, best part of my job is getting to watch the guilty pay for their crimes."

Panic rose within him.

Zane nickered as he stuck his head out of his stall door and looked toward them.

"Ah," Wyatt said, looking toward the horse, "my old boy's here." He walked by them to the horse and gave the gelding a good scratch under the mane. The horse seemed to soften under Wyatt's touch.

"This your horse?" Sabrina asked as she stepped around Wyatt like she was trying to keep him from walking farther into the barn.

"Yep," Wyatt said. "He and I have been buddies for a long time. Gwen told me you had taken them up riding, but I figured you had brought them back to Dunrovin by now."

"Actually, we just got back from our ride. We were gonna take a rest, and then bring them back to you guys in the morning." Trevor motioned outside. "In fact, we haven't even unloaded the other horse yet. If you wanted, since you're here, we could load up Zane and—"

"No worries. Gwen and I both know how it is." Wyatt

waved him quiet. "Did you guys just run the fences or did you go up the mountain a bit?"

Trevor wasn't sure if Wyatt was testing him or not, but he didn't want to give him the wrong answer. "Yeah, we ran up to the top of Rye Creek. Nice area up there."

"When you get up there in those high mountains the last thing you want to do is come back to real life." Wyatt looked to Sabrina and then back to Trevor and gave him a knowing wink. "And you can keep the horses here as long as you like. Zane isn't our main guest horse, so he's not in high demand. It does him some good to get in some trail time."

Why did everyone assume that something had happened between him and Sabrina out there in the woods? Not that they were wrong. It just hardly seemed like it was anyone else's business.

"Zane is such a good boy," Sabrina said, bridging the gap for him. "It was a nice ride."

"Did you run into the squatters?" Wyatt pressed.

Did the man know something he didn't? Or was he looking for him to supply him with some kind of information? Regardless, his questions were making him unsettled.

"Nope, but we saw a camp they may have been using as a base."

Wyatt nodded. "Good thing. That family can be a wild bunch. And they like to take potshots at people they don't know or don't like."

"Good to know."

Sabrina smiled, the effect dazzling. "Was there something we could help you with, Wyatt?"

He turned and looked toward the end of the barn like

he was some kind of damned bloodhound. "Actually, I was here because we got an anonymous tip."

"What?" Trevor asked, his voice taking on an unwanted higher pitch.

"Someone said they heard some shooting coming from out here. They said it sounded like it was coming from inside one of the buildings." Wyatt turned to them. "You guys know anything about that?"

There wasn't anyone within earshot of this place, and certainly shooting at a ranch wouldn't have rung any warning bells. Someone had called in the tip on purpose—they probably wanted Wyatt to stumble onto the body.

They'd been set up.

"Don't know anything about that. Like we said, we just got back from our ride," Trevor said.

Wyatt looked to Sabrina and she nodded in support. "Anyone around here while you were gone?"

If Wyatt looked outside and toward the house he would have likely seen Chad standing near the front window. They couldn't lie and cover his brother's whereabouts—but as far as Wyatt was concerned, he seemed to be out here for nothing more than some suspicious activity. There was no use in lying.

"Actually, my brother Chad was here. He didn't tell me he'd heard anything. And I'm pretty sure he's been watching old football games all day."

Wyatt laughed. "Dang, I want your brother's life. That is just so long as he was drinking beer and eating Doritos as well."

"You know it," Trevor said, giving his cousin's husband a jovial slap on the back. He started to move toward the barn door in an effort to get the man out of the death zone. "You want to come inside and ask him about it?"

"Sure thing. It'd be nice to meet the rest of the family." Wyatt walked toward the front of the barn.

Trevor was careful to stay behind the man so he couldn't see the blood that was likely smeared on the seat of his pants. That would be hard to explain away.

They walked back to the house and Chad met them with an open door. "Hey, bro, this is Wyatt Fitzgerald, Gwen's husband."

Chad wiped his cheese-dusted fingers on the legs of his sweatpants and gave Wyatt a quick shake. "Nice to meet you, man. What can we do for you?" Chad gave Trevor a worried look, and Trevor shook his head in an attempt to convey the fact the deputy knew nothing about the body.

"We have a report of some shooting going on out here. You know anything about it?" Wyatt asked.

Chad nodded for a moment, and Trevor could see the wheels turning in his brother's head. "Hey, yeah... Sorry, that was me. I saw a coyote out there. Wanted to scare 'im off."

Wyatt nodded. "It work?"

Chad laughed. "Not gonna lie, been a lot of beers in the belly today—that, or the aim was a bit off on the old .22."

"I hear you, coz," Wyatt said as he started to warm to them. "If I was retired I would probably be doing just about the same thing—though Gwen may have something to say about that."

Chad laughed. "There are some benefits to being a single guy."

Sabrina's brow lifted as she gave him a look of disdain. "If you keep up the sweatpants and Doritos fingers, the last thing you have to worry about is some poor woman falling in love with you."

"Oh, burn." Wyatt laughed. "It's funny how women have a way of making us step up our game, isn't it?" He looked to Trevor.

The game—that was one word to describe exactly what was going on in their lives. And this game of murder was one game he couldn't lose.

Chapter Twelve

What in the name of all that was holy was going on around here? Sabrina wished the answers would suddenly appear and everything would make sense.

As the guys continued to talk, her mind wandered. It seemed possible that the Cusslers and the other hillbilly family could have been in some kind of backwoods war, and this was their way of telling the Martins they weren't welcome at the ranch. Maybe it was the second family, and they were figuring they could kill two birds with one stone—the Cussler man, and the Martins' chance of having a peaceful life out here.

But they couldn't have known the Martins wouldn't call the police—unless they been watching them dance around the issue of the dead body in the shack. They must have been watching, and had pieced it together that the thing Trevor and his family feared most was drawing attention from the cops. And they had set the boys up to take this fall.

The thought of being under surveillance made the hairs on the back of her neck stand on end. And yet it made her feel like a hypocrite as she had been doing almost exactly the same thing to Trevor and the Martins for the last little while.

Wyatt gave her an acknowledging nod goodbye as he made his way out the door and toward his patrol unit. "If you guys need anything, or want to meet up for supper sometime, give us a call. Gwen's looking forward to getting together." Wyatt opened the door to his car and the small Chihuahua from Dunrovin jumped out and scurried off in the direction of the barn.

"Francesca," he called after the dog, and as he called the animal's name a look of embarrassment crossed over his face. "I swear I didn't name the dog," he called as he chased after the little thing.

Sabrina ran after them in hopes of catching the dog before she could make her way too far into the barn. The opportunity to tell Wyatt about the body had already come and gone, and if he found the man's body they'd all be arrested for obstruction of justice and possibly tampering with evidence.

She'd have to expose who she was and why she was here to Chad and Wyatt, and what little chance remained of her finishing this investigation and clearing the family's name would go up in dust.

"Here, pup!" Trevor called, his voice frantic.

Wyatt rushed ahead of them into the barn and disappeared.

She hurried to the door, but it was too late. The deputy stood beside the small dog, who was sniffing manically at the base of the last stall. Francesca barked, panting as she looked up to her master. The little dog looked proud of her investigative skills. It almost would have been cute if it hadn't have just blown her cover.

Trevor slipped his hand into hers and gave it a squeeze. For a second, she considered running and getting out of there, but she wasn't the kind who was going to run from her problems. She had to face whatever was coming thanks to that little dog.

She never really considered herself a full-blown cat person until now.

Wyatt stood there in silence, simply staring into the stall for a long moment before turning to them, a dark expression on his features. "How long did you guys say you been back from your ride?"

Trevor took the lead. He shrugged. "Not long. Like we said, we just unloaded Zane. Why, what's up?"

Smart. Feigning ignorance was the only plausible excuse for what the deputy had just found.

Wyatt turned back toward the stall. "I hate to tell you guys this but it looks like I'm gonna need to call out a few more friends of mine."

"Why?" Sabrina asked, she and Trevor took a few steps toward him.

Wyatt held up his hand. "Stop right there. I can't have you coming any closer. Not until I can get my team out here to investigate."

Trevor was already close enough to see the body from the open gate. He motioned for Sabrina to back up. "You don't need to see this." She wasn't sure whether Wyatt wanted to keep them away from the body to see exactly how much they knew, or if he just wanted to protect them from seeing something traumatic.

"Trevor, run inside and get Chad. He needs to know what's going on out here," she said, and leaning in close she whispered, "Don't forget to change your pants. Put them somewhere safe." She gave him a peck on the cheek in hopes it wouldn't look like she had been whispering directions.

Trevor looked unflappable, and his stoicism made her chest tighten with something much too close to love. She had to respect a man who held a great poker face even under the most strenuous of circumstances.

"I'll be right back," Trevor said, but Wyatt was focused on the body.

As Trevor rushed from the barn, she walked toward Wyatt, ignoring his request for her to stay back. She had to pretend to look at the body for the first time.

She stopped beside Wyatt as the man's body came into view. She clapped her hands over her mouth in an attempt to look as surprised as she had been a little while ago. "Do you know who this man is?"

Wyatt turned to her. "I told you not to come back here. You need to leave the barn, right now. Don't touch anything."

Reality came rushing in and Sabrina realized what she had to do. "Wyatt, we knew about the body. We had just found him before you arrived." Before Wyatt ran away with this, she had to tell him the truth…no matter how badly she didn't want to. "I'm a special agent with the FBI, currently I'm investigating a series of crimes. I'm close to cracking the case, but if you pull your men out here, I'm afraid that my cover and my investigation will be blown."

"That can't be true," Wyatt said, staring at her in disbelief.

"Call your sheriff. My people have been in contact with him throughout the investigation. He's the one we briefed when we came in, so he knew what was going on. I wasn't planning on being here too much longer. The Bureau is breathing down my neck. They want results."

"And are you going to get them?" Wyatt asked. "Did you get everything you needed?"

"I'm starting to figure things out. But with this guy's death, I'm afraid there's more going on here than I had anticipated. I need to talk to my handler about what's happened. However, I doubt I will get an extension on my assignment."

"How much longer do you have?"

"Less than a week," Sabrina said. She scuffed her boot around in the spent hay on the barn's floor, kicking up the scent of dirt and horse manure. "It's my hope that I can clear the Martins' name and head off to my next assignment."

Wyatt nodded, but he didn't say anything. The barn door squeaked as Trevor and Chad pushed it open a bit wider and walked in. Chad had the look of a deer in the headlights as he stared at Wyatt.

Wyatt cleared his throat and turned toward the brothers. "Did your brother tell you what we found?"

Chad nodded.

"I'm going to have my crew come in and investigate this man's death. It would make it a whole lot easier if you tell me what actually happened here before my team lays this on you." Wyatt stepped over to the pile of hay bales and leaned against them, crossing his arms over his chest. "You're my family by marriage and I'm going to do everything in my power to make sure you guys stay out of harm's way, but you have to tell me the truth." He looked directly at Sabrina and gave her an almost-imperceptible wink.

It did little to quell the nerves that were building within her. From what she'd heard about the Mystery, Montana, sheriff's department, their forensics team left much to be desired. Hopefully, that would work to her advantage.

But she still couldn't have anyone blowing her cover.

"Let's try this again," Wyatt said to Chad. "Was this man the coyote you were shooting at today?"

Chad rubbed his hands over his face. "I only found out about this dead guy about four seconds before I walked out here. If I had shot him, I would tell you it was in self-defense or something. But I haven't even seen the guy yet." He waved toward the end of the barn.

"The man's name is Earl Cussler. He's the second oldest of the Cussler boys. They are all as mean as rattlesnakes, so if you had admitted to shooting him in self-defense, I would've believed it. However, as it stands, this isn't going to work for me or my department." Wyatt took out his cell phone and glanced down at the buzzing device. "I want you to all go inside before I call in my team."

She turned to leave the barn, but Wyatt motioned her back. "Trevor, I'll be along in a second."

Trevor frowned at her as he made his way out of the barn. "Are you sure?" he whispered, glancing at his cousin's husband.

She nodded. "It's going to be fine."

She watched as Trevor and Chad went back to the main house. They were chatting as they walked, but she couldn't hear exactly what they were saying. No doubt it was something about how much trouble they were going to be in once everything broke. She was afraid she wouldn't be able to help them.

"Who's your handler?" he asked, pulling her attention back to him.

"His name's Mike Couer," she said, a bitter taste filling her mouth. "If you talk to him, take what he says about me with a grain of salt. He and I used to be a thing."

Wyatt chuckled, the sound out of place and haunting in the impromptu crypt. "I thought the Bureau looked down on that."

"They do, but it didn't last long—only long enough to make us realize it was a mistake."

"And to dislike each other?" Wyatt asked.

She couldn't deny it. "Let's just say, if you call him about me, I can't guarantee exactly what he's going to say. I was hoping to use this case to get out of the trenches and into another field office."

Hopefully Wyatt wouldn't judge her unfairly for the mistakes she had made. He was the only shot they had at keeping things under wraps for a bit.

"If that's all true," Wyatt said, leaning back on the hay, "then I understand why you're in a rush to end this investigation. There's nothing more fun than having to deal with your ex's crazy behavior all the time. My family knows exactly how far an ex will go to wreak havoc on a person's life."

"Yeah, Gwen told me what you guys had gone through." She hoped this commonality would act as a bridge between them, a bridge that would lead to her getting her way. "I'm sorry to hear about the mayhem.

Sounds like a lot of people died." She hadn't meant to sound so crass and un-empathetic, but her tone came out all wrong.

Wyatt looked at her with surprise, as though he had heard the hardness in her words as well. "You weren't investigating my family, were you?"

She didn't want to lie to him. "Your family drew a bit of scrutiny thanks to your recent run-in with the law, but you were all cleared. However, your name was scattered throughout my files. Just like the Martins, upon coming here and digging a bit, it was easy to see that you weren't criminals—just at the wrong end of someone's sights."

"That's an understatement. It was one hell of a Christmas."

"I can only imagine how you guys must've been feeling."

"Yeah, but even with all the upheaval, a lot of good came from my family's legal troubles."

It was no secret that everything had worked in his family's favor financially, and they had added several family members to their tree. Again, she was witness to a family that seemed to figure out how to stay together, no matter what. She'd never know what that would be like.

"Then I'm sure you can understand—maybe better than anyone—what I want to happen for the Martins." She brushed her hair out of her face. "I know what I'm about to ask isn't aboveboard, but I want you to consider it just for a couple seconds before you give me your answer. Deal?"

The darkness returned to his features, but he nodded.

"All I'm asking," she continued, "is that you give me twenty-four hours. Tomorrow at this time, regardless of if I have this figured out or not, I will call you and report this guy's death and your crew can come and get the body. You and your team will have access to everything I can give you, and I'll talk to Chad and make sure he had nothing to do with this. However, for the time being, I need you to turn a blind eye. Call this a favor for the FBI, a favor I will happily return if the need arises."

"I knew that's where you were going." Wyatt stood up and readjusted his Kevlar vest. "If I don't hear from you in exactly twenty-four hours, I will be standing on that doorstep. I will come after you, and your ex won't be your only enemy in law enforcement. Got it?"

"You can trust me, Wyatt. Thank you for this. I know it's hard to do something like this, but know you're doing the right thing."

"I hope so. I hope you realize you're not just putting your own ass on the line, but mine as well. I don't need this kind of trouble, but I've learned having friends in high places can make all the difference. Don't you be forgetting you owe me."

She had expected some of the weight to be lifted off her shoulders, but as Wyatt walked out of the barn, it was like the entire world was upon her. They'd have to get to the bottom of this fast, or her entire world—and everyone else's around her—would come crashing down.

Chapter Thirteen

Trevor hated that he'd had to leave Sabrina in the barn alone with Wyatt. He could only guess what they'd talked about, but no doubt she'd had to let him in on her secret.

Wyatt walked out of the barn and got into the squad car. Starting it up, he drove away. *Holy crap*, what had she said to him? The deputy hadn't seemed like the type who would walk away from a case like this. Family or not, he hadn't expected any sort of favors from the man.

"Dude, did you see that?" Chad asked, pointing out the window.

"I'll be right back," he said, already half out the door.

Sabrina met him halfway; her hands were up like she was surrendering to him. "It's going to be okay, Trevor. I made a deal with him."

"Is he dropping his investigation?" he asked, taking hold of her shoulders and looking her in the eye.

Her whole body tensed underneath his touch. "Far from it. We have twenty-four hours. That's it. Then all hell's going to break loose. And I would guess that at least Chad will be arrested. And you wouldn't be far behind…nor would I."

"Are you kidding me? We barely have a clue about what's going on out here. And yet you think we can solve this in a day?" She must've lost her mind. He was going to jail. They had to run. And yet if they did, it would make them look incredibly guilty. And she would have to answer for their leaving.

"Trevor, there's something I didn't tell you before. I didn't think it was important, but now with this…" She nibbled at her lip. "My handler at the Missoula resident agency, his name is Mike. He's my ex."

As she said the man's name, it looked as though she was in pain. She must hate the man. He could only imagine the kind of drama that would unfold inside the close quarters that was the FBI. It was known for being fraught with varying levels of corruption and mistrust—none more so than the last few years. Lately, it was as if everything had gone crazy in the Bureau. It was a wonder that she even had a job if she'd made the mistake of falling for her boss. In fact, this Mike guy was lucky that she hadn't gone after him for any sort of predatory behavior. The man had to be one hell of a winner if he was preying on women within his agency in order to get some.

On the other hand, perhaps she really had loved the guy and it was a relationship built upon real feelings. It was easy enough to see how something like that could come about, with forced proximity and all, but he would have thought a man in an authority position would have made the choice to not put them both in jeopardy. Then again, Sabrina was of her own mind. She had made choices—this wasn't sitting on just the shoulders of her boss. She had to have understood what kind of position she was putting herself in.

He needed to distance himself from her. Not that he didn't already know that. He just couldn't get over how sweet her lips had tasted, and how it felt when her body was pressed against him. In a weird way, his heart had felt as shriveled and emaciated as a starving man, but when she'd entered his life it was like it had started to beat again and grow stronger thanks to the nourishment that came with her presence.

Ugh, he was being so ridiculous.

"Do you still love him?" he asked without thinking.

From the look on her face, the question had clearly come out of left field. "No."

Her curtness didn't help him feel any better.

He counted his breaths until he reached ten and his heart rate lowered. He had to keep his wits about him. "Okay, so do you think this guy is gunning for you… for us?"

She chewed on her lip until a tiny bit of blood dotted its pink curve. "I want to say no, but the truth is I'm not sure. He's been pushing me hard throughout this investigation. He rushed it through the bureaucracy. What normally takes six months to get approvals for, he did in a matter of weeks. I don't know how he did it, but it may be part of the reason he needs us to get to the bottom of this so quickly."

"*This*—as in my family?" Even he could hear the hurt in his voice.

"I meant my investigation." She gave him an apologetic smile. "Mike is probably on the warpath. He likely overextended himself and promised results that, frankly, I'm not sure I'm going to be able deliver on."

"Do you think if you went to the offices that you could get a better feel for what's going on with Mike?" Part of him wanted to go with her, to ensure she was safe. Yet the last place he needed to be seen was sitting outside a federal building. Even with his connections with the CIA, those watching wouldn't appreciate his suspicious behavior.

"Mike is not the kind of guy you can get an easy read on. The FBI has trained that out of him. He's like talking to a wall."

With that kind of description, he wasn't sure how she had ever found herself falling for such a guy. Though if he looked at himself closely, he was probably cut from the same cloth as Mike. Again, he found himself lacking. He had to hope he was nothing like a possibly crooked agent. Though Sabrina hadn't always thought him capable, he was a man guided by morals. Which only made all of this more difficult.

"I think we should go, but I'll need stay out of sight. The last thing we need is you showing up to the regional headquarters with the man you are in charge of investigating." Trevor pulled the keys from his pocket.

Sabrina sniggered. "I can't even imagine how badly that would play out."

"Well, you don't have to as long as things go smoothly. In and out, okay?" he said with a raise of the brow.

"All right, but no matter what happens you have to stay out of the limelight."

He nodded. "I'll unhitch the trailer if you unload the other horse."

They made quick work of it. Sabrina wiped her hands on the leg of her pants as she closed up the barn and turned to him. "What about Chad and the cops? You don't think he'll blow my cover, do you?"

"Chad is a knot head, but he's not stupid. You're safe when it comes to my family and them keeping their mouths shut." He lifted the keys. "You want to drive?" he teased.

"If we want to get there in one piece, I better."

He threw the keys to her with a chuckle.

It wasn't too long a drive to Missoula. With each passing mile, more nerves started to fill him. It felt almost as if he was back in Adana, and the gun trade was just about to go down with Trish. This same sense of foreboding had filled him then. If something happened to Sabrina, like it had to Trish, he wasn't sure he could keep on living. The crushing blow of losing his sister had been all the tragedy he could bear. He couldn't lose someone else he loved.

"When I get out, I want you to take the wheel and drive over to the Staggering Ox. Order a sandwich, and I'll get an Uber and catch up."

He didn't like the plan, but he was in no position to argue. If something happened inside the federal building, he'd never get access in time to save her. But Mike didn't sound like a guy who would get caught making a visible threat against another agent.

Regardless of how uncomfortable it made him, he had to trust her judgment. She was going to do what she had to do for them and for their investigation. Though he had never intended on them working together, in this moment, he realized that was exactly what they were doing—inadvertently, their relationship had morphed into something new...something that *fit*.

No. He was just seeing things that weren't really possible. Sure, they could work this thing together, but that didn't mean anything for the future. This was nothing more than an isolated incident including some extenuating circumstances—circumstances that, for this moment in time, had them working toward the same goal. Once they got to the bottom of this and found their murderer they would be forced to go their separate ways.

She pulled the truck to a stop about a block away from the Fed office and got out.

"Be careful," he said, ignoring the apprehension that was gnawing away in his gut. "If you need me, I can be back within a couple of minutes."

She nodded. Her features were tight, as though she were feeling some of the same nervous energy that he was—it did nothing to make him feel better. He wanted to tell her to stop, that they could do something else, something less risky, something that wouldn't put her square at the center of Mike's radar. And yet, the leads—which all pointed at corruption—had brought them here.

This was the only way...anything else would take them far longer than the time they had been allowed.

In the meantime, he had some work of his own to do.

He watched for a moment as she walked down the sidewalk. She was still wearing her dirty clothes from the trail ride, and there was mud on her boots. She looked like anything but a special agent.

He put the truck in gear and looked up the sandwich shop on his phone, then made his way across town. The hole-in-the-wall restaurant comprised about a dozen tables, all of which were covered in inlaid comic book pages. It carried a certain charm. And as he walked toward the register, the scent of warm bread and fresh lettuce filled the air. It made his mouth water as he realized that the last time he had eaten was when they were up on the mountain. His stomach grumbled and twisted in his belly.

He ordered a couple of sandwiches and went outside to make a phone call while he waited for them to be ready.

He pulled out his phone and dialed his point person within the CIA.

She answered on the first ring. "Trevor, what's going on, man?" She sounded excited in her normal, brusque way.

"Hey. I'm working a case and I need your help."

"I thought you had taken a leave of absence," she said with a chuckle.

"You know full well that even when we're not working, we're working."

"I wouldn't know. I'm never blessed with free time, you lucky bastard," she teased.

He'd always appreciated Tina's ability to not delve down the dark and disturbing rabbit hole that was the past—she knew exactly why he had taken time away from the CIA, and why he was likely going to choose to retire, and yet she avoided bringing up his sister.

"I'm what we're calling lucky now?" He laughed. "I'd hate to see what it means to be one of the unlucky ones."

Tina laughed. "What do you want? I know you didn't call me just to be an ornery ass."

"I've been dealing with some DOAs."

"Because of course you have," Tina said, interrupting.

"Ha ha, you know if your job ever craps out at the agency, you can always become a comedian."

"I'm not half as funny as your face is looking."

"Anyone ever tell you you're a real pain in the butt?"

"Every day."

"Actually, I was calling about a friend of mine in the Bureau. We have reason to believe that there's some interoffice corruption going on."

There was a long silence on the other end of the line.

"Dude, Trevor, if you're right, you don't want to get within a thousand miles of that kind of thing. Politics has a way of ruining even the best reputations."

Tina was right, but in this instance, he didn't have a whole lot of choice in the matter—he was already deeply involved. "I hear you. I do. However, that ship has sailed. What I need from you is for you to help me run some ballistic tests. I have reason to believe that the rounds may belong to a federally issued weapon. I just need to know for sure. That something you can help me with?"

"Are you serious? Are you really asking me to stick my neck out and take part in defaming an FBI agent? You'd be putting my job at risk, you realize that, right?" Tina asked, but from her tone he couldn't decide whether or not she was being serious or kidding around. Either way he wouldn't have been surprised.

"Is that a no?"

Tina chuckled. "Pfft, come on now, you know we're supposed to be all buddy-buddy with our FBI brethren, but nothing would make me happier than knocking the hierarchy down a peg or two. Get them to the Montana State Crime Lab. I have some friends there who owe me a favor."

"I knew I could count on you," Trevor said. "I'll get the samples there as soon as I can. They should be to you within the hour. And hey, thanks."

"I've always got your back. And next time we work together, I'll make sure you get the first crappy detail that comes along."

"I'd expect nothing less."

She hung up. He sent a quick text to Chad, asking him to run out to the barn and pull the round that was embedded in the wood of the stall.

The waiter walked out of the sandwich shop, carrying a paper bag of sandwiches. "Thanks," Trevor said, handing him a ten-dollar tip.

He walked back to the truck and sat down with his sandwich. He'd forgotten to order drinks, son of a gun. He slipped his sandwich back into the bag and was just about to get out as his phone rang. It was Sabrina. Just the sight of her name made the bite of sandwich he'd eaten sit poorly in his stomach. Hopefully she was okay.

"Do you need help?" he asked, bypassing any pleasantries.

"Mike isn't here. No one has seen him in the office in a couple of days. But they were acting strange, like they were hiding something." She sounded worried.

"And no one knows where he's at?" Trevor put his phone on speaker, sat back in his seat and slammed the truck door closed. He revved the engine and screamed out of the parking lot, hurrying back to get to her.

At least he didn't have to worry about Mike taking potshots at her, and she wasn't in immediate danger, but that didn't mean they were out of the woods yet.

"It doesn't sound like he's been seen or heard from in days. People are concerned and looking into his disappearance. This kind of behavior is very unlike him."

Something was going on in her office. Something that surely wouldn't play out in her favor.

"You didn't talk to anyone about our investigation into your team at the FBI, did you?"

"No, never. I couldn't."

Trevor ran through a yellow light as it turned red. Right now, he didn't care about following rules. He just had to get to Sabrina and make sure she was safe.

"You're not driving like a bat out of hell, are you?" Sabrina asked, but there was a hard edge to her voice as she teased him.

"I have no idea what you're talking about." He glanced at the road signs. "I'll be out front to pick you up in a minute. Be outside."

She laughed, but he could hear the echo of a stairwell and her footfalls as she must have been running down stairs. "It's okay, Trevor. I'm fine. You know you don't need to worry about me."

"I'm not," he lied. "I'm approaching one block due east of the front entrance."

The front door of the building opened and Sabrina

walked outside. There was a muffled cry as she dropped her phone and it clattered onto the sidewalk. The line went dead. A group of agents surrounded her. She put her hands up and said something. She glanced in his direction, terror in her eyes. Her mouth opened, and from the distance it looked as though she was telling him to stay back.

He pulled the truck over just as the agent closest to Trevor took Sabrina down to the ground.

What in the hell is going on?

He couldn't just rush in there and fix things. If he did, it would likely only end up with him getting arrested and Sabrina getting fired for misconduct. But that didn't stop him.

He got out of the truck, only half-aware of the traffic that was passing around him. He ran down the street. "I demand you tell me what's going on here."

An older man, probably in his midfifties, sent him a dangerous smile. "I know exactly who you are, Trevor, and if you think your connections give you any right to know what is going on here, you are sorely mistaken." The man had to be Mike, Sabrina's ex. He seemed like exactly the jerk that she had described—with his salt-and-pepper hair, his silver fox looks and his arrogant swagger.

"What do you know, jackass?" Trevor sneered.

"Oh, I heard all about how you got fired from Spookville for your role in getting your sister killed." Mike stepped away and waved back the agents around him. "Sounds like you have your hands in all kinds of pots. I just wish it could have been us that found the in-

formation that proved it. As it was, Agent Parker here…
Well, she lost her edge."

He didn't know what the hell he was talking about.
Just like everything else about this investigation, it appeared as though he only had half the information—
the half that made him want to punch Mike in the face.

"Sabrina," he said, pushing the arresting officer back
and helping her up. "Are you okay?"

"Trevor, it is far from your best interest to get involved. I have it on good authority that you're just a few
days away from this happening to you as well." Mike
put his hand on the gun at his side, threatening him.
"Actually, I bet I'd get a slap on the back for bringing
you in for your role in the murders of Earl and Owen
Cussler. Former CIA or not, murder is murder."

There were a lot of things that Trevor was guilty
of, but not that. "And what genius came up with this
theory?" He looked directly at Mike. "I'm sure this is
your handiwork."

"Sounds like the words of a guilty man." Mike
looked around the group of agents like he was looking
for some sort of validation.

"That's the dumbest thing I've ever heard, Mike." He
glanced to the agents standing around them. "What kind
of motivation do we have to kill those guys?"

"It's no secret that you're trying to evict the family
from your land." Mike sneered. "Sounds like one hell
of a motivation to me. Not to mention Sabrina's hatred
for me…she's been trying to make me look incompetent
from the very beginning. She's been setting me up. I
just couldn't believe it when I learned of her role in the

shoot-out that took place with her fellow agents. I assume she must have thought she was shooting at me." He glared at her. "In case you were wondering, Agent Heath is still recovering at St. Pat's hospital."

He had been right. The people they'd been fighting on the mountain had been none other than the men from her own agency. But it didn't make sense. She should've known they were up there. Mike should have informed her that they might run into friendlies.

"Thanks to your mistakes, we have more than enough evidence to take you and your whole family into custody." Mike gave him a weighted look, like he was sure he had the upper hand.

It took all of Trevor's strength not to get up in the man's face and tell him exactly where he could stuff his theories. In fact… He pushed his way toward the man and started screaming obscenities like some outraged hillbilly. While his mouth ran wild, he lifted Mike's gun from his holster and slipped it under his jacket.

"Trevor, stop!" Sabrina said. "Just go. Before you get into trouble. I'll get this figured out. I'm innocent. We both know that. We'll get this sorted."

He stepped beside her and gave her a long, passionate kiss. Their public display of affection caused some of the agents to look away. As they did, Sabrina slipped a gun into his waistband. She leaned in close like she was whispering something sweet into his ear, and said, "This is mine. Send it to ballistics along with the one from the cabin…and Mike's."

She must have seen him take the man's gun.

She moved back from their kiss. "Now get out of here before Mike does something stupid."

As far as Trevor was concerned, Mike had already done something extraordinarily idiotic when he decided to screw over Sabrina. And now his stupidity was going to come back to bite him. Trevor would not rest until he cleared the name of the woman he loved.

Chapter Fourteen

She was innocent, and he was the only person who could prove it.

From the truck, he watched as the agents paraded Sabrina into the building—like she was some kind of prized cattle that they just couldn't wait to take to slaughter. He would've thought that there would be more comradery within the FBI, but then it shouldn't come as such a surprise. It was a dog-eat-dog world.

Loyalty was a commodity in short supply.

Which made him think about Seattle. He couldn't be completely sure, but he had a feeling that the Bureau had taken the bait—if it hadn't, Mike would have certainly arrested him when they'd arrested Sabrina. As it was, they were probably still hoping to bring him down for gunrunning. He was probably still being watched.

If he caught a plane now, he could get to Seattle with a half a day to spare—hours in which he could put his plan into action.

His first stop was to the crime lab. When he arrived at the bland brick building he was reminded of a generic apartment building in New York—maybe in the low-rent district.

Chad was just parking when he arrived, and he parked beside him. As he got out Chad flashed him a little Ziploc bag; inside was a piece of shrapnel.

"What kind of mess have you gotten us into?" Chad asked.

"If I told you, you wouldn't believe me. But on a positive note, it looks like you and I will be flying to Seattle. We need to be there before the morning. In the mood for some spoon-melting coffee?" he asked with a chuckle.

Chad sighed and handed him the bag. "And here I thought moving to Montana would give us a chance to live a slower paced life. You just love proving me wrong, don't you?"

Trevor slapped his brother's arm. "It's not about proving you wrong, it's just about keeping the standard of living to which we've grown accustomed. I'd hate for you to get bored."

"I can't say life with you has ever been boring," Chad said with his trademark half grin.

"Good, then I'm not about to let you down." Trevor flashed his brother the two guns tucked into his waistband.

"Where did you get those?" Chad asked, giving him a look of concern.

"You're not gonna believe this, but I just lifted one off of one of our local FBI agents." Trevor smirked. "Best part, I doubt he even noticed it's missing."

"You have got to be kidding me," Chad said, each word like it was in independent sentence. "No wonder you have us running. We're going to be jumping borders in no time, aren't we?"

"It all depends on what happens in that building," he said, pointing toward the crime lab.

"Please tell me that there's a Get Out of Jail Free card somewhere in there." Chad frowned. "If I end up going to jail for you, I'm going to be irate."

He would have liked to tell his brother he had nothing to worry about, but the truth was that their butts were hanging way too far out in the open for him to feel comfortable. Mike, and the agents working with him, were going to be out for blood once they figured out what he had done.

"I'm going to run in. You need to call Zoey and have her arrange for a private jet to take us to Seattle. Got it?"

Chad nodded, already reaching for his phone.

As Trevor made his way into the crime lab, he looked back. Trish would've loved this kind of thing. She'd hated FBI agents even more than he did. Though now it seemed like he may well have fallen in love with one.

Trish would have given him such crap for Sabrina. But when push came to shove, his sister would have loved Sabrina just as much as he did. In fact, Trish would've probably helped him figure out a way to make everything work, not only with Sabrina but with this cluster he found them in.

He had no idea what he would do if this didn't work.

It wasn't just Sabrina's career that hung in the balance. If this failed, not only would he likely lose all credibility within the CIA and secret services, he'd also probably end up in jail, just as Chad had predicted. He would hate to prove his brother right.

In all of his years as a independent military contractor, he had never thought he would find himself in such a compromising position. He'd done many questionable things in the line of duty—but this was by far the craziest. It seemed like some kind of karmic slap that his greatest adversaries wouldn't be some terrorists abroad, but rather American law enforcement agents.

It didn't take long to hand the guns off to the tech at the lab; apparently Tina had already made the call.

When he made his way outside to Chad, his brother pointed toward his car and said, "Get in. We will have a jet waiting for you in the morning." Chad walked around to the driver's side.

Maybe this was all going to go better than he hoped, but he had a sinking feeling that he was in some deep water.

THE NEXT MORNING, the flight took just over an hour, and when they arrived Zoey was standing out on the tarmac waiting for them. Even in the overcast gray sky that seemed to always hover over the city, Zoey's black hair picked up what little light there was, and the effect created dark blue streaks. Even with her dyed locks, she looked so much like Trish.

There was a town car and a driver waiting beside her.

"Wipe that look off your face," Zoey said. "Stop worrying. I already hacked into the FBI mainframe. This Mike guy was bluffing, but he's hoping that they can bring you in for running guns. As such, I made sure he got orders from the top to intercept our 'trade' this evening. I also contacted the DOJ. they are sending someone to look into things and find out how deep this corruption runs."

"And what about Sabrina? Is she going to be cleared?" Trevor asked.

"Depends on her level of involvement. From what Chad was telling me, sounds like you and this woman have been hitting it off."

He shot a disapproving look at his brother, but Chad just shrugged.

"What can I say, man? We're a family that hates to keep secrets from one another." Chad's half grin reappeared.

As ridiculous as his brother could be, he couldn't be mad at him. It was this open policy that was currently in the process of saving their butts.

"Sabrina and I have grown close since I got to the ranch," he admitted.

Zoey smiled. "Yeah, I knew she would be right up your alley when I vetted her for the housekeeping job."

"Oh yeah," Chad said. "I forgot that this was all your fault. Thanks a lot, sis. Maybe next time worry less about being our virtual matchmaker and worry more about whether or not the people we bring into our lives belong to the FBI."

Zoey held her hands up in surrender. "I admit, I may have overlooked the fact that her background seemed a bit sparse, but I just thought she was the kind of girl who didn't get out much."

"Well, you were definitely wrong." Trevor walked to the town car and threw their go bags into the trunk. "Then again, who am I to start pointing fingers? I assume Chad told you everything?"

Zoey nodded. "One thing for certain, you are gifted

when it comes to getting us into highly unconventional situations."

That was one way to put it.

He once again thought of Trish. Zoey gave him a mournful look. "Hey, Trevor, I know what you're thinking... It wasn't your fault."

He wasn't sure he believed her, or if he ever would.

"The family...we...none of us are upset with you about what happened back there. It was outside your control. You need to start forgiving yourself. Trish wouldn't want you to hang on to her death like you are."

It was easy enough for her to say, but she wasn't living in his shoes. "I hear what you're saying, but until we get through tonight unscathed, I'm not gonna forgive myself for anything."

Some tragedies were just too great to overcome...all he could do now was try not to repeat history.

Chapter Fifteen

Sabrina paced around the interrogation room. She couldn't even begin to count the number of times she had brought people in rooms like this one in order to get them to bend to her whims. And now here she was, on the other side of the table. There was a box of tissues and a stack of magazines at the center of the table. In the corner was a percolating coffeepot. The scent of coffee was there to promote a sense of safety, reminding people of being home and in the comfort of their own surroundings, but the aroma only made her more anxious.

At least they hadn't forced her to wear the cuffs around the building when they brought her up from her holding cell to the interrogation room this morning. It was already embarrassing enough that she had been brought in here like she was nothing more than one of their normal, run-of-the-mill murderers.

She was never going to be able to show her face around Missoula or the county again. Everyone in law enforcement knew, or had found out by now, that she had been arrested for murder. No doubt, they would have to call in an outside investigation team to review her case, but knowing Mike, he had gone out of his way to make sure she looked as guilty as hell.

What she couldn't understand was how. She'd had no intuition that they'd been watched or set up. Everything had seemed relatively...*normal*. Well, as normal as her days at the Bureau could be. Sure, not everybody came across dead bodies every few days, but in her line of work it was par for course.

Mike had to have been plotting this for some time— probably from the first moment they were sent to this remote agency from Washington.

She hadn't expected Mike to remain her friend, or even an ally, after they broke up. Things hadn't ended on the best of terms but they owed each other some amount of respect, especially after all they had been through. Instead here she was, standing on the other side of the glass thanks to his denigration of her character.

Even if she could prove her innocence, it would take some time. Certainly, the damage to her career would be nearly irreparable. Maybe she really would have to become a housekeeper. Maybe, just maybe, the Martins would hire her full time. But she had likely burned her bridge with that family, once the rest of Trevor's siblings found out about her role in the FBI.

As of the last she knew, Trevor had protected her secret, but now he'd have to out her in order to ask his family to help. Unfortunately. Even if his family did help, she wasn't sure that they would be her best allies when it came to standing in front of a judge and jury.

However, she could have sworn she'd heard Trevor say he was working with the CIA, but she couldn't believe it. If he had been working with the CIA like he said, there was no way that Mike would have sent her in to investigate the family. He had enough clearance to have that information.

But documents and proposals for the investigation had been fast-tracked through the Bureau. It was possible that either someone hadn't fact-checked properly or that Mike had known all along and had wanted her to disappear at the hands of the trained spook.

The CIA and their operatives, especially those who did not wish to be found, had been known to use their connections to make sure anyone who stepped in their way would fall prey to the shadowy nature of the agency.

There was a soft knock on the interrogation room door. "Yep," she said, awkwardly.

It didn't feel right to say anything at all, given the situation. But remaining silent also seemed equally odd. Speaking of remaining silent, she'd need to call in a lawyer.

"Good morning, Agent Parker," a female agent whom Sabrina didn't recognize said as she stepped into the room.

The woman had a pixie haircut that did nothing for the wrinkles that creased her forehead and were scattered around her eyes. Even her lips carried deep creases, like she spent one too many years smoking. As the woman walked into the interrogation room, Mike followed behind her, looking like a pit bull. He was out for blood, her blood, and seeing him made her skin prickle.

She wanted to go toe to toe with him and call him

every obscenity that was rolling through her mind, but it would do no good. She couldn't deal with the situation proactively by being angry. All she could do was play his game—a game of logic and manipulation. Hopefully, she hadn't entered the game too late.

Actually, there was no time left for hope. She was already under arrest for crimes she hadn't committed. She'd already lost.

"I want my lawyer." The words tasted like the ocean, salty and smattered with the remnants of tempests.

"I bet you do," Mike said.

The woman gave him a look to shut up—it was the same look Sabrina had given him entirely too often when they were dating.

"Agent Parker, my name is Rowena Anderson. I'm the special agent in charge from your sister agency, the Madison County resident office," the woman said, an air of authority in her tone.

"Pleasure," Sabrina said, unsure whether or not she should play nice or say nothing. It didn't seem as though it would be in her best interest to be an ass.

"Yes," the woman said. "I hope you slept well. I'm sorry it took me so long to get here."

She hadn't slept a wink. Instead she had spent the entire night staring up at the ceiling of her cell and thinking about all the ways her life had gone wrong. For both their sakes, she said nothing.

Agent Anderson pointed toward the chair beside the table and motioned for her to sit down.

She did as instructed, but she couldn't take her eyes off Mike's smug face. Looking at him, and the way he seemed to have no remorse for what he had done to her, she couldn't understand what she had ever seen in him. He was nothing but a weasel.

"Agent Parker, it is with my deepest regrets that we have to meet under such circumstances. However, I'm sure that you understand, thanks to your many years of dedicated service for the FBI, that we all must do our duty. Today, my duty is to talk to you about your role in the two deaths that occurred while you were representing the Bureau undercover." The woman walked over to the coffeepot and poured herself a cup. "Would you like some?"

The woman was stalling—it was a common interrogation technique. It was the same reason they had kept her locked up in this room for four hours before anyone had even acknowledged her presence. They wanted to make her nervous, to drive up her anxiety level to the point where she'd be easier to manipulate.

By the same token, Agent Anderson had to know that Sabrina was fully aware of her tactics.

The woman took a long sip of her coffee, staring at her through the steam—she was trying to get a read on her. No doubt, she wanted to feel her out in order to determine how she would play this interrogation.

"Sabrina, it's in your best interest to just admit you killed those two Cussler guys. We found your fingerprints all over the murder weapon." Mike smirked.

Oh, that bastard.

It was a good thing she had sat down. Her hands fell limp into her lap as the shock worked its way through her body.

Her fingerprints had been found on the murder weapon?

It was impossible.

She'd never even fired her gun—only the one that Trevor had given her on the mountain, a gun she had returned to him. Her own firearm she'd given to Trevor, so Mike couldn't have sent it off to the lab for analysis. This didn't make sense.

She wanted to cry out and to tell Agent Anderson that she had no idea what he was talking about. But she knew that they must have had concrete evidence well in advance of her arrest. Which meant they had a different gun…a gun she had likely never actually touched.

At the shanty, she had watched Trevor pick up the gun that had killed the first brother. He'd wiped it down and left it there. She'd never touched it—or even gone back inside the shack. But that didn't mean someone hadn't tampered with the evidence. If the FBI, or Mike, had gone to that shanty they easily could have planted her prints on that gun. Or maybe there was an entirely different gun. She just couldn't be sure.

If only they had just called in Wyatt and the sheriff's department when they found the body. Wyatt was probably going to have a fit when he learned where she was. If he admitted to his role in her supposed cover-up of the second Cussler brother's death, his future would be in jeopardy. Everything she had done, every choice she had made, had been wrong.

"Nothing to say for yourself?" Mike said, taunting her.

"Agent Couer, I told you that if you wished to stand in on this interrogation, you were to remain silent," the woman said. "As you seem incapable of such a daunting task, and given your familiarity with Agent

Parker, I think it best that you leave." She pointed toward the door.

Mike opened his mouth to argue, but quickly shut up. It was the smartest thing she'd ever seen him do.

If only she could tell the woman the truth. And yet this woman had no reason to believe anything she said. It was normal for the accused to immediately start blaming others. A perpetrator rarely admitted fault. And even if they did passively admit to some wrongdoing, there would always be some extenuating circumstance that explained their misdeed away. She couldn't be like one of those people. But she also couldn't sit here and be accused and do nothing.

Mike stepped out of the room, but not before giving her one last sidelong glance and an accompanying smirk. The door clicked shut behind him.

"Now, Agent Parker, back to our conversation," the woman said.

"I didn't kill anyone. I'm innocent." She put her hands on the table, palms up, the universal sign of submission and forthrightness.

The woman looked down at Sabrina's hands and then in the direction of the closed door. "I have reviewed the entire case, and the evidence they have against you. As of this moment, the evidence is not in your favor. However, I'm finding holes in Agent Couer's assessment of the situation."

Sabrina wasn't entirely sure what the woman meant, so she remained silent.

"There's not a lot of information I can give you at this time. However, if you help me in my investigation, it will not go unnoticed."

She implied she would get Sabrina a deal without directly offering anything. When interrogating, Sabrina used the same method to elicit trust from her suspects.

She couldn't get sucked into this woman's charade.

"And what is it that you would like me to do?" Sabrina asked, curious.

Agent Anderson looked back at the door, almost as though she expected it to open again at any second. If anything, it appeared as if she were more nervous than Sabrina was. "About the meeting in Seattle. We want you there. Along with Agent Couer."

"What? Why?" Did they want to publicly broadcast her shame for the rest of the Bureau? No. She wasn't going to be their whipping boy.

"I know you're gun-shy after what happened. But believe me when I say it's in your best interest to help me out." The woman reached over and gave Sabrina's hand a reassuring squeeze.

The simple action surprised her. The interrogation room was currently being filmed. Was the woman trying to tell her something that she couldn't say on camera? Or was she stringing her along?

"Trevor said he worked for the CIA. You don't think he's really involved with the illegal gun trade, do you?"

"Oh, he and his family are very involved," Agent Anderson said. "We believe he may be using it to increase his income. It's fairly common for those behind the curtain to participate in unsanctioned deals like this."

Sabrina couldn't help but feel even more deflated. The man she had fallen in love with couldn't be a criminal. He wasn't the man the Bureau made him out to be.

If they went to Seattle, she risked being made an even

a bigger fool in the Bureau, and yet she would get to see Trevor at least one more time. And she could prove that she had been right about distrusting him.

For all she knew, he wouldn't even be there and instead it would be a team of his people. It would be smart of him to call off the entire deal now that he knew that he and his family were under investigation by the Bureau.

A part of her also wanted to save him. If she went there, she could try to alert him to the danger.

She was already damned by the Bureau's standards, and probably out of a job now that she was under arrest. Even though she was innocent, she would be lucky if she didn't go to prison.

A chill ran down her spine as she thought about being stuck in a federal prison with inmates she had sent there. The situation wouldn't end well—but from the beginning of her investigation, the only thing that had gone well was the night she spent in the mountains with Trevor making love.

If only she could go back in time…to a time and place where things weren't so complicated.

Chapter Sixteen

The gun sat heavy in Trevor's hands. Though the assault rifle weighed only a few pounds, it felt as though it was imbued with the weight of everyone who depended on him.

Zoey was sitting in the corner office, out of sight from where their operation would take place. Even if he couldn't get out, perhaps she would.

Though they had planned everything to the last detail, it didn't mean that it would go off without a hitch. Things had a way of going haywire any time guns were involved. He would be lucky if he made it out alive.

Chad was sitting above him in the skywalk, and as Trevor looked up, his brother gave him a thumbs-up. In a matter of seconds, and with a rearrangement of fabric, Chad disappeared into the darkness, perfectly camouflaged. For all intents and purposes, Trevor appeared to be alone.

In the quiet of the industrial warehouse, the buzz of the fluorescent lights sounded like a swarm of bees just waiting to descend.

Between the FBI and a swarm of bees, under normal circumstances, he would take bees.

He hated that this was where they were now—playing a game of corrupt politics and misguided leadership.

Though it appeared he was standing alone in the center of the industrial building, he could feel people watching him. No doubt, by now they likely had agents set up around the building monitoring him with some hidden tech. They likely had microphones and video cameras installed in the building as soon as they heard of their plan—if they were smart, they had every inch of this place streaming live at some central command center.

His phone pinged. It was time. Everything was in place.

The metal industrial garage door clicked as someone slid it open. In front of him was Gus, the man they had hired to help flush out Mike. Gus had been working for them over the last decade, always available at a moment's notice. They paid him well, but this time he wasn't sure if they were paying the man enough to deal with what was about to happen.

This time, Gus had brought three men and a woman with him. Gus was wearing a tailored linen suit, and his gray hair was slicked back with pomade. He reminded Trevor of a Miami drug lord. The men and women standing guard around Gus all wore black, and each had a pair of Ray-Ban sunglasses perched on their head—and they looked terribly out of place in Seattle's underbelly.

He gave the man a stiff nod. "Did Ahmal send you?"

"Does Ahmal send just anyone?" Gus said, looking at him like he was a stranger he didn't trust.

He played his role well.

"You have what I asked for?" Gus asked, motioning toward the big rig that was parked by the far wall of the warehouse.

"You have our money?" Trevor asked, lowering the assault rifle in his hand and leaning on it as if it were nothing more than a walking stick.

Gus looked toward the gun at Trevor's side. "Is that one of our M16s?"

Trevor took a step forward, moving to hand the man the gun. The woman stepped between them, as though she was really there to guard the man his family had planted.

Perfect.

"Have your woman stand down," he said, glaring at her.

"Marie," Gus said, sounding tired.

The woman stepped back, but her hand had moved to the gun strapped to her side.

Hopefully, Gus had told her that this mission was nothing more than a farce. He didn't want to have to worry about drawing any unnecessary friendly fire—he had enough to worry about when it came to the FBI and what they did or didn't know. One wrong move, one misplaced statement, and all hell could rain down.

He handed Gus the gun, keeping one eye on the woman to make sure she didn't make a mistake. Gus was smart, but just like them, he probably wanted to make this seem as real as possible—which may have meant that he had left his team in the dark.

"There are a thousand more of these inside that truck." He motioned behind him. "Did you wire us the money?"

"I only work in cash. I find it comforting," Gus said, motioning for one of his guards.

As the guard stepped forward, Trevor noticed the black briefcase in his hand. The briefcase was leather and adorned with brass, perfectly antiquated. It was almost comical, and far from the kind of thing most people would've expected, but Trevor had seen a lot of eccentricity in his travels.

In fact, one of the warlords they had been investigating in Africa brought a capuchin monkey to all their arms deals. In the end, STEALTH had planted a recording device in the monkey's collar. Because of a pet monkey, a dangerous man had been brought to justice and found guilty of war crimes.

"Half a million?" Trevor asked, reaching in his pocket and taking out the keys to the truck.

"In unmarked bills," Gus said. "Show us the guns."

Trevor walked toward the truck. Each step felt like it was in slow motion, as though he were walking toward his execution.

If this was how he went down… No, he couldn't give it any thought.

Trish, and the last look on her face—the look of terror, pain and the realization that death was upon her—came to the front of his mind and a wave of nausea threatened to take him to his knees. Somehow he kept walking.

The end of the truck was open, exposing the crates. Stepping up, Gus followed him and he reached inside the open crate nearest them. The guns had been chipped, even though this wasn't that kind of deal. Everything reminded him of the last time. He'd promised himself he would never be in this kind of situation again, and as he moved toward the crate his body stopped. It was as though he was glued to the floor of the truck, and no matter how badly he wanted to step forward and look inside that crate, his body wouldn't allow it.

"You like?" Trevor asked, trying to ignore the way his body defied him.

"They are all identical?" Gus asked.

Trevor nodded. They stepped out of the truck and Gus's men closed the back end.

The guard handed Gus the briefcase.

"Do we have a deal?" Trevor asked.

Gus handed him the briefcase and Trevor handed him the keys to the big rig. Every door in the warehouse flew open. There was the percussion of a flash bang, and Trevor hit the ground.

"Get down on the ground!" a man ordered. "Hands above your head!"

The FBI agents rushed into the building, running through the smoke of the blast. Trevor watched as Mike ran toward him, his gun raised. Sabrina was nowhere in sight.

Was she in danger? He had been assured by his people at the CIA that they had spoken to the folks at the Bureau and cleared everything up. But had there been more mistakes? Had the FBI screwed up again? Or had he been set up?

Mike glanced around, making sure that he was covered by the smoke and no one was close as he stopped beside Trevor. "Stand up, jackass," he ordered.

Trevor moved to his feet as he reached for his gun.

"Oh, please do... I've been looking forward to killing you." Mike's finger tightened on the trigger of the gun that was pointed straight at Trevor's chest.

"Mike, stop! Don't shoot!" he yelled, hoping that he could alert the FBI agents around him before this thing went all kinds of sideways and they ended up in a total firefight.

A shot rang out, rising above the melee of sounds around them of men and women shouting. Everything stopped.

Instinctively, Trevor pulled his gun as he did a mental check of his body. Nothing hurt, but adrenaline had a funny way of masking pain and he couldn't risk looking down to check himself for bullet holes.

Sabrina and another female agent stepped through the smoke behind Mike, each with their weapon raised. Trevor dropped his weapon and lifted his hands. Mike lowered his arms and there was a look of shock on his face.

"What in the hell?" Mike said, turning toward the women.

Blood seeped from his back, glossy and wet against the black fabric of his suit jacket.

"Get on the ground!" the other agent with Sabrina ordered.

"But—" Mike started.

"I said, get on the ground!" the woman repeated.

Instead of following orders, Mike raised the gun, pointing it straight at Sabrina. As he moved, Trevor lunged toward the man. He couldn't hurt her. Not Sabrina. Not this time.

There was the crunching sound of bones breaking as Mike's body hit the ground beneath him.

Grabbing the gun in Mike's hand, he flipped it out of his grip and threw it to the side.

He pulled the man's arms behind his bleeding back. "Mike Couer, you are under arrest for the murder of Owen and Earl Cussler, tampering with evidence, corruption, and impeding a federal investigation. Anything you say can and will be used against you in a court of law."

The agent beside Sabrina stepped beside them and Mirandized him.

Watching Sabrina stand over Mike with her gun drawn was a thing of beauty. This time, evil didn't win.

Chapter Seventeen

The private jet was full of Trevor's family, friends and a few of the agents from the case; yet as Sabrina sat there beside Trevor, it was as if they were all alone. This wasn't how she had expected things to go. Nothing could have prepared her for the things that Rowena had told her on their way to Seattle. She had described her plan to take down of one of the most corrupt officials in the Pacific Northwest, and explained how Sabrina could help.

Mike had been transported to Seattle's Harborview Medical Center and would remain under surveillance until he was completely out of the woods from his gunshot wound. Admittedly, it had felt good to shoot the man who had threatened to take Trevor down.

She reached over and took Trevor's hand.

He looked at her. "You okay?"

Though it had only been a day, it felt as though months had passed, thanks to all the statements she'd been required to give and all the legal paperwork that needed to be completed. Rowena had been diligent in making sure that everything was filed and completed in a way that would leave Sabrina free and clear and able to jump right back into her position at the FBI when she was ready.

For the time being, she wasn't sure what she wanted to do. She definitely needed a break from things to assess her future.

"Babe? Do you need anything?" Trevor asked, pulling her from her thoughts.

"Oh no, I'm okay." Her voice sounded tired. She wasn't sure he was ready to give her what she needed now.

"It's going to be okay," he said, giving her a kiss on the forehead.

Undoubtedly, the Martins would want to leave Montana now that their quiet retirement had been upended... a situation that she herself had a role in creating. If only she had seen Mike for the man he had truly been when they were together.

As it turned out, their relationship had not only been terrible, it had been a sham from the very beginning. Mike had been using her to learn about his enemies all while sending her into this and other investigations half-cocked with spotty information—in the end, no doubt hoping to humiliate her. If only she'd realized what he was doing, smearing her name and thereby delegitimizing anything she might say about him or his dealings. She felt so used...and so angry.

But Mike would pay for his full-blown assault on her character. And she would happily take the stand should she need to.

Trevor's phone buzzed. Opening up his email, he smiled.

"What is it?" she asked.

"Ballistics came in on your gun and Mike's." He moved the screen so she could see the message. "The slug they pulled from Earl was fired from Mike's gun… not the one they found at the shack, or yours."

Rowena leaned forward from the seat behind them and tapped her on the shoulder. "It looks like we just got a little more good news."

"What do you mean?" Trevor asked.

"In addition to your ballistics, the Evidence Response Team found the hunting cabin Sabrina told me you had been looking for." Rowena showed her a photo on her phone of a graying log cabin almost completely shrouded within a thicket of barberry. "About five hundred yards from the cabin, the ERT located a shallow mass grave. It appears to contain the remains of three men—one older, who we believe may have been the father—and two women. Right now, we can't confirm or deny their identities, but it appears that they are the rest of the Cusslers. My team is looking for the other family that was reportedly in the area, but so far they haven't found anything to indicate their whereabouts."

"Do you know what happened to the Cusslers? How they died?" Sabrina asked.

"It looks like it was execution style—but one had taken a shot to the kidney shortly before the time of death. They are guessing the guy was shot in the back—probably running. There was some level of healing, which means he may have been held for a day or two before he was executed." Rowena's lips puckered.

"How long had they been dead?" Sabrina asked, thinking back to the blood she had first found behind the shanty.

"They'd been down for a few days to a week at least."

"They are going to pull DNA and confirm identities as well as run any lead they recover through ballistics," Rowena continued. "I'd bet dollars to doughnuts that they were fired from Agent Couer's gun."

"How is the man I shot… Agent Heath?" Sabrina asked.

"It looks like he took a hit up there on that mountain, as Mike said. And while Agent Heath may have been acting on Agent Couer's orders, he also may have had a role in setting you up. We believe it was their plan to pick a time and place when there were no other witnesses—but then things went haywire."

"We got lucky."

"Not entirely. We have reason to believe he retrieved the gun from the Cussler shack and planted it in your things at your house at the Martins'. Needless to say, whether or not you were the one who pulled the trigger, it was a job well done." Rowena winked at her. "He is going to be thoroughly questioned, but I have a feeling he, too, will be spending quite a while in prison."

Sabrina smiled. She'd had a soft spot for Agent Heath, but if he had anything to do with trying to take her down, she'd be fine never hearing the man's name again. "Rowena, thanks for everything. I would have gone down for this if you hadn't started digging. I appreciate it."

The woman gave a humble nod. "It's my job. And if someone tried to do this kind of thing to me, I would expect my fellow agents to see it to the end as well. Besides, we women of the Bureau have to stick together."

She wasn't kidding.

Rowena started to sit back in her seat but stopped. "Oh, and hey, I got word that there is going to be an open seat at the Missoula office…you wouldn't be interested in being the special agent in charge, would you?" Rowena said, cracking an elusive smile.

Trevor looked over at her and gave her a proud, approving grin.

What she really wanted to do was stay with him. On the other hand, her job was her life. Though her office would only be a short drive away, long hours and the stress that came with her job would inevitably drive a wedge between them. She was cut from the FBI cloth, and no matter what happened in her life, she didn't want to lose who she was.

"I'd love to take the job…you know, *if* it were to come my way," she said.

Rowena winked and sat back, taking her phone out and clicking on email. "I'll see what I can do for you."

Sabrina turned to Trevor.

"Way to go," Trevor said, but some of the light in his eyes had seemed to fade as he too must have realized what her job would do to their relationship.

"Thank you," she said, lowering her head so she could whisper to him alone. "But the truth is… I don't know if it's going to work."

"Why not?" He frowned.

She had always been told that a woman should never say *I love you* first, but she'd never been very good at being told what to do.

"Trevor, here's the deal… I love you. I know that what we had…it was probably just a forced proximity thing that was kind of convenient, but—"

"Our relationship was not *convenient*," he said, interrupting her. "I'm not the kind of guy who takes a woman to bed just for the hell of it."

"Oh yeah?" she asked, giving him a playful look. "Then you do it just for the jollies?"

He smirked. "No. I took you to bed because the second I saw you standing outside the shack that first day, I knew you were something—*someone*—special." He lifted their entwined hands and gave her fingers a soft kiss. "I loved you before we even met... I know it sounds crazy, but it was like we were made for each other...as if cosmic forces brought us together. I mean, think of the odds that were stacked against us ever even meeting, and then there we were at the same time and the same place, fighting the same side of a battle that we didn't even know we were fighting." His face flushed. "I sound ridiculous."

"No, you're cute when you're flustered," she said, happiness racing through her. "I didn't know you had it in you."

"Hey now," he said with a laugh. "If you're going to tease me, I don't have to keep going."

"No," she said, motioning for him to continue. "I like seeing you act the way I feel."

"Wait..." he started. "You didn't forget we had a bet riding on all this, did you? Turns out I was completely right about you being the target."

"Oh, yeah," she said, staring at him as they whisked through the clouds. The heat in her cheeks rose as she remembered the stakes. "Who do you think you are, Mr. Martin? Do you think you can really use a bet to get me back into bed?"

"First, I'm the man who is going to love you for the rest of our lives. And second, I would never make you do anything you didn't want to do."

"Well, we did strike a deal," she teased, giving him an impish look.

"That's what I like to hear. I can't wait to get home," he said, laughing. "By the way, what was the favor you were going to ask for if you won?"

When they made the bet, she hadn't had a clue. Everything between them had been so distorted that she hadn't even really believed that they would get to the bottom of their investigation in time for her to save her job, let alone see who won the bet. Yet here and now, she knew exactly what she should have wished for.

"Are you sure you want to hear it?"

Trevor nodded.

"If I'd won, I'd have asked you to marry me." She gazed into his eyes, half expecting him to choke and shirk away, but instead he leaned in closer so their foreheads touched. "You're right, it's like we are meant to be together. When I look at you, I see a father to my children, a husband, a friend. When we are close all I want to do is move even closer. And when I was arrested, all I wanted was to know that you were safe and taken care of." She paused. "I know my asking you isn't conventional, but I can't stand the thought of losing you. Will you?"

"Baby, nothing about us has been conventional. I'd hate for us to start now." He smiled a smile larger than any she had seen. "I'd marry you right now if we could. So, yes. Absolutely." He reached up and took her chin between his thumb and forefinger. "I love you, Sabrina Parker. And I always will."

"And I you, Trevor Martin."

He leaned in to kiss her, but she stopped him. "And one more thing," she said with a grin.

"What?" he asked, his eyes heavy with lust.

"I'm keeping Cap'n Crunch around in case this thing goes south."

"Anything for you."

She giggled as their lips met. He tasted of promises, the savories of a life filled with adventure, and the sweetness of forever.

* * * * *

COLTON 911:
FAMILY UNDER FIRE

JANE GODMAN

As I was writing this story, I was undergoing treatment for breast cancer. I'd like to thank everyone who supported me during that process, particularly my wonderful family, whose support has kept me going throughout some very difficult times.

Chapter One

Everett Colton had visited the offices of Torrington Law once before. Although he couldn't remember much about the brief meeting, he did recall the lingering odors of wet dog and fried chicken. Back then, Raymond Torrington, senior partner in the firm, had blamed both on the large, elderly bloodhound that had been sleeping in a basket behind the front desk.

Impatiently, Everett pushed open the glass front door. This was going to be a waste of his time, he didn't want to be here, he had more important things to do…and he didn't want to subject his nostrils to a repeat performance.

As he stepped inside, it became clear that at least one of those things wasn't going to be an issue. There was no sign of the dog, and the place smelled like a regular office.

He approached the reception desk, his mind on the letter he had received a few days earlier:

You are invited to attend a private reading of the last will and testament of Sean Dodd and Delilah Kennedy Dodd.

Although Sean Dodd had once been Everett's best friend, they had barely spoken in the last four years. That is, until recently, when Everett had helped his brother, Casey, arrest Sean, Delilah, and Sean's sister, Georgia, for murder and cattle rustling. Now Sean had driven his car off the road into a wall, killing himself and his wife.

Initially, a suicide note on the dash had led the Sur County Creek Sheriff's Department to the conclusion that the act had been deliberate. Everett wasn't so sure.

Not that the cause of death explained the current situation. *Sean would want me at the reading of his will because…?* He almost laughed. When had he ever been able to predict what Sean had wanted? He would find out soon enough.

"I have an appointment with Mr. Torrington."

As the receptionist checked her computer screen, Everett breathed in the improved aromas. Copier toner, coffee, some sort of holiday-season air freshener and violets.

"Mr. Torrington has been delayed for a few minutes. But if you would care to go through to his office, his other guest is already here."

"Other guest?" The invitation hadn't mentioned anyone else, and…wait. *Violets?* "Do you use Acqua Viola?"

The young woman regarded him nervously. "Can I get you some coffee?"

Everett rubbed a hand over his jaw. He'd thought he was over this. He *was* over this. It must be the stress of Sean's death. It had come on the heels of the operation his brother had undertaken, together with the woman he was now seeing, Melody Hayworth, to capture the rustlers and murderers. That, along with the speculation about what the will might hold, was triggering a return to the old fantasies. It was at least six months since the last time he'd imagined he could smell Alyssa Bartholomew's favorite perfume. Even longer since he'd experienced that stomach-churning mix of excitement and dread when he glimpsed a certain woman with long, corn-colored hair and momentarily wondered if she'd come back to him.

"Coffee would be good." He tried out a reassuring smile. From the way the receptionist scooted back in her wheeled chair, he wasn't sure it worked. If she had a panic button under that desk, he was about thirty seconds away from explaining to his bosses at the FBI field office in Phoenix why this woman had every reason to believe one of their best agents was acting weird.

"I'll bring it through." She gestured toward a half-open office door.

Everett remembered Ray Torrington from his teenage years. Anxious, pale and lanky, the other guy had always been out to impress the wrong crowd. Even though they'd been six years younger, Everett and his twin brother, Casey, had known to steer clear of the company Ray kept. Only a serious intervention on the part of Ray's dad had gotten him back on track and into law school. Which made the invitation—*summons*—currently residing in Everett's back pocket all the more irksome.

He pushed open the door with the heel of his hand,

his brain simultaneously registering two things—that subtle scent of violets was stronger here…and it was not his imagination.

The first Christmas he and Alyssa had been together, he'd scoured the department stores in Phoenix, only to come away empty-handed. How could he have known it was a rare Italian brand? On Christmas morning, when he'd given Alyssa the enamel violet on a silver chain, with an apology, she'd laughed and explained that Acqua Viola had been her grandmother's favorite perfume. Alyssa laughed a lot.

A woman was seated with her back to the door, her head bent over her cell phone, and the other thing he took in was the long blond hair, confined loosely at the nape of her neck. Tendrils were escaping the restraint and she pushed impatiently at them, the gesture achingly familiar to him. She didn't look around as he paused just inside the room.

How many times had he pictured seeing her again? Somehow, he'd always thought it would be in a bar, the scene an echo of their first meeting. Pizza and beer. That was more their style than this impersonal setting. The thought brought him back to reality with an uncomfortable bump. It was her.

"What are you doing here, Alyssa?"

She turned her head slowly, her dark blue eyes widening as she gazed at him.

"I don't know." Her hand reached up to clutch the enamel violet at her throat. "But maybe I should ask you the same question."

Her voice was calm as she spoke, but the cell phone slid from her fingers and clattered onto the floor.

ALYSSA'S MIND WAS SPINNING. Maybe she should have seen this coming? Cactus Creek was Everett Colton's hometown, after all.

But he had left this place as soon as he graduated from Cactus Creek High, enrolled at the University of Arizona and eventually settled in Phoenix. He'd told her he never missed the stifling, overfamiliar community atmosphere. She knew he rarely returned, only keeping in touch with his family and a few friends.

Of course, she'd thought of him when the invitation had arrived.

You are invited to attend a private reading of the last will and testament of Sean Dodd and Delilah Kennedy Dodd, she mused, recounting the words in her mind.

She'd only known the Dodds through their friend-ship with Everett, which had gone sour years before. She certainly hadn't enjoyed their company, finding Sean arrogant and Delilah demanding and superior. Now the couple had died in tragic circumstances, and Alyssa had no idea what, if anything, their will could mean to her.

Private. That had been the key word in that letter. *I thought it meant just me.*

All thoughts of Sean and Delilah were driven out of her head as Everett took the seat next to her. Breaking up with him had almost destroyed her, and she knew it had been equally hard on him. Under the pretense of checking her cell for damage, she risked a few sidelong glances in his direction. He was still the hottest man she'd ever seen.

With his crystal-blue eyes, tousled sandy hair and square chin, he gave off an air of brooding intensity. That was until he smiled—then he could light up a room. One of Alyssa's favorite hobbies during their time together had been making him smile.

Because his looks are the most important thing about this whole situation, right? But her reaction to him wasn't trivial. It summed up the power he still had over her. And the danger of being near him.

Although seeing him again had thrown her completely off balance, she experienced a moment of relief. After everything that had happened between them, she had never imagined Everett would speak to her again. Okay, so a curt demand to know what she was doing there was hardly friendly conversation, but at least he hadn't ignored her and walked out.

"So…" he began. Her phone was in danger of flying out of her grasp again as he turned her way, his light blue eyes catching hers. "How's the pool playing going? Did you turn professional yet?"

Alyssa made a sound midway between a gasp and a laugh. It was so like him to take her by surprise with humor when she was expecting anger, and he'd done it with a reference to their first meeting.

Her heart was in turmoil, but she figured if he could keep it light, she could, too. "No, but the Pocket Rockets have my number anytime they need a substitute."

He nodded. "I can see why Phoenix's premier women's pool team would have a recruitment drive among elementary-school teachers."

"If I remember rightly, this third-grade teacher has whipped your ass on more than one occasion—"

He checked his watch. "Less than two minutes."

The way they had slipped so easily back into a familiar, teasing rhythm was almost scary. She should stop it now. Distant and aloof, that would be the best approach… "Okay, Colton. I'll take this bait. What are you talking about?"

"Four years apart, and two minutes is all it took for your obsession with my ass to resurface." He grinned at her. It wasn't just any grin. It was *the* grin. The one that weakened her knees a little.

And that was it. All those times she'd told herself he couldn't flip her heart over with a look? Lies. Every last one.

"Sorry about the delay. That coffee machine is so slow," the receptionist said as she scooted quickly past Everett and placed a tray on the desk.

"My visitors don't need that sort of information, Brenda." The man who entered the room dabbed at his brow with a large handkerchief.

"I don't know. Sometimes it's good to know why you've been kept waiting." Alyssa regarded Everett in surprise. He was no diplomat, but he usually managed a basic level of politeness.

The other man's face reddened. "I apologize for my lateness. I was unavoidably delayed." He took a seat on the other side of the desk and gave Alyssa a tight-lipped smile. "I'm Raymond Torrington. Thank you for coming, Miss Bartholomew." The smile disappeared as he nodded in Everett's direction. "We've met before, Agent Colton."

"I'll get straight to the point." He opened a drawer in his desk, withdrew a folder and placed it in front of him. "Since their marriage, I've been Sean Dodd and Delilah Kennedy Dodd's lawyer. I am also executor of their will. Following their tragic deaths, it now falls to me to ensure that their estate is disposed of according to their wishes." He withdrew a single sheet of paper from the folder. "The will is very straightforward. There is one beneficiary who will inherit all property and investments."

"If that's the case, why are the two of us here?" Even if she hadn't known him as well as she knew herself, Everett's body language would have been easy to interpret—arms folded across his muscular chest, jaw clenched, one foot tapping out a restless beat.

"My clients wrote this will just over four years ago, not long after their marriage." Raymond scanned the sheet of paper as he spoke.

Four years. Alyssa looked at Everett, wondering if the significance of the time frame had registered with him.

Clearly it had. "That was around the time Georgia Dodd, Sean's younger sister, left my brother, Casey, at the altar." His voice was tight with remembered anger. "Sean masterminded the incident because he thought that a deputy sheriff wasn't good enough for his kid sister. Or possibly he didn't want a law-enforcement officer in the family taking a closer look at what he was getting up to. The reason doesn't matter. It was the end of our friendship."

He flicked a look Alyssa's way to let her know he hadn't forgotten the rest. Soon after that incident, but for unrelated reasons, they had broken up.

"I'm assuming that Georgia, whom I recently had the pleasure of arresting at gunpoint, is the beneficiary." Alyssa jumped slightly at Everett's words. It wasn't just the fact that he'd been involved in apprehending Georgia. They were a stark reminder of the dangers he faced every day.

"Although Georgia was released on bail, she broke the terms of her bail by attempting to leave town. She's now back behind bars but that won't affect her inheritance. So can we cut to the part where you tell us what our role is? Did Sean name us as trustees four years ago and forget to change it?"

"Georgia Dodd is not named in her brother's will. The circumstances are…unusual. There is a section in the document that involves the two of you. Twelve months ago, Sean and Delilah came to see me to check it was still legal." Raymond dabbed at his upper lip with his handkerchief. "This will be easier to explain if I invite my other guests to join us." He pressed a button on his desktop phone.

"Other guests?" Alyssa looked around as the door opened and a middle-aged woman entered the room. She leaned to one side under the weight of a large bag shaped like a pink elephant; in her other arm, she carried a sleeping baby.

"This is Patty Griffiths of the Arizona Department

of Child Safety." Raymond indicated the child. "Kennedy is Sean and Delilah's six-month-old daughter, and she has been left in your joint custody."

EVERETT'S BRAIN WAS spinning like a top. As he was trying to get his thoughts under control, the baby woke up and started to cry.

Alyssa was out of her seat in a heartbeat. Children had always drawn her in like a magnet. "Hey, honey. What's wrong? Are you hungry?"

Patty Griffiths handed Kennedy over to her with a look of relief. "She probably is. When she came to us, she'd recently started on solid food, but she still has at least one bottle of formula a day."

"Have you been caring for her?" Everett watched as Kennedy hitched in a sob and gazed up at Alyssa through tear-filled eyes. He'd had no time to come to terms with the bombshell Ray had delivered, yet he was getting the impression that events were already spiraling out of his control.

"She's been staying in one of our facilities since her parents died." Patty reached into the bag and withdrew a baby bottle in an insulated carrier. When she handed it to Alyssa, Kennedy made a cooing noise and reached out chubby hands for it. "There are some basics here in this bag, and her car seat is in the front office. Once I have your address, I can arrange to have her other belongings delivered within a few hours."

"Wait." The spell that had been holding him silent snapped and Everett finally found his voice. "We're not together, and neither of us even lives here in town.

This is all moving way too fast. We can't be expected to put our lives on hold and go along with a plan we knew nothing about."

He was conscious of Alyssa watching him as she resumed her seat, Kennedy tucked into the crook of her arm. The baby grasped the bottle, making contented noises as she suckled greedily.

"If you could leave us alone while we continue this discussion?" Ray waved a hand in the direction of the door and Patty went out. He tapped a pen on the top of his desk and shuffled his papers before continuing. "This is exactly what I said would happen when Sean and Delilah came to me with this plan. They had named you as guardians while you were still friends and had never gotten around to making the necessary changes. When Delilah found out she was pregnant, they wanted to know if they could leave things as they were. I told them that, if they left the custody details in the will without consulting you, there was every chance you would just walk away without agreeing to it."

"If it was against your advice, why did they go ahead with it?" Everett asked.

"Sean's reasoning was that although you had drifted apart, he couldn't imagine anyone who would be better parents to his daughter."

"The guy always was a piece of work." Everett shook his head, his emotions ranging between exasperation and a reluctant, lingering fondness for the man who had once been a good friend. "But we *can* say no to this, right?"

"Let's be clear." It was Alyssa's don't-mess-with-me

voice. The one she used with her students. "We aren't saying no. We're not saying anything. Not yet. We're gathering information. You said Kennedy had been left in our joint custody. If one of us is unwilling to be involved, can the other take sole responsibility for her?"

Raymond shook his head. "The will clearly states that she is to be cared for by both of you."

Alyssa's indrawn breath touched a point at the center of Everett's heart. "What will happen to Kennedy if we don't do this?"

"If you choose not to accept custody, Kennedy will be placed back into the care of the Department of Child Safety, where she will enter the foster system," Raymond said.

Everett knew what those words would do to Alyssa. When he turned his head to look at her, he could see her own past in the depths of her eyes. There was also a plea for help there. And it was aimed at him.

She was an only child, traumatized when and her father was killed by a drunk in a random knife attack when she was ten. After that, her mom had wasted away, and her death, when Alyssa was eighteen, brought an end to years of misery. The scars of growing up without any real parental presence in her life ran deep. He knew there was no way she would walk away from this child who, like her, was the innocent victim of abandonment.

But was she seriously asking him to do this? Did she believe that, after everything that had happened between them, they would somehow put the past behind them and together raise a child? And did he have to make a decision right *now*?

Four years ago, he'd have done anything for this woman. She knew that because he'd told her. But it hadn't been enough. Alyssa had needed assurances he couldn't give. At the same time, Everett had his own reasons for shying away from responsibility. It was hardly a match made in heaven.

Nothing in either of their lives had changed since, apparently. Being close to her again would mean handing her his well-being, his dreams and his life in a way that meant she could break his heart all over again. It had hurt enough the first time. Was he willing to go through all that pain again? And this time they would be adding a baby into the mix.

"We'll do it." It was only when Alyssa's eyes widened that he knew for sure he had said the words out loud.

ALYSSA GAZED DOWN at the baby in her arms. She had just become a mom. Most people, even those who hadn't planned it, had nine months to prepare for this moment. She'd barely had nine minutes. Her life had changed forever, and she was totally unprepared for how to deal with it.

The only thing she knew for sure was that Kennedy needed her and she wouldn't let the little girl down. Oh, and she would be doing this with *Everett*. The man who was now striding across the parking lot ahead of her with a pink-elephant bag slung over one broad shoulder and a car seat in his other hand.

"Wait," she called out. "Where are we going?"

"My car is over here." He jerked a thumb, indicating the dark-colored sedan parked nearby.

"And mine is in the opposite direction." Her footsteps faltered. "But that's not what I meant."

He retraced his steps, halting at her side. "I've been working on a case here in Cactus Creek and I'm staying in a rented apartment on Main Street. I'll drive us there and we can talk some more. I'll get someone to pick up your vehicle later."

The suggestion made sense. Although the sun was shining, a few clouds scuttled across the sky and the December air was cool. Kennedy wore only a lightweight sweater, leggings and socks, and the breeze ruffled her fluffy blond curls. Although she clung tightly to the front of Alyssa's blouse, she showed no signs of distress at being with two strangers.

"Let's do that, sweetie, head back to Everett's place, where we can be cozy." She bounced the little girl on her hip while they waited for Everett to fit the car seat.

"I may have misled you if you got the impression the apartment I rented is cozy. Think bland and basic." Once the seat was in place, he held out his hands for Kennedy. "And small."

"It will be cozy for her once her own stuff is delivered," Alyssa said.

"I guess so… What is this all about?" He stared in exasperation at Kennedy, who, having allowed him to place her in the seat, was now waving her arms wildly each time he tried to fasten the straps. "It's like trying to restrain an octopus."

"Do you want me to try?"

"No. I mean how hard can it be?" Each time he tried, the baby twisted in his grasp, laughing as she thwarted his attempts.

Alyssa leaned closer into the vehicle, watching over his shoulder. "Maybe it was a game she played with her mom and dad?"

Everett turned his head to look at her and she saw the pain in his eyes. She knew how Sean had hurt him when he encouraged Georgia to ditch Casey at the altar, but surely his fondness for his one-time friend hadn't completely gone away.

"Where was Kennedy the night her parents died?"

"She was staying at Georgia's place." A shadow crossed his features as he said Sean's sister's name.

"Oh." Alyssa took a moment to consider that information. "Sean and Delilah didn't want Georgia to have custody of their daughter, but they were happy for her to care for her overnight? That seems strange."

"Most things about this case are strange." Everett took a step back. "Your turn to see what you can do with squirmy baby."

"Kennedy, there's only one way to do this…" Using one hand to tickle the little girl's belly, she deftly hooked the restraints together and closed the clasp. As she did, Kennedy dissolved into helpless giggles.

"How did you know that would work?" Everett shook his head in disbelief.

"I interned in a day-care center before I got my teaching degree, remember? Delilah knew that, so I guess it could have influenced her decision about the will." Backing out of the car, she closed the door. "But just because I know about babies, it doesn't mean I get all the diapers."

"Diapers." He gave her a look of horror. "We can negotiate on that, right?"

The drive to Main Street took less than fifteen minutes. Alyssa spent most of it alternating between looking over her shoulder to check on Kennedy and studying Everett's hometown. Cactus Creek was gearing up for the holidays. All along their route, the stores were lit up with stars and bells; palm trees were decorated with red, green and gold lights. When they swung right onto Main Street, she saw the saguaro cactus plants flanking the entrance to Hoyles' Department Store had been turned into candy canes. A wide pedestrian area ran down the center of the street, from which Santa waved from the carriage of a rickety wooden train.

Everett pulled up in the parking lot of a modern block. The apartment building looked like it had been added as an afterthought at the end of a traditional row that included Pizza Paradise and the Sports Bar.

"I see you didn't stray too far from the essentials."

Pretending to be hurt, he placed a hand over his heart. "You know I can't cook. Am I supposed to starve while I'm in town?"

"Let's get this baby inside." She shook her head. "That's a sentence I didn't picture myself saying when I left home this morning."

Located on the second floor, Everett's apartment was reached by a set of stairs that led directly from the parking lot. It was one of four apartments with front doors leading off a single walkway. His was closest to the outside staircase.

Although he hadn't left her with high hopes about his rental, once Alyssa was inside, she was relieved to see that it was clean, and the furniture appeared comfortable. He was right about one thing, though. It was *small*.

From the front door, she could see a square lounge area with two small sofas and a TV, a round dining table with four chairs and a narrow kitchen that looked just about large enough for one person.

A sudden thought occurred to her. "How many bedrooms are there?"

"Two." The slight curve of his lips told her he was reading her mind. "Although one of them is more like a closet."

She thought of her comfortable apartment in Phoenix. The one she'd spent so long decorating and furnishing with carefully chosen pieces. The one from which she would need to get her clothes and other essential belongings. Then she smoothed down the sparse curls of the little girl who had no one else to care for her.

"I guess we should talk about how we're going to make this work."

Chapter Two

Everett didn't know whether to be relieved or disappointed when, before he and Alyssa could sit down to talk, they were disturbed by the security buzzer.

"The Department of Child Safety sure moves fast around here." He headed toward the front door while Alyssa took Kennedy to explore the bedrooms. "Although, when you think about it, that's a good thing. We don't even have a crib or a high chair."

Although the apartment had a speaker system, it was low-tech and didn't have the luxury of cameras. Everett could talk to the person at the front door, but he couldn't see them.

"Delivery for Miss K. Dodd."

It seemed like an unnecessarily formal way of confirming the arrival of Kennedy's belongings.

"Do you need help to carry anything up the stairs?"

"Uh. I'm good."

Shrugging, he held open the door. A few moments later, a guy in uniform with a badge that had a sprig of holly above his name tag appeared. Accustomed to checking people out, Everett registered the name first.

Joe Meyer.

Then he noticed that Joe was carrying a large, gift-wrapped box topped with a giant bow.

"That's it?" Everett peered around him. "I was expecting more."

"I just get a list of jobs each day, then I go where they send me. This time it was to pick this up from Hoyles' toy department and bring it here."

Everett had always considered himself to be reasonably intelligent. His excellent grades throughout school and college meant others had shared that opinion. Prior to joining the FBI, he'd even been headhunted into a high-flying career in corporate law. He had certainly never thought of himself as slow-witted. Even so, he was having trouble processing what was going on.

"Hoyles'? Toy department?"

"Yeah. This time of year, they're one of our best customers." Joe held out a pad and pen. "If you'll just sign here…?"

"Not until I know what I'm signing for." Everett held out his hands for the brightly packaged box. There was a gift tag attached and he turned it over to read the message:

Happy holidays, sweet girl. I'm coming for you.

A cold, bony finger of fear jabbed at his spine. He'd recently returned to Cactus Creek and had been working on a murder investigation when he'd gotten news of the Dodds' deaths. The suicide story had never felt right to him. He knew Sean. The guy was an adventurer, always looking for the next opportunity. He'd seen his arrest as the next challenge. And he had genuinely loved Delilah. Even if he'd taken his own life, Everett couldn't picture him killing his wife. Add in the fact that the suicide note wasn't in either Sean's or Delilah's handwriting and things got even more suspicious.

This message heightened Everett's distrust. Even attached to a holiday package, it felt wrong, even threatening. Who was coming for Kennedy? And what was in that box? It could be anything. Explosives? Acid? Poison?

"You said you just got this from the store? Was it already wrapped when you collected it?"

"Hey, I just—"

Everett reached into his pocket and withdrew his badge. "I need you to wait here."

The authority in his voice was enough to secure obedience. As Everett stepped back inside the apartment and closed the door behind him, Joe Meyer and his suspicious delivery were pushed to the back of his mind. How was he supposed to explain *this* to Alyssa?

Four years ago, his job had been the reason she'd walked away from him. Now, within hours of being reunited, she would be forced to face the reality of what he did all over again. And this time they weren't even involved.

Except...we are. Not the way they had been in the past, but if being the new mom and dad to a six-month-old baby girl wasn't *involved*, he sure as hell didn't know what was.

For some reason, Sean had left Kennedy in their

care. Everett might not be able to understand his former friend's motive, and he might not know anything about being a dad, but he knew what was expected of him. He would protect his new family. No matter what.

Alyssa stepped out of the bedroom. "This little lady is sleepy. I think we should set her crib up first. Oh." She regarded him steadily, her gaze going to the closed front door and his empty hands. "Is something wrong?"

She had always been able to read him like a book. Which was why there was no point in trying to hide anything from her.

"You trust me, don't you?"

"You know I do." That, at least, had never been in question.

"I don't have time to explain right now, but I have to go out. I want you to stay inside with the door locked until I get back."

"But—" Although she didn't question what he was saying, her brow furrowed. Her hand moved to the back of the baby's head, cradling the little girl closer. "I really need to get Kennedy settled. If I can't open the door, how will I get to her stuff when it arrives?"

Resisting the urge to curse, Everett drew his cell phone out of the back pocket of his jeans and opened the address book. His brother's number was at the top of his favorites list. And, unless he was out on an emergency call, his twin could always be relied on to answer.

"Are you busy?"

"I have this thing called a job." From the background noise, it sounded like Casey was in his office at the

Sur County Sheriff's Department. "It takes up most of my time."

"How fast can you be at my apartment?"

Everett had no frame of reference. Maybe it was the same with all brothers. Possibly it was more intense for them because they were twins. All he knew for sure was that whenever he needed help, Casey was there for him.

"I'm on my way."

Everett breathed a sigh of relief. The sheriff's office was close by and it would take Casey less than ten minutes to get there. He ended the call, aware of Alyssa's steady scrutiny. She was the strongest person he knew, except for one blind spot. She was terrified that anyone close to her would be snatched away violently.

Given what had happened in her early life, he figured it was natural. Throughout their relationship, he'd tried hard to help her overcome her fears. In the end, her intense vulnerability, together with his own emotional detachment, had defeated them both.

"I *do* trust you, but if there's something going on…"

"I just need to check a few things out." He gave her what he hoped was a reassuring smile. "It's probably nothing."

She rolled her eyes. "Everett, I *know* you. Remember?"

"How could I forget?" The words were out before he could stop them, carrying a world of meaning in their wake.

Timing, Colton. It never was your thing.

For a moment they gazed at each other, then an unmistakable, and very stinky, aroma filled the air.

"Oh, my goodness." Alyssa wrinkled her nose. "Where did you put the pink-elephant bag with the spare diapers?"

Everett started to laugh. "It's on the table." He jerked a thumb over his shoulder in the direction of the door. "I need to go. Casey is on his way. I'll explain everything when I get back."

"Promise me—" Her lower lip trembled.

It was like stepping back in time four years.

"I'll be careful."

ALYSSA WAS LEFT with a dilemma. It seemed like explaining their startling new situation to Everett's twin should be something they did together. Answering the door to Casey with a sleepy baby in her arms meant he inevitably gave her a look that was both startled and questioning.

"This is Sean and Delilah Dodd's daughter, Kennedy. Following their deaths, Everett and I have accepted joint custody of her."

Casey's frown betrayed his shock, and he remained silent for a moment or two.

Although she knew and liked Everett's brother, they'd never had a chance to get really close. His deputy-sheriff job kept him in Cactus Creek and, during the time that she and Everett had been dating, their lives had been in Phoenix. The two had made an effort to meet up, and family occasions with their parents had been important to them, but their busy jobs had often gotten in the way.

Casey stepped into the apartment and Alyssa locked the door behind him.

He looked around in confusion. "Where is Everett?"

"I don't know."

"Oh, I get it." The twins were fraternal, but when they smiled, the similarities between them were remarkable. "This is like the time he bet me he could beat me in a race to a bar. We both set off, then this hot girl in denim shorts distracted me by asking for my help to find her dog. It was over a year later I found out she was one of his college classmates and they split the winnings. Is he hiding in the bedroom?"

"Seriously. He said he had to go out and that you would stay with me until he got back. You now know as much as I do."

The smile disappeared as he looked around. Before either of them could say anything else, the security buzzer made Alyssa jump. If she and Kennedy were to stay here, that thing would have to go.

"I'm expecting a delivery." She hesitated, not wishing to sound overdramatic. "But Everett told me to keep the door locked."

He went to the window and twitched back the drapes. "There's a flatbed truck parked outside. It's piled high with boxes."

Piled high? With a sinking feeling, Alyssa went to stand beside him. The truck was small, but there were *a lot* of boxes. And she recognized the woman who was exiting from the passenger side of the vehicle.

"That's Patty Griffiths. She's from the Department of Child Safety." She looked down at the baby, who had fallen asleep in her arms. "She promised to deliver Kennedy's things."

"I'll get the door," Casey said.

Sure enough, the guy at the door was one of Patty's colleagues. By way of a greeting, he handed Casey a high chair. "I could do with some help getting the rest of the stuff up the stairs."

Ten minutes later, the two men had made several trips from the van to the apartment. There were now several tall stacks of boxes in the small bedroom and the floor space in the living room was rapidly disappearing.

"We only brought the essentials," Patty explained to Alyssa. "The rest of it is at her parents' home."

"Rest of it? How much stuff can one small person have?"

"I've been doing this job a long time and I've never seen so many toys and clothes." Patty pursed her lips. "They must have spent a fortune on her." She handed Alyssa a framed picture. "I know you'll want to remind her of her birth parents. This was taken recently."

It showed Kennedy sitting on a rug. Sean was lying on one side and Delilah was on the other. They were smiling as, propped on their elbows, each moved in to kiss one of their daughter's chubby cheeks.

Alyssa stared at it for a moment or two. It was hard to believe such a happy family had been torn apart so tragically. Some might say the Dodds had brought what happened on themselves, but Kennedy was an innocent victim in all of this.

"I'll make sure to put it somewhere so she can see it all the time."

When Patty and her colleague had gone, Alyssa eased Kennedy onto the sofa and sat next to her.

"If you're really doing this, you may need to get a

bigger place." Casey looked down at the sleeping baby. "*Are* you doing this?"

"We just found out about the custody request in Sean and Delilah's will a few hours ago. We were about to talk about what it meant for the future when your brother took off. It's so sad. This little girl's parents must have loved her so much…" She shook her head. "Patty mentioned their home. I guess it's part of the estate Kennedy will inherit."

"Sean may have made his money on the wrong side of the law, but Delilah was a clever accountant. She invested it wisely and legally. The Dodds had a very neat property just outside of Cactus Creek. Kennedy will be a wealthy little girl."

"I didn't know them well, and I understand that they were in trouble with the law before they died, but Sean is the last person I could imagine taking his own life," Alyssa said. "And killing Delilah, as well? It seems totally out of character."

"He left a suicide note stating that he would rather die than face prison." Casey's grim expression reminded her of the hurt that Sean had caused him in the past.

Kennedy murmured in her sleep and Alyssa soothed her by gently rubbing her shoulders. Her responsibility to the child hit her all over again. "What a dreadful start for her. It will take a lot of hard work to make sure this doesn't permanently damage her."

"If anyone can give her a normal life, you and Everett are the ones to do it," Casey said. "I guess that's why Sean and Delilah chose you. They finally got something right."

Sean Dodd was a cattle rustler who had been impli-cated in a murder. Delilah was a skilled accountant who cooked the books to make it look like his investments were honest. They had chosen a life on the wrong side of the law, but could they have foreseen that they would die this way? It felt like a step too far for a couple who had always struck her as overconfident.

And they chose us. Not Everett or Alyssa, but the two of them. It was a bittersweet reminder of how good they'd once been together. So good that the Dodds had seen something in them that they wanted for their daughter if there came a time when they were no lon-ger around.

Her relationship with Everett might have ended, but the feelings it had been built on hadn't gone away. Their shared past was one of the things that would make this new role hard.

She wished she could say she didn't walk away from a challenge. But wasn't that what she'd done four years ago? She shook away the thought. Times had changed. And this wasn't about her and Everett.

It was about working together to make a future out of a tragedy.

THE EXPRESSION ON Joe Meyer's face as he accompanied Everett into Hoyles' toy department could hardly have been described as cheery. Dodging between sales as-sistants dressed as elves and forest animals, Everett marched determinedly to the cash desk at the far end of the store. "FBI? You don't seriously think this place is pushing drugs or selling guns, do you?"

Everett couldn't blame Joe Meyer for his sarcastic comment. Hoyles' was a Cactus Creek institution and stepping through the doors brought back memories of his own childhood holidays. Ignoring the fact that white Christmases were unusual in Sur County, the toy department was decked out like an icy winter wonderland. With lavishly decorated trees, gingerbread houses, traditional dollhouses and train sets, it was guaranteed to bring a smile to the face of every kid, as well as most adults.

"I need to speak to the manager." The young cashier started to protest but was silenced when Everett held up his badge. It didn't usually see this much daylight when he was on duty. "Now."

"Wait here." After giving him a nervous look, she headed toward a nearby office and knocked on the door. A few seconds later, a tall man emerged.

"I'm Paul Denmore, toy-department manager. What can I do for you?"

Because of his suspicions about the possible contents of the package, Everett had decided not to bring it into the busy store. Instead, he had left it in Joe's delivery van, which was parked on an empty parking lot a block away. He held up his cell phone, displaying a photograph he had taken of the brightly colored package.

"I need you to tell me everything you know about this."

Denmore looked from Everett to the picture, his startled gaze taking in Joe along the way. "It looks like one of our home-delivery gifts."

Don't water an angry seed. That had always been

one of Maribelle Colton's favorite phrases. Everett could almost hear his mom saying it now as he bit back an irritated response.

"I'm aware of the appearance of this item, Mr. Denmore. What I require from you is confirmation that it did originate in your store. Once I have that, I will be able to safely open the box and check its contents." Although, having checked it over carefully, he felt confident, based on its weight and size that it wasn't a bomb, he wasn't prepared to take any chances. "Finally, I'll need details of who placed the order." A doubtful look crossed the other man's face. "I can get a warrant. Even close the store, if that's what it takes…"

"No, no." Denmore held up his hands in a conciliatory gesture. "I'm happy to cooperate. Please come through to my office."

Everett entered the room in the manager's wake, with Joe trailing behind.

"If the package is one of ours, there will be a reference number on the gift label, under the recipient's address," Denmore said.

Everett swiped through his photographs until he found a close-up of the gift label. "Does this provide the information you need?"

"Yes." Denmore went to his desktop computer and tapped on a few keys. After a moment or two, he leaned closer to the screen. "This item was ordered and paid for online three days ago." He looked up. "It's a teddy bear. The largest and most expensive soft toy we stock."

"Is there any possibility it could have been tampered

with during the packing process?" He wanted to be absolutely sure it would be safe to open that box.

Denmore pursed his lips. "I can't give a hundred-percent guarantee, but I can offer you something that comes close." He pointed to his screen, showing Everett a spreadsheet. "From the moment an order is placed to when it leaves the store, each person who handles the item records the date and time on the system. I can't see any issues with this one."

Everett released the pent-up breath that had been tightening his chest. In one sense, the confirmation that the delivery had come from Hoyles' was good news. It meant the package was unlikely to contain anything sinister. On the other hand, it provided him with only half an answer. And it raised a whole lot of unwelcome questions.

"Okay. Now I need to know who placed the order."

"Client confidentiality is important to us. We don't usually give out this sort of information. But if a crime has been committed…" Denmore typed in a few details, a frown crossing his features as the screen changed. "I'm afraid it won't be possible to give you any information about the sender."

"What do you mean?" Everett moved closer, checking out the information on the screen.

"The toy was purchased using a prepaid gift card."

Everett took a moment to consider that information. There could be any number of reasons why someone might want to remain anonymous when making a purchase. They may feel unsafe, threatened by identity fraud, or want to shield their credit-card data from hackers. They might even wish to keep the purchase private from family members.

Or they might pose a specific threat to a little girl called Kennedy Dodd.

"And there is no way of tracing who purchased the gift card?"

"None." Denmore made a helpless gesture. "This one was purchased for cash on the day the bear was ordered."

"But you have security cameras, right? You know the date and time of the purchase and which register was used. I'd like to see those images."

"Of course." Denmore turned to a table at the side of his desk. On it, four monitors displayed split screen images of the interior and exterior of the store. "The security office have a clearer view of what's going on, but this is the back-up system in case anything goes wrong."

Typing the time and date and a reference number into the keypad attached to the system, Denmore waited for one of the screens to load the information he required. After a moment or two, it switched to a single screen view of a register. There were two people waiting to make their purchases and Everett leaned closer to get a better view.

"This woman has several items, but she could have bought the gift card at the same time."

Denmore shook his head. "No. The gift card was a single purchase."

Everett pointed. "So it must be this person. He or she has no other items."

He or she. It was impossible to tell. The figure at the

desk wore dark, shapeless clothing and a jacket with the hood pulled up. Judging by the people and items around, it could have been a small man, or an average-sized woman.

"The timing shows that was the person who bought the gift card," Denmore confirmed.

"Do you have any other images of him moving around the store?"

Denmore pressed more buttons, following the figure away from the cash desk, at which point he promptly disappeared into the crowd. When the manager tried to find the guy prior to his arrival at the desk, he was equally unlucky.

"Sorry. I can get security to keep trying and let you know if they find anything."

Clearly there was no point in pursuing the matter further at that time. Everett thanked Denmore for his time and left his contact details, then made his way back through the festive scene and onto the street outside.

"Can I go now?" He'd almost forgotten about Joe.

"I need to take a look at that package."

A few minutes later, he had offloaded the box from Joe's van. Although the information from Denmore had put his mind at rest, a vague doubt remained. Carrying the package into an open space, he placed it on the ground and untied the ribbons. As he eased off the lid, his mind repeated the same question.

Even if this was a gift from a well-wisher, how did that person know where to find Kennedy?

There was no satisfactory answer. Could Sean and Delilah have discussed the details of their will with

someone other than their lawyer, possibly Georgia?
Since they hadn't shared that information with Everett or Alyssa, the people most closely affected, it
seemed unlikely. Even if that was the case, what were
the chances of that person knowing *when* Kennedy's
new living arrangements would begin?

*If we didn't know, how could anyone else have
known?*

Could someone in Child Services have leaked the
information? It was a possibility, but why would anyone do that?

Add in the fact that Everett living at a temporary address... No, whoever had sent this gift to Kennedy had
worked hard to find her. And it didn't feel comfortable.

"See. It's a bear. Just like the guy said." Joe was starting to get on his nerves.

It wasn't just any bear. It was a giant, candy-pink,
fluffy bear holding a cushion that read I Love You. Everett placed the lid back on the box and walked away.

"Hey," Joe called after him. "What do you want me
to do with this?"

"Donate it to your favorite charity."

Chapter Three

When he arrived back at the apartment, Everett found his brother on his knees assembling a crib while Alyssa unloaded baby clothes from a box. From one of *many*. His confused brain took an inventory of what had once been his living space. "What the—?"

"Kennedy's stuff arrived." Alyssa appeared way too calm for someone who was speaking to him from behind a wall of boxes.

Before he could reply, Casey got to his feet. "All done. Where do you want this?"

"Well, there isn't really space in the smaller bedroom." Alyssa cast a wary look in Everett's direction.

"I see." He wanted to adopt an outraged pose, but there was barely enough room to breathe let alone throw out his chest. "So, as well as this room being taken over by baby items, I'm also being kicked out of my bedroom. Maybe I should sleep in my car from now on?"

He knew he was being unfair but how much more was this day going to throw at him? A baby, an ex-girlfriend—and not just any ex-girlfriend. No, Alyssa was the one he'd never quite managed to get over...and then there was that mysterious delivery. Now his rented apartment, never the most organized space, looked like a natural disaster had struck it.

All of those things were bad enough, but none of them were the worst. Like a knot tightening in his chest, there was also the knowledge that he couldn't protect Alyssa from his fears. He would have to watch some of the light go out of those beautiful eyes as he told her about the teddy bear.

Aware of his twin's gaze on his profile, he turned his head. The look in Casey's eyes said it all. *Don't be a jerk.*

"You guys have a lot to discuss. You don't need me getting in the way." Casey headed toward the door, turning back to look at Everett before he left. "I'll call you tomorrow."

The message was clear. Tonight he was getting a reprieve. On the following day, his brother would want to know everything.

"I thought we could order pizza?" Alyssa said when Casey had gone. "It's getting late. And we can't eat out."

She indicated the sleeping figure on the sofa. Kennedy was sprawled on her back, snoring softly. Alyssa had placed the cushions from the other sofa in a line on the floor next to her. Something about the action both touched and frightened him. Concern for the baby's safety was an instinct that came naturally to her. He'd never have thought of this particular gesture.

I have so much to learn.

"I get it now. That's why Sean did this. No more beers after a long day. If the guys from work are going for seafood or pasta or Thai, I'll have to pass. I can't stay up all night watching movies, or go for an early morning run. And..." He clapped a hand to his forehead in mock despair. "I'll have to get a *family* car."

Alyssa regarded him with amusement. "You think your former best friend is controlling your life from beyond the grave?"

"I wouldn't put it past the guy." He drew his cell phone from his pocket. "Pizza Paradise has my regular order. How about you? Still sticking with the boredom special? Goat cheese and red onion?"

"You remembered?"

"Four years *is* a long time." It was true. Although he wasn't sure whether he was talking about the four years they'd been together, or the four years since they'd split up. One of those stretches always seemed much longer than the other. "And we did eat a lot of pizza."

"Yeah." Her smile still had the power to warm his whole body. "The same as always for me. And I checked your refrigerator." Her little shudder took him back in time. "Add some diet soda to the order, please."

He placed the order, and, when he ended the call, Alyssa had switched into serious mode. "There's something I need to speak to you about."

"I was being a jerk. I'll move my stuff into the small bedroom after we've eaten."

"Thank you. But that's not what I was going to say." She waved a hand to indicate the boxes. "Patty Griffiths said they only brought the basics. The rest of Kennedy's belongings are at the house her parents owned."

"Well, that's where they can stay. We can't fit anything else in here."

"Exactly. Everett, look at all of this." She held out a framed picture to him as she spoke. "Look how much they loved their little girl. I just can't believe that Sean would have chosen to leave Kennedy all alone by killing himself and Delilah."

EVERETT STACKED KENNEDY'S boxes neatly along one wall, which meant they could place the pizza on the coffee table. While they ate, Alyssa sat on the sofa next to Kennedy and Everett piled cushions on the floor and sprawled at her feet. It was a moment of normality in a day that had taken unreal to a whole new level. She still didn't know why he'd taken off so abruptly, or why he'd asked Casey to come over. She figured he would tell her in his own time, and already knew she wasn't going to like the explanation.

"Patty brought a cool bag with some jars of baby food, so Kennedy will have something to eat when she wakes up." Alyssa smiled as she looked at the little girl. "But tomorrow, I'll need to go shopping."

"Have you thought about what this really means?" She figured Everett was entitled to the note of skepticism she could hear in his voice. "I don't just mean shopping for diapers and formula. What about your job? Your home? My place in Phoenix?" He ran a hand through his hair in a gesture that was as familiar as her own reflection in the mirror. "And what about us? After all this time, how are we supposed to do this *together*?"

After her relationship with Everett ended, Alyssa

had accepted that theirs, like all other love stories, was unique. It was like a quilt, made of scraps and pieces that once held so much meaning. Everything they had done together had left a mark on her life. Every time she thought she was ready to move on, something would happen to remind her of those vibrant threads of color that bound her to him.

But the reality was simpler and less poetic. Breaking up had been the only logical way of dealing with her fears about his job, but she had never stopped caring for him. And leaving him had been like trying to blow up a life vest while drowning. If they'd ended things because the feelings had gone, this conversation would have been different.

But she knew what he was saying. Taking on Sean and Delilah's baby was a huge commitment. Their history would make it a thousand times harder. They had gone their separate ways, only to have their worlds shaken off-course years later in the blink of an eye by the wishes of a dead couple. In the end, it came down to one thing. The right thing.

"This is not about us. Kennedy needs a family. Today, a twist of fate made us her mom and dad. I'll do whatever it takes." She gave him a direct stare. "I took a couple of days leave of absence to come here and I'm going to email the principal of my school in the morning and request maternity leave."

There was a challenge in the words. *Over to you.*

He held her gaze for a moment or two before looking down at the beer in his hand. And that was what she had expected. Professionally, he was razor-sharp and one of the most successful agents in his field office. In his private life, Everett didn't do tough decision making. *Keep it comfortable or walk away.* During their relationship, he had never deviated from that rule.

"You're sure I can't tempt you to try a slice of pepperoni with extra anchovies?"

Ignoring the deliberate attempt to distract her with the tried-and-tested pizza line he'd always used, she forced the conversation back on track. "As far as our living situation goes, this place probably isn't ideal. But with the holidays coming up, I think we have to make the best of it for now."

"You mean we take turns to breathe?"

"I'd forgotten what a funny guy you are, Colton." She pulled a face at him. "I mean we make this a nice home for Kennedy, and we give her a family Christmas." She frowned. "Her first Christmas."

Everett was silent for a moment or two. When he spoke again, there was a new tone in his voice. "I came back to Cactus Creek to investigate a murder. Pierce Tostig was a ranch hand at Selectman Clarence Edison's OverHerd Ranch. Casey was investigating a rustling case and he found the body near the corpse of one of the stolen cows. Sean, Delilah and Georgia were behind the operation, and confessed their involvement in Tostig's death when they cornered Casey and another of Edison's ranch hands, Melody Hayworth, at gunpoint. Luckily, Melody—who is now Casey's girlfriend—made an SOS call and I was able to track their location. I arrived with a team of agents in time to arrest the rustlers."

"So when he died, Sean was awaiting arraignment for a potential murder charge as well as cattle rustling?"

"That's right." His face was turned slightly away from her, but she could see the tension in the fine muscles of his jaw. "He rammed that fancy car of his right into a wall, killing himself and Delilah rather than face prison. At least that's what the suicide note that was taped to the dash said." She noticed his fist clench tight against his thigh. "There was just one small problem with that note."

Alyssa waited. They weren't touching, but she could feel the emotion coursing through him. When he looked up, the pain in his eyes made her breath catch.

"It wasn't in Sean's writing."

"Could Delilah have written it?" she asked.

Slowly, he shook his head. "I compared it to samples of Delilah's writing, as well. Neither of them wrote that note."

KENNEDY WOKE UP just after Everett told Alyssa about the suicide note, and he was glad for a break so he could rein in his emotions. Although he had submitted a report to his senior special agent expressing his opinion that Sean and Delilah's deaths were suspicious, he had not yet been given the go-ahead to officially investigate further.

As he cleared away the remnants of the takeout meal, he watched Alyssa with the baby. Kennedy got more food on her face and bib than she did in her mouth, but she appeared to enjoy holding her own spoon and hammering out a drumbeat on the tray of her high chair.

When she was finished, Alyssa deftly wiped her down and scooped her up. The little girl chuckled delightedly.

"She needs to get into a bedtime routine." She looked across at Everett. "How about we do bath time together?"

"You mean just you and me in the tub, right? Because I'm not sure I'm ready for the three of us." Alyssa gave an outraged snort and he held up his hands. "I'm new to this parenting thing, remember?"

She quirked an eyebrow at him, letting him know he wasn't fooling anyone. "I'll get her bath ready."

Seconds later, his arms were full of warm, wriggling baby. Kennedy gave a delighted squeal as she tried to poke a finger up his nose.

"Hey." He caught hold of her hand. "I think you and I should establish a few ground rules. Firstly… Whoa! *What* is that smell?"

It was like a combination of bad eggs and rotting garbage. He regarded the baby with suspicion. Surely that aroma couldn't be coming from such a cute little body? As if to confirm his worst fears, Kennedy's stomach gave a loud gurgle. It was instantly followed by a series of popping sounds in the diaper region. The smell grew stronger.

He held the little girl at arm's length. "Alyssa?"

She emerged from the bathroom with her sleeves rolled up to her elbows. "Yes?"

"I think there's something wrong with Kennedy."

Coming to the sofa, she leaned over his shoulder. Kennedy greeted her with an aimless wave and a fresh volley of stinky blasts.

"What makes you think that?"

Was it possible Alyssa had lost her sense of smell in the time they'd been apart? "Are you serious? I've supervised a drunk tank full of men who have spent a night consuming Mexican food and cheap beer. It didn't come close to that level of toxicity."

Alyssa laughed. "Her digestive system is immature and she's still adjusting to solid food. A little gas is hardly surprising."

She headed back into the bathroom.

"A little gas?" Everett studied Kennedy's face. "I dread to think what you can achieve when you decide to fill a diaper." She gave him a cheeky grin. "That wasn't a challenge."

A few minutes later, the complex preparations were complete. There was a brief power struggle when Kennedy seemed to feel that parting with her clothing was unnecessary. Everett watched in admiration as Alyssa won the battle with ease and placed the red-faced infant in the bathtub inside something that resembled a medieval torture device.

"It's a bathing seat," she explained in response to his raised eyebrows. "It means she can sit up safely without slipping around. And we have our hands free to wash her."

It was yet another item on the growing list of "things Everett didn't know about babies." He wasn't given any more time to ponder his inadequacies. Within seconds of Alyssa beginning to rub baby shampoo into Kennedy's hair, most of the water had left the tub and was sloshing around on the floor.

Washcloth in hand, Alyssa fought on, attempting to clean every part of the shrieking, laughing little girl while Everett helped hold her still. In the end, she turned to look at Everett. "I think she's clean enough now. At six months, she's not mobile enough to get really grubby."

"Shouldn't you at least try to wash the, uh, delicate parts properly?" Everett wiped soapy water off his face and plowed back into the fray. "They get the dirtiest, after all."

Although she was giving him a look of dislike, he couldn't help noticing the way Alyssa's drenched blouse clung to her curves. He'd missed those curves.

"*You* try." She handed him the cloth and stepped back.

Kneeling at the side of the tub, he approached with caution. Kennedy, clearly aware she was dealing with a rookie, waited until he got in close, then grabbed him by the hair.

"This may be a two-person job, after all." Alyssa came to his aid, freeing him from the chubby-fisted death grip.

"I'll lift, you clean."

To howls of protest from Kennedy, they completed the maneuver before collapsing side by side against the tiled wall.

"You know what?" Everett panted. "In future, I think a thorough clean each diaper change should take care of those bits."

He ducked just in time to avoid the washcloth Alyssa threw at his head.

ONCE SHE WAS warm and dry after her bath, Kennedy was drowsy and ready for her bedtime bottle of formula.

"Why don't you give it to her?" Alyssa held the onesie-clad baby out to Everett.

He paused for a moment, then took Kennedy from her and tucked the little girl into the crook of his arm. As soon as she saw the bottle, she reached for it, pulling it to her mouth and sucking greedily. Within minutes she was asleep.

Alyssa eased the bottle away from her and placed it on the coffee table. When she looked up, Everett was watching her face.

"She's a lucky little girl to have found you."

The lump in her throat was less about the words and more about his tone of voice. *Don't do this to me, Everett. This is day one. We have years ahead of us. Birthdays, holidays, starting school, boyfriends, graduation...* The thought frightened her less than the intensity in his eyes.

"She has us both." She brushed a stray curl off Kennedy's forehead, and raised the question that had been at the back of her mind all day. "I know why I'm doing this. What about you?"

"Oh, come on, Alyssa." A corner of his mouth lifted. "When you asked Ray Torrington what would happen to Kennedy if we said no and then you gave me *that* look, you knew I wouldn't be able to resist you."

She shook her head. "Not good enough. That answer might work if we were still together and deciding where to eat out or go on our next vacation. But this is about being mom and dad to a baby. It's a life-long commitment."

He was silent for a moment or two. "First of all, you *did* influence my decision. Because there is no way I would have done this with anyone other than you."

And there goes the last of my composure...

When he spoke again, his voice was little more than a whisper. "But you're right. Just like you, I will be doing this properly, starting with a request to my boss for a leave of absence. And the reason I'll be doing it is that it's for Sean."

"Because you don't think he killed himself?"

"Even if he did—and despite his crimes—we were friends once." He tilted his head back against the cushions. "I remember one summer when we were in high school, we got into a prank war. Neither of us could back down from a challenge. Sean thought it would be funny to use duct tape to fasten the handle of my school locker closed just when we had an important assignment due in. In revenge, I coated the seat of his bike in peanut butter. The jokes got wilder, until, one day, I enlisted Casey's help. We were holding Sean down and filling his shorts with ice cubes when my mom walked in. She took one look, said, 'I'll give you boys some privacy,' and walked out again."

Although she had only met Maribelle Colton a few times, Alyssa could picture the scene. "Your mom likes to keep it classy."

"Always." He smiled. "The point is, I have a hundred stories about Sean. We kept those challenges going into adulthood, always trying to get the better of each other. But our friendship wasn't all pranks. There was the time I tumbled into the creek and he jumped in to save me. Or when he fell off a wall and cut his head open, so I rode home with him on my crossbar. He screwed up with the way he treated Casey, but the earlier memories didn't die." He looked down at Kennedy. "When he entrusted his child to me, he knew I would be there for her."

Alyssa bowed her head. In all the years she'd known him, this was the most Everett had ever opened up to her. She'd never understood why he felt the need to conceal his emotions and had spent too many hours wondering whether he was trying to prevent conflict, protect her from hurt, or avoid worrying her. Would things have worked out differently if he'd been able to express his feelings?

She gave a tiny shake of her head. It wasn't his emotional detachment that had ended their relationship. Everett had been the one to suggest taking things to the next level. He'd asked her to move in with him and Alyssa had acted like a jackrabbit when it heard the cry of a wolf. Dating Agent Everett Colton had been difficult enough. Knowing he went out to work every day and put himself in danger was hard, but she could just about switch off from it and enjoy the time they spent together. If she lived with him, if she was watching the clock, waiting for him to come home at the end of each day…?

"We should get this little one into her crib." *And leave the past where it belongs.*

Everett shuffled to the edge of the sofa and got cautiously to his feet. Carrying her as though she was a piece of priceless china, he took the baby through to the master bedroom. Earlier that evening, he had positioned her crib next to the bed, and Alyssa had placed the photograph of Kennedy with her parents on a nearby side table.

After spending a few moments shifting back and forth to find the right position, he lowered her into the crib.

Kennedy made a soft noise of protest and Everett gave Alyssa a look of pure panic. She shook her head and pointed toward the door. Like teenagers sneaking out to a party, they tiptoed from the room.

Alyssa choked back a laugh as she switched on the baby monitor she'd found in one of the boxes. "The look on your face."

"What do you mean?" he whispered, sneaking a look over his shoulder at the closed bedroom door.

"When you thought Kennedy was about to wake up, your expression reminded me of that time I started choking on my soda."

"Hey, that was scary. You nearly passed out." He threw himself down on the sofa, hands linked behind his head, long legs crossed at the ankles.

"It was your fault," she reminded him. "You made me laugh in midswallow."

"Yeah. But I wasn't expecting the whole wheezing, throat-clutching, eyes-watering response." He gave her a sidelong glance. "You frightened the life out of me."

"That's how you looked at Kennedy. She's a baby, Everett, not a time bomb. She will poop, spit up, drool, put disgusting things in her mouth and likely wake up several times a night."

"You make it sound like such fun." He sat up straighter. "I need to talk to you about something other than Kennedy's bodily functions."

"Ah." She sat down next to him. "Is this about why you disappeared today?"

Now it was here, she realized how much she had been dreading this moment. It wasn't that she believed caring for Kennedy had suddenly catapulted her into a fairy tale. Her early life had convinced her there were no such things as magic wands, golden coaches and glass slippers. And if Prince Charming existed? Well, he'd chosen a life in the FBI, and she was the anxiety-filled princess who couldn't deal with that.

No, she was realistic enough to know that bringing up a baby would be hard. But she'd have liked more than a few hours to adjust to the idea before things got weird.

He nodded. "A delivery came. It was a Christmas gift for Kennedy."

She frowned, her brain trying to make sense of what he was saying. "How could anyone have known where she was?"

"Exactly."

Her first instinct was to rush into the bedroom, wrap Kennedy in a blanket and dash out into the night with her. But where could she take her that would be safer than right here with Everett? He was experienced at protecting people who were at risk. For the first time ever, she saw his job as a blessing instead of a curse.

"Is she in danger?"

"I couldn't find out who sent it." He reached across the space between them and covered her hand with his. "I won't let anything hurt her—or you, Lyss."

The old term of endearment slipped so naturally from his lips she wasn't sure he even noticed it. From her perspective, it was soothing. And, goodness, she would take all the comfort she could get right now.

"Do you know have any idea who could have sent it?"

"I don't have enough information to start speculating." She sensed he was holding something back. Did he have a suspect in mind? Was there even anything to be suspicious of at this point? She figured he would give her any information she needed to keep Kennedy safe.

"It could have been innocent," he said.

"You don't think that." She turned her head to look at him. His expression was grim.

"No, I don't." He heaved a sigh. "When Sean and Delilah died, Georgia made it clear she thought they had been murdered. She also said she wanted to take care of Kennedy."

"Oh." She looked down at her hands. "But you said she was in jail because she broke her bail conditions. How could she send the gift if she's behind bars?"

"I don't know. But it makes me want to know more about the way Sean and Delilah died."

Chapter Four

Everett had always been a light sleeper. He had trouble drifting into slumber and struggled to get back to sleep if he woke in the night. Things had gotten worse over the last few years, and he'd tried every tip and gadget that came his way. Recently, he'd found a combination of an eye mask, headphones and white noise playing on his phone worked best. It was awkward going to bed wired up, but at least he felt human in the mornings.

Even with his support system in place, he lay awake for several hours after his conversation with Alyssa. There were so many thoughts competing for his attention, it would be surprising if he ever slept again.

The first, and most important thing, was that he'd become a dad. It was not the way he'd always pictured it would happen, but he was determined to make the best of it. For Sean, for Kennedy and for this new little family. It was exciting, scary and intense. And he still couldn't quite believe it was happening. He couldn't help wondering how Kennedy would fit into his life. Was it really possible to love someone else's child? He had made a commitment to care for Sean's daughter and protect her, but would he ever care for her the way he would if she had been his own? It wasn't important. If the love didn't come, he would make sure Kennedy never knew.

He just wished he didn't have to get to know her alongside the mystery surrounding her parents' deaths. His thoughts turned to the call from Casey telling him Sean had killed himself. Even though it had been four years since they'd spoken, Everett's first reaction had been guilt. Should he have known? Could he have done something to prevent it?

Next came disbelief. Not Sean. Not his energetic, arrogant, laugh-in-the-face-of-danger ex-friend. And that was what stayed with him. Maybe everyone felt that way, but Sean had always believed he was invincible. He'd never had a moment's self-doubt in his life. But Sean's open disapproval of Georgia's relationship with Casey had ended up with his brother heartbroken at the altar.

You hadn't seen him in four years. A man can change a lot in that time.

Except… Everett *had* seen him. He'd headed the FBI team who had chased down the cattle rustlers. After not speaking to him in years, Sean's first words had been a quiet, mocking whisper when Everett had read him his rights.

"I'm going to enjoy making you look dumb in court, Colton." The familiar gleam in his old friend's eye said it all. Sean hadn't changed a bit. Even though it was malicious, he saw this as an extension of the duct-tape and peanut-butter games. Sean played to win, and he was looking forward to a new challenge.

Of course, Everett accepted that no one ever knew for sure what was going on inside another person's life, or head. But when his focus shifted from Pierce Tostig's murder to the Dodds' deaths, his concerns became professional as well as personal. The suicide note was just part of the problem. There were too many other things that didn't add up.

Even if he allowed himself to picture Sean committing suicide, he could not accept that the man he had once called his friend would have killed his wife. With a new baby to care for, it was likely she'd have faced a reduced charge and might even have escaped a custodial sentence.

Sean and Delilah were two of a kind, each drawn to the other's reckless streak. They had a six-month-old baby whom they both clearly loved. Their criminal activities hadn't halted when Kennedy came along but they had gone to the trouble of enlisting a neighbor to help with the babysitting. Even if he'd thought of taking Delilah's life, would Sean really have taken the drastic step of depriving Kennedy of both parents? Yes, she had an aunt, but would Sean have considered Georgia a suitable person to care for his child? Everett doubted it. It came back to that same question. If his mind had been disturbed, who knew what his reasoning might be?

The night they died, there were signs at their house of a disturbance. It appeared that the couple had been eating at the kitchen table when chairs were overturned and plates tipped onto the floor. There were marks suggesting someone had been dragged along the gravel drive between the house and the garage.

Had Sean forced Delilah out the door and into the car against her will? That suggested an impulsiveness at odds with a written suicide note. As did driving his vehicle full-speed at a wall. Death wasn't guaranteed, and Sean was nothing if not precise. If he had wanted to die, he had a safe full of guns that would have been a safer bet.

Thank goodness Kennedy had been staying with Georgia that night...

It was the first time in his life Everett had been thankful for Georgia Dodd, the woman who had almost been his sister-in-law. When they were kids, Sean's little sister had been trouble. As an adult, she had embraced rather than outgrown the label. When she'd gotten engaged to his twin, Everett had done his best to put aside his misgivings. Dumping Casey at the altar had sealed his dislike for her. Sean might have urged her to do it, but Georgia had a mind of her own. The decision to walk had been hers.

She was Kennedy's only surviving close relative. She was behind bars and, if she was found guilty, that was where she would stay. It was one more thing he would have to deal with now his life had taken this new, unforeseen turn. In one day.

But the most painful twist the last twenty-four hours had thrown at him was bringing Alyssa back into his life. And he didn't know how to deal with that.

When they broke up, he'd learned the hard way that heartache really did hurt as much as people said. He'd lost count of the number of times he'd picked up his cell phone and gazed at her number on the screen, rehearsing what he was going to say. But he'd known there were no words to make it right. The damage had been done before they met.

For Alyssa, it had happened way back when a random drunk stabbed her dad. Casey would say that, in Everett's case, it had been more recent, dating back to his brief stint in the world of corporate law. Did that make it harder to deal with?

I'll leave the amateur psychoanalysis to my brother.

Friends told him the pain of a breakup got better with time. It didn't. He just found ways to push aside the ache of missing her. Instead of staring at her picture like a man dying of thirst would stare at an out-of-reach bottle of water, he threw himself into his work, went for long runs, worked out and took aimless drives with his music turned up loud to tune out the memories.

He'd even tried dating again. If possible, that had made him miss her more. After a few attempts, he'd given up. It was unfair to the other women, who didn't know they would never be enough for him because they weren't Alyssa.

Four years had passed, and he still thought about her every day. She was imprinted on his heart. Now she was in the next room…

A sound penetrated his sleep defenses. It was a series of squawks followed by a child's distressed sobbing. Everett was on his feet, with wires trailing, and ran into the master bedroom.

"What's going on? Is she okay?"

Alyssa was out of bed and pacing the floor with Kennedy in her arms. The dim glow from the night-light next to the bed shone on the baby's tearstained, red cheeks.

"I've tried everything I can think of to settle her," Alyssa said. "She started whimpering a little, so I gave her some formula. Her diaper is clean and dry, so that's not the problem. Her body temperature is fine. She likes being rocked, so I tried that. I think she may be cutting a tooth and her gums are sore."

"What can we do about that?" Under Alyssa's interested gaze, he removed his sleep aids as he spoke. She'd never seen him wired up. The sleep problems had gotten worse since the breakup.

"We can give her an infant pain reliever, but I didn't see any in the boxes I unpacked."

"There's a twenty-four-hour drugstore a couple of blocks away. I'll head over there."

"See if they have any teething toys for her to chew on." Alyssa held up a reddened thumb. "I'm running out of fingers for her to bite."

Going back to his own room, he threw a jacket over the sweatpants and T-shirt he'd worn to bed and pulled on his socks and boots. He grabbed his car keys and cell phone, then headed out into the cool night air.

Cactus Creek was not a party town, and, since it was after midnight, most businesses on Main Street had closed their doors several hours earlier. It was unusual to see anyone around at this time of night, so as he started down the steps, Everett's attention was caught by a vehicle parked directly opposite from his apartment.

The single occupant hunkered down in the driver's seat, woolen beanie hat pulled down low and scarf wrapped around the lower part of the face. Everett had worked enough stakeouts to know what he was looking at. It was amateurish, but unmistakable. There was only one place in plain view. Everett's apartment was at the top of the steps. The guy was watching *his* front door.

Going down the stairs two at a time, he approached the vehicle at a run, cell phone in hand as he snapped a picture of the license plate. Catching sight of him, and anticipating his intention, the driver gunned the engine into life, turning on the main beams at the same time. Caught in the glare of the lights, Everett threw up an arm to shield his eyes.

As the car's tires squealed, he had a split second in which to process what was happening. Instead of heading out of the parking lot, the driver had hit the gas and was speeding straight toward him. Diving to one side, Everett managed to roll into the space under the steps just as the car bounced off the curb where he had been standing.

Like cluster bombs exploding inside his skull, his brain fired off a series of instructions. This guy had signaled his intentions, and they weren't good. A stakeout was bad enough. Taking the opportunity to try to kill a federal agent took the situation to a whole other level.

Everett was currently pinned in position. If he moved from his place of security, he risked being mowed down. If he stayed where he was, Alyssa and Kennedy could be in danger.

Hunkering down in the darkness, he was preparing

to call Casey when the car engine started revving up again. Risking a quick glance out at the parking lot, he was in time to see the vehicle make a 180-degree turn before it bumped across a flower bed and screeched out onto the road.

Uncurling his long legs from their cramped position, Everett exited his hiding place. As he headed toward his car, he made a mental to-do list.

Get Kennedy her teething meds, send Casey the picture he'd taken of that vehicle...and add some agility training exercises to his workout regime.

WHY WAS EVERETT taking so long? As soon as the thought hit, Alyssa groaned out loud. It was starting again. She had been in his company for less than twenty-four hours and already the old anxieties were resurfacing.

This time, she had to find a way around her fears. Not because they were together. But because of this new commitment. For Kennedy's sake, she couldn't freak out every time he was gone. She couldn't live on a knife edge forever, and she wasn't prepared to pass on her insecurities to a helpless little girl.

"There must be a way. Other people do this." She drew Kennedy closer, and the baby hitched her breath in a tired sob as she tucked her head into Alyssa's neck. "How about I try to get you to take a sip of cold water while we're waiting?"

Although more water dribbled onto Kennedy's chin than into her mouth, the cool liquid soothed her. By the time Everett returned, her tears had subsided and she was almost asleep with her head on Alyssa's shoulder.

"Are you limping?" As soon as the words left her lips, Alyssa wished them unsaid. So much for her vow— made minutes earlier—to overcome her worry. Instead of toughening up, she was coming across as whiny and needy.

Everett appeared not to notice. "How about we settle this little one, then I'll tell you all about it?"

If the fact that there was an "it" didn't escape her attention, neither did the reassuring smile in his eyes. He was here and, for now, that was enough to make her feel safe and warm.

It wasn't enough last time...

She shrugged away the thought. Everything had changed when Kennedy came along. Maybe she should get that made into a lapel pin?

The painkiller syrup came with a small, needle-free syringe. Having filled it to the required dose, Alyssa tilted Kennedy's head and put the syringe into her mouth, aiming for the back corner.

Everett watched the maneuver with concern. "Won't she choke when that goes down her throat?"

"If I pointed it directly down her throat she might gag. But I'm going to release it slowly into the back of her mouth." Alyssa pressed the stopper gently as she spoke. "It's no good putting into the front of her mouth. She'd simply push the medicine back out with her tongue."

As she released the medicine, Kennedy regarded her with wide, hurt eyes. Clearly, the little girl was questioning the reason behind this breach of baby etiquette. Once she had taken all the painkiller, Alyssa removed the syringe and, as she had anticipated, Kennedy started to cry. Holding the baby close, she rocked her back and forth while crooning an old lullaby her own mom used to sing.

After a few minutes of tearful protest, Kennedy's eyelids began to droop and she was soon asleep.

"Poor little girl." Alyssa pressed a kiss onto one soft cheek. She looked up, meeting Everett's gaze with a smile. "Let's hope she gets a good night's sleep now."

He followed her as she carried the baby to the bedroom and placed her in the crib. She pulled the quilt over Kennedy and Everett leaned closer.

"It's hard to believe she's only been with us a few hours." There was a husky note in his voice that could have been tiredness. Alyssa turned her head to look at him. In that moment, his expression was an open book. He wasn't tired.

Kennedy's dad had been part of his life, and that emotional connection had never been fully severed, despite the pain Sean had caused him. Love stretched over time and space as if those dimensions didn't exist. Could he get past the hurt and form a genuine bond with Kennedy for the child's own sake? If it didn't happen naturally, Alyssa saw a new role for herself as the person who would need to intervene.

She pointed to the door. As she entered the living area, she switched on a lamp. The room felt cool and she wrapped her arms around herself. "You said you'd tell me why you are limping."

He hesitated, and she knew he was trying to figure out the least painful way to explain things to her. Suddenly, instead of being afraid, she was annoyed. She was unhappy at herself for needing to be handled with care.

"Just tell me." The words came out faster and harsher than she'd intended.

She'd always found it hard to hide from that piercing gaze, but now she looked him in the eye. After a moment or two, he shrugged. "There was a guy watching the apartment."

A tiny part of her wanted to crumble, but she squared her shoulders. "Did you get a good look at him?"

"No." He grimaced. "I was too busy running away when he tried to run me down."

"Everett!" She moved closer, pushing him down onto the sofa. "Why didn't you tell me this straight away? Are you badly hurt? Did you call 911?"

He held up his hands in a gesture of surrender, a slight smile touching his lips. "I'm not badly hurt. Just stiff, because my muscles took a pounding when I rolled away from the vehicle. I didn't call 911, but I got a picture of the car and I sent it to Casey. And I didn't tell you straight away because—"

"You didn't want to worry me?" She knew it was true, so why did it hurt?

"Partly. But also because it was important to settle Kennedy." He tilted his head back to get a better look at her. "Because she comes first from now on. Right?"

"Of course." She curled into a corner of the sofa, all

thoughts of sleep long gone. "This guy must be linked to the parcel that came for Kennedy."

"I was prepared to keep an open mind about that… until he drove straight at me. And since we already have a dangerous situation, it seems safe to assume they could be connected. After that, I figured he could be a bad guy. Don't ask me why. Just a bizarre hunch." As she glared at him, he held up his hands. "Sorry. I don't mean to sound like I'm taking this lightly. It's just been a long day, you know?"

"I know." Her own sigh was even heavier. "I've been right here with you."

EVERETT HAD FORGOTTEN how refreshing he always found the sight of Alyssa in the mornings. With her hair caught back in a ponytail, her eyes bright and her skin soft and glowing, she looked like an advertisement for good health. He'd always thought of her as a golden girl. Petite, blonde, with those glorious eyes and wide, full lips.

He was also having trouble concentrating on anything other than the way she filled her gray fleece pajamas. She looked a lot like someone he wanted to hug. For a very long time.

Kennedy appeared to have recovered from her teething problems and was seated in her high chair, splashing in a bowl of oatmeal.

"What are the plans for today?" Everett clutched a mug of coffee and leaned against the kitchen counter.

"Lots of shopping." She started ticking off items on her fingers. "The first thing is more storage for Kennedy's clothes and toys. Then we have to stock up on formula, food, diapers and other day-to-day items."

"Other day-to-day items?" He didn't like the sound of that.

"Trust me. You are missing some basics here. Also, I've asked a friend to send some of my clothes from Phoenix. I know you've had my car brought over and I have the bag that was in in it, but I'll still need to buy myself a few things." Her smile broadened. "And there's Christmas."

That smile brought so many memories with it. Alyssa loved the holidays, and when they were together he had entered into the spirit right along with her. Cozying up and watching classic movies, sitting by the tree and wrapping gifts together, shopping for matching silly sweaters, Alyssa preparing dinner while Everett made eggnog…and sneaking up on her with a bunch of mistletoe.

Now, there were practical considerations to take into account. "Alyssa, if you're planning on turning this apartment into Santa's workshop—"

She laughed. "I know what you're going to say, but I'm sure we can find room for a small tree."

He gestured around the cramped space. "What should we sacrifice so we can fit in some holiday decorations? Do we really need a kitchen? And I, for one, am tired of sitting down. Let's get rid of these chairs and stand while we eat in the future."

"You are such a grump in the mornings, Colton." Her cheeks reddened as she realized what she was doing.

Turning away, she fussed over Kennedy, wiping oat-meal off the little girl's cheeks.

Yeah. It was too easy to fall into that old, familiar routine. *Because it was fun, and we enjoyed it.*

Everett's cell phone buzzed, providing a welcome distraction. It was Casey, and as he answered it, Alyssa signaled that she was taking Kennedy into the bedroom to get ready. He nodded, glad for the chance to talk freely to his brother.

Casey got straight to the point. "First things first. Who is trying to kill you?"

"I sent you a picture of the car that tried to run me down," Everett said. "I was hoping you'd be able to trace the license plates and answer that question for me."

"The car was stolen in Tucson two days ago and was found burned-out on wasteland in the early hours of this morning. It's not going to tell us a damn thing."

Everett bit back a curse. "Then neither of us has the answer to the question about who it is." He quickly told Casey about the delivery of the teddy bear addressed to Kennedy. "I'm not a betting man, but I'd put money on the package from Hoyles' and the guy staking out my apartment being linked."

"I wouldn't bet against you in this instance." Casey sounded serious. "As well as who, we need to know why."

"Sean was ambitious," Everett said. "He had quite the criminal enterprise going on with his gang of cattle rustlers. And with Delilah cooking the books to make it appear that his business was legitimate, he had a lot of money stashed away. And there's the house as well.

Kennedy inherits it all and Delilah made sure that any-thing connected to Kennedy was completely clean."

Casey whistled. "So whoever gets custody of Ken-nedy has access to Sean's money and property?"

"Pretty much." He waited a moment or two. "Can you think of anyone devious enough to use a child to enrich themselves that way?"

Casey didn't answer immediately. "At her arraign-ment, Georgia pled not guilty. She got bail, but, as we know, she blew it by trying to leave town. I, for one, and glad to know she'd behind bars."

"I didn't mention Georgia."

"You didn't have to. As soon as you said the word *devious*, her name sprang to mind. I'm just giving you the facts," Casey said. "I know how destructive Georgia can be, remember? You won't find me defending her."

"Georgia wasn't behind bars when Sean and Delilah died," Everett pointed out.

"If you're right, and the Dodds were murdered, it was a very tight window of opportunity. How many people do you figure knew about the time period between the three of them being arrested and their arraignment? It's not like they had a wide circle of friends and family."

Casey had a point. Neither Sean nor Delilah had any other close relatives besides Georgia and they had delib-erately shut out old friends. The reason was clear now, of course. As Sean's criminal activities had grown, he must have wanted fewer people close enough to ques-tion what was going on.

Everett gazed at the parking lot. Black tire marks slashed across the tarmac surface ending at the ruined flower bed. Georgia had been his number-one suspect all along. The only reason he'd hoped it was someone else was that Sean's younger sister was likely to prove a devious and volatile opponent. And, of course, she had to have help. If she was behind bars, there was no way Georgia had been the person who drove that car at him on the previous night.

"Can we get a sample of Georgia's handwriting?" he asked. "I need an FBI analyst to do a comparison with the suicide note."

"Leave it with me." There was a pause and Everett guessed what was coming next. The unique connection between twins was something most people couldn't understand. Most of the time, Everett viewed it as a gift. Now and then, it could be a curse. "Are you sure you want to get involved with Alyssa again?"

Everett cast a glance in the direction of the master bedroom. "We're not involved."

"Right. Because nothing says distance like raising a baby together." Casey sighed. "You don't want to hear this, but I have to say it. It's the twin thing. I know what breaking up with her did to you last time. I don't want you to go through that again."

Casey knew? He had never said anything. Once or twice, Everett had felt his brother watching him as if he was wondering whether to ask him how he was doing. But Casey had never crossed that line. *The twin thing.* They'd always been there for each other. Maybe he had figured Everett would tell him if he needed him? If that was the case, he hadn't known how badly Everett was hurting.

"It's not the same." Why were his throat muscles so tight? He reached for his coffee and swallowed some of the lukewarm liquid.

"Be careful. That's all I'm saying. Some feelings aren't easy to keep locked away. Even you, who work so hard at that, are going to struggle with this." When did his kid brother—younger by two vital minutes—get so wise? Maybe it was when he'd recently moved on from his own heartache with his new love, Melody. "I'll keep you informed if I hear anything relevant to the Dodd inquiry."

Chapter Five

Alyssa's mom had always tried to make Christmas memorable. Growing up, the holiday had been a brief escape into fantasy. After her dad died, it had become a break from a childhood filled with fear that her mom was about to crack under the strain.

As a result, she unapologetically loved the yuletide season and viewed it as a magical time. Although Kennedy was too young to know what was going on, Alyssa wanted to make their first Christmas together special.

She was determined that, as Kennedy grew up, the little girl would know how much Sean and Delilah had loved her. At the same time, she wanted her to look back on this transition as a positive point in her life. The holiday celebration, with its traditions and colorful cheeriness, would always be "their" time. The anniversary of when Kennedy came to them. She wanted pictures and mementos and laughter as reminders.

One of Alyssa's favorite parts of the holiday had always been the shopping. The bright lights, tacky window displays, delicious food smells, tinny pop music—as far as she was concerned, it all added to the atmosphere. Of course, the presence of a six-month-old baby complicated the whole process of immersing herself in it this time.

"This is like a military operation." Half an hour after they started out, Everett loaded the pink-elephant bag and the stroller into the trunk of his car. "How much stuff can one baby need for a trip to the shops?"

"Maybe I should pack more diapers?" Alyssa, who was carrying Kennedy, cast a look back toward the apartment.

"This is Cactus Creek. It's a small town, but we have stores here that can deal with a diaper emergency." He steered her toward the vehicle.

The baby was looking particularly cute in a fluffy pink coat and a matching hat. She eyed the car seat thoughtfully but allowed Alyssa to strap her into it without any resistance. When Everett handed her a teething toy, she bit into it with obvious delight.

"I still can't believe her aunt might be behind the attempt to run you down," Alyssa said, as Everett pulled out onto the road.

"That's because you've never met Georgia Dodd. She's not like any person you've ever encountered."

Although she was pleased that he'd shared the details of his conversation with Casey without holding anything back to protect her, she was concerned at the turn events were taking. In her imagination, Georgia had become the caricature of a child stealer, and she couldn't shake the foolish image. Even if Sean's sister was behind the attempts to scare them, how much harm could she really do from behind bars?

"She created a very dramatic moment in court, wailing, clutching Kennedy to her, while she screamed that her brother and sister-in-law had been murdered," Everett said.

"I guess it must have been an emotional time for her." Even so, Alyssa was picturing the impact of that moment on Kennedy and hoping that, in the same situation, she'd have tried to keep things calm for the sake of the baby.

"You could say that." Everett's voice was grim. "Or you could say that Georgia likes to make a scene."

Casting a sidelong glance in Everett's direction, Alyssa decided to tackle another subject that had been bothering her. "What will you tell your parents about Kennedy?"

"Now that is an interesting question."

Alyssa had met Ryker and Maribelle Colton a few times when she and Everett were dating. Everett's dad was an oncologist and his mom ran the Cactus-Creek post office. The kindly couple had always been friendly and welcoming toward her and she had enjoyed the warm family atmosphere at their home.

"I'll tell them the truth, of course." A slight smile crossed his lips. "When they get back from visiting their friends in El Paso."

"When will that be?" Alyssa asked.

"They are coming home for the holidays. Casey and his new girlfriend, Melody, are staying with them for Christmas." He flicked a glance in her direction. "Which doesn't give me much time to plan what I'm going to say."

"I guess they'll be shocked?"

He pulled into a space in front of Hoyles' Department Store. "Well, the circumstances aren't exactly normal. But I'm counting on the fact that my mom has been dropping hints about becoming a grandma."

"Kennedy is a cutie," Alyssa said. "Your mom will find her hard to resist."

"Let's hope so." He brought the car to a stop and turned to look over his shoulder at the baby. "My mom plays a key role in the Cactus Creek community. Not just because of her job, but also because she does work for good causes. She's a feisty lady, and she'd defend me and my choices to anyone, but—"

"She will find this hard to explain," Alyssa said, finishing for him.

"I'm still struggling with it," he admitted, as they got out of the vehicle.

A few minutes later, they had Kennedy strapped into her stroller. Like everything else the Dodds had purchased for their daughter, it was made of the finest material and Alyssa suspected it had come with an eye-popping price tag. With its leather trim, supersoft cushions, and both rear- and forward-facing options, it was surely the ultimate in designer baby transport.

"It will be comforting for Kennedy to be able to see us and hear our voices while we shop," she said as she instructed Everett to turn it to face the rear.

They headed toward the entrance of the store. It appeared to Alyssa that the whole town had decided to go shopping at the same time. As they entered the brightly lit foyer, she looked approvingly around her. When it came to an over-the-top Christmas, Hoyles' could compete with any of the stores she had seen in bigger cities.

"Everett!"

She sensed Everett stiffen and turned to look at him. His face had taken on an almost comical expression of dismay. Together, they swung slowly around to face the person who had called out his name.

"Mom?" Everett managed to sound pleased as well as stunned. "I thought you were out of town."

Maribelle Colton's build was statuesque and her bearing regal. With her dark brown locks, prominent cheekbones and deep-set eyes, she cut a striking figure as she strode toward her son.

"We had car trouble." She rolled her eyes. "You know what your dad is like. He doesn't trust anyone except Brian at Bauer Motors with his precious baby. So he had a quick repair job done in El Paso, then we left early. He's at the shop now getting the car fixed." The bright gaze that missed nothing took in Everett's companions. "Alyssa. How lovely to see you again. Goodness, what a beautiful baby."

Everett turned to Alyssa with a rueful smile. "So much for planning."

"I don't understand." Maribelle looked from one to the other. "Whose baby is she?"

"Mom, this is Sean Dodd's daughter, Kennedy," Everett said.

"Oh." Maribelle's expression softened. "The poor little sweetie. Heaven knows I didn't think much of her father, but—"

"Alyssa and I have custody of her now."

For a moment or two, it appeared as if Maribelle hadn't understood. A blank look washed over her face, like her brain cogs couldn't turn fast enough to take in the information she had just been given. Then, with slow, robotic movements, she reached into her purse and withdrew a lily-white handkerchief. With a hand that wasn't quite steady, she dabbed at the corners of her mouth.

"Is this one of your jokes, Everett?"

"You know I wouldn't joke about something like this. I was hoping to find a more diplomatic way to tell you." He placed a hand under her elbow. "Why don't we go to the coffee shop? We can sit down there and talk some more."

She shook her head. "I was supposed to meet your dad ten minutes ago. You know what he's like. He'll already be pacing and checking his watch. Five more minutes and he'll call Casey to see if I've been in an accident." She looked down at Kennedy again. "And I think I need a little more time to digest this news."

Everett kissed her cheek. "Call me in a day or two and we'll bring Kennedy to visit."

"So nice to see you again, Alyssa." She waved a hand. "A new baby in the family. Oh, my."

Alyssa watched her disappear into the crowds. "She seemed less than overjoyed."

What else had she expected? If anything, Maribelle's reaction had been remarkably tame. Most women in their sixties, when confronted with the news that their son had suddenly acquired a child, would have been stunned. The knowledge that the child belonged to a criminal once responsible for ruining the happiness of her other son could easily have tipped Maribelle over into fury.

Her protective instincts toward Kennedy were developing fast. The little girl had already lost so much, and Alyssa wanted to give her a happy life. It would be wonderful if her future included grandparents who would love and support her. That vision was starting to fade.

"She'll be fine," Everett said. "Seriously. By the time Mom gets home, she'll be planning for Kennedy to have her own room in their house." Alyssa gave him a skeptical look. "Trust me. Her love of kids will outweigh any other consideration."

"I hope so." She gripped the bar of the stroller and consulted the store guide. "Which way to the toy department?"

An hour later, Everett was in danger of disappearing under the pile of the things they'd bought and Kennedy was getting cranky.

"She probably needs something to eat before she has a nap," Alyssa said.

"You mean we can finally head to Hoyles' coffee shop?" Everett asked hopefully.

"You get a table while we go to the ladies' room." Alyssa turned the stroller toward the elevators. "A diaper change is called for before nap time."

Although there were restrooms on each level, the baby-changing facilities were located on the third floor. As Alyssa waited for an elevator, Kennedy began to cry in earnest.

"Oh, hey, sweetie." She squatted beside the stroller.

"We'll soon have you feeling clean and fresh. Then you can have lunch and a nap."

A bell dinged, signaling the arrival of the elevator. Relieved, Alyssa pushed the stroller in and pressed the button for the third floor. The doors had started to close when a man suddenly stepped in.

With his hood pulled up, hands in his pockets and his shoulders hunched, he drew her attention for all the wrong reasons. Was he a shoplifter hiding his face from the security cameras? Acting on impulse, she placed herself between him and Kennedy.

"I'm going to the third floor. You?" She was proud of the way her voice sounded so calm.

He didn't answer, keeping his back to her as he faced the elevator doors. With her heart pounding, she kept her eyes fixed on the display showing them moving up the floors. When the red light showed the number three, the doors opened. The sight of shoppers moving around nearby made her feel safe again.

"This is my floor."

He stayed where he was, blocking her exit.

"I need to get out."

Nothing. When he reached out a hand toward the buttons, Alyssa knew she had to act fast. If those doors closed, she and Kennedy would be trapped inside again with this creepy stranger. Gathering all her courage, she pushed the stroller forward. At least Kennedy was facing her and couldn't see what was going on.

Offering up silent thanks to the Dodds for their expensive tastes, she hit him hard in the shins with the heavy wheel guard. As he grunted in pain, she kept on going, barging past him and out through the doors. Once she had gained the freedom of the store, she drew a breath and looked around for a security guard. It was too late. The elevator doors were already closing.

She stooped to kiss Kennedy's cheek, then drew her cell phone from her bag with shaking hands. As she leaned against a wall, she called the only person who could make this situation right.

"Everett?"

"HAVE YOU EVER considered that there could be such a thing as too many holiday decorations?" Everett looked down at Alyssa with a twinkle in his eye as he stood on a chair and finished hanging a garland above a door in his apartment. He was trying to keep the mood up after the frightening incident at the department store a few hours earlier.

"No." Although her expression was prim, her eyes danced. "Just like there's no such thing as tacky tinsel or an ugly Christmas sweater. Bows, bells, baubles, stockings… I want Kennedy's first Christmas to have it all."

He stepped down and waved a hand to indicate the brightly lit tree that now occupied one corner of the room. "So this is all for Kennedy?"

"I can't pretend I won't enjoy it along with her." The look of anticipation dissolved into a frown. "I just wish there wasn't this shadow hanging over us."

He knew Alyssa was still upset to think that one of Kennedy's own relatives might act in such a malicious way. Since she'd never met Georgia, it was hard to explain that Sean's sister was unlikely to be a warm and loving aunt toward her niece.

She was even more distressed at the realization that, if Georgia was responsible, she must have an accomplice. The idea of an unsavory character recruited to watch over and threaten them had taken hold of her imagination. It had become even more real since the incident in the elevator at Hoyles'.

When Alyssa had called him in the store and told him what had happened, his initial reaction had been one of fear. As he had rushed past the other shoppers, images of her and Kennedy in danger had crowded his mind.

Once he had seen they were physically unharmed, the sight of Alyssa's pale face and trembling lip had pushed his anxiety aside.

His anger had been like lava bubbling up inside a volcano, erupting from him in waves. He'd kept it hidden for Alyssa's sake, but its silence made it even more powerful.

And the memories it evoked... He'd shaken the thought aside. This was about Alyssa, not what happened all those years ago.

Now they were home, his fury had cooled a little. But it was still there. Waiting to resurface when he found the guy who had threatened his family.

Casey had acquired the security-camera footage from the store and inside the elevator, but it wasn't helpful. The same guy who had gotten into the elevator had shown up a few other times, lurking close to Everett and Alyssa as they made their way around the store.

Although it looked like he could have been following them, he had kept his face hidden the whole time. Everett had sent a copy of the film to the FBI laboratory for enhancement, but he wasn't hopeful that it would reveal any clues to the guy's identity.

They would also run a comparison with the picture he'd taken of the car that had tried to run him down. Again, he didn't have high hopes of a positive outcome. On both occasions, just as with the person who had purchased the gift card, the individual had taken great care to disguise his or her features.

He turned his attention to Alyssa. He could tell she was trying hard not to let the intimidation get to her, but now and then she would look out of the window at the parking lot, or check on Kennedy in her crib for no reason.

In addition, she was dealing with new-mom issues. Sleep deprivation, the baby's teething, trying to work out Kennedy's likes and dislikes, while also keeping up with the sheer amount of tiny clothes that had invaded the laundry. They were both discovering that becoming parents was an even bigger change than they'd anticipated. Bringing a baby into their lives had turned their emotions upside down, as well as their living arrangements.

"Kennedy is such a sweetheart. I can't bear the thought of anything bad happening to her."

Instinctively, he moved toward her. As he reached out his hands to grasp her shoulders, he paused. Was touching her a good idea? His intention was to reassure her but was that how Alyssa would see it? He gazed at her lovely face, and briefly questioned his own motives. Maybe comfort wasn't the only thing on his mind.

"I won't let anything hurt her." He let his hands drop back to his sides. "Or you."

"Oh." Darkness bloomed in her eyes. "This is turning out all wrong."

"What do you mean?"

"I always saw your job as something to be feared." She made a helpless gesture, and he knew she was thinking of their breakup. "In the end, it was a worry I couldn't live with."

"I understood that." After all this time, it still hurt so much to talk about it. "I didn't like it, but I respected your decision to end things between us."

"But don't you see what's happening here?" A corner of her mouth lifted, but there was no humor in the smile, only sadness. "I'm depending on your job—the cause of so many of my nightmares—to keep us safe from this threat. Everything has gone into reverse."

This time, he didn't stop to think. Closing the distance between them, he drew her into his arms. When she rested her head against his chest, warmth glowed deep inside him.

"Isn't life supposed to be all about timing?" He ran a hand down the length of her hair. His mind hadn't played tricks. It really was as silky as he remembered.

"If that's the case, this sucks." Her voice was muffled by his sweater.

"And I'm not sure I want a dangerous situation to be the reason you see my job as a positive."

"Positive? Let's not get carried away. I'm forced to

rely on your role as an FBI agent to get us through this. I didn't say I see what you do as a good thing." She took a step back. "Now how about you get back on that chair and put the star on top of the tree so Kennedy can see it when she wakes up?"

He threw her a jokey salute. "Whatever you say, o festive commander."

She gave him a little shove in the direction of the tree. Before he could step onto the chair, her fingers lightly brushed his wrist. "Thank you."

He raised questioning eyebrows. "For putting a star on the tree?"

She smiled again, this time with no trace of sadness. "Among other things."

"SEAN AND DELILAH got married four years ago. They'd been together for three years before that." Everett started talking almost as soon as Casey entered the apartment the following morning. He might have taken a leave of absence, but there was nothing he could do to stop his brain from working on the investigation. "During that time, had your department ever been called out to deal with any domestic-disturbance incidents involving them?"

"Not that I'm aware of, but I'll check it out." Casey went straight through to the kitchen and helped himself to coffee. "What are you thinking?"

"The night they died, it appeared that they had been eating at the kitchen table when a disturbance took place. Chairs had been overturned and plates of food were smashed on the floor. There was a small amount of Delilah's blood on the floor and the front door had been left wide open. Have I got this right so far?"

Casey nodded. "It looks like you've memorized every detail of the investigation report."

"There were marks on the gravel drive that could have been consistent with someone having been dragged from the house to the garage."

"That was speculation on the part of the first officer at the scene," Casey said. "I'm not saying he was wrong, but there could be any number of explanations for those marks. Sean and Delilah could have moved an object earlier in the day, something that needed to be pulled over the gravel."

"Or they could have had a fight and he hauled her from the house to the car," Everett said. "That's why I want to know about any previous history of domestic disturbances. They'd been together for seven years. Wouldn't it strike you as odd if this was the first time things got physical between them?"

"They both were under intense pressure," Casey pointed out. "On a countdown to prison sentences."

"That wasn't how Sean saw it. You know what his ego was like. The guy straight-up said he was looking forward to making me look stupid in court. And even if he did think prison was a possibility, why would he turn nasty with Delilah? He worshipped her."

"The suicide note said he couldn't face spending time in prison."

"Ah, yes. The suicide note." Everett nodded. "It seems odd that it didn't mention his reason for wanting to kill Delilah, as well."

Casey shrugged. "You just said yourself that he worshipped her. Maybe he couldn't stand that she'd get time, too?"

Everett fell silent as he tried to make sense of the Dodds' last night. Even if what Casey was saying was true, if Sean couldn't bear the thought of Delilah going to jail, where did Kennedy fit into the picture? Everything he had learned told him that she had been the center of her parents' world. Even if he removed every other doubt about Sean's suicide, he couldn't get past the biggest one of all.

He would not have left his little girl without both parents.

"Where was the suicide note found?"

"In the car, taped to the dashboard." Casey poured more coffee. "It was all in the report. By the way, why are you mashing green slime?"

"It's avocado and kiwi fruit. Kennedy loves it." Everett returned to the conversation. "Doesn't the location of the note strike you as strange? Sean writes a letter, explaining that he is going to kill himself rather than go to jail. At what point does he place it on the car dash? Is it before he goes down to the kitchen and gets into a fight with Delilah over his intentions? Or does he drag his wife to the car and then write it?"

"Does it matter?" Casey regarded him with something like fascination.

"I'm trying to piece together what happened that night. And don't get me started on why they would leave Kennedy with Georgia on that night. If there was ever a contest for irresponsible aunt of the year, Sean

Dodd's younger sister only had to show up to be handed the crown."

"Speaking of Kennedy... Where is she now? And where is Alyssa?" Casey looked around the apartment with raised eyebrows. "It's not like there are many places to hide around here."

"Both asleep." Everett scrubbed a hand over his unshaven chin. "Kennedy is teething and was awake most of the night. When she does sleep, we take turns to join her."

His twin regarded him with interest. "And do you want to tell me the story of how you got that bruise on your head?"

Everett laughed as he rubbed his forehead. "I forgot to open my bedroom door on the way to deal with a crying baby in the middle of the night. The smack it made when I struck the wooden panel with my skull was impressive."

Casey gave him a sympathetic look. "You're finding this whole thing tough, huh?"

"It's the hardest thing I've ever done. I didn't sign up for this, yet my life is suddenly all about sterilizing bottles, changing diapers, washing clothes, wiping up sick..." He sucked in a breath.

"I'm guessing you'd advise against parenthood?" Casey said.

Everett felt the smile warm his face. How could he explain his feelings to his brother? Being a new dad was scary. In a good way. It was like being on a roller coaster that he never wanted to get off.

All those times recently when his mind had been

preoccupied with adult worries, like how they would they fit everything into the apartment or what was going on with the investigation. Then he'd look down and see her tiny hand in his and wonder how it was possible to have come to care for another person so much in such a short time.

"No. Just the opposite. Hearing Kennedy laugh when I tickle her makes it all worthwhile. Her big, cheeky grin warms my heart and, even though I'm so tired I don't know what day it is most of the time, I'm loving all these new experiences."

"And Alyssa?"

"Oh, she adored Kennedy from the moment she saw her. And she's better at being a parent than I am."

Casey shook his head. "Yeah. If it makes you feel better, you can pretend that's what I meant."

Chapter Six

The linen closet was located next to the bathroom. When Everett opened the door on the following evening, it was like he was in the wrong apartment.

"Alyssa?" When he called her name, she emerged from the kitchen. "Where did all these towels come from?"

"I bought some new ones."

"Why? There were already plenty of towels."

"There were *enough* towels. For one person." She gave him a pitying look. "Although some of them were past their best. Now you have enough towels for two adults and a baby, plus a few spares in case we have guests."

He snorted. "If we have guests, we are going to need to get rid of the towels so they can stay in the linen closet. And why do we have those little fancy towels on the shelf over the bath?"

"They're for decoration."

He started to laugh. "We can't move in this place because of all the baby stuff and Christmas decorations, but you decided what we really needed to make our lives easier was some decorative towels?"

"Just make sure you don't use them." She whisked past him with an armful of laundry. "Where do you keep your iron?"

An hour later, he was watching her arrange his shirts on hangers, while listening to a lecture about the correct way to fold socks. It was like entering a scary parallel universe.

"I get it. From now on, I will hang my work shirts in the same direction and color-code my T-shirts." He gave her a smile. "Are you trying to domesticate me, Lyss?"

He'd seen this happen with enough colleagues. They moved in with a partner or got married, and the complaints started. *She moves my stuff. I can't just drop things on the floor anymore. She changes the sheets before they even* look *dirty.* Then came the acceptance. *It's kind of nice to know where everything is. A clean washcloth every day* is *the way to go. Never going back to the old sniff-'em-and-see sock test.*

If Everett was honest, he was enjoying this introduction to domesticity. He just couldn't resist the temptation to tease her a little.

She bit her lip. "Was I coming on too strong? I just like things organized."

He draped an arm around her shoulders. "You may just have met your biggest challenge."

From the glint in her eye, it was possible he had just said the wrong thing.

A few minutes later, he heard an exclamation of annoyance from the kitchen. When he went in there,

Alyssa pointed to the dishwasher. "It didn't close properly. Again. So it hasn't completed the cycle. We need to call the landlord or get someone to fix it."

"Or I can get my tools and do it."

She gave him an interested look. "You have tools?"

He waggled his eyebrows at her. "Many. I just don't have anywhere to keep them in this itty-bitty space. Fortunately, there is a tool shed downstairs for the use of all tenants. I'll go get them."

When he returned, he pulled off his shirt. The job was simple and undemanding, but he'd seen the light in Alyssa's eyes when she said "tools." She'd always liked his muscles, and… Oh, hell. What was he thinking? Now he felt like a jerk.

"Can I watch?" She hoisted herself onto the counter. *Maybe not such a jerk…*

He could see the problem immediately. Would it be wrong to exploit the situation by stringing it out a little? It wasn't every day he got to feel like a blue-collar god in front of the woman of his dreams. Lying on the floor on his back, he spent some time explaining to Alyssa exactly what he was doing. She leaned over, listening intently. Damn, she looked beautiful when she was upside down.

Finally, Everett reached the point where he couldn't keep procrastinating. He clipped the seal on the door back in place, put his tools back in their box and got to his feet. Alyssa slid from the counter, standing inches in front of him.

"I can't believe we were together all that time and I never knew you could do things like that."

The glowing look in her eyes embarrassed him. "It's just a kitchen appliance. No big deal."

"It is to me. I've paid hundreds of dollars for similar jobs," she said. "You must be thirsty now. Let me get you some water."

She went to the fridge and brought him a glass. As she handed it to him, her hand shook slightly and some of the icy liquid spilled down his chest. Everett sucked in a breath. Alyssa's eyes widened as they dropped to his abs.

Totally worth removing the T-shirt.

"Oh, hey…let me get you a towel." They both started to laugh. "Not a decorative one."

ALYSSA NOTICED THAT Everett was endlessly fascinated by Kennedy's sense of humor.

"She's only been on this planet for half a year, but she knows when something is funny," he said to her. "Watch this."

Abandoning her attempt to make a casserole, she came to sit on the rug beside him. Everett handed his car keys to the baby, who jangled and chewed them happily. When Everett tried to take them back, Kennedy appeared to be about to willingly hand them over. Then, at the last minute, she whipped them away again quickly, all the while watching his face with a mischievous grin.

"She's teasing me." He shook his head. "She's so tiny, yet she knows that's amusing."

Watching them together brought Alyssa a level of joy she'd never dreamed of just a few weeks ago. They had become obsessed with Kennedy in such a short time and seeing her growing and learning new things every day deepened their family bond. Their little girl had been given a tough start, but when she was with them, she was their chubby-cheeked, doll-wristed darling. And she was loving life.

"This is what we wanted for her."

As Everett nodded, Kennedy grabbed his finger and pulled it toward his mouth. "Hey, it's not dinner time—Ouch!"

"What happened?"

"She bit me." He withdrew his finger and held it up. "Look." There was a faint red mark on the tip.

"Kennedy, do you have a tooth? You're such a clever girl."

"Clever?" Everett examined his finger. "She almost drew blood."

Alyssa rolled her eyes but was too busy trying to get a look inside Kennedy's mouth to take much notice. The baby, clearly deciding this was some sort of new game, determinedly clamped her jaw closed and refused to open her mouth.

She gestured to Everett. "Give her the keys again."

He handed them over, so Kennedy grabbed them and waved them around gleefully. After a moment, she lifted them to her mouth and Alyssa pounced. "I can't see any tooth."

"I suppose you think I did this to myself?" Everett raised his finger again.

"Maybe you already had a mark?" Alyssa gave him a sympathetic glance. "Her gums are really hard. She can hurt when she tries."

Just then, there was an unmistakable clunking noise from the direction of Kennedy's mouth. "I'm probably imagining that," Everett said.

Carefully, Alyssa slid her finger along the baby's bottom gum. "There." She took another peek inside. "It's like a tiny grain of rice."

"With a razor edge—" As Alyssa shoved him hard in the ribs, Everett toppled over. Lying on his side, he looked up at her with laughter in his eyes. "Is this how it's going to be from now on? Two girls against one guy?"

"If you don't stop being such a wuss, this is exactly how it will be," she said. "I need to finish making this casserole. Do you think you will be able to change Kennedy's diaper? I know you're injured…"

He lunged for her, preparing to tickle her, but she ducked out of his way. Laughing, she got to her feet and headed for the kitchen.

HAVING RECLAIMED HIS KEYS, Everett carried Kennedy through to the changing table in the bedroom. Giving her a toy to distract her, he commenced the routine of removing her sweatpants. What he saw when he removed her used diaper had him reeling back in shock.

"Alyssa, I need you to get in here now." He'd wanted it to be a forceful shout. It was more of a croak. He tried again. "Lyss!"

She came running, obviously summoned by the note of pure panic. Staring at the baby in horror, she clutched his arm. "What happened?"

"Nothing." His hand shook as he raked his fingers

through his hair. "I just undid her diaper and that's what I found."

Kennedy, who was lying in a diaper soaked in blood, grinned up at them and babbled delightedly. She didn't seem to be in any pain.

"I don't know what's wrong with her, but we need to get her to the ER. Right now." Thoughts of serious infant illnesses filled his mind, dragging him down into dark places. Kennedy looked fine, but the crimson mess in her diaper was telling a whole other story.

Whatever it took. They would get her through this. She was their little girl and the three of them were in this together.

"Wait." Alyssa was way too calm for this situation. "Baby poop and pee often comes out the same color as the food that went in."

"You think she drank a blood smoothie when we weren't looking?"

"No, but she did have beet puree for her lunch."

"Lyss." He bent over with the force of his exhale. "You really think she's okay?"

The scary moment receded, but the knee-knocking, heart-pounding reality was even more terrifying. Kennedy was so vulnerable, and the world was full of bad things just waiting to happen to her. The knowledge that he would be powerless to stop some of them was like a punch in the gut.

"I really do." Alyssa stepped forward and deftly removed the disgusting diaper.

"I didn't know parenthood would be like this. Good

or bad, we're responsible for everything that happens to her."

She looked up from the task of cleaning up Kennedy. "It's scary, isn't it?"

He straightened, feeling the panic receding. "But worth it. Did you know how much you'd love her?"

Her eyes were bright as she shook her head. "I guess nothing could have prepared us for that. But at least, in future, we'll be ready for the beet poop."

ALYSSA PURSED HER lips as she studied the new storage bins she'd purchased for Kennedy's belongings.

"Patty Griffiths said she had brought the basics from Kennedy's home. The truth is, someone must have gone to the Dodds' house, grabbed handfuls of clothing and thrown them into those boxes. A lot of this stuff is way too small for her and we just don't have room for it here."

"What do you suggest?" Everett asked.

She was serving lunch: homemade tomato soup with chunks of cornbread. Everett had suggested covering the whole apartment in a plastic sheet before they attempted to feed the baby. Although, as long as they avoided beet puree, he was willing to give anything a try. While she waited, Kennedy was playing her favorite game of throwing her spoon on the floor.

"I think we need some information from Ray Torrington about our status. We have custody of Kennedy, but who are her trustees? It's clear that she has been left a substantial amount of money. Who will ensure that it is invested wisely until she is old enough to take control of it herself? You and Casey have talked about the house that she owns. What will happen to it? It can't be allowed to fall into ruin." She carried bowls from the kitchen to the table. "We were so blindsided by the custody issue that we didn't consider these other things."

"You got all that from thinking about her clothes?"

"I got all that from thinking I'd like to go to the Dodds' house and sort out Kennedy's belongings. I need to get rid of all the things that are too small and make sure she has enough of everything in the right size." She took the seat next to his. "You know me. I like to plan ahead."

You know me.

The simple phrase hung in the air between them. She wasn't the easiest person to get close to, but he knew her better than anyone. Even though he'd taken a peek into her heart, he'd stuck around. She'd told him about her father's murder and how scared that made her that she'd lose someone else in a similar way. He knew how she'd struggled to connect to her mom, the woman who hadn't wanted to stay alive once the man she loved was gone. He'd dried her tears and held her through the nightmares.

Their gazes remained locked together for too long. Alyssa was finding it difficult to breathe, difficult to do anything other than lean a little closer. As she did, Kennedy let out a demanding squawk, the message clear.

Hungry baby requires attention.

"Do you have protective clothing? I'm thinking a reinforced face shield would come in useful about now," Everett said.

Alyssa pulled a face at him and placed a bowl of soup on the tray of Kennedy's high chair.

"At least take the spoon away."

"I've been reading up on this. It's important for her to learn as early as possible—"

She broke off as Kennedy brought the spoon down into the center of the bowl. Red liquid sprayed upward in a jet, most of it landing directly on Alyssa. She gasped and tried to wipe the worst of her homemade tomato soup out of her hair and eyes. Everett jumped up to help.

"Get the spoon off her." Through a soupy mist, Alyssa could see the baby preparing for a replay.

He lunged but missed by a split second. With baby-perfect timing, Kennedy picked up her bowl. "Oh, no you—" Crimson bloomed in the center of his chest as the bowl hit him then dropped to the floor. "If that was deliberate, the Cactus Creek Divas are going to want to give you a tryout in about sixteen years."

"She's six months old. It was a lucky shot. Can we have less talk of ladies' softball and more cleaning?" Alyssa could feel soup running from her sweater into her jeans and underwear.

"I've been to murder scenes that are less gory. And as for you, young lady…" Kennedy fluttered her eye-lashes at him, and he sighed. "You eat your cornbread."

Everett pulled his sweatshirt over his head, then dropped it to the floor. He grabbed a few of Kennedy's baby wipes and turned to Alyssa.

"Hold still." He gripped her chin and tilted her face up to his. "You have soup on your eyelashes."

In all those empty years, when she had fantasized about Everett Colton's muscular chest, he had murmured many different words as he leaned close. Some had been romantic. Some erotic. Some had featured heart-stopping accounts of what he would like to do to her once he got her into the bedroom. *You have soup on your eyelashes?* No. Not once had her overactive imagination featured him uttering that phrase.

Still got you weak at the knees, didn't it?

Gently, he wiped the soup from her eyes, then moved on to the rest of her face. Alyssa held still. His touch ignited so many memories; she could stay like this all day.

"You go get a shower while I clean up here." Now *those* words had featured in some of her Everett-related fantasies… Heat bloomed in her cheeks as she opened her eyes and blinked at him.

He studied her face. "You okay, Lyss?"

"Yeah." *Just picturing you naked.* "I'll, uh…" She jerked a thumb over her shoulder toward the bathroom.

"Hey. So the spoon thing went wrong. Look at her." They turned to look at Kennedy, who was tearing chunks off her cornbread. For each one that went into her mouth, two more were carefully dropped onto the floor. Everett turned Alyssa back to face him. "You're doing a great job."

He dropped a light kiss onto the tip of her nose.

It meant nothing to him. Just the same sort of kiss he'd give Kennedy.

That was what she told herself as she headed to the bathroom. The problem was she now had heat in her lower regions that had nothing to do with soup.

LUCKILY, ALYSSA'S CLOTHES had arrived from Phoenix on the previous day. Although it meant they had to cram yet more items into the already overcrowded, overdecorated apartment, she at least had plenty of outfit changes. With Kennedy around, it was a bonus.

When she emerged after her shower, she was wearing tight-fitting jeans tucked into boots and a cornflower-blue sweater that highlighted every curve and reminded Everett that he was a red-blooded male. Not that he'd needed prompts lately. After four years of wondering if there might be something wrong with him, his sexual urges had been back in working order.

Working order? You mean "overdrive."

Which meant he had a problem. He'd pretty much already figured it out, but there was no ignoring it now. He was a one-woman man. And that woman was right across the room from him, swinging Kennedy up into her arms and laughing about her being a tomato-soup monster.

Alyssa had already made it clear she couldn't contemplate a future with a man whose job put him in danger. That left Everett with a stark choice. He could have a half life with Alyssa, sharing responsibility for Kennedy, caring for her and watching her grow up, while keeping his true feelings buried. Or he could give up the job he loved. Just as he was in line for a promotion.

Having just gone through one major upheaval, he was probably not in the right frame of mind for a second life-changing decision. With Alyssa looking so tempting, he was having trouble making up his mind about leaving the room.

"I'll go clean up and then we can pay Ray Torrington a visit."

"Should I call his office first?" Alyssa asked.

"Trust me." He grinned. "Years of law-enforcement training have taught me it's best to just turn up."

Forty minutes later, Ray Torrington rose from behind the desk as his receptionist showed them into his office. He looked down at Kennedy, who was asleep in her stroller. "You agreed to the terms of the will. You can't just return her like an unwanted gift."

Although they weren't touching, Everett felt every line of Alyssa's trim figure stiffen. Since he was instantly equally tense, he understood her response perfectly. "We have no intention of parting with our *daughter*, Mr. Torrington."

"Oh." He looked sheepish. "I just... Won't you sit down?"

They sat in the same chairs they'd used at their last visit and, although it had only been days earlier, Everett couldn't help reflecting on how much his life had changed in that short time. He watched as Alyssa tucked the baby's blanket more tightly around her. She was a natural mom. It had taken him longer to adjust but he liked to think he was getting there.

"There are some things we want to ask you about the will." He fixed his gaze on the lawyer's face. Some people just made him suspicious. Ray Torrington was one of them. "Specifically, what arrangements were made for Kennedy's financial future?"

"I'm not sure I understand the question." The lawyer had "shifty" written all over him; he showed an his inability to make eye contact and made nervous hand gestures.

"When we came in here the other day, you read us the part of the will that dealt with custody of Kennedy. That was, of course, important. But Sean and Delilah must have made other provisions. You said that there was one beneficiary. If Kennedy is that person, she is too young to manage her own finances. Delilah was a skilled accountant. She would have known the best way to provide for her child's future as she was grow- ing up. I would assume that the Dodds named a trustee, or trustees, to care for their daughter's estate until she was old enough to do it herself."

As Everett was talking, Ray moved restlessly in his seat. Was it possible the lawyer had been hoping to de- fraud Kennedy? Everett wouldn't put it past him. A glance in Alyssa's direction told him she was thinking the exact same thing.

"Mr. Torrington, is there a legal mechanism by which we can get an order to see the whole will?"

Everett had never heard that tone in her voice be- fore. It was like ice tinkling in a glass. Motherhood had clearly aroused new and dangerous protective in- stincts in her.

"That won't be necessary, Miss Bartholomew." Ray's shoulders slumped. "I will provide you with a full copy, including the information you require. I am one of Ken- nedy Dodd's trustees." The next words came out on something resembling a snarl. "Agent Colton here is the other one."

"That's kind of an important piece of information.

You must have forgotten to mention it to us when we met before." There were few things Everett disliked more than a crooked lawyer. Ray was going to pay for this blatant attempt to cheat Kennedy. In a few days, agents from the FBI fraud team would be crawling all over his paperwork like ants.

"I assumed the custody issue would be your first priority and that everything else could wait." Ray tented his fingers beneath his chin and leaned back in his seat. A nasty grin crossed his face. "It may soon be unimportant, anyway."

"Why is that?"

"Sean's sister, Georgia Dodd, is contesting the will. She is hoping to inherit her brother and sister-in-law's estate *and* gain custody of her niece."

IT WAS LIKE going back in time. Ten-year-old Alyssa had experienced this same uncertainty over her future. It had been worse back then, of course. Her dad had been dead, and her mom had been unable to cope with her grief.

The parallels with Kennedy's situation hit her again. Thankfully, the little girl was too young to know what was going on.

Even so, as she walked to the car at Everett's side, fear wrapped around her like a prickly old rug. Just as she was learning to love Kennedy and her new family, it could all be snatched away.

A strong hand gripped her elbow. "Let's get into the car. The forecast is for snow and, although it's rare in this area, and only likely to be a few flakes, the temperature is dropping."

Turning her head to look at him, she registered the look of concern on his face. "A white Christmas in southern Arizona? We don't get many of those." Her attempt at a smile wasn't a complete failure.

"You wanted it to be perfect for Kennedy." Her smile faded and he shook his head. "Georgia is in *prison*, Alyssa. No court will let her near Kennedy. Not this Christmas. Not any time in the future."

Working together, they got the sleeping baby out of her stroller and into the car seat. In a short time, they'd perfected the routine. While Everett stowed the stroller in the trunk, Alyssa covered Kennedy with a blanket. Within minutes, they were ready to go.

"Do you still want to go to the Dodds' house?" Everett asked.

What she really wanted to do was drive as fast as they could back to his apartment, run inside, lock the door and never come out again. Just the three of them. She would protect that with everything she had. It was a thought so fierce it rocked her back in her seat.

They hadn't planned this new life, but they were making it their own, and it was working. Better than that. It was good. Georgia wasn't going to take it away from them.

"Yes." She gave a determined nod. "Why should we change our plans for her? Georgia has no control over our lives."

He gave her an approving glance. "There's just one

thing that bothers me. How much do you think Kennedy remembers about her time there?"

"I hadn't thought about it." She frowned. "Do you think taking her back there might bring back memories of Sean and Delilah?"

"I don't know how much a six-month-old child can remember. Even if she recognizes the house, will she associate it with her parents? Does she have any sense of missing them?" Everett mused. "We've been focused on her physical care, but we may also need to think about the emotional trauma she has been through."

"At least she wasn't in the house the night they died. It sounds like the events leading to their deaths were so harrowing they could have imprinted themselves into the mind of even such a young child," Alyssa said. "If we take her into the house and she shows any sign of being troubled, we can always leave. I only want to drop off these clothes that are too small and pick up some larger ones."

They drove through Cactus Creek in silence. Once the town had been left behind, they were on a long stretch of straight, narrow highway with craggy hills rising on either side. Before long, a sign indicated the turn for the Old West Fairway.

"The Fairway is an exclusive golf club, established in the canyon basin about eighty years ago," Everett said. "My dad and most of his hospital colleagues are members. In recent years, a number of luxury houses have been built on the edge of the canyon with views over the course."

"Luxury houses?" Alyssa raised her eyebrows. "Casey described the Dodds' home as 'a neat property.'"

"I think you'll find my brother was understating the case." There was a wry twist to his lips as he drove past the entrance to the golf club and along a private road.

Intrigued, Alyssa watched the scenery roll past for a few minutes. When they reached a set of ornamental gates, Everett used the electronic fob Ray Torrington had given him. The gates slid open and they entered a different world.

"Is this...?" Alyssa turned wide eyes in Everett's direction.

"Kennedy's home? Yes. This is Paradise Palms."

"But it's a mansion." As Everett halted the car in front of the house, she leaned forward to get a closer look. The brick-built, two-story property was centered on a courtyard with a mosaic-tiled fountain in front.

"Six bedrooms and seven bathrooms," Everett said. "All of the entertaining rooms have access to the outdoors and views of the canyon. When Sean and Delilah bought the place there was an infinity pool, a golf simulator, a basketball court and a fitness center with a steam room. They added a games room, a home theater and an outdoor kitchen."

"If you lost touch with Sean, how do you know all this?" Alyssa asked as they got out of the car.

"I told you how competitive we were with each other. There was no way Sean was going to let this slip by me. He sent me an email with details of the house and a one-sentence message." Everett looked up at the beautiful property with a slight smile on his face. "It said 'Enjoy your two-bedroom apartment, G-man.'"

"G-man?" She lifted Kennedy, who stirred slightly in her sleep, from the vehicle.

"It's a slang term, meaning 'government man.' It refers to employees of the US government, specifically FBI agents. Sean always used it in a derogatory way."

"Well, at least your two-bedroom apartment was paid for with honest, hard-earned cash." There was a touch of heat in her voice as she thought of the way in which Sean had earned his money. How dare he sneer at Everett? "If this was purchased with laundered money, shouldn't have been forfeited to the government?"

"If you look at Sean's accounts, I'm sure you'd find this place was purchased honestly, too."

She snorted. "Delilah must have been mightily creative if she pulled that off."

He took Kennedy from her and placed the little girl in her stroller. "She was. Her role in the family business was to make sure the financial side of things was legal. She couldn't have foreseen what was going to happen, but she made sure her daughter's future was secure. What matters now is that we protect Kennedy's inheritance."

His words gave her a sudden chill. "She is already in danger. I don't know why, but Ray Torrington tried to trick us by not informing us of the true details of the will. Now Georgia is attempting to have the will overturned. Those are the two sources that we know of. What if neither of them is responsible for the threats we've been getting?"

"I've already thought about that. In my job, you make enemies." He took her hand and placed it next to his on the handle of the stroller. "But Kennedy has us to take care of her. Together, we'll make sure nothing bad happens." From his pocket, he withdrew the bunch of keys Ray had given him. "Are you ready?"

She placed her fingers over his, feeling the strength and warmth of his hand. Were there any certainties in life? Sean and Delilah had stepped outside the law in an attempt to buy happiness and had died horribly. Alyssa's own method was to turn her back on anything that might bring her hurt. The result had been four years of misery.

Looking up at the beautiful house, the scene of so much drama, she wondered if the best way was to let fate take its course.

"Let's do this."

Chapter Seven

"Kennedy had her own *suite*?" Alyssa turned a full circle in the vast room. When she faced Everett again, she started to laugh. "We could fit our whole apartment in here and still have space to let her have a puppy and a pony."

He paused for a moment to consider how much he liked hearing her say "*our* apartment." Yeah. Maybe he liked it a little too much.

"Do you have house envy, Alyssa?"

She shook her head. Hard. "No. I would not want this lifestyle. Not knowing it was bought with stolen money."

Even though her childhood had been tough, Alyssa's moral code was unshakable. Before his death, her dad had passed on his strong sense of right and wrong. Despite her own struggles, her mom had kept those values alive. Contrasting that with Sean and Delilah, who had taken the easy way and opted for a life of crime, Everett spared a thought for the tiny figure in the stroller.

Kennedy's life with him and Alyssa would be so much richer, because it would be about more than money.

There was a small dressing room off the main nursery, and they found what they were looking for in there. Two whole walls were taken up with drawers and rails that were filled with baby clothing. Clearly, Delilah had believed in planning ahead, because there were items still in their packaging that wouldn't fit Kennedy for several months. A glimpse at the price tags was enough to make Everett's eyes water.

Quickly, Alyssa transferred the smaller items they had brought with them to the drawers, exchanging them for clothing that would fit Kennedy now.

"It seems such a waste to just leave them here." She was kneeling on the expensive rug, looking up at Everett, as she placed onesies in a drawer. "I wonder if we could donate them to a nonprofit organization in Cactus Creek?"

"As one of the trustees of Kennedy's estate, I think it's something we should look into," he said. "My mom would definitely know of families in need who could use some."

As he spoke, Kennedy, who had napped for longer than usual, gave a whimper and opened her eyes.

"Hey, there, sleepyhead." Alyssa went to her and the baby blinked at her in confusion. "Are you hungry?"

"Silly question." Everett reached into the pink-elephant bag for the thermos that kept Kennedy's formula at the right temperature. "This little lady is always hungry."

For once, Kennedy decided to prove him wrong. When he offered her the bottle, she fussily turned her head from side to side, all the while uttering soft cries.

"Maybe she's uncomfortable in the stroller and wants to be held?" Alyssa suggested. "There is a chair in the nursery. I'll take her through there."

As soon as she released the baby from the stroller, Kennedy clung to her like a monkey, twisting her hands into Alyssa's hair and burying her face in her neck. Bemused, Alyssa exchanged a glance with Everett.

"Could she be confused because she fell asleep in one place and woke up in another? It might all feel strange to her, even as though she's in the middle of a dream."

He accompanied her through to the nursery. "Or is it possible she's remembering this place?"

Alyssa sat in the rocking chair that had been placed near the wide windows. Cradling Kennedy close, she tried to get the little girl to take some of her formula. Although the baby seemed happy to be snuggled, she refused to take her formula.

"She's not happy. All she wants to do is hide her face. If she has memories of this as her home, surely they would be pleasant ones? We know how much her mom and dad loved her."

Everett leaned over and stroked Kennedy's head. "We've got what we came for. If Kennedy's unhappy, the reason doesn't matter. Let's go."

Alyssa carried the baby while Everett pushed the stroller. The bags of clothing were stashed in the shopping basket in the stroller's base. Quickly, they made their way back toward the front entrance, heading along the wide central hall. When they drew level with the state-of-the-art kitchen, Kennedy gave a high-pitched cry that pierced Everett's heart.

"What is it, sweetie?" Although Alyssa spoke soothingly to the baby as she looked at Everett, her expression was one of concern. "She's trembling all over."

Kennedy was screaming in earnest now, the sound like a siren signaling fear and distress. Over and over.

"Her face, Everett. Look at her face."

The tiny features were bright red and balled up tight, but it was Kennedy's eyes that drew his attention. She was staring into the kitchen. With a look of horror, her gaze was fixed on the table in the center of the room.

"Don't you see what this means? Kennedy was here." Alyssa tucked the little girl's face into her chest and started to walk quickly toward the door. "She was in this house the night her parents died."

ONCE THEY GOT HOME, it took Alyssa about an hour to comfort Kennedy. Holding her close, rocking her, singing to her—all of those things gradually relaxed the baby's tense muscles and she eventually fell asleep again.

When she placed her in her crib, Alyssa watched over her for a few minutes before going to the kitchen. Everett observed her closely as she poured herself a glass of water.

She may as well say it before he did. "You think I'm making it up."

"I didn't say that. It's just… Can a child as young

as Kennedy really be trusted to remember a bad experience?"

"You saw what she was like." Alyssa tilted her chin determinedly. "You can't tell me that was a normal reaction."

"I guess not." He ran a hand through his hair. "But I don't know what we can do about it."

"I need to make a call."

She went through to the living room and retrieved her purse from the table. Rummaging inside, she found the card Patty Griffiths had given her. Although it was late in the afternoon, she hoped the child-care worker would still be available.

Sure enough, Patty answered her call almost immediately. "Patty? It's Alyssa Bartholomew. We met in Raymond Torrington's office when I took custody of Kennedy Dodd."

"I remember." Patty sounded pleased to hear from her. "I think about little Kennedy a lot and wonder how she's getting along these days."

"She's doing really well. This may seem odd, but I'm calling with a general child-welfare question. It could be something you can't answer, or you may be able to direct me to one of your colleagues who could assist me with it."

"I'll do my best to help." Alyssa could hear a trace of bewilderment in the other woman's voice.

"I'm wondering if a very young baby—say one aged about six months—would be able to remember a traumatic event?"

"Ah, now that's an interesting question," Patty said.

"Most people are under the impression that infants don't recall distressing incidents. But this has recently been disproved by child mental-health specialists. New research shows that even very young babies can later remember episodes that scared them, and they will leave a lasting impression."

"It sounds like this is an area of expertise for you?" Alyssa said.

"I'm doing a part-time degree in child psychology and I've studied infant trauma as a cause of extreme separation anxiety. If you need any more information, let me know."

After she ended the call, Alyssa relayed the details of the conversation to Everett.

"This is too much." He slumped onto one of the sofas, rubbing his temples with the tips of his fingers. "If Kennedy was in the house, that means Georgia was lying about looking after her for the whole night. The first cop on the scene at the house reported that there was no sign of the baby, and Casey, who knew the family circumstances, suggested contacting Georgia. She confirmed that Kennedy was with her. There's only one reason I can think of for her to lie."

"You think Georgia needed Kennedy to be her alibi?" She sucked in a breath, trying to loosen the tightness in her chest. "Because Georgia was the one who killed Sean and Delilah?"

"It looks that way, but how will I ever prove it?" Everett groaned. "It's not like Kennedy's testimony will stand up in court."

Alyssa sat next to him, curling into a corner of the

sofa. Kennedy's distress earlier in the day had been heart-wrenching. The little girl had been beyond upset and watching her suffer had been devastating. Trying to process this new development on top of that was using up all her emotional resources.

"Being in the house upset her, but it was when she looked *into* the kitchen that she became really triggered," she said.

Everett sat up straighter. "Of course. If the baby was in her room, how would she know if anything bad was going on elsewhere in the house? Kennedy had to have been *in* the kitchen with her parents when the disturbance took place."

"Oh, my goodness." Alyssa raised a shaking hand to her mouth. "You're right. Our poor little darling must have witnessed the whole thing."

"Wait." He slammed a fist down onto the cushion at his side. "What did Patty Griffiths say at our first meeting with her in Ray's office? When she came into the care of the Department of Child Safety, Kennedy had recently started eating solid food."

Alyssa picked up his train of thought. "Which means, if she was in the kitchen, she'd have been in her high chair."

"I need to find out which officer was the first to check out the house after the bodies were found." He reached for his cell phone. "And if any photographs were taken."

While he made a few calls, Alyssa went to check on Kennedy. The baby was sleeping soundly, her breathing regular and her temperature normal. Tears briefly blurred Alyssa's vision as she gazed down at the sweet face with its fluffy halo of hair.

She had already acknowledged that there would come a point in the future when they would need to handle the issue of what had happened to Kennedy's birth parents. The photograph of Sean and Delilah was in its usual position beside the crib. It was another reminder, if they needed one, of how much Kennedy had been loved.

Losing her mom and dad at such a young age had been bad enough. But had she seen the events leading up to their demise? Alyssa had been ten when her own father's death had caused the emotional scars that had affected her all the way into adult life. What sort of impact could a similar trauma have on a fragile baby?

"We'll get through it together." The bonds that bound her to Kennedy drew even tighter. "The three of us."

EVERETT WATCHED IN amazement as Kennedy devoured a second bowl of oatmeal. "I think we can safely say her appetite hasn't been affected."

After sleeping for several hours, the baby had woken in a cheerful mood and appeared to have forgotten her earlier distress. The only difference in her behavior was a tendency to get tearful if she couldn't see both Everett and Alyssa at all times.

"Casey is coming over with Bob Andrews. He's a deputy in the Sur County Sheriff's Department and he was assigned to go to the Dodds' house after the bodies were found. I figured he would be the best person to tell us exactly what the scene looked like that night."

As he spoke, he used a baby wipe to get as much oatmeal as he could out of Kennedy's hair. Watching him, the little girl chuckled and batted her eyelashes at him.

Alyssa placed apple slices on the tray in front of Kennedy. After checking that the baby was engrossed in her food, she moved away slightly, indicating that Everett should follow her.

"I know she can't understand what we're saying, but I don't like talking about these things if she can overhear us." She smiled fondly as Kennedy used one chubby fist to pound apple into mush. "I just..." She crossed her arms over her body as though fending off a chill. "I'm having a hard time picturing how it happened, you know? How do you kill someone by getting them to drive their car into a wall?"

As he stepped close, he could see the tension in her jaw and the tightness in the fine muscles around her eyes. Alyssa, who had always turned away from danger, was being forced to confront it head-on. Although she was finding it tough, he was amazed by the inner strength she was developing. Imagining a murder scene was about as far from the peaceful life she had created for herself as it was possible to get, but, for Kennedy's sake, she was prepared to face this nightmare and defeat Georgia.

Drawing her into a hug, he ran his hands along her shoulders. A shudder ran through her slender body and she rested her head against his chest.

"It's a question I've thought about a lot, but it's best not to torture yourself with trying to picture what went on," he said. "One thing I've learned is that murderers can be creative. If we're right, and Georgia is guilty, that's all we need to know. The details will all become clear once she's charged with their murders."

She tilted her head to look at him. "You sound so confident."

"As confident as I was that time I tried walking a tightrope on Valentine's."

Her laughter rang out immediately, just as he'd hoped it would. "I'd forgotten about that."

He placed a hand over his heart. "Forgotten? That was my finest hour, Lyss, and it was all for you."

"Ah, yes." Her eyes twinkled deliciously. "There you were. Poised like an orangutan in a safety harness, wobbling six inches above the padded floor, with a rose between your teeth—"

"You just don't know how to appreciate a romantic gesture."

He moved his hand up to lightly tug her ponytail. It was a familiar, teasing action, but it took on a new meaning in that instant. Sparks flew between them and Alyssa's eyes widened as they both moved closer...then jerked quickly apart at the sound of the security buzzer.

"I should, uh—" Alyssa pointed to Kennedy. "While you—" She gestured to the door.

Equally flustered, Everett waited until his breathing had returned to normal before he pressed the button for the speakerphone.

"It's Casey. Take your time." Even the electronic system couldn't disguise the sarcasm in his twin's tone.

When he opened the door, Casey was accompanied by another man in uniform.

"This is Bob Andrews." Casey had to raise his voice above the commotion coming from the direction of the high chair.

As soon as she'd seen the two men, Kennedy had started to cry. By the time Alyssa had unfastened her from the chair, the tears had turned to full-blown screams.

"My sister adopted a baby boy," Bob sympathized. "He was the same whenever he saw a stranger. What did she call it? Separation anxiety."

Alyssa cuddled the baby close. "But we were strangers to her when she came to us and she didn't act like this."

"My nephew had been abducted when he was a baby. There were triggers that reminded him about it, and he'd get anxious and refuse to leave my sister." He offered a reassuring smile. "He's just started kindergarten and is fine now."

Kennedy was gradually calming down in Alyssa's embrace. What Bob was saying fitted with what they'd seen earlier that day. She now saw Everett and Alyssa as her caregivers, but was aware of a time when something bad had happened to others who had been in those roles. The visit to her former home had reminded her of that event and clinging to the people who made her feel safe was her way of acting out her distress.

It felt like further confirmation that Kennedy had been at the house on the night of her parents' deaths. Everett felt his determination harden. He would do whatever it took to get to the truth.

He served coffee and they sat at the table. Kennedy

chewed on her teething toy, watching the strangers cautiously from the safety of Alyssa's lap.

"First off, I wanted to let you know that I checked back through the records to see if there were any domestic-disturbance calls involving Sean and Delilah during the period when they were together," Casey said. "And the results came back negative."

"That supports what we already believe. The Dodds might have been criminals, but they had a loving relationship," Everett said. "Unless they had problems that went unreported to the police."

"Casey explained that you want to know what I saw when I went to the Dodds' house on the night they died." Bob gave an apologetic shrug. "I don't know if there's much I can add to the investigating officer's report."

"You described plates of food on the floor and overturned chairs," Everett said. "We're more interested in how the table was set out. I don't suppose you took photographs?"

"Not of the table. I have pictures of the mess, the smashed plates and the chairs that had been tipped over." Bob reached into his top pocket and drew out a notebook. "I do have the quick sketch that I did at the time, if that helps?"

Everett nodded. "Yeah. That will be really useful."

Bob flipped through the pages until he found the one he wanted. Placing it in a position on the table where they could all see it, he pointed to the rough diagram. "I'm not much of an artist. These are the chairs that had been flipped over, and here are the plates on the floor. You can see that I've indicated the other chairs that were left in position."

Alyssa leaned forward and pointed to a smaller square at one end of the table. "What was this?"

He leaned closer to get a better look at his own drawing. "That? Oh, that was the baby's high chair."

EVERETT HELD UP a hand, silencing the burst of conversation that had broken out around him. "Unless we can prove that Kennedy was actually in her high chair that night, Bob's sketch means nothing."

Alyssa frowned. "You saw that house. It was a designer's paradise. Baby items would spoil the look of the place. That high chair wouldn't be in the kitchen unless the baby was eating with her parents."

He pointed to the high chair Kennedy had recently vacated at their own table. "We leave that in the same place all the time. Maybe Sean and Delilah did the same."

"Your approach to interior design is laid-back," Casey said. "The Dodds' place, on the other hand, was done by a famous designer who'd won awards."

"None of that matters," Everett insisted. "No jury in their right mind would accept this sketch as evidence that Kennedy was actually there."

Alyssa huffed out a breath. "But she *was* there. We know it because of the way she reacted when she saw the kitchen. We don't know if her parents were killed there but we know she saw something bad happen that night."

"We have to prove it." He lightly touched the back of her hand. "Beyond doubt."

Silence fell as they drank their coffee and considered the situation.

"The Dodds had a cleaner who came in each day," Casey said. "I'll ask her if the high chair stayed in place, or if it was only brought out at meal times."

"That's a useful line of inquiry." Everett turned to Bob. "What about the photographs? Do you have copies?"

"I deleted them from my cell phone, in line with department policy, but I emailed them to Captain Forman, the investigating officer." Bob cast a sidelong glance in Casey's direction. "I could access them through my emails, but I don't know if I should get permission first."

Casey rolled his eyes. "Everett is FBI. How long do you think it will take him to bypass the sheriff's department and get those pictures?"

Bob hesitated for a moment longer, looking from one twin to the other. Finally, he retrieved his cell from his pocket.

"Because I wanted to show that there had been a disturbance in the house, the only pictures I took were of the chairs that had been tipped over, the broken plates and the food on the floor. There are two of them."

He handed the phone to Everett. Alyssa leaned closer, studying the screen with him. She could understand why Bob had wanted to capture these images. There were eight high-backed chairs around the marble table, four on each side. With the high chair in position at one end, two places had been set for dinner, one on either side of the baby's seat. Alyssa pointed that out to Everett, and he nodded, his expression grim. If the high chair wasn't being used that night, why had Sean and Delilah chosen to sit next to it?

There were the two chairs that had been tipped over. Next to the table, as though swept aside by an angry hand, a water pitcher, glasses, plates and a large bowl of salad were smashed on the tiled floor with water and food splattered around them. Alyssa viewed the devastation with dismay. She'd been expecting to see evidence of a disturbance, but the feeling she got from the scene was one of rage.

"We already know that the blood splatters—" Everett pointed "—were Delilah's. Was there evidence that anyone else had been injured?"

"No," Bob said. "But there was no sign of how Delilah came to be hurt. Her blood wasn't on any of the broken glass or crockery. Just those splashes on the tiles."

Unsure what more she'd expected to gain from seeing the pictures for herself, Alyssa studied the pictures from every angle. Eventually, she pointed to the image of the food on the floor. "Can you enlarge this section?"

Everett obliged, stretching the photograph to zoom in on the mess that had been Sean and Delilah's last meal.

Alyssa's gaze became intent. "There!"

Everett's shoulder bumped hers as he took in the portion of the picture she was indicating. "That's it." He gripped her hand tightly. "You've found it. It's the evidence we needed."

"Found what?" Casey tried impatiently to get a look at the screen over their shoulders. "What is it?"

"There's a sippy cup and a jar of pureed food half-buried by the spilled salad," Everett said. "Although it's evidence that Kennedy was there that night, it doesn't prove Georgia killed her parents."

"But it does confirm that Georgia lied when she said Kennedy was with her that night." Alyssa was outraged. "Why else would she do that if she wasn't covering up her guilt?"

"Because lying comes as naturally to her as breathing?" Casey's smile was faintly self-mocking. "I've known for a long time what a lucky escape I had when she dumped me at the altar."

"You know Georgia better than most people. She helped kill Pierce Tostig. Do you think she's capable of murdering her own brother?" Everett asked.

Casey was silent for a moment or two. "If she was cornered, I think she'd be capable of anything."

Chapter Eight

Bob Andrews had already left in his own car, but Casey paused at the door. "Are you spending the holidays with Mom and Dad?"

"We haven't discussed it yet." Everett cast a swift look over his shoulder in Alyssa's direction. "I kind of caught Mom by surprise with the news about Kennedy."

"Yeah." Casey grinned. "She hasn't stopped talking about it since."

"What stage is she in?"

"We recently reached the I-trusted-you-to-tell-me-if-there-was-a-problem-with-your-brother phase."

Everett laughed. "I like that one better than when she gets to 'you have no idea how hard it was to raise twin boys.'"

After a few minutes of reflecting on their mother's various ways of guilt-tripping them, Casey's expression became serious. "Are you okay?"

"A ready-made family is hard enough. This other stuff takes it to a new level," Everett said. "In a way, I wish we could find conclusive proof that Sean did kill himself and Delilah. That way, we could move on."

"I think we all know that's not going to happen." Casey lowered his voice further. "I didn't want to say this in front of Alyssa, but Georgia is in court again tomorrow."

"Do you know why?"

"No idea, but I plan on being at the courthouse to find out."

"I'll meet you there," Everett said. He would welcome an opportunity to look Georgia in the eye. He didn't expect her to give away anything, but it would be an opportunity to see if he could make her squirm. "Why don't you and Melody come over for dinner tomorrow night? We can plan our strategy for the holidays."

Casey laughed. "You mean how do we deal with Mom when she reaches the come-because-you-want-to-not-because-you-feel-obliged-to phase?"

"I'd forgotten about that one. I had moved on and was picturing Dad's response."

They recited Ryker Colton's closing argument together. "Your mom wants you here. Show up."

When his brother had gone, Everett found Alyssa dealing with a sleepy baby.

"It's been a tough day. I think she needs to have an early bath and go straight to bed."

Everett had learned a few things since Kennedy's first bath time. "I'll put some towels on the bathroom floor and change into a pair of shorts. Then I'll run her bath and help you get her ready."

He headed toward the bedroom, but as soon as he was out of her field of vision, Kennedy started to whimper.

"She's doing that thing again. It upsets her when she can't see us both," Alyssa said.

"Okay." Everett gave the situation some thought. "We can get the bath ready together. I don't have to wear shorts this time."

As he spoke, Alyssa started wrestling Kennedy out of her clothes. The baby, who wasn't a fan of getting dressed or undressed, had the ability to impersonate a wriggling worm while rolling around her changing mat. Everett stepped in to distract Kennedy with a toy while Alyssa removed the rest of her garments.

Everett pulled off his own sweatshirt. "Do you want to take off some of your clothes before we start?" he asked Alyssa.

She cast a quick glance in the direction of his bare chest. They had gone from wearing regular clothing at bath time, to changing into old garments, then into shorts and tanks. Her look said it all. *Next step, naked?*

"I'm good, thanks."

He shrugged. "You know what it's like when Tidal Wave Dodd gets started."

"She's tired tonight. I'll risk it."

Her confidence turned out to be well-placed. Instead of being her usual wild and squirmy self, Kennedy was content to relax in the warm water and let herself be washed. At the same time, Everett was happy for once to take a step back and let Alyssa care for the baby. He watched the softness in her eyes as she murmured to Kennedy, soothing away the cares of the day. It was like they had always been mother and daughter, and she had never been more beautiful to him than in that moment.

He knew he'd been staring for too long when Alyssa looked up at him with a question in her gaze.

"Time for bed?" He cleared his throat. "Not for us. I have no reason to suggest that. Why would I even be thinking it? I meant for Kennedy…"

A slight smile flitted across Alyssa's face. "Where's her special towel?"

"In the linen closet. Because I forgot to bring it." He got to his feet but as soon as he reached the door, Kennedy started to cry. "Ah…"

Alyssa pointed to the shelf. "We can wrap her in one of the new towels and carry her through to the bedroom together."

"Wait. *She* gets to use one of the decorative towels, but I don't? Shouldn't we have a family meeting about this? Take a vote—" He broke off laughing as Alyssa dug a finger into his ribs. "Oh, I get it. They're *emergency* decorative towels."

"Stop talking and start moving, Colton."

Although Kennedy was dwarfed by the fancy bath towel, she was happy to be fussed over by both of them. By the time they reached the bedroom, she was drowsy, and even getting her into a fresh diaper and a clean onesie posed no problems.

Alyssa lowered her into the crib. "Once she's asleep, we'll be able to leave the room without her noticing," she whispered.

"Are you sure about that?" Everett asked as, even with her eyes closed, Kennedy maintained a tight grip on the front of Alyssa's shirt.

His note of caution turned out to be justified. Although Kennedy allowed Alyssa to tuck her into her crib, as soon as either of them tried to move away, the baby's big blue eyes opened wide and she hitched in a tearful breath.

"Maybe we should sit on the bed and wait it out until she's fully asleep?" Everett suggested. "How long can it take?"

Two hours later, Everett rolled from his back onto his side.

"Serious question. How are we going to get pizza and beer into this room without Kennedy noticing that one of us has gone?"

Alyssa, who was sitting propped against the pillows, pressed a finger to her lips. "Shhh."

He lowered his voice. "What do you say, Lyss? We place a takeout order and, when we hear the buzzer, you cause a distraction while I make a run for it. I'll do it. For your sake."

She snorted. "For the sake of your stomach, you mean."

"Look at me." He took her hand and placed it on his rock-hard abs. "I'm wasting away."

The heat of his flesh against her palm did something sinful to her nerve endings. The only light in the room was the soft glow from Kennedy's night-light. She hoped it was faint enough to hide the blush that stained her cheeks. Touching Everett was a dangerous pleasure. One she shouldn't allow herself.

"Make your call. We'll find a way of getting to the pizza when it arrives." She chuckled. "It's better than trying to explain to Casey how come you're too weak to crawl to the door in the morning."

"Yeah. If he found us shut in here, he might suspect my exhaustion had another, more physical, cause."

Alyssa gasped. "You wish."

"Oh, come on. You never could resist this body."

She was still smothering her laughter in the pillow when he finished his call to the pizza parlor.

"Do you remember the night we met?" Everett's whisper and the dim light made the question intimate and secretive.

"Of course I do. I nearly got thrown out of my apartment. My landlord really did *not* appreciate it when you decided to serenade me from the sidewalk at four o'clock in the morning."

"How else was I supposed to find out which apartment was yours?" He edged ever-so-slightly closer and she pretended not to notice.

"I'd already given you my number. You could have called me," she pointed out.

"There you go again. So unromantic. Although, you were quite poetic in the pool hall, when I sat next to you at the bar."

She rolled her eyes. "And you love to remind me about it."

"I told the bartender to keep the alcoholic drinks coming until you said I was handsome." Even in half darkness, she could tell he was grinning. "And you said you only needed water."

She turned her head, unable to resist his smile. "I must have already been drunk."

Everett shook his head. "You picked the wrong guy for that line, Lyss. I know you too well. I've seen you tipsy a handful of times, but you don't get drunk."

The silence between them lengthened and became meaningful. When he reached up and twisted a strand of her hair around his fingers, she sighed. She'd always loved the feel of his hands on her hair.

"Tell me what you're thinking." His voice was husky and persuasive, his breath warm on her cheek.

Did he really believe she was capable of thinking right now? "It's not important."

"Everything about us is important."

His lips were achingly close and all she could think about was how they would feel on hers. She knew his kisses so well. His mouth was demanding and passionate, but it could be tender at the same time.

Four years ago, she had walked away from the vulnerability she felt around this man. Now he was back in her life and her defenses had been stripped away once more. She was standing on the edge of a chasm, unsure whether to step over the edge, or turn and run.

I'm so tired of being safe.

She touched her lips to the corner of his mouth. Instantly, Everett's arms came up, drawing her tightly into his embrace as he pulled her down next to him and took possession of her...and safety became a distant memory.

Although the kiss was soft and slow, desire reverberated through her and she clung to him. How had she survived four years without *this*? Without being held and cherished? Without feeling passion burning through her veins? Without her heart developing an insistent extra beat?

Her lips parted, welcoming him inside, and she savored the velvet heat of his tongue. Memories of other intimacies flooded back, and she murmured softly. The kiss was a sweet, familiar dance, exploring and retreating, fanning the flames between them.

Cradling Alyssa's face in his hands, Everett broke the kiss. He was so close, she could see the tender light in his eyes and feel his warm breath on her cheek. The kiss had taken them closer to the edge and this was a now-or-never moment. Was she ready to keep going?

"I can guess what you're thinking," she murmured.

"I imagine you probably can." His voice was shaky.

"That pizza's taking too long. Am I right?"

IT WAS DAWN when Everett woke with his arms full of Alyssa. They were both fully dressed—except for his missing sweatshirt—and she'd kept him firmly at arm's length after they'd kissed. He didn't care. The kiss had been magical, and she'd fallen asleep next to him. After four years apart, just holding her was a dream come true. Anything else could wait.

The one thing he wasn't happy about was the reason they'd been forced to share a bed. Although he'd joked about making a dash for the pizza when it was delivered, it hadn't been far from reality. As soon as he'd left the room, Kennedy had started crying. Their little girl was only happy when she had both of them with her.

He was her dad and he wanted to make things right for her, but it gave them a real problem, and not just in terms of the baby's emotional well-being. Apart from the logistics of day-to-day living, there was the immediate issue of Georgia's court appearance. Everett intended to be there, but he didn't plan on taking Alyssa and Kennedy along. If, as he suspected, Georgia had played a role in Sean's and Delilah's deaths and Kennedy was a witness, he didn't want the child anywhere near her aunt ever again.

Of course, Georgia had declared her intention of filing for custody of her niece. Everett was confident she wouldn't get it, but stranger things had happened. It meant he couldn't be completely confident about keeping Georgia away from Kennedy.

He was uncomfortable about the reason for the forthcoming court appearance. He didn't trust Georgia Dodd. Now that Sean was dead, was she going to pull a stunt and blame all their crimes on him? Everett wouldn't put it past her. He could almost hear her now, claiming that her brother had forced her to help him steal cattle and kill a ranch hand...

"What time is it?"

The sensation of Alyssa's body stretching against his drove every other thought out of his head.

"Early."

She turned her head to look at the crib. "She seems to be in a really deep sleep. I think you could sneak out now."

He gave an exaggerated sigh. "Kicking me out of bed, Lyss?"

"Go get a shower and take your beer bottles with

you. And, Everett?" He had started to move away, but he turned back to look at her. "Do it silently."

An hour later, he was making toast for Kennedy while Alyssa took a shower. Although the baby was still inclined to be cranky if one of them wasn't around, it wasn't the big drama it had been on the previous day. She was currently distracting herself with a new activity.

"I see. You throw the teething toy on the floor and shout for me to pick it up," Everett said. "As soon as I give it back to you, we start all over again. Great game. The rules are a little one-sided and I'm not sure anyone over six months old would find it fun. But maybe I'm missing something."

Kennedy gave him her cheeky grin and melted his heart a little. When he placed the toast in front of her, she studied it before carefully smearing one of the small squares onto the tray.

"I guess you're wondering how anyone can spend so long in the shower?" he asked. "I used to ask myself that when I first got together with your mom. Alyssa-mom, not your other mom. I think it has something to do with all the mysterious bottles she keeps in the bathroom. They fill the place. I expect you'll be the same when you get older."

Kennedy gurgled and waved her toast.

"It's okay. I'm allowed a razor, toothbrush and deodorant. I found a little space for them at the back of the cabinet."

"What are you guys whispering about?" Alyssa

emerged from the bathroom in jeans and a T-shirt with a towel wrapped around her head.

"It's daddy-daughter stuff. Moms are not allowed," Everett said. "I have to go out soon. You know what to do, right?"

"Keep the door locked and don't answer it to anyone I don't know." She recited it like a poem. "Where are you going?"

The moment of truth had arrived. "Georgia is appearing in court this morning."

Alyssa moved closer to the high chair. "Will she be released?"

It was tempting to be protective and tell her there was no way that could happen. But she had asked him for honesty.

"I'm not sure what today's hearing will be about. Although we suspect there may be new evidence relating to Sean's and Delilah's deaths, I haven't reported those findings yet. That means the charges against Georgia haven't changed. My guess is that this will be related to her bail."

"What does that mean?" Alyssa asked.

"When Georgia was originally granted bail, the judge would have taken into account a number of factors. He considered the seriousness of the charges, Georgia's criminal history, if she presented a danger to the community and if she could be considered a flight risk. He'd also have been trying to weigh whether she was going to turn up for her trial. She was given bail, but she broke the conditions by attempting to leave town."

"He sent her to jail, so he must have considered her a flight risk," Alyssa said.

"Exactly. But her attorney may have put together a case for why bail should be offered now. If he can suggest ways the court can mitigate the danger of flight risk and harm to the community, the judge may agree." He watched her face, hating the nervous look that came into her eyes. "That means she would be released again."

"She killed Sean and Delilah. We know that." She drew in a shuddering breath. "And if Kennedy saw what happened, she may come after her."

"As far as the law is concerned, we know nothing." He went to her and took her hands in his. "I seriously don't believe Georgia will view Kennedy as a threat to her safety or freedom. Remember what Patty Griffiths said? Most people don't think very young children can remember things that have happened to them." His lips hardened into a line. "Although Georgia is trouble, she's not stupid. She knows she'd have me to deal with if she tried anything with Kennedy."

He could tell she wasn't convinced, but it was the most he could do. Part of him wondered if the best scenario might be for Georgia to be freed and attempt to harm Kennedy. Even though it was the last thing he wanted, he knew he would be able to deal with her and then put her back where she belonged for a long time.

"What made Sean and Delilah turn out the way they did?" Alyssa asked. "People aren't just born bad."

"When we were growing up, Sean and Georgia weren't raised with the same sort of boundaries as me and Casey. At the time, I envied their freedom. It's only when I look back that I can see what a nightmare their childhood must have been. Their dad was always out chasing the next quick buck, or a new woman. Left to bring up two kids more or less on her own, their mom resorted to desperate measures."

"In what way?"

"I don't know all the details," Everett said. "I just remember the kids were always given pitying looks."

Alyssa grimaced. "I can understand how stepping out from that shadow would have been hard for them. But lots of people have tough childhoods. They don't all go on to steal cattle and commit murder. On the contrary, many of them are determined not to repeat the mistakes of the past."

"Of course they do." Everett knew she was thinking of herself. Of the hardships her mom had endured, and the way Alyssa had turned them into lessons for life. "But the Dodd kids were fighters who thought the world was against them."

"So Sean and Georgia had a poor upbringing, a bad example and a grudge against the whole town?"

"And the arrogance to do something about it. Neither of them have ever lacked nerve." Everett put on his jacket as he spoke.

"But Casey was going to marry Georgia," Alyssa said. "She must have some redeeming qualities."

He paused. "Although I never liked her, I truly think marrying Casey was the one thing that could have turned her around. My brother is one of the good guys." He shrugged. "But she blew it."

She stepped up close, catching hold of the front of

his jacket. "Even though we didn't know who you were fighting, I used to tell you to be careful every time you went to work."

"This time the bad guy—or gal—has a name." He lightly kissed her forehead. "Nothing else has changed."

"You think?" Even though she stooped to pick up mangled toast slices from the floor, he got the feeling she was talking about more than Kennedy.

Chapter Nine

Since the weather wasn't really warm enough for a walk, Alyssa didn't mind staying indoors with Kennedy. Determined to keep busy while Everett was out and not focus on what might be happening at the courthouse, she sat on the rug with a collection of the baby's toys and books.

Kennedy was already sitting independently and, when she was lying on the floor, she could roll from her front to her back. She was also showing early signs of wanting to crawl, lifting her bottom in the air and rocking backward and forward.

"I dread to think what life will be like when you're mobile," Alyssa said. "In this tiny space, you'll be able to cause havoc in seconds."

It was a reminder that their living arrangements were temporary. She'd gotten her maternity leave and, after the holidays, they would need to have a conversation about what happened next. Although Alyssa knew it was necessary, she was oddly reluctant to move on. It felt like the rest of the world had currently been put on hold. Even though they were dealing with a menacing figure who wanted to disrupt their lives, the little apartment had become a place of safety. Within these walls they had learned to become a family.

One of Kennedy's favorite games was peekaboo. She never tired of searching for an object that had been hidden under her blanket and squealed with delight at her own cleverness when she found it. For the first time, when Alyssa clapped, the baby copied her, bringing her hands together in an aimless applauding motion. At first, Alyssa thought it was a coincidence, but Kennedy did it each time.

"Oh, clever girl. You're clapping. Wait until Ev— until Daddy sees this."

She was just withdrawing her cell from her pocket to take a video when the security buzzer sounded. She wished that noise didn't make her so jumpy. Okay, so they weren't expecting anyone, but Georgia was in court at this very moment. There were a hundred reasons why someone could be at their door.

Which is why I should answer it.

Checking that Kennedy was safe on the floor, she got to her feet and went to the door. Was there a way of sounding bright and confident? Unlike a woman alone with a child?

"Hi." That should do it.

"It's Ryker and Maribelle Colton." She recognized Everett's dad's voice. "Is our son home?"

"He's not, but please come up."

A quick glance around the apartment confirmed that it was clean and tidy, apart from baby toys on the floor. Alyssa picked up Kennedy and went to let in Everett's parents with the baby on her hip. Maybe she should have been more nervous about the situation, but she had always liked Ryker and Maribelle. And it wasn't like she was under scrutiny as a future daughter-in-law.

With his usual old-fashioned courtesy, Ryker stood back to let his wife enter first. He was exactly as Alyssa remembered him. In his late seventies now, he was straight-backed and slightly disheveled, with a kindly face and a twinkle in his eye when he smiled.

Maribelle's gaze went straight to the baby. "Oh, I've been thinking about this little sweetheart ever since we last met."

"Would you like to hold her?" Alyssa asked.

"My darling girl, there is nothing I would like more."

Ryker nodded approvingly as Alyssa handed Kennedy over. "Smart move," he murmured as they all moved into the living area.

"Can I get coffee for anyone?" Alyssa gestured to the sofas.

"Is it too much to hope that my son has remembered to buy some English breakfast tea?" The regal effect of Maribelle's words was ruined slightly as Kennedy yanked on her necklace, pulling her head forward.

"Coffee would be perfect," Ryker said. "For both of us."

While she was in the kitchen, Alyssa took a moment to straighten her ponytail. She considered sending Everett a text message to let him know his parents had arrived but decided against it. If he was inside the courthouse, his cell phone would be switched off. By the time he got the message, he would be on his way home, anyway.

When she returned to her guests, Ryker and Maribelle were sitting close together and were both engrossed in the baby. Alyssa halted a few steps away and watched them. Where was her child's fear of strangers that had been so apparent on the previous day? Although her smile was shy, there was no question about it. Kennedy felt comfortable with Everett's parents.

Alyssa experienced a new rush of warmth toward this good-natured couple. She also felt a profound sense of relief. Kennedy's problems weren't over, but perhaps they weren't as severe as she'd feared.

"Maribelle tells me you and Everett have adopted this little lady." Ryker patted the sofa cushions, inviting Alyssa to sit next to him.

"That's not quite how it happened." They were both so easy to talk to that, under their interested stares, she found herself pouring out the whole story. Minus Creepy-Elevator Guy, Teddy-Bear-Delivery Guy, Parking-Lot-Attempted-Murder Guy, Cheating-Lawyer Guy and Villainous Aunt. She didn't want to see those smiles turn to looks of horror as they grabbed the baby and headed for the nearest social worker to explain that this poor child should not be left alone with some woman who made up wild stories.

"It's quite a commitment," Maribelle said.

"One that will do Everett good." Ryker's voice was firm.

Alyssa bowed her head as an unexpected rush of tears threatened to overwhelm her. After everything they'd been through, hearing those words from Everett's traditional, upright father meant more than she could say. When she looked up, he gave her an understanding nod.

"You have quite an adventure ahead of you."

She gave a shaky laugh. "You have no idea."

"Oh, I know my boys." The smile deepened. "I know I can't contact either of them this morning. I also know Georgia Dodd is back in court today."

Alyssa gave a start of surprise, but before she could answer, Maribelle shuddered. "Don't say that name in my presence. Casey is better off without her, but when I think of what she put him through—"

Ryker patted her hand. "Let's not think of it, my love."

"I'm happy to turn my attention to this little one." She bounced Kennedy on her lap. "You'll join us for the holidays? Casey is bringing his new girlfriend. It would make it such a special occasion to have the whole family together. After all…" She turned to Ryker with shining eyes. "This is our first grandchild."

"Alyssa and Everett may have other plans," he said in his gentle way.

"We haven't really talked about it—"

"Then it's agreed."

Maribelle clasped her hand. "How wonderful to see both my boys settled."

A blush heated Alyssa's cheeks. "We're not… Everett and I…" She floundered. Taking a deep breath, she continued. "We're not in a relationship."

"Goodness." Maribelle looked at the baby for long,

silent moments. "Don't you think it would be better if you got married?"

Alyssa's initial reaction was to instantly dismiss the suggestion, but she didn't want to hurt the other woman's feelings. Maribelle came from a different generation. If only life was that simple…

In some ways, taking responsibility for Kennedy meant they had to act like they were married. Their lives had become intertwined, they now divided up the labor in a way that made sense, and, at some point in the near future, they would have to do something similar with the finances. Alyssa hadn't thought through their own futures, but either of them dating seemed out of the question for the moment, or, at the very least, a complex arrangement. Even so, getting married for any reason other than love felt plain wrong.

Guess that means I never get to go wedding-dress shopping.

It was a fleeting thought with only a tiny sting in its tail. How could she be sad when her no-wedding reason was Kennedy?

"Kennedy came to us in an unconventional way, as part of a civil contract," she said. "For that reason, Everett and I feel we can raise her together without the need for a marriage certificate."

Although she hoped there was enough finality in her tone to end the discussion, she could tell Maribelle was already in wedding-planning mode. "But, my dear, have you really thought it through? About how it looks to other people? What about when she starts school? Other children can be so cruel."

"Alyssa is a teacher, remember?" Ryker intervened in his soft-spoken way. "We can trust her to deal with any issues that arise."

It was clear that Maribelle wasn't finished with the subject, but she turned her attention back to Kennedy, asking questions about health checks and doctors. Thanks to Delilah's diligent record-keeping, Alyssa was able to answer them all easily.

"Physically, she's fine. We're just a little concerned about the impact of her parents' deaths," she explained. "We'll watch her closely and seek professional help if necessary."

"At this age, there's no substitute for lots of love and cuddles." Maribelle put action to her words by snuggling Kennedy close.

"I'm going to add my professional support to that opinion," Ryker said. "And now, we'll leave you in peace. I do hope we'll see you during the holidays."

"I hope so, too." As she took the baby from Maribelle, Alyssa realized that she meant it. Since her father's death, she'd never really known a family Christmas. Her mother had tried hard, but her declining health had made it difficult. Spending time at Everett's childhood home would be a pleasure.

As they got ready to leave, Ryker stooped to pick up a folded piece of white paper wedged halfway beneath the door.

"Looks like someone couldn't wait for you to go down to the mailbox." His bright eyes scanned Alyssa's face as he handed it to her. "Are you okay?"

"I'm fine." She tucked the note into the back pocket of her jeans. "Everett will be sorry he missed you."

Ryker laughed. "We all know that's not true."

Maribelle kissed Alyssa's cheek. "Twins are such a blessing. If you like blessings that team up and make you spend your whole life worrying about them."

When they'd gone, Alyssa leaned against the wall and released a long, slow breath. Reaching into her back pocket, she withdrew the piece of paper. She studied it for a moment or two, debating whether to unfold it. There was no reason to suspect it contained anything sinister, but the way things had been going lately...

She could just wait for Everett to get back. But that wouldn't change anything. If the note contained bad news, she might as well find out now. Tentatively, she opened it and read the words that had been written in black felt pen.

Enjoy playing happy family while you can. Dead babies don't play so good.

THE CACTUS CREEK courthouse was close to the sheriff's office, and Casey was waiting outside when Everett arrived. He held cups of fast-food coffee in each hand and as his brother approached, he held one of them out.

"Turbocharged. Three sugars. No cream."

"There are days when I'm glad you're my twin." Everett accepted the beverage gratefully.

"There are days when I almost feel the same way."

They stood on the sidewalk for a few minutes,

drinking their coffee and watching the entrance to the courthouse.

"How do you feel about this?" Everett asked. "Seeing the woman you almost married up in court on such serious charges has to be hard."

Casey continued to sip his drink for a moment or two. Everett wasn't concerned. He knew his brother would give him an honest answer.

"It just feels like that part of my life happened to someone else, you know?" Casey shook his head. "We were childhood sweethearts, me and Georgia. Getting married was what we were meant to do. Don't get me wrong, I knew she had a wild side. But I figured she'd settle down. Now I'm happy with Melody and I look back and wonder how I could have been such a jerk."

"Don't be so hard on yourself. You loved her."

"Did I? I'm not so sure." Casey drained his drink. "I loved who I thought she was. I sure as hell didn't love the woman we're about to hear about in this courthouse."

They went through the double doors and into the marble-tiled lobby. Casey checked his gun at the reception desk, and they signed in, using their badges as identification. Passing the Court in Session signs, they entered the main courtroom. Judge Morley Ackerman was already seated at the bench talking to the district attorney, Warren Marano, and a younger man.

"That's Jacob Cardell, Georgia's defense attorney," Casey murmured.

"Good? Bad?"

"Expensive."

They had just taken their seats when Georgia, escorted by a female prison officer, was led in through the rear doors. Immediately, Jacob Cardell was at her side, first pulling out a chair and then pouring her a glass of water.

Everett studied the woman whom he'd known since she'd had pigtails and been missing her front teeth. Now, as an adult, there was no doubt about Georgia's physical beauty. She had tawny skin, sultry eyes and a slim body. As she licked her lips and glanced about, the way she tossed her dark wavy hair around was more reminiscent of a nightclub than a courtroom. But that was Georgia Dodd. Her wild-child tendencies couldn't remain hidden for long.

Although her attorney was talking earnestly, her gaze continued to wander. When it finally fell on Everett and Casey, her eyes widened slightly and a tiny smile touched her lips. Everett kept his eyes on hers, answering her with a cold, stony stare of his own. Georgia's smile faded and she looked away first.

Score one for the good guys.

The public seats were mostly empty. There was plenty of interest in the case because there was a murder involved and the double suicide of Georgia's brother and his wife had gripped the imagination of the citizens of Cactus Creek. But since today's hearing was likely to be administrative and over quickly, only a few journalists and the most hardened court watchers had shown up.

Judge Ackerman called the court to order and announced that the session was in progress. He asked Cardell to state why he had requested this additional hearing.

"She wants bail," Everett murmured.

"Ackerman is a tough nut to crack," Casey whispered back. "Once he's made up his mind, he'll take some convincing."

"Your Honor, my client fully understands the reasons behind your decision to impose a custodial sentence after her bail conditions were broken." From the sulky look on Georgia's face there was a possibility that Cardell's opening statement may have lacked truth. "However, we would respectfully request a review of that ruling."

"On what grounds?" Judge Ackerman was clearly a man of few words.

"Firstly, my client is willing to submit to any additional conditions the court may impose, including relinquishing her passport, wearing an electronic monitoring device or daily reporting to a police station."

"Big deal," Casey muttered.

"Secondly, my client wishes to appeal to the court for leniency on compassionate grounds. As you are aware, her brother and his wife died recently in tragic circumstances, leaving their infant daughter orphaned." Everett sat up straighter. What did any of this have to do with Kennedy? "Although the baby was left in the care of others, my client wishes to overturn the will and apply for custody of the child. It will be easier for her to go through the legal processes involved if she is not in jail."

Anger burned its way up from somewhere deep inside Everett's gut. By the time it reached his face, it was so red-hot he was in danger of giving off steam. His knuckles whitened as he clenched his fists on his thighs and gritted his teeth, forcing himself to remain silent.

Casey sent him a sidelong glance. "You want to take a few minutes? Maybe step outside?"

Slowly, he shook his head. "I need to hear this."

Judge Ackerman scribbled a few notes. "You said the child is in the care of others, Mr. Cardell? Presumably this was in accordance with the parents' wishes?"

Before Cardell could answer, Georgia tugged at his sleeve. Everett could see her muttering furiously to him. "Yes, Your Honor, but my client feels—"

"Was this in accordance with the parents' wishes, Mr. Cardell?" the judge repeated.

"Yes, Your Honor."

Ackerman scribbled again. Georgia, clearly feeling that her attorney had let her down in some way, scolded him under her breath while they waited. When the judge looked up, Cardell flapped a hand to silence her.

"Your offer to submit to conditions doesn't influence my decision. As for the care of your client's niece, I don't feel that there is any pressing need for this to influence your client's custodial status. The child is currently being cared for by the people named in her parents' will."

Although Georgia gave an audible hiss, the judge continued.

"In case you hadn't noticed, Mr. Cardell, your client is facing some serious charges here. There will be time to consider overturning her brother's will, if she manages to walk away from them a free woman."

"Your Honor, may I ask—"

"You may not. Your request for reconsideration is denied."

"What?" Georgia got to her feet, facing the judge with wild eyes. There was a ripple of interest in the seats near Everett and Casey. "They got to you, didn't they? The FBI agent and his kid-brother deputy…"

Cardell quickly pulled her back down into her seat, and the prison officer was at her side in a flash. Within minutes, she was being led out of the room.

"Whew. Nothing to see here, folks." Casey got to his feet. "At least she showed her true colors *and* she stays behind bars. She can't hurt you while she's in prison."

With perfect timing, Everett's cell phone pinged to indicate the arrival of a message. When the picture from Alyssa appeared on his screen, adrenaline had him heading for the door at a run.

"What is it?" Casey was close behind him.

"You think Georgia can't threaten us from a cell?" Everett showed him the message: Dead babies don't play so nice. "Think again."

"It's been a stressful day," Everett said. "We can cancel dinner with Casey and Melody. They'll understand."

Alyssa shook her head. In the past, she'd have let the threatening note tip her world off-course, just as the sender intended. But things had changed the day she'd walked into Ray Torrington's office and become a mom.

Caring for Kennedy meant facing up to her fears, not running from them.

"Georgia is not going to win this fight." Stubbornly, she placed a dish onto the counter. "And I've already started preparing dinner."

He nodded approvingly. "There is one thing we have to consider." She raised inquiring eyebrows. "Around the time that note was being pushed under the door, Georgia was being brought from the jail to the courthouse in a police car."

"We know she didn't do it herself. That means she has an accomplice. We already considered that possibility."

"I agree that a sidekick is the most likely scenario," Everett said. "I'd also like to pay another visit to Ray Torrington. And I think I'll take Casey with me next time."

Alyssa's brow wrinkled. "You're the FBI agent, but Ray doesn't strike me as the type to try to run you down in a parking lot."

"You're probably right. He's more likely to commit his crimes on paper." He sighed. "How's Kennedy been today?"

"Really good. She loved seeing your mom and dad." She pointed toward the bedroom. "She's sleeping off the effects."

Everett shook his head. "My parents are incredible. How many times was Christmas dinner mentioned?"

Alyssa laughed. "It may have entered the conversation."

He watched as she stirred the sauce. "Would it bother you if we went there for the holidays?"

"Bother me? No. I'd like it." She dipped a spoon into the pan and held it out for him to taste. "And I think it would be good for Kennedy."

"You do?" He ran a hand through his hair. "Then let's do it. Let's take our little girl to her grandparents' for the holidays." He pointed to the pan. "More pepper, by the way."

Alyssa went to the window. "Oh, look! It really is snowing. And it's settling."

Everett smiled. "It will be Kennedy's first glimpse of snow. When we were kids, there was a freak snowstorm and my dad took us to make snow angels in Henderson Park. If we wrap her up warm, I guess half an hour in the cold won't hurt her."

She was already running toward the bedroom. "She has the prettiest little snowsuit…"

Henderson Park was close to the center of town. Everett explained that it was often used in summer for outdoor events, such as live music, or fireworks displays. Despite the fact that the snow hadn't been falling for long, a surprising number of people were already taking advantage of the rare Arizona weather and were sledding, throwing snowballs and building snowmen.

At first, Alyssa had dressed Kennedy in so many layers that the baby resembled a tiny sumo wrestler. Eventually, a more common-sense approach had prevailed, and the little girl now studied the white landscape from her stroller clad in her snowsuit and bundled in a blanket. A knit hat and matching gloves completed her outfit. She appeared unimpressed with her apparel and the world in general.

"Great." Everett studied his cell phone. "We have a series of images of you and me grinning like idiots while Kennedy frowns at us."

"That may well be the story of our lives from now on—" She let out a squeal as Everett caught her unaware by shoving a handful of snow down the back of her neck. "You…"

As she attempted to retaliate, chasing him around the stroller with her own handful of snow, she reflected on how easy it would be for anyone watching them to imagine their lives were normal. Whatever that might mean. It certainly didn't mean living in fear of the woman who had almost certainly killed Kennedy's parents. A woman who was now dominating their lives.

Only if we let her.

"It's getting colder," she said at last. "Let's go home before Grumpy Baby catches a chill."

Everett moved toward the stroller and Alyssa launched her master-plan. The snowball she'd been hiding behind her back arced through the air, hitting him full in the face. As he spluttered and wiped snow out of his eyes, even Kennedy started to laugh.

When he caught Alyssa around the waist, she resigned herself to whatever icy fate he had in store for her. As his hands cupped her cheeks, she saw the light in his eyes change and she gave a tiny gasp that had nothing to do with the cold.

"Lyss." He bent his head toward her, closing his eyes as he caressed her mouth with his own. The taste of his lips was magical, and she wrapped her arms around his neck with a soft moan of pleasure. Growing more possessive, he slid his arms around her, drawing her close and kissing her deeply.

Alyssa molded her own body to his, her lips equally demanding. Desire licked through her and she was only half aware of her surroundings when Everett broke the kiss and drew back. "Bad timing." His smile was rueful as he indicated Kennedy in the stroller. "But I feel a lot warmer now."

The late-afternoon light was fading fast when they reached the car and Everett turned the heater up full as they quickly loaded Kennedy and the stroller inside. It was only as Alyssa was climbing into the passenger seat that she noticed the folded slip of paper under one of the wipers.

"It takes dedication to go out and about leaving flyers on car windshields in the snow." Even as she spoke, reality hit her.

"Ours is the only car that has one." Everett reached around and snagged the slip of paper. "I'm guessing this is not a special offer."

Sure enough, when he unfolded it, the familiar scrawl, written with a black felt pen, stared up at them.

Looks like you had fun. Snow or death. Guess which one will hit you in the face next?

Chapter Ten

Two hours later, Everett was opening the door to Casey and Melody while Kennedy yelled loudly in the background.

"Oh, my stars." Melody looked slightly alarmed. "Is there a problem?"

"It's a new game. She blows spit bubbles, then screams with delight at her own cleverness." Everett led them into the living room. "Now she's teaching Kennedy how to do it."

"Oh, I see. So I'm the one who's spitting?" Alyssa laughed. "This brother of yours. Was he always such a funny guy?"

"He always thought he was," Casey said. "This is Melody Hayworth. Melody, I told you about Alyssa. She and Everett have accepted joint custody of Kennedy Dodd."

"That's a big job, but it must be so rewarding." Melody came over to the high chair. "And she's gorgeous."

Alyssa found herself instantly warming to the other woman. Melody was friendly and down-to-earth, and her praise of Kennedy helped. The baby, sensing a new admirer, fluttered her eyelashes and blew another spit bubble.

"I didn't know what we were eating, so I brought wine and beer." Casey placed the bottles on the table.

"We're having chicken tagine. It's Alyssa's signature dish, and wine or beer works equally well." Everett went into the kitchen to get glasses. On his return, he poured drinks for everyone. "Kennedy has been a little cranky since we took her to her parents' house yesterday. For that reason, we've decided to dispense with her usual routine and let her stay up until she falls asleep."

"It may be a decision we regret," Alyssa said. "But the alternative would have been that all four of us ended up trapped in the bedroom with her until morning."

She left Everett recounting the story of the previous night while she went to check on the food. When she returned, the conversation had moved on and was about the threatening message she had received.

"What about the handwriting?" Casey asked.

"A distinctive scrawl in black felt pen." Everett shrugged. "The sender may as well have typed it. That reminds me, I got the report back from the labs about the sample of Georgia's handwriting. They did the comparison with Sean's suicide note."

"And?"

"Inconclusive. Whatever the hell that means." Everett ran a hand through his hair. "Put simply, there's a possibility Georgia wrote it and disguised her handwriting well enough to leave the experts with some doubts. Or the mystery accomplice did it for her. It's been passed on for further analysis but that could take weeks."

They returned to the subject of the note that had been delivered to the apartment. Casey had been making inquiries to see if he could discover who had left it. "There are no security cameras on the entrance to this building, and none of the neighbors saw anything suspicious."

"It was pushed under the door within a very specific time frame," Everett said. "It wasn't there when Mom and Dad arrived. They stayed with Alyssa and Kennedy for about half an hour, so we know it was left during that time."

"And that half hour just happened to coincide with Georgia's arrival at the courthouse," Casey pointed out.

"You think it was a message?" Everett raised his eyebrows and took a slug of beer as he considered the matter.

"Yeah. The only question is what sort of message."

Alyssa turned to Melody. "How about we give them an ultimatum? They stop being cryptic, or we take the beer away?"

"Sounds good to me," Melody responded with a smile.

"It was either a message that confirms Georgia's innocence," Casey said. "Because, on the face of it, she couldn't possibly have sent it."

"Or it was Georgia, and she was letting us know just how dangerous she can be," Everett finished.

"You mean she was demonstrating that she can still get to us from her prison cell?" Alyssa asked.

He nodded. "We either accept that the timing was coincidental, or we consider that possibility."

"I have another option for us to think about." Everett raised his eyebrows at Alyssa. "For the next hour or two, let's forget about Georgia and focus on dinner."

He smiled. It was a tiny, secret exchange meant just for her. A moment that acknowledged how far she'd come. And—*goodness*—didn't she know it. The old Alyssa could never have said those words. She'd have obsessed, over and over, about the source of the threat, wanting reassurances that couldn't be given.

The new Alyssa still had fears. She was still peeking over her shoulder to see if Georgia Dodd was hiding in the shadows. But she had a better idea of how life worked. And she was learning how to trust.

She took a moment to reflect on when "new Alyssa" had emerged. It could have been when she'd walked out of Ray Torrington's office with Kennedy in her arms. It might even have been a few minutes before that. Seeing Everett again had certainly shaken her out of her comfort zone.

The meal was a huge success. The food turned out perfectly, and the four of them got along in a relaxed way that felt like they'd been a friendship group for years. Kennedy fell asleep while drinking her suppertime formula and then Everett took her to the crib, settling her with no problem. Over the baby monitor, they could hear the occasional soft snore or mumble.

After dinner, they lingered over their drinks, chatting idly, and the subject turned to Everett and Alyssa's living arrangements.

"What's the best thing about living with a guy?" Melody asked.

Alyssa considered the question with her head tilted to one side. The best thing about living with Everett was that she had gotten to know the real him. The good, the bad, the up-all-night-with-a-baby him. She had seen sides of him she hadn't suspected existed and her feelings for him had remained steady. Even grown, becoming deeper and warmer, with a feeling of constancy.

In the tiny space they currently inhabited, there was no hiding place. In a very short time, they had learned how to be there for each other and for Kennedy. They'd become a team. And she loved it.

"You are taking way too long to answer this," Everett teased.

"The best thing is the socks." She kept her face straight as she answered Melody's question. "They are everywhere. They sort of creep up on you. Go to bed and the place is sock-free. Wake up and it's become a sock-infested twilight zone. I'm thinking of opening a non-matching-sock emporium. I could make my fortune."

Laughing, Melody turned to Everett. "Same question to you. What's it like living with a woman?"

He gave Alyssa a mischievous look and she groaned. "I think 'cheat day' comes near the top."

"What's 'cheat day'?" Casey asked.

"It's a girl thing," Alyssa and Melody chorused together.

"But, if you live with a girl, you get to be part of it," Everett said.

"You didn't swear him to secrecy?" Melody asked Alyssa.

Alyssa hung her head. "Forgot."

"Is anyone going to tell me about 'cheat day'?" Casey demanded.

"Women talk about eating healthily, and maintaining their ideal weight, right? But then they have this thing called 'cheat day.' Bad day at work? Glass of wine. Is it Monday? Chocolate. Your boyfriend didn't notice the new dress? Pizza. That's how 'cheat day' works."

"Genius." Casey shook his head. "And that's not the best thing?"

"I think organized laundry comes second." From the twinkle in his eye, it was clear Everett was enjoying himself. "Before Alyssa moved in, I used to think I was doing okay. I got out of the house each day looking decent enough. Now I have one drawer with underwear and socks, another with shorts and workout clothes and everything else is on hangers in the closet. I now know I was living a clothing half life."

"Seriously?" Casey looked from Alyssa to Melody and back again. "You all do this?"

"It's in the code," Melody said. "Once we get you in our clutches, we teach you how to fold a fitted sheet and there's no going back."

The light in Everett's eyes as he turned made Alyssa's breath catch in her throat. "But then comes the times when I sit on the sofa and watch you with Kennedy. The look in your eyes and the way you sing to her. Sometimes I watch you when she's not there." He laughed. "Not in a creepy way. And you'll start to dance while you're cooking or cleaning even if there's no music playing. And, yeah. That's the best thing about living together."

Although the words made Alyssa feel special, the note in his quiet voice held a reminder. Of how his lips made her skin tingle, of how his tongue felt when it stroked hers, of how his strong arms wrapped around her, warming and protecting her.

And in his eyes…did she see a promise? Melody gestured to Casey. "Drink up. We should go."

"Oh, hey. It's not late. We don't have to—"

"I think we do." Melody gave a tiny jerk of her head in Everett's direction as though she had noticed something important. "Good night, guys."

REALIZING THAT CASEY and Melody had gone because he'd pretty much poured his heart out in front of them, Everett took a moment to catch his breath before going into the kitchen. His confession had taken his, as well as them by surprise, but he figured it was about time. He just wondered what Alyssa was thinking.

When he went through to the kitchen, the tension he'd been expecting was missing.

Instead, Alyssa jumped guiltily. "Oh."

"Are you eating leftovers without me?"

It was hard to make out what she was saying because she was frantically trying to swallow the food in her mouth. "Might be."

He laughed, relieved that he hadn't ruined everything with his disclosure. "Let's take a plate and a couple of beers through to the living room. Cleaning up can wait." She looked nervously at the dirty dishes. "It can, Lyss. Believe me. Mess doesn't go away."

They collapsed companionably onto the sofa with the food between them.

"Melody seems nice," Alyssa said.

"She really does," Everett agreed. "It's so good to see Casey happy. It will be fun to see them again for Christmas dinner."

She shot him a measuring glance. "Your mom felt strongly that we should get married. For Kennedy's sake."

He jerked, spilling beer down the front of his shirt. Muttering a curse, he grabbed one of the napkins he'd brought with the food and mopped up the mess.

"She *said* that?"

"I told her that, because we aren't in a relationship, it wouldn't make sense for us to do something just because it's what other people expect. I don't think I convinced her."

Everett sank back in his seat, thinking about what his mom had suggested. He'd always seen marriage as a scary step. Making a promise that was meant to last forever? It had always felt as chancy as gazing into a crystal ball. Now something had clicked into place and he got it. When people got married, they hadn't reached a point where they knew exactly what the rest of their life would look like. They had no clue what was ahead. But they were prepared to make a promise to stick with one person through all of it. And that was comforting instead of scary.

Could he explain his change of thought to Alyssa? He drained his beer. He could try. Maybe he could even convince her that his mother was right...

"She does have a point." Aware that Alyssa was giving him an are-you-serious? stare, he plowed on. "I mean, this is a small town and people have expectations of what a family looks like. And marriage does have its advantages."

"Sure it does. For people who are in love." Her slim body visibly bristled with tension.

This was all going horribly wrong. He needed to come up with a compelling reason. Fast. "If we were married, Georgia wouldn't stand a chance when it came to a counter claim for custody."

"She doesn't stand a chance, anyway. She's a criminal, remember?"

"Even so, we could make doubly sure that no one can ever take Kennedy from us." He reached for her hand. "Don't worry, we can always get a divorce in a few years."

The speed with which she sprang away from him would have done credit to a puma. Without speaking, she marched through to the kitchen and, after a moment or two, he heard the sound of plates being loaded into the dishwasher.

Guess I just blew my first marriage proposal.

Tentatively, he followed her. "Lyss—"

She swung around to face him, and he was shocked at the raw emotion on her face. He knew he'd angered her, but he hadn't realized, until that moment, that he'd also hurt her.

"Don't say any more." She twisted a dishcloth in her hands as she spoke. Her voice shook and she battled to get it under control before she continued. "When we were together, I dreamed of a future with you, Everett. And my fantasies included the day you proposed to me."

"Let me—"

"No. You had your turn to talk. This is my time." Her hand shook as she brushed away a tear. "I've always known there was a part of yourself you keep shut off from me. I figured that, one day, you'd tell me why. And that when that day came, we'd be able to plan for a future together. At no point did I see this… A proposal that included a get-out clause. Like 'Hey, baby, we can always get a quickie divorce and walk away in a few years.'"

He froze. His mind replayed the words *part of yourself you keep shut off.* How could he open up to her about that, when he didn't know how to deal with it himself?

It's time to tell her. All of it.

When he opened his mouth to try, the words wouldn't come. At the most critical moment of his life, he couldn't speak. With a sound midway between a laugh and a sob, Alyssa turned away and continued loading dishes.

Tightening his fist against the door frame to keep from punching the wall, Everett watched her for a few seconds before heading for the front door. Fresh air. That was what he needed. He'd clear his thoughts, come back and start again. This was too important to leave unfinished.

He stepped outside with no real idea of where he was going. The snow had stopped, but the night air had enough bite to make him catch his breath. Regretting the impulse that had driven him out in a T-shirt and high-tops, he ran down the steps and into the parking lot.

Although he wasn't dressed for a run, he contemplated a quick circuit of the block. Perhaps a burst of exercise would take away the sensation that his muscles were burning with red-hot tension.

He was preparing to start jogging when he sensed a movement behind him. His nerve endings fired out an alert. The person approaching was moving fast... And they were heading straight toward him.

His instinct was to swing around and confront the impending danger. Every self-defense class he'd ever attended came back to him, and he maintained his position, only turning at the last second. Clad in dark clothing with a hood pulled up to hide the face, the figure darting toward him was small and slight. He tried to find something distinctive in that fast-moving figure to latch on to, something to remember if he needed to give a statement... The only thing that caught his attention was the unusual sneakers. They were edged with a pattern that looked like alligator teeth. As Everett swung onto the balls of his feet, he kept his arms relaxed and open, ready to block or grab his opponent.

The glint of security lights reflecting off a blade caught him by surprise, and he sidestepped with a grunt as the knife arced low. This wasn't a random mugging. By aiming for his stomach, the attacker was clearly planning to do him some serious damage.

Everett had been an FBI agent for long enough to know that attempting to disarm a knife-wielding assailant in an anything-goes, street-fight situation was a very bad idea. Focusing on not getting stabbed and getting the hell out of there was a much better plan. Unfortunately, no one had told the aggressor about those rules.

The figure doubled back, knife hand extended once more. Everett took a moment to consider his options. He could grab the outstretched arm and break it, but the offender might still be able to escape. And he really wanted to get a look at that covered face.

This time, as the assailant lunged forward, Everett backed away and pretended to fall down. Facing the attacker, he propped himself on his elbows and waited for his opponent to move in close. When the moment was right, he slammed his right foot hard into the antagonist's leg.

With a grunt, his foe staggered and went down on one knee. Everett seized the assailant's knife arm, intending to smash it into the ground. With an agility that amazed him, the other person rolled to one side, driving the blade deep into Everett's forearm and breaking free at the same time. Warm stickiness trickled over his palm as he watched the hooded figure run off.

Staggering to his feet, he headed toward the apartment building. Black spots danced in front of his eyes and he forced one foot in front the other. As he reached the first stair, his vision blurred and he dropped to his knees.

WHEN EVERETT WALKED OUT, Alyssa's first reaction—kicking in alongside the hurt she was already feeling—was anger. Why must he be so determined to avoid his feelings? Whenever emotional issues were discussed, his coping mechanism was to lighten the mood or change the topic. If that didn't work, he physically left the scene. Exactly as he'd just done.

Why should she care any longer if he thought being strong and unfeeling was the "masculine" thing to do? Even though they were co-parenting a child, they weren't together. His insecurities were not her problem anymore.

Except… She still cared about him. Just because Everett could pretend to turn off his feelings, it didn't mean it was easy for Alyssa to do the same. Even though he had chosen not to open up to her, she sensed he was fighting the same inner battle he always had.

She bowed her head, gripping the countertop. This was all wrong. They were both hurting. Why did it have to be this way? Surely they could talk it over.

But how was she supposed to go after him with the baby asleep in the apartment? At least she could go out onto the top of the steps, see if he was still around and ask him to come back.

After grabbing her cell phone in one hand and the portable baby monitor in the other, she opened the front door and stepped outside. A scan of the parking lot revealed no sign of Everett, and the night was cold enough to drive her straight back inside. She was taking one final look around when a faint sound caught her attention.

Hesitantly, she leaned over the rail to get a clear view of where the noise was coming from. There, at the base of the steps, a man was lying on his side in the snow.

She paused, wondering if it might be a trap, then he moaned and she threw caution to the wind.

"Everett!" She darted to the top of the steps.

"Stay there." Faint and rasping, the voice was barely recognizable as his own.

Alyssa watched in growing dread as he crawled up the steps on his hands and knees. When he reached the top, the full horror of his appearance became apparent. A large knife protruded from the muscle of his right forearm and the flesh around it was shiny with blood. His clothes were covered with dark crimson splatters. His face was drained of color, with even his lips appearing white. Using the handrail, he pulled himself upright. As Alyssa ran to him, he swayed and leaned against the wall.

"I'll call 911."

As she made the call, Everett slumped into a sitting position. Alyssa finished speaking to the emergency dispatcher and squatted next to him. "The paramedics are on their way. What happened?"

"Guy…" His teeth chattered. "Came out of nowhere."

"You're freezing. I'll get something to wrap around you."

She ran back inside and went into her bedroom. Thankfully, Kennedy was still sound asleep as Alyssa pulled on a warm sweater and grabbed a fleece blanket from the closet. She hurried into the bathroom to snatch a hand towel from the shelf and locate the first-aid kit, then dashed back to Everett.

As she draped the blanket around him, he leaned his head briefly on her shoulder. "Call Casey. Tell him the guy was wearing sneakers with a pattern just like a row of alligator teeth. Could still be around."

"He'll know from the 911 call what's happened. I'll message him now and call him from the hospital."

"What about Kennedy?"

"She can come with us in the ambulance. Stop worrying, Everett. Let me take care of the practical stuff." The knife sticking out of his arm looked gruesome, but she remembered from mandatory training courses she'd attended that impaled objects should not be removed. Instead, she wrapped the towel around his arm below the stab wound, using a bandage from the first-aid kit to tie it in place. "It should stop the bleeding until the paramedics get here."

"He was waiting in the shadows." He leaned his head back against the wall.

"For what? Someone to rob?"

He shook his head. "For me."

The chill that swept over Alyssa had nothing to do with the night air. Right here, right now, she was living her worst nightmare. Ever since her father's death, fear had controlled her like a battery-operated toy. Yet now that she was here—plunged into the scene she had dreaded—her rational self took over. All that mattered was that Everett was okay. And she could play her part in that.

"Painkillers." She found the bottle in the first-aid kit and shook a couple out. "You could probably use some of them."

As she held them out, he gripped her hand. "Lyss, what I said... What I should have said—"

She shook her head. "We don't have to do this now."

He mumbled something under his breath that she didn't quite catch. *Never a right time?* She wasn't quite sure, and as the sound of an approaching siren brought a welcome rush of relief, she shifted her focus back to the practicalities.

As KIDS, EVERETT and Casey had spent more than their fair share of time in the Sur County Hospital. For some reason, twin life had seemed to bring double the quantity of bruises, sprains and fractures for each of them.

"This place hasn't changed much," Everett commented to Alyssa as he was wheeled from the ambulance into the emergency department. The stronger painkillers he'd been given by the paramedics were kicking in and he was able to talk normally.

He studied her face, looking for signs of panic. So far, there were none. Although she was pale, she seemed to be in complete control. With a sleeping Kennedy wrapped in a blanket in her arms, her composure had been remarkable. She'd calmly answered the paramedics' questions about what had happened and in detail. No one watching her would ever guess how difficult this sort of situation was for her.

Not that it would have been easy for anyone. His arm looked like a poster for a slasher movie.

A nurse led Alyssa to a seat at one side of the small cubicle as the emergency team got to work.

"Once we start any procedure, I'll have to ask you to leave," the nurse told her. "But you can wait here while we do an initial assessment."

"Thank you." For the first time, there was a quiver in her voice.

Everett didn't know why, but it helped to know that, if he craned his neck, he could just about see the toe of one of Alyssa's boots.

"Okay." A doctor started examining him. "We have an adult male patient with a piercing injury to his right forearm. He reports that he was assaulted and stabbed about a half hour ago. I take it the sheriff's office has been informed?" There was a murmured confirmation. "There is a knife blade penetrating approximately four centimeters into the front and midline—the anteromedial aspect. Vital signs?"

"Blood pressure, pulse rate and body temperature are all within normal limits." He could tell by the voice it was one of the paramedics who had treated Everett at the scene that responded.

As the doctor gently moved his hand and arm, Everett gritted his teeth. Fingers of fire licked through his damaged nerve endings.

"There is movement in the right wrist and elbow, but the patient finds the examination painful."

You don't say. Maybe that has something to do with the blade sticking out of my flesh?

"Tetanus vaccination and antibiotics will be required to counter the effects of this foreign body penetration. Removal will be made under general anesthesia." He spoke directly to Everett for the first time. "With such a deep-seated injury, the only way we can be sure we don't injure the surrounding tissues as we take the blade out will be to knock you out."

Everett frowned. His mental processes were clear, thanks to the painkillers, and, while he understood what the doctor was saying, he didn't like the idea of Alyssa and Kennedy being alone and vulnerable when he was on the operating table. He needed Casey to get down here. Fast.

And there were other things worrying him… "Will there be any lasting damage to my arm?"

"This sort of injury is difficult to manage because the associated potential vascular and nerve injuries can be extremely serious. That's why I'm not going to attempt to remove the knife here. In the operating room, I can perform the procedure while scanning your arm to see exactly where the blade is in relation to any vital structures. I can't make you any promises at this stage, but I'll do my best to limit any permanent harm."

"Thank you." There was a flurry of activity, and he sensed the medical team were getting ready to move him. "Alyssa?"

"I'm here."

"I need to see you."

She stepped into his line of sight, cradling Kennedy against her shoulder. Although she was pale and the fine lines around her eyes were etched a little deeper, she still had the power to take his breath away.

"You okay?" When he spoke, his throat felt like he'd swallowed a cup of sand.

"Yeah. Neither of my arms have knives sticking out of them." Although she smiled, her eyes were a little too bright.

"Call Casey," he told her. "He'll know what to do.

He'll also know the best way to tell my mom and dad about this."

"Calling him is the first job on my list." She lightly touched his left hand. "You focus on letting the doctors make you well."

"Sorry, but we have to go," a nurse said.

"I'll see you soon." Alyssa kissed the hand she was holding.

"Yeah." As the gurney started to move, he turned his head. "And, Lyss?"

"Yes?" She craned her head to watch him.

"You do know that divorce comment was a trick? Just my way of giving you a get-out so you'd say 'yes' to the whole marriage plan…"

Her soft laugh was the last sound he heard as they wheeled him out of the room.

Chapter Eleven

"Alyssa!" Half an hour later, Melody dashed into the waiting room with Casey close behind her. "Oh, my stars. Are you okay? How is Everett? What can we do to help?"

"Maybe we could start by asking one question at a time?" Casey suggested. "Beginning with, can we get you anything?"

"Some water would be good." Alyssa gestured to the machine in the corner of the room. "I worry about disturbing Kennedy if I try to move."

Although she was happy to see them, their arrival triggered a change in Alyssa. It was like a dam had burst inside her. Until now, she'd been numb, able to function because of a curious lack of feeling. Now the old fear found her, pouncing on her with glee. Its cackling voice whispered in her ear, telling her knees to go weak, her stomach to lurch and her heart to pound. In response, she bowed her head.

"Hey." Melody came to sit next to her, then rubbed her back with a circular movement. "He'll be okay."

"You didn't see it." Her throat felt like she was trying

to swallow dry breadcrumbs. She waited until Casey handed her a glass of water. After taking a long slug, she started again. "There was a knife…" She gestured to her own arm. "Sticking out of his skin."

Casey closed one fist and smacked it into his other palm. In that moment, Alyssa could see her own feelings reflected in his eyes. They both wanted to shout, have a tantrum and beat their hands on the ground like a toddler. They also wanted to run away and hide.

It occurred to her that this could all be a nightmare. So far, she had been playing along with the bad dream. What if she refused to comply from now on? Would it be over faster? Or would it get worse…?

"The doctors know they need to preserve the knife for evidence, right?"

"I think they are more concerned about saving your brother's arm."

Casey swung away, every line of his body rippling with tension. "They may be able to do both. I need to speak to someone."

He stalked from the room and Melody placed an arm around Alyssa's shoulders, drawing her close. "He doesn't mean to be insensitive. He's worried about his brother and is dealing with it the only way he knows how. And he had to call his parents with the news. That was hard."

"It's okay." Alyssa said. "Everett and I were together for four years. His default setting in a crisis was law enforcement as well."

"Everett is in the hands of a medical team, but I'm worried about you right now." Melody's kind voice almost tipped Alyssa over the edge into tears. "You've had a terrible shock."

Those words set the scene for the next three hours. The time they spent in that waiting room took on the quality of water. Sometimes, it passed slowly, a drop at a time. Now and then, it rushed past with the speed of a river in flood. Once or twice, it froze and refused to move. Yet the clock on the wall showed it was constant, moving with a regular, unfailing tick-tock.

No matter how the time passed, Alyssa's insides grew increasingly hollow, and her skin became colder. A nurse wheeled in a portable crib and blankets. Placing Kennedy in it relieved the ache in Alyssa's shoulder muscles but did nothing for her heart. Casey paced up and down like a caged tiger and she couldn't decide whether she wanted to join him or throw something at him.

"He should be out of the OR by now." Casey checked the time on his cell-phone screen, clearly mistrusting the clock. "I'm going to see if I can find out what's going on."

As he marched from the room, Kennedy gave a soft whimper in her sleep.

"She'll wake up soon and be hungry." Alyssa bit her lip. "When I dashed out, I didn't think to bring her nighttime bottle with me."

Melody patted her hand. "Let me see what I can do. The staff here must be used to dealing with families in every kind of emergency."

As she went in search of a nurse, Alyssa leaned over the crib. *Family.* The word had the power to ground her.

"We're his, and he's ours," she whispered, watching Kennedy's rosebud lips puff in and out. "It's scary but true."

A movement caught her attention, and she looked up, thinking Melody or Casey had returned. Instead, there was a hooded figure standing just within the room. Alyssa's gaze dropped to the distinctive sneakers.

Just like a row of alligator teeth...

Instinct replaced rational thought. Acting fast, she snatched up her water glass and threw it. Although the intruder ducked, the glass shattered against the wall at the side of his head. At the same time, Alyssa screamed for help with all the power she had in her lungs. The stranger spun around and sprinted from the room.

Seconds later, Casey and a security guard almost collided in the doorway.

"What happened?" Casey was in uniform, but he still showed the other guy his badge to establish his seniority.

"He was here." Alyssa was trembling so hard she could barely get the words out through her strained airway. "The guy who attacked Everett was right here in this room."

Casey didn't waste time questioning how she knew it was the same person. "Get someone on the security cameras, then start a search," he told the guard. "He may still be on the premises."

The guard set off to follow his instructions while Casey made a call to the sheriff's department and got someone to clean up the glass. Kennedy, disturbed by the loud noises, started to cry. Alyssa lifted her from the crib, then rocked the little girl in her arms.

Inside her stomach a snowball was building, gaining layers in time with the machine-gun fire that was her heartbeat.

"Why did he come *here*?" she demanded when Casey finished his call.

"Isn't it obvious? He came to the hospital in search of Everett." Casey gave a short bark of laughter. "The knife is already on its way for processing, but the guy either wants it back, or he's planning to finish the job he started back in the parking lot."

"No." The negative thoughts were coming hard and fast, like waves pounding on rock. She started pacing, holding Kennedy with the baby's head tucked into her shoulder. "If that was the case, he had no reason to come to *this* room."

Casey stifled a curse. "You're right. There's a good chance he came looking for you and Kennedy."

Luckily for Alyssa's overwrought brain cells, Melody returned carrying a bottle of Kennedy's usual formula. As the baby drank, she gazed up at Alyssa with trusting blue eyes. Determinedly, Alyssa channeled all her concentration into making sure her little girl was okay. Kennedy was going to grow up strong and confident. Alyssa was not going to pass her own fears onto her. Kennedy would know she was loved, no matter what had happened in her parents' lives. This night would become a horrible memory, not a defining moment.

Having finished drinking, Kennedy sat up and gazed around her with interest. Clearly having decided that

Melody and Casey had come to this new place to see her, she entertained them with wide, new-tooth smiles and chuckles.

"At home, she would go straight back to sleep after her nighttime bottle." Alyssa smiled as Kennedy bounced up and down with excitement. "Tonight, she's ready to party until dawn."

Melody held out a hand to the baby, who grabbed her finger and tried to bite it. "At least she hasn't picked up that there's anything wrong."

"And she doesn't seem to be missing Everett." Alyssa cast a longing look in the direction of the door. "Not yet."

"I have to ask this, even if you tell me to mind my own business," Melody said. "But why aren't you and Everett still together?"

"This." Alyssa leaned back, resting her head against the hard cushion of the chair. "Knives, hospitals, bad guys hiding in the shadows. Those are just a few of the reasons why I can't be with him. It's what split us up last time. It's just too hard for me to see him in danger."

Casey looked perplexed. "So the reasons were all on your side?"

She frowned at him, confused by the question. "What do you mean?"

"Oh, nothing. It's been a long night and I'm talking nonsense." She could tell he was embarrassed, was instantly backtracking and trying to cover up for what he'd just said.

Alyssa wasn't fooled. There had always been a nagging doubt at the back of her mind. How many times had she tried to figure out what was behind Everett's emotional disconnection? Whenever he became tongue-tied about his feelings, hadn't she sworn there was a cause he was hiding from her?

"Are you trying to say Everett had his own reasons for why he couldn't be with me? Was it about something that happened in his past?"

Casey held up a hand in a backing-off gesture. "Hey. That's something you'd need to speak to Everett about."

"What is?" They all turned at the sound of Everett's voice from the doorway.

He was seated in a wheelchair, watching them. A porter wheeled him right into the room, then activated the brake before departing. Everett's right arm was in a sling and his face was pale but, otherwise, he appeared healthy. His gaze went from Alyssa to Casey and back again, missing nothing in the process.

"Oh, thank goodness." Overwhelmed with relief, Alyssa hurried toward him. "What did they say? Can you come home?"

He gripped her shoulder with his good hand as she knelt beside him. "First things first. What does Casey think you need to speak to me about?" Looking past her, he gave his brother a challenging stare.

"I was wondering whether you, Alyssa and Kennedy should come and stay at my place for a few days." The idea may have been on Casey's mind, but Alyssa thought his response was a little too smooth. And if she thought that, chances were his twin could see right through him.

"Thanks, but we'll be fine at home." Everett's smile

encompassed them both. "And, although that was a nice try, I'd still like to know what you were really talking about."

THE SURGEON WHO had done the procedure on Everett came into the waiting room to see him. "Luckily there was no nerve or blood-vessel damage and no fracture of the forearm. I removed the knife slowly, then repaired the muscle that had been injured by the stab wound. After that, my concern was the flesh surrounding the penetration site." He gave a small, tight smile. "Even after my best efforts, you will have quite a scar."

"But I can go home, right?" Everett asked.

Before the doctor arrived, Casey had briefly filled him in on the details of what had gone on while he had been in the operating room. Since then, his brain had been working on two levels. One was in this room, responding to the conversation that was going on around him. The second was in basic caveman mode. He had to protect his family. Injured or not, that was his only job.

"I see no reason to keep you here," the doctor said. "The procedure was lengthy, but it was successful. The range of movement in your hand and elbow should be back to normal within two weeks and I'll arrange for you to see a physiotherapist. Don't overdo it, but don't rest, either. Keep the arm movements undemanding but regular and try to rebuild your strength gradually."

After Everett had thanked him again for his help, he left.

"Before we get into the conversation about how I drive you home when I don't have a baby seat in my cruiser, how about I take your statement?" Casey regarded his brother with a touch of sympathy as he reached into his shirt pocket for his notebook.

Intense weariness washed over him, and Everett was tempted to tell his twin in no uncertain terms exactly what he could do with police procedure. But he knew as well as Casey did how important it was to get a witness's statement as soon as possible after the event. Although he wanted to get Alyssa and Kennedy back to the apartment, where he could keep them safe, he also wanted his attacker caught.

"Okay." He shot Alyssa an apologetic glance. "Let's get this over with."

His account of the attack was factual and concise. He'd taken enough witness statements to know exactly what Casey needed from him. Although his brother had a series of questions to go through, he raced ahead, anticipating each one and answering it before Casey had even begun to ask it. Scribbling frantically to keep up, his twin frowned as Everett finished his account.

"It was late. Why had you gone outside at that time?"

Everett glared at him. He had hoped they could dispense with supplementary questions. "I needed some air."

Casey tapped his pen against the page. "You were at the exit to the parking lot, almost on the road itself. Yet you weren't wearing a jacket, or even a sweater. On one of the coldest nights of the year, after a rare heavy snowfall. You want to tell me more about that breath of fresh air?"

"I was thinking about going for a run." Could Casey tell he was gritting his teeth? Everett sure as hell hoped so.

Tilting his head to one side, his brother glanced at his worn sneakers without comment.

So help me, Casey, I hope I get to interrogate you in similar circumstances one day. It wasn't true, but the thought allowed him to release a little frustration.

"Tell me about your impressions of the guy who attacked you."

Everett shrugged. "It happened so fast. The only real sense I got was that he was small and slight. He was also fast and nimble. It could even have been a woman."

Alyssa raised frightened eyes to his face and cradled Kennedy closer. "You don't think—?"

"That it was Georgia?" He took her hand. "How could it have been?"

Her shoulders slumped. "You're right. I know you are." She returned the pressure of his fingers. "But who else would be waiting in the dark? With a knife?"

"Probably the same person who tried to run me down. And the list could include any number of people I've put behind bars. My job as an FBI agent doesn't win me many friends among the criminal community," Everett said. "Sorry. But it's the truth."

Casey flipped through his notes. "You said you think this guy was waiting specifically for you."

"That was how it felt. He made no attempt to rob me. Just came out of the darkness, straight at me, and tried to stab me."

Casey appeared lost in thought for a moment of

two. "How long do you think he was there before you came out?"

"I'm not a mind reader." Everett rolled his eyes in Alyssa's direction. "And it didn't occur to me to start a conversation while he was trying to gut me like a fish."

"You're missing my point, smart guy. I don't know why you went out for a 'run'—" he put air quotes around the word "—on a snowy night in sneakers and a T-shirt. Since you are my brother, I trust you and believe it wasn't for any villainous reason, so I don't care. But think about it from the attacker's perspective."

Everett looked down at his arm resting in its sling. "Any particular reason why he gets to have a point of view in all this?"

"He, or she, was also out tonight. By the targeted nature of the assault, it seems likely he was waiting for you. But he couldn't have known you'd come out when you did. It's not like you went for a regular 'run' at that time. I'm not a gambler, but I'd say the odds of you emerging from the apartment at all in the snow, and at that time, must have been close to nil."

"You can stop with the air quotes." Everett gave his brother a warning look. "Just get to the point."

"Unless he was there tonight, and every night, waiting around in the hope you'd show, he had another motive for being outside your apartment with a knife."

Alyssa gave a little cry as Casey's meaning became clear.

"He wasn't waiting for me to come out." Everett's lips tightened into a thin line. "He was planning on coming in."

KENNEDY STUDIED HER bowl of fruit with all the interest of a food critic about to deliver a scathing review. Picking up a piece of banana, she carefully rubbed it between her thumb and forefinger. Holding out her hand to Everett, giving him her sweetest smile, she offered him the slimy mess.

"You know what? I think I'll stick with coffee."

Undeterred by his lack of interest, Kennedy found an orange segment and began to suck on it noisily.

"She's the only one who got any sleep." Alyssa smothered a yawn as she spoke. "It doesn't matter to her whether it was in her crib or in my arms."

"Why don't you take a nap now?"

She could hardly believe the guy with the face the color of curdled milk and the black bags beneath his eyes was telling *her* to get some rest.

"Uh, because one of us has to watch Kennedy, and you need sleep more than I do?"

He hunched a shoulder. "I have too much to do."

"You're on a leave of absence." As soon as she said the words, their irony made her flinch.

"Right." He carefully flexed the fingers of his right hand. "Tell the guy who left his knife in my arm about that."

"What will you do?"

"Probably exactly the same things Casey is doing right now." He gulped coffee like it was his lifeline. "Look for similar crimes. Search the databases for anyone matching our suspect, even though we don't have much to go on. Check out the weird alligator sneakers and see if they are sold in any local outlets. Go through my arrest list, see if any of them are carrying a grudge, then cross-check that with who is out of jail free and likely to be in this area. Find out if any of Georgia's associates are mixed up in this."

"You said you planned to visit Ray Torrington again."

"Are you okay with this?" He shook his head. "What a dumb question. What I mean is—"

"What you mean is 'why aren't I freaking out in typical Alyssa style?'"

"That's not what I said." His voice was gentle. "I know what you went through when your dad died."

She bowed her head, taking a few moments to stir her own coffee. "When we were together, your job was there, but it was distant. I never had to face its consequences. In my imagination, that made it grow into some kind of beast that was lurking on the edge of our lives just waiting to pounce. I couldn't rid myself of fear—even the certainty—that you would be killed in the line of duty. Since we've started to care for Kennedy, I've been plunged into the reality of what you do."

"I wish it didn't have to be this way—"

"So do I. But now I've been forced to confront your world, I see it for what it is." She looked up to find him watching her with a puzzled expression. "You mentioned the positive side of your job. Although I don't know if I'm there yet, I do know your training and experience are what Kennedy and I need to keep us safe. The reason I'm not freaking out is because the things I once hated are the very things I now appreciate."

Everett placed his hand over hers. "Is that what you were talking to Casey about at the hospital?"

"Partly. I told him we broke up because I couldn't bear to see you in danger." She held his gaze. "It was funny. He seemed to think there could be another reason. He said I needed to talk to you about what that was."

Watching him, she glimpsed everything she was hoping for. Momentarily, his expression was stripped of all pretense—the armor he wore was gone, and his fears and vulnerabilities were on display. Her breath caught in her throat. Was she about to find out a truth she had barely been aware of?

Then the light in his eyes changed. It pained her to see the battle taking place inside him. His dilemma was clear. He could let go of the defenses he'd worked so hard to build and risk being hurt, or leave his armor in place and never rebuild their relationship.

Four years ago, she'd reasoned that, if he loved her enough, he would one day tell her what had hurt him. Although she'd speculated about the cause of his emotional distance, he had never given her even a glimpse behind the walls he'd put up. Now, she decided he needed a prompt...

As she reached for his hand, the security buzzer broke the moment and Alyssa—the mild-mannered third-grade teacher—muttered a curse. "One of these days, I swear I am going to rip that thing out."

Everett raised an eyebrow at her. "Really? I've never heard you use words like that before."

"Long night." She pressed the backs of her hands to her burning cheeks.

He spoke into the speaker system and returned looking slightly bemused. "It's two of my FBI colleagues."

Alyssa's heart rate kicked up a notch. "What do they want?"

"I guess we're about to find out." Everett went to open the door. A tall, competent-looking woman and a younger stocky man entered. "Alyssa, meet Agents Karen Hayes and Shawn Heath."

They nodded a greeting. Although Agent Hayes glanced at Everett's arm in its sling, she made no comment. "I'll get straight to the point. You submitted a report expressing your concerns that Sean Dodd didn't commit suicide and kill his wife at the same time, but that both were murdered. The senior special agent saw enough merit in that to have it investigated. Since you are on a leave of absence, the case was assigned to us."

"There have been a few developments you should know about," Everett said.

The two agents exchanged a glance. "That's exactly what I was about to say to you."

"What do you mean?"

"Georgia Dodd escaped from her prison cell yesterday," Agent Hayes said. "I don't know if she has a reason to stay in the area—"

A loud hiccupping noise from the direction of the high chair drew their attention. Kennedy, having tired of eating her fruit, was now dropping it piece by piece onto the floor. Finding she had a new audience, she clapped her hands and waved.

"Georgia has a very powerful reason to stick around," Everett said. "I don't know why she would want her niece, particularly if she murdered her brother and sister-in-law, but she won't leave Cactus Creek until she gets what she wants."

Chapter Twelve

Alyssa shook her head as she surveyed the living area. When she had first seen it, she had wondered how they would fit two adults and a baby into the cramped space. Now it contained three FBI agents and a deputy sheriff, as well as her, Kennedy and Melody.

"Maybe I should go." Melody squeezed around the kitchen counter with a fresh pot of coffee in her hand.

"You stay right where you are." Alyssa gave her a stern look. "I need all the support I can get in this testosterone-charged atmosphere."

"One of them is a woman," Melody whispered.

"I think they give out macho swagger with the FBI badge," Alyssa murmured back. "Regardless of gender."

They directed a shared glance of female sympathy in the direction of Agent Hayes, who was doing her best to ensure her male colleagues conducted the investigation on her terms. The developing closeness Alyssa felt toward Melody was just what she needed right now.

Having had such a turbulent childhood, she found it difficult to trust anyone to be there when she needed them. Right from the start, Melody seemed different.

Somehow, Alyssa knew that, if she was ever stranded in the middle of nowhere, Melody would set off in her pajamas in the middle of the night to find her. If she was in a car wreck, she'd open her eyes to find Melody at her hospital bedside holding her hand. Finding her had been like coming across a rare and priceless jewel. Alyssa wasn't planning on letting her go anytime soon.

Maybe she should apply the same principle to finding the right man?

Her eyes shifted across the room to Everett's face. His tiredness appeared to have vanished as he spoke heatedly, vetoing one suggestion and agreeing with another. Although the four law-enforcement officers seated around the table were equal in rank, there was no doubt who was in charge. The others deferred to Everett, with only Casey questioning him now and then, or offering suggestions to supplement his ideas.

"You said you split up because of his job." She became aware of Melody watching her. "But you knew he was FBI when you met. Was there something specific that led to your decision?"

Alyssa picked up the baby monitor and led Melody into the kitchen, where they could talk undisturbed while she prepared Kennedy's lunch. The baby, having been overwhelmed by the desire to entertain her visitors, had grown tired and fallen asleep in the middle of an energetic game of peekaboo.

"Everett had only just joined the Bureau when we started dating," she said. "When he first graduated, he worked for a high-powered law firm as a paralegal. I don't know the circumstances, but it didn't work out.

My dad was killed in a violent attack and I…well, I've always been scared of losing anyone else I get close to in the same way. But we were just goofing around at first, you know? I was twenty-two. I wasn't thinking 'Is this is the man I want to spend the rest of my life with?'"

"But he was?"

Alyssa was chopping carrots, but the question stilled her fingers and blurred her vision.

Of course he was. Why had it needed a surprise baby and a crazed attacker to make her see what she'd always known?

"Everett loved his job. He didn't see the danger. For him, it was about righting wrongs." She laughed. "That makes him sound like a modern-day Robin Hood. I guess it was his way of helping people. As our relationship grew more serious, and I started to get spooked, I asked him if he wouldn't consider going back to his old job. Wasn't there a chance he'd get the same sense of satisfaction from helping people in the legal world?"

"I'm guessing it wasn't a popular suggestion?" Melody said.

Alyssa thought back to the way Everett had responded, to the way his jaw had clenched and he'd stared out of the window in silence for several minutes. At the time, she'd taken it as a signal that he didn't care for her interference in his career. Now? She wasn't so sure. It was almost as if he'd seen a ghost.

"He didn't really answer me. Just gave a strange sort of laugh and said there were more dangerous ways to earn a living than facing a terror suspect with a live device."

"Was he trying to fob you off? Change the subject?" Melody asked.

"Probably." Alyssa continued with her chopping. "We continued as we were. I tried to push the knowledge of what he was doing to the back of my mind, but the closer we got, the harder it became. Then, one night, I switched on the TV and started watching the evening news. There was live coverage of a hostage situation at a drug dealer's home. I couldn't make out the shadowy figures in the darkness, but I just knew Everett was there. Even though I didn't want to watch, I couldn't help myself."

It had been her idea of torture played out in front of her eyes. As the siege deteriorated into a battle, with shots being exchanged and agents scaling the walls of the dealer's mansion, she had been convinced that Everett was lying dead or dying in the uproar. When he finally walked through the door in the early hours of the morning, he had been tired, dirty and bloody, but mostly unhurt.

"Making the world a safer place is what I do, Lyss," Everett had said. He'd sounded helpless as she sobbed in his arms. "Another bad guy was taken off the streets tonight."

"A few days earlier, he'd asked me to move in with him. That night, he questioned if I would ever get used to his job." Her voice was a whisper as she placed the carrots in a saucepan. "I said I couldn't. That was four years ago. I didn't see him again until I acted on the letter inviting me to attend the reading of Kennedy's parents' will."

"Do you still feel the same?" Melody took the saucepan from her shaking hands and placed it on the heat. "Can you find a way to live with what he does?"

Alyssa blinked rapidly as she tilted her head back. "All I know is we don't have luxury of getting it wrong this time. We have Kennedy to think of…"

Her head ached with the pressure of thinking about everything that was going on. At the same time, her heart was being flung in every direction as she tried to decipher her feelings. One thing she had already realized was that she didn't lack courage. From deep within herself, she had found the strength to face her fears. Now, she had to make the right choice, for herself and for her daughter.

"That's not an answer." Melody brought her back to the original conversation.

"It's all you're going to get." Alyssa managed a slight smile. "Because, when I do figure out how I feel, I don't think you should be the first to know."

Everett and Casey arrived at the Torrington Law office at 9:30 a.m. the following morning and found the building still locked.

Casey peered through the window. "Looks like Raymond may be sleeping in today. Either that, or he's having himself a vacation. Tell me again why we need to talk to him."

"I'm certain that the guy was planning to cheat Kennedy when he didn't tell me that I was one of her trustees. That doesn't necessarily mean he's mixed up in anything else, but it makes me suspicious. I'd like to ask him how much he knows about Georgia's custody bid. Or anything else to do with Georgia, for that matter."

"You think Georgia could have recruited him to help her?" Casey asked.

"Stranger things have happened," Everett said. "Let's ask the neighbors what they know."

The adjoining store was a Western outfitters. As kids, it had been one of their favorite places. From the buffalo head and Apache artifacts on the wall, to the boots and hats displayed on top of barrels, everything about Freeman and Hicks was a magical taste of Cactus Creek's heritage.

Tom Hicks, the owner, was one of their dad's golf buddies. A living advertisement for his own products, he tipped his Stetson in greeting as he strode forward to meet them.

"Hey, guys. Did Ryker tell you about the sweet deal we've got on hand-stitched leather boots?"

Casey quirked an eyebrow in Everett's direction. "No, but if anyone is wondering what to buy me for Christmas…"

"Judge your timing," Everett growled out of the corner of his mouth.

"I'm sensing it's something I should work on."

They explained to Tom that they were there on business and accompanied him through to his office. Once he'd shifted stacks of plaid shirts out of the way, they were able to take a seat in the two chairs opposite his desk.

"This won't take long," Everett said. "We want to ask

a few questions about Torrington Law. Specifically, if you know how long the office has been closed?"

Tom tented his fingers beneath his chin. "Ray shut the place up yesterday. Said he had a family issue and he had to leave town. I asked him when he'd be back, but he couldn't say."

Everett flicked a glance in Casey's direction. Was it a coincidence that Ray had gone away on the same day that Georgia had escaped? He supposed it was a possibility. It was just that he had never liked the words *coincidence* and *possibility* in connection with criminal acts.

"You don't have a contact number for Ray's receptionist, by any chance?"

"Brenda Caplin? I don't, but my wife will. They are both members of the Cactus Creek Community Choir."

Ten minutes later, they were back in Casey's car and Everett was ending a call to Brenda.

"Anything?" Casey asked.

"Only some fairly bitter words about what it's like working for Ray. He didn't tell her he was closing the office. She just turned up for work as usual and couldn't get in."

"He always was a slimeball. Even when we were kids. Remember when he smashed the church window and blamed it on Philo Harper? Then Ray's dad paid a small fortune to the church fund to keep the truth quiet."

"Ray's dad." Everett pointed to the ignition. "Of course. It's time we paid Robert Torrington a visit."

Casey groaned. "The guy has spent his whole life covering up for his son. Nothing has changed since then."

"That's not true." Everett flexed the fingers of his

right hand, feeling the pull deep in his damaged muscles. "I've changed."

Casey kept his eyes on the road. "You need to tell Alyssa."

"That I've changed?" *Keep it light.* It was the tactic he used for making the big stuff go away. It worked pretty well most of the time. The only person who didn't get the message was sitting right next to him. Casey figured that twin thing gave him additional rights. Everett couldn't carry a grudge. It worked both ways.

"Am I the only person who knows?" They were on a quiet stretch of highway, heading out of Cactus Creek, and Casey flicked a glance in his direction. "You've never gotten any counseling, or other support?"

"I don't need—"

"Sure you don't," Casey snorted.

"Let's not do this."

When Casey spoke again, his voice was softer. "All I'm saying is, tell Alyssa what happened, or lose her." Everett held up his good hand, palm facing his twin. "Okay, I'll leave it there." They completed the rest of the journey in silence.

ROBERT TORRINGTON LIVED with his second wife, Renata, in an elegant colonial-style mansion. The acid-tongued lawyer was still considered a force to be reckoned with, despite having been wheelchair-bound for the last ten years.

As his twin drove up the sweeping drive with its towering palm trees, Everett viewed the house. "I've never heard any rumors about Torrington Senior operating on the wrong side of the law. You?"

Casey shook his head. "The guy is a major pain, but he's an honest one. The son? There are rumors, so I'm not sure."

Everett thought back to his most recent encounter with Ray, and the guy's bungled attempt to defraud Kennedy of her inheritance. "I'm certain Ray Torrington is a crook. There's only one reason I can think of for wanting to keep me out of the loop. He wanted to get his hands on the money the Dodds left their daughter. Was he smart enough to plan that himself, or did he have someone giving him advice? Someone who knew the details of Sean and Delilah's estate? That's what I'd like to ask him."

"I wouldn't recommend sharing your suspicions with his dad."

"Robert may expect other people around here to quake in their boots every time he speaks, but I intend to get some answers."

When Everett left Cactus Creek, he had shaken off its expectations and hierarchies. Although coming back had brought him an unexpected sense of satisfaction, he wasn't about to step back into the small-town mindset.

As soon as they halted in front of the house, the front door opened. Alighting clumsily from the vehicle as he struggled to get used to his sling, Everett found he was being scrutinized by a tall man in black pants and a white shirt. Not quite a uniform, it nevertheless proclaimed his status as an employee.

Although Everett held out his badge, the guy's gaze

skimmed right past him and landed on Casey. "Deputy Colton. I don't believe we were expecting this visit."

"That's right." Everett spoke before his brother could answer. "Law-enforcement officers don't need to make appointments."

"This is Deval Holden," Casey said as the other man's eyes finally dropped to Everett's badge. "He's Mr. Torrington's butler."

"While an appointment may not be a requirement, Agent Colton, it does signify a level of courtesy to an elderly gentleman." The butler hadn't shifted from his original position and was effectively blocking their entrance to the house.

Everett wasn't about to fall into the trap of justifying his actions. "As you've already correctly assumed, I'm here to speak to Mr. Torrington."

He kept on walking, daring Holden to stop him. At the last moment, the butler stepped back, holding the door wide. "Mr. Torrington had a bad night. I'll see if he's well enough to talk to you."

He escorted them into an elegantly furnished living room and left them there without any further conversation.

"I know this is hard for you, but you might want to tone down the bad cop and dial up the good cop," Casey said. "Just a little."

Everett drew in a deep breath, then let out a long and slow exhale. The action restored a little of his calm. "Someone stabbed me. That person is threatening my little girl. And scaring Alyssa."

"We'll catch whoever it is." Casey gripped his shoulder. "I just don't think it's Robert Torrington. And he's more likely to respond to flattery than hostility."

"Right. So now we offer a choice of interrogation styles?" Although Everett grumbled, he knew his brother was right. He was letting his emotions cloud his judgment. There was too much at stake for him to mess this up.

"Oh, my goodness." The words were accompanied by a swish of silk and a waft of heavy perfume. "Two handsome men in my house, and I wasn't expecting either of them. What did I do to deserve this?"

The woman who entered the room was probably in her fifties, but she was so perfectly styled and made-up that she could have claimed to be twenty years younger. Everett had a vague memory of returning home from college for a visit and listening with half an ear as his mom recounted the latest gossip. One of those stories had included an account of how Robert Torrington had scandalized the community by dumping his loyal wife—Ray's mom—in favor of a lap dancer. This, Everett figured, must be Renata Rose-Torrington.

"Mrs. Torrington? I'm Agent Colton of the Phoenix FBI office, and this is Deputy Colton of the Sur County Sheriff's Department. We're here to ask a few questions about your stepson."

"Ray? Oh, he had to go away." Renata took a seat on a plush white sofa and indicated the chairs to either side of her. "It was all kind of sudden."

A witness who wanted to chat. She was every law-enforcement official's dream. Resisting the temptation to exchange smiles with Casey, Everett took the seat she had indicated. "I hope everything is okay?"

"I don't know what's going on. All I know is, he turned up here during dinner in a state of panic. He and Robert locked themselves away for an hour. After that, Ray was out of the door like a shot from a gun." Restlessly, she smoothed down her skirts. "It's not like anyone ever tells me anything around here, but this time they just completely bypassed me."

"Do you have any idea where Ray went?" Everett asked.

"I may have overheard some of the conversation as I was passing the door of Robert's study." She examined her nails, favoring him with a pout that told its own story. Renata was jealous of the relationship between her husband and his son, and unhappy at being kept out of this latest crisis. "My husband told Ray he should go to relatives in Denver and lay low for a while. He told him he'd screwed up for the last time. Cheating clients should be easy, but he'd brought the Feds into it. If he didn't smarten up, Robert would cut him loose."

"Renata." Robert Torrington's voice was a bark as he rolled his wheelchair into the room. "Don't you have somewhere else to be?"

His wife's demeanor changed instantly. All traces of her former flirtatiousness vanished and as she got to her feet, she reminded Everett of a wilting rose. "Can I ask the housekeeper to bring you gentlemen some refreshments?"

"Thank you, but we won't be staying."

"Well, you got that much correct." Robert positioned

his wheelchair directly in front of Everett. "Perhaps you'd be good enough to explain the reason for this enforced federal presence in my home?"

"Your son and I are joint trustees of a child's estate. I need to make some decisions about her finances, and I'd like to get in touch with him," Everett said. "Do you have his contact details?"

He could tell his approach had taken both Robert and Casey by surprise.

"I'm sorry, Agent Colton, that you've had a wasted journey." Robert gave him a smug smile. "If only you'd called first, I could have told you that my son doesn't have a cell phone. Since he is currently traveling, I have no way of getting in touch with him."

Everett returned the smile. "You must have the address of the relatives in Denver with whom he's staying, however."

He figured the frown that descended on the other man's brow was generally considered some kind of storm warning. "Did my wife tell you about that?"

"Mrs. Torrington told us she had not been included in any conversations about your son's whereabouts."

Everett gained a measure of satisfaction from Robert's petulant expression as he barked out the address for his cousin in Denver but that was short-lived. By the time he was able to get in contact with the Denver police and give them a list of questions for Ray, Robert would have tipped off his son. The tricky lawyer would be long gone.

The truth was, of course, that Everett didn't really suspect Ray of being the person behind the threats and attacks. The guy was a sleazy bottom-feeder, but it was stretching the imagination way too far to picture him killing his wealthy clients just so he could get his hands on their daughter's fortune. It was still possible he could be working with Georgia, hoping that, if she got custody of the baby, he would be in line for some of the inheritance money.

Whatever was going on, it all came back to that curious question. How would anyone have murdered Sean by getting him to drive his car into a wall?

Stranger things have happened.

And that was why, even though, when it came to suspects, Ray was way down the list, they had to eliminate him. He flicked the piece of paper Robert had given him with a scrawled address in Denver written on it.

"What if he's not there?"

Robert puffed out his chest. "What are you implying?"

"I'm simply thinking of the child. Can a trustee who does not fulfill his duties to the required standard be removed?"

"It's a matter for the courts." Robert gave him a look of intense dislike. "Technically, an incapable, or incompetent, trustee must be replaced by another suitable person."

"Thank you for your help." Everett got to his feet.

Robert blinked up at him. "That's it?"

"I'm sure you'll be in touch if you think of anything that might help our inquiries."

"What inquiries might they be, Agent Colton?"

"For now, I only have reason to suspect your son of

plotting to defraud a newly orphaned child of her inheritance." Everett let the polite facade slip. "If I find out he is involved in anything more, I'll be back."

"You can't threaten me in my own home—"

"My brother doesn't make threats," Casey said, as Everett headed toward the door. "He makes promises. Then he keeps them."

Chapter Thirteen

"I do not have an online shopping problem."

Alyssa reasoned that if she said the words often enough, they might turn out to be true. Although, right at that moment, she was fighting a losing battle. There were just so many things she wanted to buy for Kennedy.

Melody had called in earlier for a coffee and a chat, but her job at OverHerd Ranch didn't allow her much free time. It was fine, Alyssa had assured her. Everett wasn't planning on being out for long. That had been three hours ago. Since then, she had cleaned the apartment, done the laundry and prepared dinner.

She swiped through a few pictures on her cell phone. "It's his own fault if he comes back to find I've bought a life-size sleigh and a real reindeer."

Kennedy, who was lying on her back on the play mat, trying to eat one of her own feet, chuckled happily.

"And, if he's not careful, Everett is going to find himself unwrapping this cute, fluffy bathrobe on Christmas morning." Alyssa tilted the screen to show Kennedy. "What do you think? Too much?" Hampered by a mouthful of toes, the baby made a gurgling sound. "You could be right. He's not really a snuggly, teddy-bear kind of guy."

In a corner of the room there was a stack of parcels that had been delivered when Melody was still there. Just the thought of their contents sent a flood of excitement pouring through Alyssa's veins. Later, when Everett was home, she would open them and hang Kennedy's stocking next to the tree. Then, when the baby was asleep, she would wrap her presents...

"Oh, I know what that one will be." Jumping up, she retrieved the smallest package from the pile.

This item had been the most expensive and well-researched of all her purchases. She'd initially been unsure whether it was possible to place a GPS tracker on a baby, but in a short time, Alyssa had become an expert on the tool. Convinced Everett would think she was paranoid, she hadn't told him about her plans.

Now she held in her hands a box containing a tiny bracelet, a button that clipped inside a child's clothing and details of how to activate her subscription. One of her main priorities had been to find a method for tracking Kennedy's whereabouts that didn't look obvious. She figured that if someone—*Georgia*—managed to abduct the little girl and found an electronic device on her wrist, they would simply remove it. A pretty pink bracelet would be more likely to survive.

For a moment, the image of Georgia abducting Kennedy, or even gaining custody of the little girl, swamped Alyssa's thoughts. Although the idea of her daughter in danger was paramount, the loss of her new parenthood scared her as well. It was a mirror of her own child-hood and it filled her with dread. Brushing it aside, she focused on the tracking device.

Minutes later, Kennedy was wearing her bracelet and button, her movements corresponding to a flashing dot on Alyssa's cell phone. "That's it, honey. No secrets for you for the next eighteen years."

It was a tiny victory in an otherwise harrowing time. The knowledge that someone was out there, hunting them like prey, was emotionally draining. It wanted to consume her thoughts and eat away at her peace of mind. The only things that stopped it were Everett and Kennedy. Now an app on her phone screen was helping.

"Where *is* he?" Just as Alyssa was checking again to see if there were any messages, she heard Everett's key in the door. Instantly, her tension lifted like steam rising from hot coffee.

Resisting the temptation to run to him and wrap her arms around his neck—*because...where did that come from, anyway?*—she watched as he kneeled be-side Kennedy.

"Don't swallow those toes, sweetheart." He indi-cated the foot that Kennedy was still chewing. When he kissed her cheek, the baby cooed contentedly. Alyssa shook her head to dispel the sudden rush of emotion.

Maybe he is a big, snuggly teddy bear, after all.

"I'm sorry." He looked up at Alyssa and she saw the lines of weariness around his eyes. "I should have called." Quickly, he outlined the details of his visit to the Torrington Law office and Robert Torrington's house.

"Is it possible Ray was the person who stabbed you? He could have panicked and decided to go on the run."

"Whoever attacked me was smaller than Ray," Everett said. "In my opinion, he's lying low because he knows he's in a world of trouble because he knows I suspect him of trying to cheat Kennedy." He caught sight of the pile of boxes. "You've been busy."

"This is the last of the Christmas shopping. I want—"

He laughed. "I know. You want it to be special for Kennedy."

"For all of us." She would never be able to convey how much it meant to her to have a family of her own this Christmas. Instead, she changed the subject. "Kennedy won't remember her first Christmas, so I want to capture lots of magical moments."

"Alyssa." He gave her a measuring look. "Do any of your plans involve me wearing a silly sweater?"

She hung her head. "Just for the photographs."

He gave an exaggerated sigh. "Show me."

Going to the stack of parcels, she found the one from the online sweater store and opened it. "Promise you'll keep an open mind?"

"How bad can it be?" Everett asked. "Or are you intending to get me drunk before you answer that question? Like last time?"

"There are three sweaters, one for each of us." Alyssa held them up, one at a time, smiling a little at Everett's reaction to the snowflakes and sleigh bells. "Mommy Elf. Daddy Elf. And, for Kennedy, there's one that says Raised by Elves." He put his head in his hands, but from the way his shoulders were shaking, she guessed he was laughing. "I thought it would make the cutest family portrait."

When he looked up, the laughter was gone. Even though his expression was unreadable, his gaze warmed her from her head to her toes. "Yeah. That was my plan for the holidays until a few weeks ago. The cutest Christmas."

"Well, excuse me if Kennedy and I spoiled your single-guy holiday of beer, pizza and video games—"

"What's this?" Everett interrupted Alyssa's half-joking rant.

When she'd moved the packages, a folded piece of white paper had slipped out from between them and fallen to the floor. Reaching for it with his good hand, he clumsily opened it. The message, like the last one, was in that familiar scrawl and had been written in black felt pen.

Looks like the knife did some serious damage to the tough guy's arm. Can't wait to see what the next one will do to the baby.

"WHO DELIVERED THESE?" Everett was on his feet, cell phone in hand, any traces of tiredness gone.

Alyssa stared at him, her face chalk-white and her eyes wide. He could see her chest moving in time with each shallow, rapid breath. As she lifted a shaking hand to her lips, Everett bit back an exclamation.

What had he been thinking? She'd just seen a gruesome threat to kill Kennedy and he'd responded by barking a question at her as if she was a suspect. He could try using the excuse that he was in shock as well, but…really? Would making this about him help?

Don't go there, Colton. Just this once, get it right.

He closed the distance between them and drew her close, tightening his uninjured arm around her. "I'm a jerk and I'm sorry."

She melted into him, her whole body quivering. "You *are* a jerk." The words were muffled by his shirt.

"What was that? I didn't quite catch what you said. Something about a jerk, but also incredibly hot?"

She leaned back and the tears in her eyes made his heart ache. "You're impossible."

"But also incredibly hot?" he asked hopefully.

She managed a slight smile, along with a loud sniff. "I need to blow my nose."

She disappeared into the bathroom, returning a few minutes later. Her eyes were red and her face was blotchy, but she shook her head when he raised an eyebrow at her. "Ask your questions. I know it's important."

He took a seat on the sofa and patted the cushion next to him. "Who delivered your parcels?"

Alyssa sat down, frowning in an effort to remember. "It was a regular courier service. When the guy pressed the buzzer, I looked out of the window. His vehicle was in the parking lot and, because Melody was here, I figured it would be okay to open the door."

He didn't like her reasoning. Two women and a baby alone in the apartment… The person at the door could have been armed or taken Alyssa by surprise and overpowered her. His mind skittered away from the disturbing images. Once he'd dealt with the immediate matter of the letter, he'd come back to the issue of tightening security.

"Can you remember the name of the company?"

"No, but the company logo was something about smiles." She wrinkled her nose. "'Sending smiles'? No, that's not right."

"'Delivering smiles.'" Everett clenched his right fist a little too hard and felt the pull on his damaged arm. "The company is Blaze Couriers."

"That was it. How did you know?"

"Because it's the same firm that delivered the teddy bear on Kennedy's first day with us."

"Oh." She went to the baby, lifting her into her arms. Kennedy snuggled sleepily into the crook of her arm. Although his mind was focused elsewhere, Everett observed Alyssa fiddling with a bracelet on the little girl's chubby wrist. He hadn't seen the item before and, although he wouldn't normally have chosen to put jewelry on a baby, it looked pretty.

"I don't suppose you saw the guy's name tag?" Alyssa shook her head. "Could you describe him?"

"He was average-looking. Early twenties. Slim build. Brown hair. I didn't notice his eye color. Nothing made him stand out to me."

"It could be Joe Meyer, the guy who delivered the bear," Everett said. "I need to pay him a visit."

He stared at Alyssa, taking in her soft, golden beauty and the protective way she held Kennedy. Just watching her brought him so much mingled joy and pain. Until now, he'd never dared dream of eternity. His past had made him scared to look beyond tomorrow. But in that instant, he wanted to hold out his hand to her and ask her to be brave enough to trust him again.

As he moved across the room toward her, Alyssa must have sensed his intention because she shifted Kennedy's weight to her shoulder. Mindful of the sleepy baby between them, Everett lowered his head until his lips grazed across Alyssa's skin, tracing a line from the hollow beneath her ear to her jaw, until he reached the trembling pulse at the base of her neck.

Her tiny indrawn breath told him everything he needed to know. Brushing his lips across hers, he toyed with her, tempting her until she gave a little moan.

When he slid his open mouth over hers, she edged her tongue just far enough between his parted lips to taste him.

With a low growl, he fastened his mouth on hers, still arching away from her to avoid disturbing Kennedy. The muscles of his shoulders trembled as it took all his strength to keep his hands away from her body.

Their mouths moved together in a kiss that was both tender and passionate. Everett devoured her mouth, caressing her tongue with his and sucking on her lower lip.

As Alyssa leaned into him, the baby murmured and stirred and they sprang guiltily apart.

"I—" She hitched in a sharp breath as Kennedy tugged on her hair. Laughing, she untangled the strands from between the baby's fingers and started again. "I don't want to stay here alone while you go out again."

Everett wanted to ask her what she'd really been about to say. He wanted to talk about the kiss and if it meant as much to her as it did to him...

"Let me make some calls."

A few minutes later, he finished speaking to Casey, and explained the details of their conversation to Alyssa. "If it's okay with you, I'm going to take you and Kennedy to my parents' house. They are both at home today. After an attempted break-in last year, my dad installed a hi-tech security system, complete with cameras. In addition, Casey has put a red alert on your cell phone. If you call 911, or the sheriff's department main number, it will be flagged for an immediate response. He'll also send a cruiser out to check on this apartment, and my mom and dad's place every hour. And, of course, we have an alert out for Georgia but no luck so far in finding her."

Her shoulders relaxed. "As long as your parents don't mind?"

"My mom has been desperate to get her hands on Kennedy." He grinned. "If she starts with the wedding hints again, you may be the one who minds."

She matched the grin with one of her own. "Maybe I should distract her with the novelty sweaters?"

"That conversation is not over." He removed Kennedy from her arms and pointed her toward the bedroom. "I'll get this little one ready for the journey while you get the pink-elephant bag for all eventualities."

ANY FEARS ALYSSA may have had that Ryker and Maribelle's home would prove too imposing were soon put to flight. The property was certainly large and luxurious, but it was also comfortable and welcoming.

She drove close to the house, halting just in front

of the steps that led from the wraparound porch to the drive. Maribelle was already heading toward the car with her arms outstretched.

"Let me get that sweet little girl out of the cold and into the house."

With all the skill of a woman who had clearly been practicing to be a grandmother for many years, she had the baby out of her seat and was heading up the steps. Alyssa watched them disappear inside. She should probably follow them, but it was no good. There was something she had to ask first.

Everett was in the passenger seat and she shifted her position to face him. "You'll—"

He flexed his right arm. "Be careful? You have my promise."

It didn't feel like enough, but she couldn't think of anything else to say. Actually, that wasn't true. She could think of a hundred things, none of them relevant to this moment.

"Not being able to drive is frustrating the hell out of me." Everett turned to look behind them and she knew he was scanning the area for signs of Casey's arrival.

She should be glad his whole focus was on catching the bad guys, right? She didn't want him to be distracted, not even by thoughts of her. There would be time to think about the future when they knew if there *was* a future. Leaning closer, she kissed his cheek.

"Hey." He looked surprised but pleased. "What was that for?"

"Luck. Memories. Thanks. Does there have to be a reason?"

"I guess not." He smiled, taking her hand and placing it on his knee.

They sat in silence for a few minutes until the sound of Casey's car approaching broke the mood. "I'll be back as soon as I can."

They exited the vehicle together with Alyssa heading toward the house while Everett went in the opposite direction. Before she started up the steps, Alyssa took a glance over her shoulder. Casey swung the car into a U-turn, ready to exit the drive. As he drove away, she was just in time to see Everett raise his left hand and press his fingertips to the point where her lips had recently connected with his cheek. It was a sweet ray of light on a dark day.

Once she was inside, she found Kennedy had taken over the house. In the short time she had been there, Ryker and Maribelle had become her devoted servants. Seated on the rug, with cushions piled around her, the baby only had to wave in the general direction of an object and Everett's parents went scrambling on all fours to get it for her.

"These belonged to the twins when they were babies." Maribelle got to her feet. "They've been stored in the garage since then."

Alyssa laughed as Kennedy whacked Ryker over the head with a stuffed toy. The respected oncologist rolled around pretending to be injured and the baby squealed with excitement.

Maribelle's eyes shone with pleasure. "It's wonderful to hear that sound within these four walls again."

When Ryker sat up, his hair stood on end as if he'd

been given an electric shock. "I'm sorry to hear about these awful threats. I'm sure Everett will catch the person responsible very soon."

"Oh, goodness, I hope so," Maribelle said. "It makes me shudder to think that such evil exists." She slid Alyssa's hand into the crook of her arm. "Why don't you come through to the kitchen with me while I finish getting lunch ready? Ryker can keep the baby entertained."

An hour later, Alyssa felt as though she had known these people forever. It wasn't Maribelle's fresh-baked lemon cake, or her beautiful china, or even the hand-picked flowers from Ryker's conservatory that made this place feel like she'd come home. It was the smiles, love and warmth.

After lunch, Kennedy fell asleep and Alyssa placed her on a sofa in the cozy lounge, tucking her favorite blanket around her. Maribelle came to sit next to them.

"I know she's not his biological child, but the way she's lying right now reminds me of Everett." Her expression was tender. "He was such a sweet baby." She laughed. "I know I complain about raising twins, but they really didn't give me much bother, only the usual rough-and-tumble boy things. At least..." A troubled look came into her eyes. "Not until the summer after Everett graduated. He was dealing with some things that caused him a few problems."

Alyssa's heart began to thud. That would have been the summer before they met. "Do you know what happened?"

Maribelle shook her head. "We hadn't seen him for over a month and, when we did, we were shocked at the change in him. He was quiet and withdrawn and had lost a lot of weight. He'd recently started a job as a para-legal with a big law firm in Phoenix. Ryker and I were seriously concerned about his well-being, but when we tried to talk to him, he brushed our concerns aside. Our only hope was that he might confide in Casey. Not long after that visit, he quit his job and joined the FBI. We never did find out what had affected him so badly."

She should leave this alone. Casey had summed it up. *Speak to Everett.* If he wanted her to know about his past, he would tell her. She should not go digging without his permission…

"What was the name of the firm he worked for?"

Chapter Fourteen

As they drove toward the head office of Blaze Couriers, Everett and Casey discussed a recurring theme in the case.

"Sean drove his SUV at speed into a wall. How could Georgia—assuming it *was* her—have gotten him to do that?" Everett had studied every report and photograph of the scene until his head ached. He still couldn't make any sense of it.

"There was speculation in the press that Sean and Delilah were killed elsewhere, and their bodies were placed in the car wreck after it happened. Forensics confirmed that wasn't the case. Sean was driving that vehicle when it hit the wall. Their injuries were devastating." Casey's mouth thinned into a line. "I got to the scene before the bodies were removed. There was no way they could have survived."

"What are the other theories? The car was tampered with in some way?"

Casey shook his head. "There was nothing wrong with the vehicle. It was subjected to a thorough check and it passed every test."

Everett drummed his fingers on his thigh. "I'm reaching here, but could a remote-controlled device have been used? Something that meant Sean was unable to apply the brakes when he needed to?"

"Why wouldn't he have swerved?" Casey asked. "If he found himself unable to slow down, there were less devastating actions than driving into a wall."

"Maybe all the controls were taken over remotely?" Everett shrugged. "That sounds like something from a movie, I know, but I'm just speculating."

"Anything is possible," Casey conceded. "All I know is that nothing has been found so far."

"That means it was probably something simple." Everett felt his mood lower further as he stared out of the window. "And untraceable."

Blaze Couriers had an office located just outside Cactus Creek, on the road to Tucson. The business consisted of a small reception office, behind which there was a long, low building that Everett assumed was the handling depot for parcels. There was also a fenced yard in which several of the firm's vehicles were parked.

When he and Casey entered the office, the uniformed guy behind the desk waved them to a seat without looking up. "Be with you in a minute. Make sure you have ID. No ID, no parcel."

Everett stepped up to the counter. "I've got ID." He checked out the guy's name tag before holding out his FBI badge. "Is this good enough for you, Antonio?"

"Uh. Right." Antonio scrambled to his feet. "What can I do for you, officer? Er, agent? I mean…sir?"

"I'm looking for one of your delivery drivers. Name of Joe Meyer."

"Joe? He's out on a job." He reached for a clipboard and flicked through a sheaf of papers. "Although he is due back soon for his next pickup."

"Soon. What does that mean?" Everett asked.

"Ten minutes." Antonio's eyes flickered nervously to Casey, who was leaning against the door. "Maybe sooner if he finishes his last job quicker than expected."

"We'll wait here for him."

"Should I call him? Tell him you're here?"

Everett smiled. "No, Antonio. You absolutely should not do that."

Casey moved to watch one of the windows and Everett took the other. It was almost exactly ten minutes later when a delivery van pulled into the yard and Joe Meyer alighted from it.

"Our guy?" Casey quirked a eyebrow at Everett.

"That's him."

He watched Joe approach the office. Could he have been the person who came out of the darkness and stabbed him? Joe wasn't a big guy. Alyssa had described him as average build, but he was possibly smaller than that, and he was light on his feet. Even so, Everett wasn't convinced. When he compared his own size to his attacker's, he wasn't sure there was enough of a difference between him and Joe.

Still have a few questions for you, Joey boy...

The door swung open and, whistling cheerfully, Joe entered. As he stepped up to the desk, Everett and Casey moved into place behind him.

"Nice to see you again, Joe."

Swinging around sharply, Joe looked from one to the other and back again.

"Hey, I remember you. You're the teddy-bear guy, right?" His grin failed miserably and he looked like he wanted to cry.

Casey looked his brother up and down. "Teddy bear? That's not how most suspects describe him."

Joe's face dropped even further. "Suspect? What do you mean?"

Everett ignored the question. "Is there somewhere private here? We need to talk to you."

"Sorry. Got too much to do." Joe's gaze swiveled to Antonio in a help-me-out plea. "Isn't that right?"

"There's an office at the back." Antonio gave a helpless shrug as he beckoned them around the counter. "FBI, man," he said as Joe glared at him.

The office was more of a storage closet. Everett rested his hip on the edge of a packing crate while Casey took up his usual position against the door. Joe backed unhappily into a corner.

"I told you all I know about that teddy bear."

"You made another delivery to my apartment today, Joe," Everett said. "Tell me about that one."

Joe tried for a flash of defiance. "I don't remember every job I do."

"You'll remember this one." Carefully, Everett removed the letter—now encased inside a plastic folder—from the file he was carrying and held it up so that Joe could read it. "Because either you are guilty of sending threatening letters or someone gave you this to deliver with the other packages you brought to my apartment."

Joe licked his lips. "I've never seen that before."

Everett turned his head to look at Casey. "That's good. Will it work in court?"

Casey shrugged. "It's a risky defense. A jury might believe a mystery person smuggled the letter into the stack of packages while he wasn't looking. Did you sign for them when you collected them from the depot, Joe?"

"Um...yeah."

"And you lock your vehicle each time you do a delivery?" Casey continued.

"Of course."

"Then you'd better get yourself a good lawyer. Any half-decent prosecutor is going to hang you out to dry when you say you haven't seen that letter before."

"And threatening a baby?" Everett shook his head. "I can't see you getting much sympathy from a jury for that, Joe."

"She said it was a joke." The words burst from Joe's lips, and he slumped against the wall. "A family thing. She told me you'd see the funny side."

"She?"

"Georgia." He turned his head, whispering the name into the brickwork. "Georgia Dodd. The woman I love."

WHILE KENNEDY SLEPT, Ryker went out to tend the plants in his conservatory and Maribelle chatted to Alyssa as she organized her charity paperwork. Surreptitiously, Alyssa checked her cell phone for details on Alexandria and Foster, one of the largest, oldest and most well-respected law firms in Phoenix. Specializing in corporate and finance litigation, it had a client list that included some of the largest banks in America.

It was also rumored to have a cutthroat approach to winning awards. This obsession with excellence and perfection had come under the spotlight eight years ago, when the firm's hiring policies were criticized following the attempted suicide of a young intern.

Eight years ago. Alyssa gazed into space, her mind racing with possibilities. Could Everett have been that person who was driven to the point of suicide by the pressures of his job? She needed to stop this *now*. She was getting way ahead of herself. Giving him a history that she knew nothing about was dangerous territory. Determinedly, she put aside her cell phone.

"Is there anything I can do to help?" she asked Maribelle.

A few minutes later, she was immersed in Maribelle's unique filing system. Since it was unlike anything she had ever come across before, it required all her concentration. It was a curiously therapeutic way to spend an hour.

When Kennedy woke up and noisily demanded food, Alyssa held her bottle out to Maribelle. "Would you like to feed her?"

"I would love to." Maribelle and Kennedy settled into a large rocking chair together, and Alyssa watched them with a smile. All those expensive presents back at the apartment were meaningless next to this.

A few minutes later, Everett and Casey arrived.

"Did you find him?" Alyssa wasn't sure whether an affirmative, or negative, answer was the one she wanted.

"We did, and he confessed everything." Everett placed an arm around her waist.

She turned her face into his shoulder, relief washing over her. "I don't understand. Did he have some sort of grudge against the Dodds? Against you?"

"No. He's been working with Georgia. She picked him up in a bar just after the Dodds were killed and convinced him that she was the love of his life. The poor sap would do anything for her."

Her short-lived happiness soured. "So she's still out there somewhere?" Why did the thought of Georgia Dodd always make her want to look over her shoulder?

"We'll catch her," Casey said. "Joe is in a cell downtown, singing his heart out about everything he's done for Georgia. The only thing he hasn't given away is her hiding place." He jerked a thumb over his shoulder. "On that subject, I want to get back to the office."

Maribelle waved a hand in his direction. "We'll see you on Christmas Day."

"What happened to 'can't even stay for a five-minute chat with your mom these days'?" Casey murmured.

"She has a new love interest." Everett indicated the contented baby. "Be prepared for her to forget your name in a week or two."

When Casey had gone, he turned to Alyssa. "It's only a matter of time before she's caught."

"I'm worried about what she can do in that time." She indicated his right arm. "She's proved she means business, and she was planning on getting into the apartment the night she stabbed you." She frowned. "Unless it was Joe?"

"No. He has an alibi for the night I was attacked. He confirmed Georgia was the one who stabbed me the night she escaped from jail. Is that what you're worried about? That she'll succeed next time she tries to break in? Would you rather stay here?"

She weighed the options. The apartment was cramped and inconvenient. As soon as she moved a single item, the place became untidy. It was also unsafe because Georgia was targeting them there, although it was hard to see how she could get in without tripping over holiday decorations or baby gear. This house, on the other hand, was simply lovely. Big, cozy and with every convenience. And it was secure. There was no choice.

"I want to go home."

As they drove back through the center of Cactus Creek, the holiday lights were starting to glow against the falling darkness. Offices were closing and overloaded shoppers walked along the sidewalk carrying bags and parcels.

The ice rink that had been erected at one end of Main Street was busy, but the queue for the Santa Express was dwindling as dinner time approached. Accompanied by reindeer, the little wooden train took passengers on a festive journey into the hills around Cactus Creek.

"It was one of our favorite holiday traditions," Everett said, as he pulled up at an intersection. "Each December, Casey and I would count the days until we could board the train to the 'North Pole.'"

"We should do it," Alyssa said.

"Good idea. Next year, when Kennedy is old enough…"

"We're trying to make memories for her this year."
She pointed to a parking space. "Let's take her before
we go home."

He frowned. "Are you sure? It's been a stressful day.
We could always come back tomorrow."

"It's quiet now," she said. "Any other time, we may
have to join a line."

She had a point. The journey in the rickety wooden
carriages only took an hour, but the wait time could
often be three times as long. Although Everett wasn't
convinced that Kennedy would get anything out of the
ride, he could appreciate what Alyssa was trying to do.
She wanted to be able to share these experiences with
Kennedy in the future so that their little girl knew she'd
had a rich and loving start to her life with them.

And wasn't there a part of him that wanted to put
aside all the stress of recent events and clamber aboard
the train that had been one of the biggest thrills of his
childhood? It would be worth it just to see Casey's face
when he told him how he'd spent the evening.

He pulled into the parking space and turned to look
at Kennedy. The baby had been sleeping, but she was
now looking out of the window, studying the holiday
lights with fascination. That settled it. She would love
the color, vibrancy and fun of the Santa Express.

The booth was decked out like a gingerbread house
and they were given candy cane entrance tickets.

"I don't quite follow how we travel from old Arizona

to the North Pole," Alyssa whispered as they boarded the train.

"That's the magic of Christmas," Everett told her solemnly.

There were eight seats in each carriage, and, during the journey, Santa made his way through the train delivering gifts. Holiday music played, festive lights twinkled and elves danced.

As the train chugged off on the start of its journey, Everett relaxed. Maybe this was exactly what they needed to put things in perspective. With Kennedy on her knee, Alyssa was waving to the people they passed. The baby was watching the lights with wide eyes and clapping along with the Christmas music. It was a reminder that there was a whole other world that had nothing to do with Georgia Dodd and her threats.

The high point of the journey was when the train reached Santa's workshop in the "North Pole." Passengers were able to alight and feed the reindeer before being served hot chocolate and cookies.

"And, of course, Santa has his own store up here in the hills with lots of special offers," Everett said. "Just in case the passengers have any last-minute shopping to do."

Alyssa wasn't listening. "I just need to get a closer look at those baby elf slippers—"

"Seriously? She can't walk yet, but she needs slippers?"

She gave him a pitying look. "Yes. But Kennedy mustn't see them."

"Of course not." He rolled his eyes. "I'll take her

back to look at the reindeer again while you indulge in a little retail madness."

Five minutes later, the elves were encouraging the passengers back onto the ride with a merry jingle, but there was no sign of Alyssa.

"All aboard." One of the elves waved Everett toward the train.

"I'm looking for my—" He paused. How was he supposed to describe Alyssa? "Partner." That was probably the closest. "She went into the store."

"She's probably waiting on the train for you, sir."

While that might be a reasonable assumption for other people, Everett knew Alyssa wouldn't have boarded the train without him and Kennedy. She knew he'd taken the baby to look at the reindeer, so, once she'd finished her shopping, she'd have come to find him.

"No, she must still be inside the store. Please check."

The elf looked slightly less cheerful as she shook her head. "The store is closed now, sir. You need to board the train."

Everett looked around. He was the last person on the platform. The driver gave an impatient toot of the festive horn. Was he really considering his next action? He would be remembered as the guy who tore apart a Cactus Creek tradition...

He leaned closer to the elf. "The Santa Express is not going anywhere until I find her."

ALYSSA WAS GETTING ANNOYED. The elf behind the counter was the least efficient person she had ever encountered. And he was way too tall to be an elf.

"Is there a problem with my card?" She knew that couldn't be the case. She had transferred a large chunk of savings to her checking account only a few days ago to cover every festive eventuality. She asked the question in the hope it would prompt him into moving a little faster.

"Uh…no. It seems to be a problem with our systems. I'll just check with my colleague."

Okay, so he was an inexperienced elf. Maybe he was a stand-in holiday sprite, or something. Alyssa sighed as she waited for him to return.

The store was emptying rapidly as the passengers returned to the train and she was starting to wonder if the elf slippers were worth the effort or the price tag. But they were cute. Kennedy was going to look adorable in them on Christmas morning.

"I'm sorry." The elf returned at last. "Your transaction has now been processed."

"What was the problem?" she asked as he handed her a brightly colored bag and her card.

He cast a furtive look over his shoulder. "I probably shouldn't tell you this, but the cash register had been unplugged from its power source."

Alyssa gave him a sympathetic look. "Technology, huh?"

She reached for her purse to return her card to her organizer. Except… Her purse wasn't where she'd left it. Her heart gave a heavy, downward thud. Taking a step back, she scanned the area around the checkout. But she already knew what she was doing was in vain. Her purse had been right next to her. Now, it was gone.

"My purse has been taken." It was the only explanation.

With a flare of annoyance, she noted the exchange of glances between the elves. When did she become *that* customer? The one who provoked the raised eyebrows and the polite eyeroll? The last one in the store who kept everybody waiting only to have her bag turn up exactly…

"Is this your purse, ma'am?" One of the employees stooped and picked up an item near Alyssa's feet.

"Oh." Embarrassed, she felt the heat rise in her cheeks as she took it. "Thank you. It must have fallen, and I didn't notice."

Alyssa wanted the floor to open up and swallow her. She knew her past had affected her, but when had things gotten this bad? Without noticing it, had she reached a point where she was suspicious of everyone around her?

"The other passengers have all boarded the train now, ma'am." It was amazing how judgmental someone in big ears and a pointy hat could sound.

Stuffing her card into her pocket, she hurried out of the store and dashed onto the platform, where Everett was waiting with Kennedy in his arms. Conscious of the other passengers staring through the windows, Alyssa hooked her arm through his and dragged him onto the train.

"What kept you?" Everett asked.

"There was a malfunction." She shuddered. "Both of the cash register and of my brain."

Even though there had been a tinge of awkwardness attached to it, Alyssa was glad they had taken the ride. As they returned to the car, they were wrapped in a glow of pure sentimentality that could only come from the sort of holiday kitsch provided by the Santa Express.

"I know you wanted to leave behind the small-town feel of Cactus Creek, but do you ever miss it?" she asked as they drove home.

She could see him giving the question some thought. "Cactus Creek is one of my favorite places in the whole world, and leaving it never meant I thought I was better than it. But there are things I don't miss about this place. I don't miss that I can tell you exactly what's happening at every point in the year. I still know when the pageants will take place, and when the two high schools will play their football game. I like having boundaries between myself and my neighbors, and I don't just mean physical ones."

As he gazed out of the windshield, she could see his expression softening.

"But there are other things that I do miss. I miss being able to stop by and see my parents and my brother whenever I want to. I hate that I can't sit on the porch with my dad and watch the stars come out. I can't get used to the way sirens have replaced the chirping of crickets. I wish I could meet my friends for a beer without months of planning and coordinating schedules. As my mom and dad grow older, I don't like the worry that one day I might get a call with bad news and not make it home in time." He turned his head to look at her. "Why do you ask?"

"Just curious. I only arrived here recently, and a lot of uncomfortable things have happened since I came, but I like your hometown."

"You do?" He sounded surprised.

"It feels..." She searched for a description. "Like all the connections go to the right places. Does that make sense?"

"Weirdly, it does."

They had reached their apartment block and he stopped the car in the parking lot. When Alyssa turned around to look at Kennedy, the baby was sound asleep, still clutching her candy cane balloon.

"I need to get a picture."

She opened her purse and reached inside for her cell phone. Her fingers encountered a sheet of folded paper, and she withdrew it with a frown.

"What's this?"

Everett leaned closer as she unfolded it and they read it together by the orange glow of a street light.

Nice slippers. Be sure to check them carefully for broken glass.

ALYSSA WENT OVER one more time exactly what had happened from the moment she'd stepped into the Santa Express store.

"I knew where I'd put my purse," she stated angrily.

"It seems likely someone followed you in there, tampered with the cash register, then, while you were distracted, placed the note in your purse," Everett said. "But you didn't notice anyone close by?"

She shook her head. "The place was busy, and the train was ready to leave. I was getting frustrated at having to wait. I barely noticed the people around me."

"Another note to add to our collection." He sighed, weariness making his eyes hurt. "I'll send the slippers to the lab and have them checked over. If you still want them?"

"Yes, I do." Alyssa looked outraged. "Georgia Dodd isn't going to spoil this for us."

Everett kept his eyes on Kennedy's face. He wasn't too weary for her. Those chubby cheeks, shining eyes and saucy smile were more fascinating to him than the biggest blockbuster. Had there really been a time when he thought he might not bond with her? Everything about his little girl lit up his world. Even diaper changes weren't all bad. He'd sing a happy song while he wiped and tell Kennedy about how he was going to share these stories with her friends when she was in her teens.

She was watching him, so he wiggled his eyebrows at her and stuck out his tongue. When she chuckled, his heart popped with joy and he planted a kiss on her cheek. Although, when he tried to play with her...

"Why does Kennedy keep hitting me over the head with her toys and laughing?" He rubbed his scalp. Catching a glimpse of himself in the mirror on the opposite wall, he noticed how much he looked like his father and quickly smoothed down his hair.

"It's her new game. Your dad invented it. You have to fall over and pretend to be injured," Alyssa explained.

"Remind me to thank my dad for this when I see him." He groaned as a wooden dinosaur connected with the top of his head.

"Bath time." Alyssa scooped up Kennedy as she reached for a toy train.

"I think you just saved me from a serious brain injury." Everett started a one-handed toy cleanup.

Although they had a nighttime routine, they had also learned that there was no such thing as organized when there was a baby involved. On this particular evening, everything went to plan, and they were able to high-five each other as they tiptoed out of the bedroom, leaving Kennedy snoring lightly in her crib.

Neither of them mentioned the fact that, although Kennedy had mostly recovered from her fear of being separated from them both, they had continued to sleep in the same bed in the master bedroom. Convenience. That's what it was. They could share Kennedy's care more easily if they were all in the same room.

"Did you ever picture us with a baby?" Everett asked.

"Yes." She walked away without elaborating, and he took it as a signal not to question her further.

When she returned, Alyssa was carrying rolls of festive paper and everything she needed for a lengthy present-wrapping session. Sitting cross-legged on the floor next to the tree, she started to sort through her many packages. With the twinkling lights casting a golden glow on her hair, she was Everett's perfect Christmas fantasy.

"I think there's a bottle of wine in the fridge. I can't vouch for its quality, but I'll risk it if you will."

She smiled up at him. "Wine instead of beer? Are we celebrating something?"

"Getting Kennedy bathed and into bed without a fight?"

"I'll drink to that."

When he returned with the glasses of wine, she was humming a carol under her breath and his heart flipped over. Everything clicked into place as he realized how happy he was, how happy she made him and how much he cared for her. After everything they'd been through, he couldn't screw up this second chance they'd been given.

He placed the glasses on the coffee table. "Stay right there."

Alyssa watched him with a combination of amusement and bewilderment as he headed for the smaller bedroom. When he returned, he had his good hand tucked behind his back. "You're not the only one who did some Christmas shopping."

Kneeling beside her, he withdrew the sprig of mistletoe he'd been hiding and held it over her head.

Alyssa started to laugh. "You remembered."

"Of course I did. I remember every second of our time together."

Her little gasp was all the encouragement he needed. He leaned in close, taking a second to look into her beautiful blue eyes, then touched his lips lightly to hers. When he drew back, Alyssa slid a hand behind his neck, pulling him down to her. This time, he didn't hold back. He kissed her tenderly, gently tasting her lips and breathing in her familiar scent. And she kissed him in return, closing her eyes and murmuring softly as he ran his fingers through the silky length of her hair.

It went on forever, stirring memories of past kisses and igniting sparks of arousal throughout his body.

When Alyssa drew away, she was breathing hard, but

her expression was determined. "I need you to tell me about what happened the summer after you graduated."

He sat back on his heels, the sweet warmth of the kiss fading. Placing the mistletoe to one side, he considered his usual tactics. Humor wouldn't work. How about deflection?

"Who told you about that? My mom or Casey?"

"It doesn't matter. You spent the four years we were together hiding behind a wall. We both knew it, but we did nothing about it because I was too busy dealing with my own problems." She smoothed a crumpled piece of wrapping paper. "But we have a baby to care for now. We owe each other—and *her*—honesty." When she raised her gaze to his face, her cheeks were pink. "And if there is to be any follow-up to that kiss, we can't keep secrets."

At the same time that one part of his brain was telling him to run and hide, another part was registering that she'd just suggested there could be a follow-up to the kiss. And that was what it came down to. Did he carry on listening to the cowardly voice, the one that shook with fear and that advised him against taking responsibility for other people?

You'll only make the wrong decision, or crack under pressure.

Or did he follow his heart and tell Alyssa the truth? For an instant, the fears came flooding back. She would see him as a failure. He would risk seeing the smile in her eyes turn to contempt…

She placed her hand over his. "Did I tell you I haven't dated anyone else in four years?"

He made a choking sound. "Seriously?"

"Well, I've been out for dinner with a few guys. Nothing more. They were all jerks." The corners of her mouth turned down. "Actually, that's not true. They weren't you."

Using his good arm, he pulled her back against him so hard that they sprawled on the floor. Ignoring her protest about the wrapping paper, he kissed her again.

"The only person I've ever told is Casey. I don't even know where to start."

"Just talk. See where it takes you." She wrapped her arms around his waist and rested her head on his chest. "I'm not going anywhere."

Until she heard his story… He always tried so hard *not* to think about that time, that opening his mind to the memories hurt even more than he'd believed it would.

"A recruiter from one of the top law firms in Phoenix contacted me in my final year of college. The way he spoke made my head spin. He said they only hired the very best to work with them as paralegals. They didn't just want graduates with the best grades. They were seeking people who 'looked the part,' and who could withstand the pressure. That last part was a clue about what was to come. The salary I was offered made me go weak at the knees."

Lying on the floor under the Christmas tree in his tiny apartment with Alyssa pressed up close and Kennedy asleep in the next room, it was as if he was talking about someone else's life. And in a way, he was. But it was a life that had affected his every thought and action since that time.

"I knew, almost immediately, that it wasn't for me. Working in law enforcement can be dangerous, and it's definitely tough, but one of the key skills you need is empathy. Even when you're getting the bad guys off the streets, the job is about people. At the risk of sounding corny, you are making the world a better place. The summer I spent in that law firm was all about outdoing the other guy, whether it was another firm, the person in the next office, or winning an award."

"It sounds cutthroat," Alyssa said.

"That place made cutthroat seem merciful." He shuddered, and her arms tightened around him. "I'd gotten friendly with one of the interns, Caroline, and we were working together on an account. It was minor compared to some of the clients the firm was dealing with, but the competitive push was still there from our managers. Then, one day, something happened that changed everything."

The pain was always there, lodged deep in his heart. Now it blazed back to life like a burning piece of coal and he clenched his teeth together, startled by its intensity.

"Why don't we have some wine?" Alyssa suggested.

"If I stop now, I won't start again." Everett took a second or two to gather his thoughts, then plowed on. "We were working late. Caroline went to the records room to track down some papers. She'd been gone a long time, so I decided to take her a cup of coffee. When I got there—" He sat up abruptly, dashing a hand across his eyes. "I can't. I'm sorry."

"Hey." Alyssa kneeled beside him, taking his good

hand between both of hers. "If this is too hard, you don't have to continue."

He briefly rested his forehead on her shoulder. "No, you may as well hear all of it. As I went into the room, one of the senior partners was coming out. He pushed past me as if he was in a hurry. At first, I couldn't find Caroline. Then I heard a sound from under one of the desks. She was huddled there. Her clothes were torn and her face was so badly bruised and swollen I barely recognized her. She'd been…" He choked over the word.

"Raped?"

He nodded. "When I started to call 911, she stopped me. It was him, the senior partner I'd seen leaving the room. He'd said that if she told anyone what happened, her career would be over."

"But that's awful," Alyssa gasped. "No one should be allowed to get away with that."

"I tried to persuade her to go to the police, but she refused. She wouldn't even contact a rape crisis center." Everett scrubbed a hand over his face. "After that, she was in a terrible state, deteriorating daily. Her work was suffering, and she was being threatened with dismissal. It was killing me that I couldn't help her. And when I saw him—" He shook his head. "Then she tried to commit suicide and all hell broke loose."

"Did the reason become known?" Alyssa asked hopefully.

"No. It was assumed that it was because she was struggling in her job. There was an internal investigation." He snorted. "From the start, it was just a cover-up. It found there was nothing anyone in the firm could have done to help her. But I knew, Lyss. And I did nothing."

"What could you have done?" He heard the tears in her voice. "If you'd gone to the police, they would still have needed Caroline's evidence."

"I should have done something. Spoken to the other partners. Gone to the press. Talked to her family. Anything, rather than just walking away. I failed her."

"This is probably not what you want to hear, but all of those things required a measure of proof you didn't have. You saw the senior partner leave the room. After that, you saw Caroline in a distressed state, and she told you he'd raped her. I'm sure that's exactly what did happen, but you had no evidence. If you'd shared the story with a wider audience, you risked damaging your own career and reputation."

His lips twisted into a bitter line. "He admitted it."

"Pardon?"

"The day I left, I went to his office," Everett said. "I wanted to look him in the eye when I said her name. The plan didn't quite work and while I had him up against his office wall by the throat, he tried to tell me she led him on. 'Just like all the others.' That was the phrase he used. We, uh, exchanged a few more words and he confessed that he might have been mistaken. I told him that, from that moment on, I would be watching him. If he ever stepped out of line again, my threats would become reality."

"What happened to him?" Alyssa asked.

"He left the company soon after that. It didn't matter. Caroline's next attempt was successful. She died of an overdose a month later." Everett bowed his head to look at the floor. "She needed me, but I couldn't protect her."

Alyssa caught hold of his left arm. "That's not true. You did what you could, but the culture at Alexandria and Foster—"

He looked up, pain darkening the depths of his eyes. "I never mentioned the name of the firm."

Chapter Fifteen

Everett was lying on his side with his back to Alyssa. An hour had passed and, although she'd thought of a dozen things to say to him, every time she opened her mouth to speak, something inside her froze. In the end, she placed her hand on his shoulder and said the only thing that was important.

"I'm sorry."

His muscles tensed, and he remained silent for a few long moments. "You asked me for the truth, Lyss. And giving it was one of the hardest things I've ever done. But you'd already checked me out."

"Your mom told me the name of the firm." He was right. This was about honesty. "And, yes, I looked them up online. But I didn't know anything about what had happened in your past. If I had, do you think I'd have ignored what you were going through?"

With his arm in a sling, turning over wasn't an option for him. Instead, he shuffled awkwardly into a half-sitting position. "I think you'd have every right to question my value in your life."

Watching his face in the half light, she knew she

only had one chance at this. Finding the right words now was one of the most important things that would ever happen in their relationship.

"Everett, we were together for four years and you never once let me down during that time." She smiled. "You made it fun and magical, but you also made sure I felt cared for. I was able to open up to you about my childhood in a way I'd never been able to do before. My life was finally okay, because *you* accepted me. You made me feel at home."

When his jaw muscles relaxed slightly, her heart soared.

"We split up because of my problems, not because of anything you did, or didn't do. And I have had four years of regrets."

"Lyss—"

"This is my big speech. Let me get through it." Her lip quivered as she tried to smile. "When we came back into each other's lives, fate gave us a new perspective. The fun-loving days are over. We're parents now, and we've been tested to the limit of our reason. Throughout everything, you've made sure me and Kennedy are your first priorities. You've kept your family safe. What happened to Caroline was horrible, but it hasn't shaped you. It's simply added another layer of empathy to the fine man you already are."

He bent his head and took possession of her mouth, pressing hard and hot against her. The caress of his lips was enticing, and his tongue penetrated her mouth in a slow, seductive movement. Alyssa felt boneless as she molded herself to him, giving herself up to the sensations that swept through her. His body was as powerful and strong as she remembered, and the raw power he exuded stirred erotic memories alongside new passion.

"Uh." She placed a hand flat against his chest. "Aren't we forgetting something?"

"I have protection." He nipped the lobe of her ear as he spoke. "I may not have had any use for it in the last four years, but those old habits are hard to break."

"I'm glad to hear it. But I was thinking more about the fact that we have company." She pointed in the direction of the crib.

Everett groaned. "I didn't even think. I mean... I would have remembered. Eventually."

She chuckled. "There is another bedroom. We can take the baby monitor with us."

"Who said romance was dead?"

"You go first." She gave him a gentle shove. "And don't make a sound. Because if you wake her, it won't just be romance that's dead."

A few minutes later, she joined him on the narrow bed in the smaller bedroom.

"Sneaking around trying not to get caught." His eyes gleamed as he dimmed the light. "It makes it more exciting."

"*You* are what makes it more exciting."

Her hands slid under his shirt and along the sculptured muscles of his chest. Everett nipped at her lower lip, then, as she moaned softly, he began to devour her in long, hungry kisses. Her whole body was on fire as her hands glided over his chest and back.

Turning their bodies, he separated her legs with his

muscular thighs, his hard erection pressing against her heated core through his sweatpants and her pajama bottoms.

Leaning back, he slowly undid the buttons on her top while raining kisses along her eyelids, jawline and down her neck. When the garment was fully unbuttoned, he pulled it open to reveal her breasts.

"You're so beautiful, Lyss. I want to lose myself in you."

His fingers on her skin left trails of static electricity. It had always been this way. His touch was a perfect pleasure, each time more intense and intoxicating than the last.

"More than chocolate-chip cookies."

The reminder made her smile. It had been their private joke that they were more addictive to each other than their favorite foods.

"Better than buttered popcorn."

The touch of his hands on her skin as he cupped her breasts almost sent her into orbit. When he bent his head to capture the tip of one nipple in his mouth, she arched her back and cried out. For Alyssa, sex was about so much more that physical pleasure. It was giving herself, body and soul. An expression of the deepest bond, an intimacy that was a declaration of belonging.

Although, right now, the things Everett was doing were *all* about physical pleasure.

His tongue flicked and swirled across her taut nipples, his teeth gently scraping before he tugged one tender tip into his mouth. Her hips lifted and gyrated as she ground against him. Slipping his uninjured hand between them, he moved it down inside the waistband of her pajama pants.

"I'm not exactly agile right now. Losing the clothes would help me a lot."

While Alyssa wriggled out of her pants, he clumsily removed his own garments and took off the sling.

She slid a hand down his body, reminding herself of its delicious contours. "You're not doing so badly."

As he tipped her onto her back and positioned himself between her legs, Alyssa's body arched to meet him. His mouth claimed her breasts again, licking, swirling, teasing and sending shudders of delight through her. Taking his time, Everett stroked the length of her body until every nerve ending was inflamed. Molten heat raged through her veins.

His fingers trailed lower until one finger slid inside her and his thumb circled. Her writhing body rippled with unimaginable pleasure as the slow-burning fire grew, then blazed out of control.

Within seconds, her head was spinning. He could always do the most amazing things to her, the connection between them making a fireball out of every touch. Everett's mouth claimed hers, his tongue plunging inside in the same rhythm as his finger. Four years of being prim and proper, now she was biting back her screams as those magical fingers swirled and teased and did the most amazing things to her.

A bolt of pure pleasure ripped through her, taking her over the edge. Bursts of color flashed before her eyes and a series of volcanic eruptions had her thrashing wildly. Everett's eyes locked on hers.

"I need you."

"Yes." It was more a gasp than a coherent word.

He reached into the top drawer of the nightstand at the side of the bed and found a condom. Holding up the foil-wrapped package, he gave Alyssa a rueful smile. "I can use my right hand for some things, but this needs a little more precision."

"I'll help."

Taking the condom from him, she opened the wrapper. Everett eased back, watching her with a playful smile as she grasped his length, positioned the rubber over his head and rolled it down.

"You're good at that." His voice was husky.

She shifted his position until they were face-to-face. "I've seen you do it often enough."

He groaned, pulling her to beneath him again. Holding her hips, he opened her legs wider with his thighs, pressing his erection against her.

"Look at me, Lyss. I want to watch your face."

He pushed into her, his movements measured as he gave her time to adjust to his size. Alyssa lifted her hips, urging him on. Slow and steady could wait. She wanted more this time. Her fingers dug into his shoulders as her pelvis ground against his. Everett responded with a single powerful thrust that buried him deep inside her. His single groan was everything she needed to hear.

He pulled back slowly, then drove deeper into her again, sending darts of pleasure searing her nerve endings. The breath left her lungs, leaving her pulsating, burning, flying. Her muscles were already spasming around his hardness as she gasped for more. And he gave it. Driving faster and harder, consumed by the need to push deeper into her body. Raising her hips to meet his thrusts, he lifted her higher into a continuing spiral of ecstasy.

Her body tightened around his, gripping and pulling him deeper. As the first shudders of her orgasm started, Everett's own release hit. Harsh and hard. He threw back his head and joined her in a mind-shattering climax.

The last four years melted away as their bodies stilled and he held her close, warm and snuggled and safe.

ALYSSA WAS HIS DRUG. One touch and Everett was addicted all over again. Not that he cared. He was happy to sink deeper into this enchantment.

"I missed this so much." Her lips tickled the curve of his neck.

He buried a hand in her hair, testing its softness. Tilting her face to his, he stroked down her cheekbones to her lips. Kissing her was like tasting heaven and they moved together like dance partners who knew the routine but were excited by the endless interpretations. Their bodies fitted together perfectly, made for this moment, falling into a natural rhythm.

He got to his feet and held out his hands. Regarding him warily, Alyssa bounced into a kneeling position.

"You're injured."

"I can still do this." He hoped he was right. If not, he was about to fall flat on his face and take her down with him. Not the best look for a guy hoping to keep the rekindled romance alive. "Grab another condom and wrap your legs around me."

Her trust in him was absolute and she instantly did as he asked, tightening her arms around his neck and her legs around his waist. Holding her with his hands on her hips, he walked to the bathroom. Alyssa squirmed against him, her movements sending a series of electric shocks pulsing along his hardening shaft.

Keeping his left hand under her buttocks, he turned on the shower, adjusted the temperature, then stepped right in. The water cascading over them heightened every sense. Pinning her against the tiles, he grasped her hips again. Bending his head, he lapped at the water trickling between her breasts.

Wriggling out of his grip, Alyssa gave him a mischievous smile before placing the condom on the soap dish and dropping to her knees. Using the wet tiles to help her shimmy closer, she halted when her face was level with his erection. Using the tip of one finger, she traced around the head, then up and down the shaft, tilting her face to watch his reaction.

Everett leaned back, mesmerized as she took him firmly in her hand, and opened her lovely mouth. Her tongue flicked out, licking the tip, lightly probing and he sighed as fireworks went off inside his head.

"You were always amazing at this."

Right there, as he was swept up in the intensity of an erotic moment that made his eyes bulge, he realized his heart was mended.

And I didn't know until now that it had been broken.

Alyssa smiled at the compliment, using her tongue

in a circular motion to lick him like an ice cream, before traveling down his shaft and back up again. Finally, she held his length between both hands and lowered her mouth over his head, sucking in, then pushing out. All the while, her probing tongue teased, and her hands massaged. Everett saw stars.

The blood pounding in his ears drowned out all other sounds. When his jaw clenched and his eyes closed of their own accord, he knew he was dangerously close. Reluctantly, he eased away from that magical mouth. Alyssa looked up at him with a question in her eyes.

"I won't last." His voice was raw as he pushed her up against the tiles again.

This time he tore open the condom packet with his teeth and they got the protection on together. Taking hungry possession of her mouth, he drove his hard length straight into her. Alyssa gasped and tipped her head back.

"Don't stop."

He was fiercer this time, sure of himself and of her, driving them both to the edge hard and fast. Her body moved in time with his, meeting his demands and driving him onward. Lava coursed through his veins, consuming him. Four years without her. How had he survived?

The fire that Alyssa had started with her lips was growing and spreading, roaring through him. He felt her start to contract, her muscles clamping him tighter and drawing him deeper as her whole body thrashed.

A primal growl escaped him as the first explosions of his own volcanic release hit. Then he was soaring high, barely breathing, clinging to Alyssa, who was boneless in his arms.

He didn't know how many minutes passed before she spoke.

"I think I can stand now." Her voice was faint.

"Are you sure?"

"I'm worried about your arm."

He managed a breathless laugh. "I think it's healing well. Although I won't share the details of how I've gained that information with my physiotherapist."

Holding her against his chest, he lowered her until her feet connected with the tiles. Making sure she was steady before he released her, he left her for a few minutes while he took care of the condom. When he returned, they showered together the way they had always done.

Afterward, he wrapped her in a towel, dried her all over, then carried her into the small bedroom and placed her gently on the bed.

"We're staying in this room?" Alyssa smirked. "Does that mean we're not done for the night?"

He gave her a mock leer. "I may have other plans for you before morning."

When he'd finished drying himself, he lay next to her, cocooning them both within the warm bedding. As he drifted off to sleep, he reflected that there was nothing in the world like the feel of Alyssa's naked body cradled protectively in his arms.

WHEN ALYSSA WOKE, she took a moment to let her surroundings sink in. Warm hard body pressed tight up against her back. Muscular arms wrapped around her. Delicious postsex glow. She smiled as the memory of the previous night came back.

But there was something wrong. Her smile quickly faded as she realized what it was. The room was in complete darkness.

But we left the lamp on...

Her hand went out, reaching for the baby monitor. Instantly, her worst fears were confirmed. The green light that indicated it was working wasn't on. When she tried the switch on the lamp, nothing happened.

"Everett!" She was on her feet, scrabbling in the darkness for her clothes.

"What's happening?" She heard the bed move as if he was sitting up.

"The power is out."

They burst from the room at the same time, Everett in his boxer briefs and Alyssa halfway into her pajamas. The master bedroom was lit by the glow of Kennedy's battery-operated night-light. And the crib was empty.

Alyssa's knees buckled and she covered her face with her hands. "She's gone. Our baby girl..."

As Everett used the light on his cell phone to check the windows and doors for signs of a break-in, she sank to the floor, sitting with her back to the wall.

When he returned, Everett hauled her to her feet. "You can faint when we've found her. Right now, Kennedy needs us both."

Shocked at his harsh words, Alyssa sucked in a breath. "This is all your fault. If you hadn't distracted me with sex, I wouldn't have left her alone!"

"Keep yelling if it gets the adrenaline pumping and makes you feel better, but get dressed while you do it." He gripped her shoulders, giving her a push toward the closet. "The person who took the baby disabled the alarm from the outside, then pried the kitchen window open. He, or she—I'm going with she—was small enough to squeeze through it. After cutting through the electrical wiring it looks like they picked up Kennedy and walked right out through the front door."

Alyssa pulled on jeans and a sweater. "I'm calling 911." Picking up her cell phone, she stared at its screen.

"It's a good plan," Everett said. "Any reason why you're hesitating?"

With fingers that shook wildly, she opened the tracking app she'd activated the previous day. Holding it up, she showed him the screen. "I know where Kennedy is."

He studied the map with its flashing dot for a moment or two. Dragging on his own clothes with lightning speed, he grabbed his car keys. "Throw some bottles of formula and bananas into the pink-elephant bag. You can explain on the way."

"Wait." She had to run to keep up with him. "Will you be okay to drive?"

He flashed her a quick glance over his shoulder. "My arm held up okay when I was distracting you in the shower. I think I can manage to turn a wheel."

As they followed the tracking signal along the still dark roads, Alyssa alternated between feeling completely numb and totally terrified. Dark thoughts clouded her mind. If Kennedy wasn't around, would

Georgia inherit the Dodds' money and property? Was that what this was all about?

"I wanted to find a way to keep Kennedy safe if Georgia tried to snatch her." Tears trickled down her cheeks as she explained how the bracelet and button linked to the app on her cell phone. "I never imagined we'd be putting it to the test so soon."

"Why didn't you tell me about it?" Everett asked.

She blew her nose on a tissue. "I thought you'd laugh at me for being overprotective."

He briefly placed a hand on her knee. "I'm so thankful for your overprotectiveness."

She glanced at the map, her fears increasing as she noticed the direction in which the tiny dot was heading. "Could Georgia be planning to take Kennedy across the Mexican border?"

"If she is, she hasn't taken the most direct route," Everett said. "I'm not going to rule it out, but the main thing is to catch up with her. I've messaged Casey and told him to put more pressure on Joe Meyer. If he knows where Georgia's hiding place is, we may find that's where she's heading."

"She won't know how to care for Kennedy." Alyssa choked back another sob. "Our baby will be so scared when she wakes up and we're not there, especially if she recognizes Georgia as the person who hurt her mom and dad."

"We're going to find her and bring her home." He was so resolute that she let his words soothe her and drive some of her doubts away.

After about half an hour, the dot on the map stopped moving. "Where is that?" Everett asked.

"It's near Deming, New Mexico." Alyssa checked the location. "But it isn't a town or city. It appears to be the foothills of Cookes Range."

"I don't know the area, but it sounds like the perfect hiding place for someone on the run."

Chapter Sixteen

Everett used the hands-free system on his car dashboard to talk to Agent Karen Hayes. From her base in the Phoenix FBI field office, she liaised with Casey, and also her colleagues in El Paso.

"From the coordinates you're giving me, El Paso believes the location is a disused seven-thousand-acre ranch in the New Mexican desert. Specifically, your signal seems to be coming from a horse barn on the property."

"How reliable is that information?" Everett asked.

"I'm hearing from Casey that his suspect, fearful of being caught up in a child-abduction charge, has become more communicative. Apparently, Georgia has links to the area we're looking at. Prior to the theft from OverHerd Ranch last month, she was briefly involved with a ranch owner in the Deming area. Although they split up when the rancher sold and moved away, Joe Meyer told Casey she has been using this guy's place as one of her hideouts."

"Sounds promising." Everett checked his GPS. They were on I-10, approaching the exit for Deming. It had been fully light for some time and fluffy clouds scudded across wintry blue skies. Although the landscape had a bleak beauty it was far from welcoming. He didn't want to communicate his fears to Alyssa, but the thought of their little girl out here with a suspected killer made his stomach churn. "We have no further updates. The app has shown Kennedy in the same place for over an hour."

While he was talking, he sent glimpses in Alyssa's direction. Her demeanor worried him. Slumped in her seat, she reminded him of a rag doll that had been thrown aside by a careless child. On her pale cheeks, spots of color burned too bright. Her limbs were bent at awkward angles as though poised for action that wasn't going to happen.

"We're nearly there." He touched her hand and was alarmed at its iciness.

"But what will we find when we arrive?"

Everett left the highway. Using his own GPS together with the instructions given by the local FBI agents, who were using satellite images, he followed a route that would take him to a point on a ridge above the barn where they suspected Georgia was holed up.

"If we approach her in a vehicle, she's going to hear us and be spooked," he explained to Alyssa. "The only way to do this will be to sneak up on her."

She continued to gaze out of the window at the vast, arid nothingness. He figured she was thinking the same as him. If Georgia decided to take off, there was no easier place to get lost, and no harder terrain through which to track her.

Eventually, he saw a ridge up ahead. The rocky formation stretched across the horizon as far as he could see, but his GPS showed a path leading upward. Trusting the technology, he followed the instructions on his dashboard screen and his vehicle was soon cresting the ledge at what felt like a dangerously steep angle. When they reached the top, he stopped several yards away from the edge to ensure the car couldn't be seen by anyone in the valley.

"I have binoculars in the trunk." He made his way to the rear of the car and retrieved them. At the same time, he tucked his licensed weapon into the shoulder holster that was hidden beneath his jacket. Although the muscles of his right arm were not in full working order, he would trust his ability to put a bullet in Georgia at close range if she attempted to harm Kennedy.

Taking Alyssa's hand, he drew her with him to the edge of the ridge. Crouching down, they surveyed the valley. Immediately below them, Everett could see a large two-story barn. Beyond that, the only break in the barren scene was way off in the distance.

"That could be the ranch house." As he took the binoculars from their case, he drew Alyssa's attention in that direction.

Looking through the glasses, the scale and layout of the ranch became clear. In addition to the main house, there were a number of outlying buildings, including what appeared to be log cabins. Possibly they were staff quarters, or the owner might have rented out accommodations. Either way, if Georgia knew of this place, it was an ideal hideout.

But the app on Alyssa's cell phone showed that Kennedy was in the barn below them. Or that's where her tracking bracelet and button were. The app had no way of telling them whether they were attached to a living, breathing baby…

Stay positive.

He refocused on the shape of the barn. It was two floors, with a pitched roof. He didn't have a background in ranching, but he figured the lower floor was for stabling and tack, and the loft was possibly storage or even living quarters for a groom. Maybe that was why Georgia had selected this place. If anyone came looking for her, they would search the main ranch house and possibly overlook the barn.

Where had she left her car? Maybe she'd hidden it somewhere close by and then walked here with Kennedy in her arms. Quickly, he fired off a message to Agent Hayes, describing the barn. If she was planning to send other agents into this hostile terrain, she would need all the help she could get. He also suggested they search the area for Georgia's vehicle. Taking it out of action would be helpful if she decided to make a run for it.

"We have to get down there without Georgia seeing us." The side facing them had a window overlooking the ridge, but the adjoining wall was a blank expanse of wood. "If we move along the ridge a few yards, and then climb down, we can approach from that angle. Do you think you can get down there?"

Her expression shifted from fearful resignation to grim determination. "It's for Kennedy. Just watch me."

True to her word, within minutes, she was slithering down the steep slope on her bottom, kicking up loose rocks along her way. It wasn't the most graceful descent Everett had ever seen, but it was easily the most effective. Since he figured it would also be the kindest on his injured arm, he prepared to copy her... Although he wasn't sure how his butt was going to feel in a few hours.

When they reached the valley floor, Everett caught hold of Alyssa's hand and ran the short distance to the barn. Pressing close up against the wall, he listened for any signs of life from within. There was nothing.

"Check the app," he whispered to Alyssa.

She had kept her cell in her hand the whole time, charging it on the drive from Cactus Creek. She quickly consulted it now and held it up to show him. The red dot that represented Kennedy filled the screen and was flashing wildly.

"She's right here."

"Then I'm going in."

As Everett crouched low and moved along the barn wall, the twin smells of old hay and stale manure assailed his nostrils. Momentarily, it took him back to visits to his uncle's farm when he was a kid, so he had to shake his focus back to the present.

He had motioned for Alyssa to stay where she was, but when he glanced her way, she had moved up and was close behind him. Had he really expected compliance from her when she thought Kennedy was nearby? Sending her a warning frown, he continued to approach the corner of the building.

The lack of any sound bothered him. Kennedy should

have woken up by now, and she would be hungry. If she didn't get her food on time, she would be distraught. Add in the fact that Everett and Alyssa weren't around? He'd have expected the team of FBI agents to be led across the desert by her cries. And then there was the issue that she was with Georgia. If they were right and Kennedy had witnessed a scene during which her aunt had attacked her parents, she wouldn't just be upset. She would be terrified.

He had reached the point now where he could peer around the corner and see the open front of the building. His guess about the purpose of the first floor had been correct. The area was divided into stalls and, although his view was hampered by the need to remain hidden, he figured there were six. Cautiously, he crept farther along the wall. Then froze.

The sound was faint, but unmistakable—he could hear a radio station playing rock music. It was coming from the second floor. If Georgia was up there, it could mean he was safe to enter.

His cop instincts went to war with his new-dad longing to hold his baby girl in his arms again. Years of training and experience told him not to assume that Georgia was alone or that there was no trickery involved. What kind of rookie mistake would it be to assume she was upstairs, enter the building on the heels of that belief and take a bullet in the back of the head from an accomplice?

But his gut was telling him Kennedy was in there. And she was quiet… Which meant there was something very wrong. Just as he was weighing his options, with the cop-versus-dad argument playing over and over in his head, Alyssa pushed past him and his decision was made.

He caught her easily, but not until she was already stepping inside the barn. Gripping her by her upper arms, he held her against him. She didn't resist, but her whole body quivered with tension. "Lyss, please. You have to leave this to me."

"She's in here, Everett." The anguish in her face matched the ache in his own chest. "I don't need an app to tell me that. Our baby is here, and I have to go to her."

Over her head, Everett scanned the barn. Weak sunlight sifted through the wooden boards onto the old hay that was scattered carelessly around. A broom was lying on the floor and a broken saddle hung on one wall. And there, drawing his attention like a beacon on a dark night, were two items that chilled his blood.

The first was Kennedy's tracking bracelet.

When she saw it, Alyssa moaned and covered her mouth. Everett held her tighter as she swayed against him. "Don't give up hope. You told me this is the reason you wanted the button as well. The app is picking up signals from them both, remember?"

"But the button is smaller. It could be hidden in the hay." She gulped back a sob. "And what's that? It looks like some kind of *drug*."

Going down on one knee, Everett picked up the small white carton and read the details on it with a growing sense of disbelief. Kennedy was here. And now he knew why she wasn't crying...

"What is it?" Alyssa whispered.

"It's the packaging from an over-the-counter anti-histamine for infants." He clenched his fist around the flimsy box, fury tearing through him and driving out any earlier hesitation. "It says 'may cause drowsiness.' I dealt with a case once of a mom who used this to keep her baby son quiet on a long-haul flight. He suffered serious side effects—" He decided against finishing the story.

"Georgia drugged Kennedy to keep her quiet?" Alyssa's own anger, usually a slow burn, was already alight in her eyes.

Thinking fast, he caught her arm again before she could march toward the steps that led to the loft. "Let me go first."

"Neither of you has to go anywhere." Georgia always did like to make a big entrance. "I'll come to you."

THE WOMAN ON the stairs was not what Alyssa had expected. Smaller and prettier, Georgia Dodd appeared more vulnerable than the wicked-witch image Alyssa had built up in her mind. That was all the time she spared for Georgia's looks. Her mind was too busy registering two other things. One was that the other woman was holding Kennedy at an awkward angle, propped against her shoulder. The second was the gun she had leveled at Everett's chest.

"You Coltons refuse to know when you're defeated, don't you? Just like when we were kids."

"Is the baby okay, Georgia?" Alyssa didn't know how he kept his voice so calm. "How much antihistamine did you give her?"

"She's fine. I only used a little more than the rec-ommended dose." Alyssa couldn't stifle the groan that rose to her lips, and Georgia gave her a pitying look. "What's the problem? You found me, anyway."

"She's so little. Can I take her? Check her over—?" She would beg if she had to.

Georgia snorted. "Right. Meanwhile, Agent Colton here puts a bullet between my eyes. The baby is my ticket out of here. I don't really care if she screams the place down. It was just easier not to draw attention to myself when I took her, and on the drive." She waved her gun at Everett. "By the way, lose your weapon."

Obediently, he unzipped his jacket and removed a gun from his shoulder holster. As he dropped it on the floor, Alyssa—who hated weapons of any kind—had the sense of their last chance receding.

"Do you have any others?" Georgia asked.

"No. I'm carrying an injury to my right arm. I don't have the flexibility to reach for anything."

Georgia laughed. "I only wish I'd gotten that knife into your gut instead of your arm. No hard feelings, Everett, but you were the one I wanted off my tail."

"It doesn't have to be this way, Georgia. Come back to Cactus Creek. Tell the story of what really happened to Sean and Delilah—"

"You already know what happened." Slowly, keep-ing the gun trained on him, she descended the rest of the stairs. "Everyone else was buying into the suicide story. Then you turned up."

"I wasn't there on the night they died. I only have suspicions." Alyssa could see him slipping into a practiced rhythm. This was why he was so good at his job. She could see him reading the scene, measuring Georgia's mood and reacting accordingly. "You are the only one who knows what really went on and can put the record straight."

"You seriously expect me to tell you? What is this? Revenge for what I did to Casey? Hero cop gets murderess to admit all? Death Row Georgia says, 'He made me see the light'?"

"Escaping from prison, abducting a child and going on the run is not exactly the right way to go about building your defense," Everett said. "I'm guessing you haven't told your attorney everything. There may be something in the true story that can help you. I'm not going to lie to you. I don't think you're walking away from this. But, who knows, you could be looking at a reduced sentence."

"He's good, isn't he? I often wondered if I picked the wrong brother." Georgia rolled her eyes in Alyssa's direction. "Okay. You want to hear it so badly, I'll tell you. All about how your friend Sean was going to frame his little sister for the cattle-rustling organization he'd been running for years. Do you see me with a big fancy house, swimming pool, foreign holidays and vintage-car collection? No. But all of a sudden, I'm the brains behind the operation."

"You must have been able to prove it was Sean."

She shook her head, her dark hair flying in every direction. "He had his secret weapon. As always, Delilah was there behind the scenes, cooking the books. That was how they built up their fortune. Sean made the money, she grew it. Now, she was using all her skills to make him look legitimate and throw the blame on me. And if I was behind the cattle rustling, that meant I was also to blame for Pierce Tostig's murder."

"But you and Sean were always so close. Couldn't you have worked something out?"

Although Alyssa's focus was on Kennedy, who remained still and silent, clutched against Georgia's chest, she could see what Everett was doing. Yes, he was establishing a bond with Georgia, but each passing minute was also bringing his FBI colleagues closer. Was he buying them enough time? With every fiber of her being she hoped so.

"They refused to talk to me when I asked!" The words burst from Georgia with such force that the gun in her hand jerked alarmingly. "Oh, I know who was behind it all. Sean would never have turned his back on me unless Delilah encouraged him. But she had him right where she wanted him. And when Kennedy came along, it was all about them and their little family. I didn't stand a chance. I was getting desperate, so when I went to the house that night, I took a few weapons of my own along. Mine were not-so-secret ones."

Georgia started pacing up and down, her movements jerky. "They were eating dinner and, although they didn't want to invite me in, I guess Sean found the barrel of a gun in his belly improved his manners. We went inside and things quickly became heated when Sean tried to grab the gun from me. We struggled. Plates got smashed and chairs were tipped over. Delilah yelled at us to stop. Someone was going to get hurt and it might be her precious child."

Alyssa closed her eyes briefly, picturing the scene, almost feeling Delilah's panic. The other woman had done a lot of things she didn't agree with, but she could identify with that need to protect her baby. Now she was in the same position. Helplessness tried to overwhelm her, but she fought it hard. For Kennedy's sake, she had to stay strong.

"That was when I saw my chance. I could force them to listen to me if I used the thing they loved the most as a bargaining chip. When I went toward the baby, Delilah came at me like a tiger. I had the knife in my hand, and she got cut. It wasn't bad, but there was blood on the floor. She was screaming and crying, trying to get the baby away from me. I hadn't thought about killing her—not then—so I was fighting her off the whole way from the house to the garage. At one point, she was holding on to my leg, getting pulled along the drive with me."

Alyssa thought of Everett's description. Of how he'd wondered if Sean had dragged Delilah to his car against her will. How different the truth had been.

"What was Sean doing while this was going on?" Everett asked.

"What could he do? I'd told him I would shoot Kennedy in the head if he moved out of the kitchen." Georgia flashed him a smile. "You must remember how hard it was to get the better of my big brother. Gotta tell you, that felt good."

Alyssa pressed a fist into her stomach, riding the

wave of nausea that hit her. Kennedy had been there while this was going on. She had already known that, but hearing Georgia describe what had happened in such detail made it even worse. As for Georgia... How could anyone take pride in such horrific acts? And Everett was staying so calm, letting her talk about her crimes without giving a glimpse of his own disgust. Alyssa's pride in his professionalism increased with each passing minute.

"When I got to my car, I realized the flaw. There was no seat for Kennedy. Luckily, the keys to Delilah's vehicle were in the garage, so I made her take the seat from that and put it in my car. I knew they'd follow me, of course, so I took them on a chase." She laughed. "Man, that was a wild ride."

"That leads me to the most important question of all," Everett said. "How the hell did you persuade your brother to drive his car into a wall?"

By now, Georgia appeared to be losing control. She clutched Kennedy tighter, her gaze swiveling back and forth, as though seeking an escape route. "I didn't persuade Sean, I *forced* him. For the first time in our lives, I was in charge. The baby was in my vehicle, and Sean was chasing us. Delilah was in the passenger seat with him. She was on her cell phone, talking to me, trying to get me to slow down, offering me anything I wanted if I would just give them Kennedy. Everything she said just made me more mad. She tried to frame me. Suddenly she wanted to play nice?"

Alyssa became aware of a tiny change in Everett's stance. He was focused on something outside the barn.

Hope flared inside her. Was it the FBI? Would they be able to get close to the barn without Georgia noticing them? Right now, she was so caught up in her story, it was unlikely she would notice if a brass band marched through the place. Even so, they didn't want anything to spook her when she was already dangerously disturbed.

"It was when I reached Sheldon Street that the idea came to me. The entrance to the shopping mall parking lot is only wide enough for one vehicle. I swung into a U-turn, so I was facing Sean, then backed into the parking lot. As I came back out, I drove straight at him. He was going so fast, he didn't have time to brake. His only choices were to hit my car head-on and risk his baby's life, or swerve and drive into the wall."

"So Sean did what every loving parent faced with the same decision would do." Momentarily, Everett stopped hiding his feelings and the pain in his voice tore into Alyssa's heart. "He saved his baby's life at the expense of his own and Delilah's."

"I might have known you would try to make my brother sound like some sort of saint." Georgia sneered. "I told my attorney I'd never get a fair trial if the Colton brothers had anything to do with it."

"A fair trial? You forced Sean to drive his car at speed into a wall. How soon after you checked he and Delilah were dead did you come up with the idea of planting the fake suicide note on the dash?" Everett asked.

Georgia's lips drew back in something close to a snarl. "I checked on them and knew immediately they had died instantly. Once I knew they were dead, anyway, it didn't matter what story I told, did it? I could make it work for me."

Alyssa's stomach rolled uncomfortably. She had never seen pictures of the crash scene, or heard it described, but from Everett's and Casey's expressions when they talked about it, she knew it had been horrific. Yet Georgia's first thought after seeing the mangled bodies of her brother and sister-in-law had been how she could use their deaths to save herself. It was further confirmation that she was a cold-blooded killer.

And she has our baby...

"When I went back to my own vehicle and saw Kennedy in the car seat, I realized I already had the perfect alibi. I wrote the note with my left hand and placed it on Sean's dashboard. Then I drove back to their house and took some of Kennedy's clothes and food away with me to support the fake alibi that she was at my place that night. I figured the signs of a struggle in the kitchen worked in my favor. It looked like Sean and Delilah had been fighting. I was the doting aunt who had been caring for the baby when her beloved brother took his own life. I was in the clear. I *should* have stayed that way, until you came sniffing around."

"Didn't you ever once consider telling the truth at the arraignment? If you'd come clean about Sean's cattle-rustling operation, you could have gotten a reduced sentence."

"You aren't listening to me. You know what my brother was like. They were going to blame it all on me." Georgia's voice rose to a screech. "Yes, the cattle rustling was all Sean's idea. So was the murder of that meddling Tostig guy. But with Delilah forging the evidence and me working with them, I couldn't fight them. I would get sent down for all of it."

"When you escaped, you could have gone on the run. Why did you come back for Kennedy? Is she your way of getting Sean's money?" Alyssa asked.

Georgia glared at her. "Why shouldn't I have his money? When Ray Torrington contacted me and told me about the will, he said I should try to get it overturned. He said he'd help me if I gave him a share of the estate."

"Good old Ray," Everett muttered. "No wonder he did a disappearing act."

"That's not the only reason I want her." Georgia gazed down at Kennedy's face. "I want to take care of her, even though we'll be spending our lives on the run."

"But in the letters you sent, you threatened to kill her." Could Georgia tell that Everett was moving closer to her as he spoke?

"That was to scare the two of you, to get you to back out of the custody arrangement." A slight smile flitted across her lips. "I've never had any trouble picking up guys in bars, and Joe Meyer was smitten within minutes. I gave him a sob story about being framed by the FBI agent whose brother I dumped."

At the mention of Casey, Everett's jaw clenched, but he kept his emotions in check.

"So while you were behind bars, Joe was delivering the notes?" he asked. "Was he also the person who drove his car at me and followed Alyssa into the elevator in Hoyles'? And let's not forget the Santa Express store."

"Yeah. He turned out to be quite creative." She looked down at Kennedy. "I'd never hurt her. She's all I have left now."

Her gun hand wavered and Everett seized his chance. He lunged and grabbed Kennedy, then began running in a zigzag pattern toward the exit. Bending almost double, he cradled Kennedy against his chest. As he reached Alyssa, he pulled her down to the same level and, with an arm around her waist, dragged her along with him.

When Georgia screamed in fury, Alyssa risked a glance over her shoulder. She was in time to see the other woman raise her weapon and take aim. Then a sudden volley of shots rang out from the loft space and Georgia pitched forward onto her face.

Even with the threat from Georgia neutralized by his FBI colleagues, Everett didn't stop running until they were outside. There were a number of vehicles close to the barn and, seeing Casey crouched beside his cruiser, Everett placed Kennedy in Alyssa's arms and thrust them both toward his brother.

"Keep them safe. And get a paramedic to check Kennedy over."

Alyssa watched in dismay as he headed back inside the barn. Casey found a warm throw in the trunk of his car and placed it around her shoulders before guiding her into the back seat. Kennedy gave a few hiccupping sobs then, after exploring Alyssa's face with her fingertips, heaved a huge, sleepy sigh. Alyssa rocked her and sang some of her favorite songs.

When the paramedics came, they checked the baby's vital signs, but pronounced her fine. "Give her plenty of fluids and keep her warm, but she seems happy now she's back with Mom."

Alyssa promptly burst into tears, only managing to stop long enough to fish her keys out of her pocket. Tearfully, she asked Casey if he could find Everett's vehicle and bring her the pink-elephant bag. When he returned with it, Kennedy gulped down her formula and fell asleep while Alyssa changed her diaper. After that, the minutes seemed like hours as Alyssa strained her eyes waiting for Everett to reappear.

"What's happening?" Despite the throw, her teeth were chattering wildly as she spoke to Casey, who came to sit next to her. Together, they watched the barn.

"Even though the suspect is down, they have to secure the scene," he replied.

It must be so hard for him to stay professional, Alyssa thought. In this case "the suspect" had been his childhood sweetheart, the woman he once thought he'd marry. Now he had no idea if she was dead or alive. Part of him had to be remembering the past and feeling sorrow for everything Georgia Dodd had once meant to him.

Finally, they saw a movement at the entrance. Alyssa slid down the window to get a better view. Everett was exiting the barn slightly ahead of a small group of other FBI agents, all of whom wore body armor.

He hadn't been wearing any protective gear when he snatched Kennedy from Georgia. Although the thought made her shiver even more, she knew he had done the right thing. Acting on his training and instincts, he had judged when the moment was right and saved their little girl's life.

It's who he is. This is what he does. She had never been more proud of him.

After talking to his colleagues for a few minutes, he joined them in the back of Casey's vehicle, sandwiching Alyssa between the Colton twins.

"Georgia is dead." Everett closed his eyes as he tilted his head back. "The paramedics did everything but they couldn't save her."

After a few minutes, Casey straightened. "I'll give you some time alone while I speak to Agent Hayes."

When he'd gone, Alyssa wrapped the throw around the three members of her little family, and they sat in silence for a long time.

"It never gets any easier when someone dies," Everett said at last.

"This must be so much harder. You knew Georgia as a child."

He nodded. "I keep looking back and wondering if there were any signs back then that it would turn out this way."

"Don't do that to yourself. Georgia was responsible for what happened to her today." She nodded to a lone figure. Casey had returned and was standing a few feet from the vehicle. "But I think someone else may be torturing himself with memories and guilt."

He caught her hand and kissed it. "I need to go to him. Will you be okay here?"

"Me and my girl are doing fine." It was true. She couldn't say she was untouched by what had gone on, but she had new resources that would help her through.

Motherhood. She watched Everett as he went to

Casey and placed an arm around his brother's shoulders. *And something else.*

The two men leaned on the hood of one of the unmarked FBI cars, sometimes talking, occasionally lapsing into silence. After about fifteen minutes, they returned to the cruiser. Alyssa handed Kennedy to Everett so she could climb out. Stretching her limbs, she shivered as the cold hit her. It was a good shiver. The shiver of someone enjoying the fresh air, hungry for food and able to think about the future without fear. A survivor-shiver.

"Lyss?" Everett took her hand. "I don't know what you're smiling about, but it's Christmas Eve."

She pulled him in the direction of the ridge. "What are we waiting for? Get our car down here. We need to get home *fast*. Remember those superorganized holiday plans of mine? I haven't even wrapped the presents."

Chapter Seventeen

Alyssa spent the rest of the day determinedly plowing on with her festive preparations. On Christmas morning, she woke feeling as though she'd been hit by a truck. *And maybe I have. Emotionally.*

"Do you think Kennedy will be okay?" she asked Everett, as they drank coffee in bed and waited for their daughter to wake up and open her mountain of presents. "She was abducted and saw her aunt killed."

"She was drugged, so she wasn't aware of any of that. And the paramedics confirmed that she's physically fine. The only issue may be if she has a memory of Georgia coming into the apartment and taking her from the crib. But we already know that we have to watch her for signs of PTSD. If that happens, we'll deal with it." He placed an arm around her shoulders. "How are you holding up?"

She leaned against him. "Mostly okay. I get a little shaky now and then when I think about what could have happened. But I'm just grateful to have my family back together."

He drew her closer. "Speaking of families, Mom wants to know if we're still okay for dinner?"

"Of course. I wouldn't miss it for anything."

"And, on a scale of one to ten, how festive are you feeling right now?" There was a familiar gleam in his eyes.

Alyssa gave a little wriggle of pleasure as he twined his fingers in her hair. "Were you planning on giving me a present?"

He lowered his lips to her neck. "I was thinking more of starting a new tradition…"

SEVERAL HOURS LATER, they arrived at Ryker and Maribelle's house. Although the mood around the table was subdued, there was an unspoken pact not to let recent events spoil the occasion. It was Casey and Melody's first holiday as a couple, as well as Kennedy's first Christmas. "I have a family of meat eaters," Maribelle explained. "Although they just had turkey at Thanksgiving, it's a Colton tradition to eat it again at Christmas."

"But Dad cooked it, right?" Everett exchanged a nervous glance with Casey.

She rapped the back of his hand with a wooden spoon. "I don't know where this myth that Mom can't cook meat originated. But, yes, your father did roast the turkey and he baked a ham."

"She only has to look at a piece of beef to incinerate it," Everett whispered to Alyssa out of the corner of his mouth. "When we were growing up, we thought the smoke alarm was the dinner bell."

She choked slightly, and he gave her a wicked grin as he patted her on the back.

"Is everything okay, dear?" Maribelle asked.

"I think a cornbread crumb got stuck in my throat." She glared at Everett.

"Mom is in charge of sides and desserts." This time he said it louder, tilting his wineglass toward Maribelle. "And she is incredible at both."

It was true. The table groaned under the weight of mashed potatoes, gravy, green-bean casserole, rolls, brussels sprouts and carrots, cranberry sauce and sweet-potato casserole. In the kitchen, pumpkin pie and pecan pie were waiting to be served with ice cream once everyone's digestive capabilities had returned to normal. Alyssa figured that might be around mid-January.

Kennedy, seated in her high chair at the head of the table, was in her element. Food and an audience were two of her favorite things. She really liked this particular group of people, and today they had all given her presents. She was approaching the screeching stage.

"I don't understand why she kept hitting me with the doll we gave her." Casey felt the top of his head carefully. "Didn't she like it?"

"Ask Dad." Everett rubbed his own scalp reminiscently.

Ryker laughed. "All babies like rough-and-tumble games. Don't they, little one?"

Kennedy grinned and offered him a half-chewed piece of green bean. Solemnly he took it and pretended to eat it.

"What will you do now?" Maribelle asked Everett.

"I mean, now this is all over, won't you have to go back to Phoenix? And Alyssa's job is there…"

Ryker covered her hand with his own. "This is not the time, my love."

Everett sent a sidelong glance in Alyssa's direction. "Maybe the time to answer that question would be after we've discussed it with each other."

After dinner, Everett and Casey cleared everything away and loaded the dishwasher.

"Maribelle, you raised your boys right," Melody said.

"Some Christmas traditions are worth keeping." Maribelle kicked off her shoes and refilled her wineglass.

Kennedy, exhausted by the strain of being the main attraction, fell asleep. Alyssa placed her on the sofa and tucked her favorite blanket around her. Ryker placed a hand on her shoulder as he stood next to her gazing down at the baby.

"Thank you for giving Maribelle and me our best Christmas present."

"Oh." Her throat tightened, and she reached up to grip his hand. "She loves you, too."

"You'll work it out."

From where they were standing, she could see into the kitchen. Now and then, she caught a glimpse of Everett, and heard him laughing with his brother.

They *had* worked it out. At least, she thought they had. They wanted to be together. But what would that look like from now on? Was Everett's together the same as hers?

A few minutes later, he emerged from the kitchen. "Want to take a walk?"

Leaving Kennedy under four pairs of watchful eyes, they wrapped up warm and headed out into the garden. Remnants of the freak snow shower still clung to the ground and Ryker's outdoor flower beds looked forlorn in the icy, gray light. Everett took Alyssa's hand and tucked it into the crook of his arm, guiding her around the yard and pointing out the places where he and Casey played as a child.

Turning to face her, he drew in a deep breath. "I've been thinking."

"So have I." What if his thinking wasn't the same as her thinking? "But you go first."

"I can turn down the promotion and take a desk job." The words came out on a rush. Everett Colton was more nervous than she'd ever seen him. It was a sight to behold. "That way, you don't have to worry that I'll be in danger at work."

"You'd do that for me?" He nodded. "But you love your job."

"I love you more." His eyes were bright. "When I say 'more,' I mean more than you'll ever know. More with every passing moment, with each breath I take and with every single kiss or touch. Most of all, I want you to know that, if I'm lucky enough to hear you say you love me, too, my answer will always be 'I love you more.'"

With a little sob, she reached up and cupped her hands on either side of his face. "There's no 'if' about it. I fell in love with you eight years ago. That didn't change just because of the distance between us. If anything, it made my love for you even stronger. Since we've been back together, the obstacles that have been thrown in our path have only reinforced what we have."

She pressed a kiss onto his lips. "But I don't want you to quit your job."

"What about your fear that I'll be in danger?"

"Maybe a little part of that will always be with me, but the way you've cared for me and Kennedy, and watching you save her life, have made me see things differently. I can't let what happened to my dad continue to rule my outlook, and I can't let it affect Kennedy's future. I love you, and I'll take what comes with that—the good, the bad and the reality of your job."

He swung her off her feet, kissing her until she was dizzy and breathless. When he set her down again, the blaze of love in his eyes did nothing to restore her balance.

"Wait. You said you'd been doing some thinking as well."

"Okay. Hear me out on this." She smoothed down the front of his jacket with her hand. "I don't want you to change your job, but how would you feel about relocating to the Tucson field office?"

He frowned down at her. "Any particular reason?"

"I'd like to formally adopt Kennedy and raise her here in Cactus Creek." She watched his reaction carefully. "I know you left this place because you wanted to move on from the small-town atmosphere, but that's exactly the sort of experience I want for her. And I want her to be close to her new family."

"There are no objections from me about adopting Kennedy, but what about *your* job?"

"After the holidays, I could speak to the principal of the Cactus Creek Elementary School. I'd only want to work part-time when my maternity leave is over. Kennedy has been through so much. And I thought your mom and dad might like to care for her while I was at work. If they can fit that in with their own work schedules, of course. If not, I can speak to Patty about suitable daycare."

He whistled. "You've really given this some thought. Where would we live? The Dodds' mansion?"

She shuddered. "Not a chance. That place is tainted. As Kennedy's trustee, you should look into selling it and investing the money for her future."

"I'll bear it in mind." He took her by the shoulders, turning her until she was facing away from his parents' home. "See that property close to the tree line? That's Casey's place." He shifted position slightly. "And that plot of land over there belongs to me. How would you feel about designing our own home? Right here? We could make sure there was plenty of space for towels."

She clapped a hand over her mouth. "You've been thinking about this as well."

He laughed at her surprised expression. "For a long time, I was happy to stay away from Cactus Creek. But now I have a family of my own, I can see its advantages."

She leaned her head against his chest. "Despite everything that's happened. This is turning out to be a happy Christmas."

"It's about to get even better." He reached into his inside pocket, then pulled out the slightly squashed sprig of mistletoe. As he held it over their heads, he smiled. "And just so you know, I plan on distracting you with sex *a lot*, Alyssa Bartholomew. Start getting used to it."

* * * * *

COMING SOON!

We really hope you enjoyed reading this book. If you're looking for more romance, be sure to head to the shops when new books are available on

Thursday 12th December

To see which titles are coming soon, please visit

millsandboon.co.uk/nextmonth

MILLS & BOON
MEDICAL
Pulse-Racing Passion

Set your pulse racing with dedicated, delectable doctors in the high-pressure world of medicine, where emotions run high and passion, comfort and love are the best medicine.

JOIN US ON SOCIAL MEDIA!

Stay up to date with our latest releases, author news and gossip, special offers and discounts, and all the behind-the-scenes action from Mills & Boon...

 millsandboon

 millsandboonuk

 millsandboon

It might just be true love...

LET'S TALK
Romance

For exclusive extracts, competitions
and special offers, find us online:

f facebook.com/millsandboon

🐦 @MillsandBoon

📷 @MillsandBoonUK

Get in touch on 01413 063232

For all the latest titles coming soon, visit
millsandboon.co.uk/nextmonth

MILLS & BOON
Desire

Indulge in secrets and scandal, intense drama and plenty of sizzling hot action with powerful and passionate heroes who have it all: wealth, status, good looks… everything but the right woman.